D0823945

THE BOOK OF RENFIELD

A Gospel of Dracula

TIM LUCAS

A TOUCHSTONE BOOK
Published by Simon & Schuster
New York London Toronto Sydney

TOUCHSTONE
Rockefeller Center
1230 Avenue of the Americas
New York, NY 10020

TOUCHSTONE and colophon are registered trademarks
of Simon & Schuster, Inc.

For information about special discounts for bulk purchases,
please contact Simon & Schuster Special Sales at
1-800-456-6798 or business@simonandschuster.com.

Designed by Melissa Isriprashad

Manufactured in the United States of America

1   3   5   7   9   10   8   6   4   2

Library of Congress Cataloging-in-Publication Data
Lucas, Tim.
The book of Renfield : a gospel of Dracula / Tim Lucas.
p.   cm.
"Touchstone book."
1. Dracula, Count (Fictitious character)—Fiction. 2. Whitby
(England)—Fiction. 3. Vampires—Fiction. I. Title.
PS3562.U238B66   2005   813'54—dc22   2005042531

ISBN 13: 978-0-7432-4354-4
ISBN 10: 0-7432-4354-4

FOR MY LADY

also for Lori Perkins and Allyson Edelhertz Peltier, my midwives, who spent years believing and pacing and keeping the water aboil for this book's delivery;

for my dead father and absent mother;

for my unwitting co-author, Mr. Bram Stoker—and, because he would want it that way, for Hommy-Beg;

for the Pets whose companionship has enriched my life over the years, and whose names (to date) are scattered throughout this text as a sign of my affection;

for Dwight Frye, Thorley Walters, Klaus Kinski, and Peter MacNicol, whose portrayals were particularly inspirational;

and with thanks to Kim Newman, Anca Vlasopolos, and Richard Harland Smith for their valuable counsel and contributions.

The ravings of the mad are the secrets of God.

—Bram Stoker

Editor's Note.

As will be stated in my great-grandfather's Foreword, the bulk of the following manuscript consists of materials originating from different media, which have heretofore been suppressed—in accordance with his wishes. That said, some excerpts from his personal diaries appeared previously in the book known as *Dracula*. These were edited and, in some instances, rewritten by John L. Seward before he provided them for the use of Mr. Bram Stoker, at the request of Mr. and Mrs. Jonathan Harker. Such passages have been **Bolded** in acknowledgement of their first publication. In an effort to make the material easier to digest, the entries from Doctor Seward's personal and professional diaries will be treated without distinction. The passages in the text labelled "Commentary" were added by my great-grandfather circa 1939.

Martin Seward, 2005

PART ONE

Now John was clothed with camel's hair and wore a leather belt around his waist and ate locusts and wild honey.

And he preached, saying, "After me come he who is mightier than I, the strap of whose sandals I am not worthy to stoop down and untie."

—Mark 1:6–7

R. M. R.—I'll be quiet, Doctor. Tell them to remove the strait-waistcoat.

J. L. S.—It was already unwise of us to move you bodily in this condition, Renfield. To remove this garment might make you feel freer, but it would also very likely cost you your life.

R. M. R.—But you shall remove it—later? Promise me, you will empty my pockets?

J. L. S.—You have my word.

R. M. R.—I have had a terrible dream, and it has left me so weak that I cannot move. . . . What is wrong with my face? Was I smitten? It feels all swollen, and it smarts ever so dreadfully. I must not deceive myself; it was no dream, but grim reality. If I were not sure already, I would know from the way you are looking at me. I am dying! How is this possible?

J. L. S.—Please, Renfield, you promised to lie quietly. Professor Van Helsing, all this blood . . . Is there nothing we can do?

V. H.—Let him speak. We must attend to all this poor wretch has to say. His words may be worth many lives . . . It may be that there is a soul at stake!

R. M. R.—I feel that I have but a few minutes, and then I must go back to death . . . or worse! *I have something that I must say before I die—or before my poor crushed brain dies anyhow . . .*

J. L. S.—Yes? What is it, Renfield?

R. M. R.—It was that night after you left me, Doctor Seward, when I implored you to let me go away. I couldn't speak then, for I felt my tongue was tied. But I was as sane then—except in that way—as I am now. I was in an agony of despair for a long time after you left me; it seemed hours. Then there came a sudden peace to me. I felt as though I was about to be touched by the Hand of God.

He came up to my window in the mist, as I had seen Him often be-fore, but now He was solid—not a mist, not a ghost . . . and his eyes were fierce like a man's when angry. *They were charged not with anger, but with sheer power.* **He was laughing with His red mouth . . . His sharp white teeth glinted in the moonlight when He turned to look back over the belt of trees, to Carfax, where dogs were barking.** He wanted to come in . . . here, into this place. There was something here that He desired and would have as His own. That is when I realised . . . this is why I was here; this was why I had been chosen—because there would come a time when only I would stand between the Master and that which He desired. It wasn't anything to do with me at all, really. Oh, Doctor Seward, I felt such . . . resentment! **I wouldn't ask Him to come in at first, though I knew He wanted to, just as he had wanted all along.** I had done so much for Him . . . consecrated my very life to Him. I needed for Him to express to me that I was more to Him than a com-mon door-man . . . for surely I was more than just that! **Then he began to as-**suage me and to soothe me by **promising me things—not in words, but by doing them.**

J. L. S.—Promising you things . . . by doing them?

R. M. R.—Yes. **He simply made them happen . . . just as He used to send**

6

in the flies when the sun was shining. Great big fat ones with steel and sapphire on their wings. And big moths, in the night, with skull and cross-bones on their backs. He began to whisper: "Rats, rats, rats! Hundreds, thousands, millions of them, and every one a life. And dogs to eat them—and cats too! All lives! All red blood, with years of life in it, and not merely buzzing flies!"

I laughed at Him, for I wanted to see all that He could do, I wanted to possess all that He would give me—as my rightful reward! Then the dogs howled, away beyond the dark trees in His house. He beckoned me to the window. I got up and looked out, and He raised His hands and seemed to call out, but without using any words. A dark mass spread over the grass, coming on like the shape of a flame of fire. And then He moved the mist to the right and left, there in the clearing were thousands of rats, their eyes blazing red—like His, only smaller. They were moving in a vast carpet of teeming life! He held up His hand, and they all stopped, and I heard a voice in my head promise me, "All these lives will I give you—aye, many more and greater, through countless ages—if you will fall down and worship me!" I fell . . . oh yes, I fell. And then he said, "Now arise, my chosen one, to do my bidding!"

A red cloud, like the colour of blood, seemed to close over my eyes, bending my very will, and before I knew what I was doing, I found myself opening the sash and saying to Him, "Come in, Lord and Master!" The rest of it no longer mattered, now that I had seen and been promised what was rightfully mine . . . But then . . . the rats were all gone—gone before they were given me!—and He slid into the room through the sash, though it was only open an inch wide, just as the Moon herself had often come in through the tiniest crack and stood before me in all her size and splendour. He moved past me, a figure of ghastly splendour, but transient . . . as He dissipated once again into the mist and escaped through the observation trap in my door.

7

All day today, I waited to hear from Him, but He did not send me anything, not even a blow-fly! By the time the Moon got up, I was pretty angry with Him. I told myself that I would not grant Him entry, should He come back again . . . I stood guard by my window, watching the skies turn from azure to cyan, from beryl to sapphire around the bright coin of the Moon, remembering how Father had helped me to overcome my fears, so long ago. And all the fears I had shed re-attached themselves to me as I felt the twin drapes of Father's cape mantling my shoulders once again. It was the cape of the Master— standing behind me! He had slid in through the window cracks, though it was shut, as a mist, and did not even knock! He towered over me as though I was a child again! He sneered at me, His red eyes gleaming, and went on as though he owned the whole place, and I was no one. He didn't even smell the same as He went by me. I thought that, somehow, Mrs. Harker had come into the room. He was steeped in the smell of her, a smell that came not from her perfume, not from her flesh, but deeper—from her blood.

I should have known! When Mrs. Harker came in to see me this afternoon she wasn't the same. She was like tea after the teapot has been watered. I didn't know that she was here till she spoke, and she didn't look the same. I don't care for pale people; I like them with lots of blood in them, and hers all seemed to have run out. I didn't think of it at the time, but when she went away I began to think, and it made me mad to know that He had been taking the life out of her! And then I realised that it was I who had made it all possible, that the Master had wanted to enter this place because Mrs. Harker was a guest here, in your house! I had given her to Him to feed upon, while He had offered me nothing but rubbish! And after all I had sacrificed!

So when He came tonight, I was ready for Him. I saw the mist stealing in, and, summoning all my strength, I grabbed it tight. I had heard that madmen have unnatural strength. And as I knew I was a madman—at times, anyhow—I resolved to use my power. Aye, and He felt it too, for He had to come out of the mist to struggle with me. I held on tight, and I thought *for one foolish moment* **that I was going to win, for I would not stand that He would take any more of her life ... and then He turned on me,** *showing me what so few others have seen ... He showed to me His true and final face. It was much as described by Enoch, who walked with God and looked upon His face. It blazed like iron made burning hot in a fire and brought out, incandescent and emitting sparks. His breath kindleth coals and a flame goeth out of His mouth . . . multiple tongues wrestling forth like mighty eels ... I cower before the task of describing Him, as He was so very marvellous and awesome and supremely terrifying.* **His eyes, they burned into me, and my strength became like water. He slipped through** *my hands,* **and when I tried to cling to Him, He raised me up and** *I found myself so close to His face, so near that which cannot be bourne by human eyes, that I was reduced to begging, pleading, gibbering like an animal. Oh, how I screamed . . . desperate to flee the full weight of His final punishment.*

C. W.—I 'eard him scream, sir. "GOD! GOD! GOD!"—just like that! Like to froze my blood, it did.

J. L. S.—Not now, thank you, Watkins.

R. M. R.—I was twisted in His giant hands. I wanted to chew a hole into my own belly and crawl deep inside myself to hide ... My sight blacked out— once, twice, and again—and I had a glimpse of the hell which is to come for me. And, with each view, a different pain brought me back here, to suffer more at the Master's hands before my ultimate suffering. He raised me high above His head, high enough to crack my head on the ceiling, like an egg, and then He **flung me down,** *leaving the yolk to run out.* **There was a red cloud before me, and a noise like thunder, and the mist seemed to steal away under the door.** *Then all was darkness . . . until you revived me and I saw you good gentlemen assembled around me . . . Doctor Seward . . . Professor Van Helsing . . . Lord Godalming . . . and your American friend, Mr. Morris . . .*

9

Q. P. M.—Rest easy there, poor fellow.

R. M. R.—The madness which has been my life . . . it is lifting from me like a fog. I can see that my life was lived in confusion, but not in vain. You do not yet have the benefit of such wisdom, Doctor, but your time will come. Fear not, for I can see that God is with you. . . . The real God, not the one I have worshipped.

J. L. S.—Shall I summon Father Reville?

R. M. R.—There isn't time, I fear . . . and I still count him a fool. I would much rather keep this moment . . . amongst friends.

J. L. S.—As you wish, Renfield.

R. M. R.—The room is darkening now, and the last thing I shall see in this life is your four faces, looking down on me with such compassion . . . so, perhaps God has not entirely forsaken me. You imagine I have been cheated of my immortality, don't you, Doctor? But that is where you are wrong. It is true that the man in the mist—whom I now renounce as my Master—will not make me immortal. But perhaps, Doctor Seward . . . you shall. Pray, all you good people assembled around me, heed my dying words: Si vis pacem, para bellum.

V. H.—He is no more! God rest his poor, demented soul. The Devil has lost a disciple.

C. W.—Good heavens, Doctor! What was that he said just then?

J. L. S.—He spoke to us in Latin. I can't believe my ears. He spoke Latin.

C. W.—But what did he say?

J. L. S.—Si vis pacem, para bellum.

V. H.—"If you want peace . . . prepare for war."

Foreword

by Dr. John L. Seward.

1.

"GOD'S WILL BE DONE!"

These were the words spoken by Mrs. Wilhelmina Harker, *née* Murray, on the evening of 3 October 1885, following her rescue, upon learning of the violent death of my patient, R. M. Renfield, at Carfax Asylum. The official record, which I was obliged to certify, specified Mr. Renfield's death as being caused by injuries sustained as a result of falling out of bed. A preposterous explanation for a completely shattered body, I grant you, but in the coldly appraising eye of the average medical official, infinitely more acceptable than the truth: that Renfield had been annihilated by his Un-Dead "Lord and Master," Count Dracula.

At some point—shortly before or after he left Renfield's cell inhabited by only the merest spark of life in a pool of blood—Dracula sought to silence his pathetic minion utterly by unearthing the records of his verbal histories, as well as my own diaries of the period—transcribed from Edison/Bell cylinders by my secretary, Mr. Ralph Morrison—and hurling them into the fire-place of my private study. When the monster was put to his overdue death not long after, he died unaware that a second complete set of transcripts also existed—a precaution I did not take with all of my patients, but which I did take with poor Renfield, after I became convinced that he was under Dracula's control. Once collected and deemed as complete as could be, these papers—some reconstructed from Morrison's original short-hand manuscripts—and a handful of original cylinders which had survived through sheer accident were then secured in my office safe, where they remained undisturbed until the spring of 1892.

To understand how and why these long-suppressed documents should now come to light, the reader must understand that the destruction of Count Dracula, outside his castle in Transylvania, brought no particular relief to those of us who effected it. Indeed, once my friends Lord Godalming (Arthur Holmwood), Jonathan and Wilhelmina Harker, and I had returned to our homes in London and Purfleet, Sussex, from the Balkans—our good companion and mentor Professor Abraham Van Helsing having returned with our eternal gratitude and fond wishes to his home in Amsterdam—the four of us found ourselves unexpectedly driven apart by our shared memories of the mission.

At first, I considered that our instinctive rejection of one another's company was our shared response to the untimely deaths of our beloved friend and sister, Miss Lucy Westenra—the woman to whom Godalming was betrothed, and the woman I loved—and our brave American comrade, Mr. Quincey P. Morris. But as the years accumulated behind our victory and those losses, I came to understand that we had all independently decided to avoid one another's company in future for a reason that we did not consciously understand: because the very fact of our fellowship was a chilling confirmation that such profound Evil had actually existed . . . walked the earth, touched our lives, and known each of us by name. Away from one another, we could more easily forget the ways in which we had each been compromised by our involvement in that awful adventure.

As I look back now on my early years as the founder and chief superintendent of Carfax Asylum, I suppose I had noted some shade of evil within almost every patient I housed or treated. Whether it was characterised by hatred, frustration, neglect, jealousy, or feelings of inadequacy, each of these malign shadows was usually traceable to the abuses of a parent plagued by similar grievances of his own, which had gone undetected, or at least uncorrected. My experience had taught me that not all mental disturbance was caused by disease; in many cases, mental illness was not unlike a festering secret bequeathed by one generation to the next, perhaps reaching all the way back to Adam. Too often did I reflect that many of the men and women under restraint at my asylum were innocent, while those who had infected them with madness were still at liberty. It shames me to admit that—in the wake of my encounter with a more potent, if not original, strain of Evil—these sad and banal realities took on an overbearing quality that I found un-manageable, and I sought oblivion in the use of morphine and other drugs.

As time passed and my indulgence deepened, I began to noctambulate through a practice which had lost all satisfaction for me, while dispassionately observing the un-ravelling of the most meaningful bonds of my life. It troubled me that, just as my friends and I had brought an end to Dracula's centuries-old reign of terror, so had he severed our precious connections to one another. In a sense, he had the last hurrah.

I began to loathe myself. Eventually, there came the blessed night when my self-hatred could no longer be tolerated. Marshalling my will-power, I denied myself my indulgences and forced myself to acknowledge from the depths of my averted heart that I had looked upon the face of Evil incarnated. As I forced this admission from myself, I felt an over-whelming chill of terror so vivid I feared it might re-manifest that Evil in the very room where I knelt in prayer.

I had helped bring an end to Count Dracula, true—but I had not begun to obliterate the Count Dracula in me. And so I resolved, in the spring of 1892, to dare the unthinkable and look once again upon the naked face of Evil by re-visiting my diaries and Renfield's personal histories—to re-live, in a sense, those nightmarish events of 1885.

2.

In a coincidence that seemed to bear the seal of Divinity, my estranged friend Jonathan Harker, independently of me, had been noting many of the same emotions in himself. The morning after my first night of retrospective reading, Jonathan changed the future course of our lives by making an appointment with me, via my secretary, who conspired to keep his impending visit a surprise.

At our first sight of each other, before exchanging a single word, the two of us walked into a strong and absolving embrace; seven long years were bridged in an instant. Then, without letting go, we held each other at arm's length to regard one the other, warmly searching each other's faces for signs of how time had changed us—and we laughed.

I asked after dear Mina, and Jonathan shared with me the wonderful news that she was with child. (I had heard rumours that Mina had suffered a miscarriage in years past, but, so joyful was our reunion, I did not broach the subject of this private sorrow.) I invited Jonathan to take the wing chair nearest my desk, and we spoke at length of the turns taken in recent years by our respective lives.

In time, Jonathan produced from his coat pocket two small volumes bound each in red and blue: the 1885 diaries of Mr. and Mrs. Jonathan Harker. He placed them on my desk without comment. With this gesture, of course, his visit transcended mere coincidence.

"What have we here?" I asked fatuously.

"Jack," Jonathan said with grave solemnity, "some years ago, Mina and I lost a child, in the sixth month. It nearly killed poor Mina. Yes, she almost died, yet I could not bring myself to come to you. I found myself praying at night for an answer as to whether I could even bring myself to grieve with you, were I to lose her."

His candour left me quite speechless.

"Do you know?" he continued. "Ever since . . . *that time* seven years ago, Mina and I have never spoken . . . *his name* . . . or acknowledged the claim he once had on her."

My friend—more brother than friend, if truth be told— was barely in control of his unsettled emotions; it was up to me to be strong.

"That 'claim' perished with him, Jonathan," I said.

Jonathan closed his eyes, squeezing their lids gently, as if to confirm that he knew this, in his heart, to be true . . . yet I intuited that something in his head, if not his heart, was telling him otherwise.

"Yes," he acknowledged impatiently, "but do you not see, Jack? Our silence is prolonging his power." He tapped the red leather cover of his own diary, which lay near the green blotter on my desk. "There was a time when this diary of mine alerted you to an Evil of which you were completely oblivious, an Evil which had infiltrated the very walls of this, your asylum. My diary, along with those of Lucy and Mina, confirmed what our old friend Van Helsing could only suspect. It was unthinkable for so long, but last week, I resolved to open my diary again—and read it."

I leaned forward in my chair with heightened interest. "Why now, of all times?" I asked.

"Because this time next year, God willing, I am going to be a father. Already the Lord has gifted us with this expectant miracle, which we didn't dare hope for, so I believe, this time, it shall come to pass. I am fully aware that Mina and I are bringing a child into a world where Evil does exist. I am not willing to shut my eyes a second time and ignore the reality of Evil, because that—I have learned—is precisely when Evil strikes. The words in these little books give an account of Evil . . . yes! But they are also a testament to the values of friendship and cooperation and love. If I deny the Evil, it follows that I must also deny the Good. And I've done that for much too long. We all have."

Jonathan proceeded to tell me how Mina, seeing him darkly absorbed in his diary by night, ventured no comment;

16

yet she noticed a slow but unmistakable brightening of his demeanour by day. She was pleased that her husband had determined to confront the past we had all sought to avoid; at the same time, she was reticent to re-open her own diary of the period, superstitious of what effect its exhumed words might have on her unborn child—but Jonathan encouraged her to do so, for the very reasons he was expressing to me. As it happened, he said, her reading exacted a similarly healing effect on her spirit, and when she finished, they had the idea to exchange diaries.

"Somewhere in the midst of those accounts of horror were the stories of our love, the agonies we suffered when apart, and the early days of our marriage," Jonathan said. "It was important for us to be reminded of that."

"I'm very happy for you both," I told him, "but why bring them to me?"

"Call it 'glad tidings.'" Jonathan smiled. "Besides, Jack, you have never read our complete account."

"That's true," I realised. "When I last read your journals, we were only half-way through the crisis, yet they gave me the instruction I needed to gird myself—as a Christian soldier."

"Nor had we the courage to read them in their entirety before now," Jonathan confessed. "I can't explain it, Jack, but we both found the experience strangely reassuring. And we thought it of the greatest importance to extend that reassurance to you, as you truly are our dearest friend."

I conveyed my gratitude to Jonathan for his thoughtfulness, and more for him to convey to dear Mina.

"Tell me, Jack," Jonathan said when I had finished, "do I

remember correctly—that you also kept a record of those times?"

"Oh yes, certainly," I owned. "My hand-writing has never been very good for purposes of re-reading, so then as now, I made use of Mr. Edison's invention. I record everything, speaking aloud, onto wax cylinders. They hold only two to four minutes of information, so it forces me to be concise and to the point. My secretary, Morrison, then transcribes the cylinders and collects the pages, which are later bound. Your own good wife transcribed some cylinders for me, once upon an unhappy time."

Jonathan furrowed his brow as he studied me. "Forgive me for saying so, Jack, but you have such a deuced mysterious look on your face as I have ever seen!"

"Well, this really is most uncanny, Jonathan," I admitted. "By the most amazing coincidence, I too recently found the courage to dip into my diaries of that fateful year. Indeed, it was only last night that I started, reading one such volume from cover to cover."

In the enthusiasm of our reunion, my old friend had inched forward to the edge of his seat, closer to me—but now, my revelation punched him back, deep into its cushions.

"The devil you say!" he said in time, over interlaced fingers. "Look, I know this is asking a great deal, but . . . Well, would you consider allowing us—Mina and me—to read it, Jack?"

I reflected for a moment on the peculiar twist he had worked into his request, introducing Mina into it, as if his own asking might not be persuasive enough.

"With my diaries, it's a bit complicated," I hedged. "I

would have to be selective in what I shared with you, by the nature of my profession. You would be welcome to anything of a personal nature; under the circumstances, I can see no reason to refuse you that request. I am not proud of it all, you understand . . . but I don't believe there is anything therein that you two good people would read without compassion. But then there are the entries which are professional in nature and touch upon the private lives and problems of my patients. These are held in strictest confidence and cannot be shared. Surely, you understand."

"Oh yes, perfectly."

As long as we were speaking so candidly, I felt entitled to note the obvious: "Do I remember correctly, Jonathan . . . that Lucy also kept a diary?"

He flashed a small, wincing smile of hurt. "Yes, it was bequeathed to Mina and me following the death of her mother. Mina also has some correspondence. I didn't bring Lucy's diary with ours because . . . well . . . to be perfectly frank, Jack . . . they mention you. Your meeting, your proposal of marriage. I didn't know that you would want . . . or would be prepared to read her interpretations of moments that I am certain were most precious to you. After all, she was so carefree, so vivacious . . . *young*, as we all were then . . . unaware of how short her life would be."

"That's very thoughtful of you, Jonathan," I said, "but half measures will accomplish nothing, don't you agree?"

"Very well," he allowed. "Mina and I shall arrange to have her diary and letters delivered to you by special messenger."

Our reunion was not yet half over. Needless to say, I reciprocated the use of Jonathan and Mina's diaries by offering them my personal papers dating from May through December, in the year of our Lord 1885. I agreed to meet with the expectant parents for dinner and to compare notes on Saturday night—"just the four of us," as Jonathan beamed.

3.

That very evening, I immersed myself in Jonathan's diary, in which the Dracula saga truly began. Following Jonathan's lead, I was attentive to the dates in Mina's diary, and when the two volumes offered entries of a simultaneous nature, I read them both side by side and felt unexpectedly excited by their entwinings of drama, adventure, and—yes!—horror. I had read portions of both before, as the adventure was in progress, but at the time, they were akin to a compass, providing us with our bearings—nothing more. But now, read in their entirety, with the knowledge that there was no longer a present danger, I had the perverse reaction of feeling almost entertained.

The relation of certain events in these diaries reminded me of those same events as I had portrayed them in my own records, and when our disparate reports came together in holy harmony, I experienced a keen elation. I was pleased to see, as Jonathan had noted, that when his entries faltered or fell silent, Mina's voice appeared to carry the ball; even in epistolary form, the Harkers were harmoniously wed. As they likely discovered that very night, my own diaries were significant to our collective chronicle as the almost exclusive source of material related to poor Renfield—though my personal records excluded any detailed discussion of events which took place between us in privacy.

I read the Harkers' diaries through the night and closed them at the crack of dawn feeling a chaos of re-awakened emotion. I felt very warmly inclined towards Jonathan and Mina, who were now closer to my heart than they had ever been, and a pronounced pang of regret after reading the peculiar and well-reproduced cadences of Professor Van Helsing, which none of us would hear again, as he had died of heart failure on a ship bound for the Middle East several months earlier, on what mission I do not know. I also felt a giddy, almost shameful sensation of being alive—the sort of feeling a scholarly bachelor experiences all too seldom in his sheltered life.

The Harkers' diaries had shown me, amongst other things, what a miracle it was to find and claim the perfect mate. Also, while our journals did vividly describe the repugnant Evil we had sacrificed so many years of friendship to shed from memory, our shared perspectives framed that description with an omniscience which expressed—more eloquently than any of us could express individually—that friendship was a gift from God.

Perhaps for this reason, after seeing Lucy and Quincey portrayed afresh as living, thinking, feeling people—and then to re-experience their deaths (and, in my beloved Lucy's case, Un-Death) as they were directly felt by my friends—the afterglow of my reading was also tainted by suffering, as my long-healed grief bled freely from a re-opened wound. I lamented that our American friend had kept no diary of his own, a pastime unsuited to his boisterous and outgoing personality, but my greatest agony would be reserved, in the days ahead, for my reading of Lucy's largely unfilled, unfulfilled little book, in which she had written rhapsodically of young love, fearfully of bad dreams, and petulantly about the garlic that Van Helsing had draped around her room, whose obnoxious bouquet had in fact granted her one final night of unmolested slumber. She had been too full of fun, too delightful to wish to inter any part of her sunshine in a book—but the few entries she wrote brought her fully back into my presence. Seeing for the first time those pages written in her florid hand, I could not resist pressing my lips to them; nor, when I saw those precious pages on which she had inscribed my own name and called me "handsome" and "clever," could I help but press them to my chest as I wept.

Thus I formed an appreciation of our interwoven documentation as a new gospel, an account of how the most insurmountable Evil imaginable had been vanquished—in modern times—by the qualities most exemplary of human nature: love, friendship, cooperation, and moral vigilance. What gladder news could be brought to a world on the brink of a new century, which threatened to make such advances in the realms of science and technology as to antiquate common faith, and supply the vagaries of Evil with an infinite variety of new and infinitely more obscure masks to wear? Like many Victorians, I anticipated the coming century—the last before the Millennium—with feelings of superstition and dread. As I write these words, many years later, one global war is already behind us, and England has declared war on Germany for its invasion of Poland, so I cannot say that those trepidations were altogether unfounded.

As my eyes skimmed along those different strains of hand-writing—Mina's perfect script, Jonathan's forward-leaning scribble, and Lucy's girlish yet gradually weakening calligraphy—always in the back of my mind was that I held in my possession yet another adjunct of this new gospel, of which the Harkers were completely unaware.

I had The Book of Renfield.

4.

These professional diaries reposed—along with the few surviving cylinder recordings and a humble notebook in which my zoöphagous patient kept his own accounts—in a floor safe in my home study, where I kept all my important private documents.

After reading the Harkers' diaries, I felt a powerful compulsion to re-acquaint myself with those suppressed materials in preparation for our forthcoming dinner conversation—not that I planned to reveal any of their contents, of course; merely to immerse myself more completely in the mood of those times, the better to confront them and to discuss, as we no doubt would, the effect they had on our lives.

It was not until I opened that safe with the express purpose of consulting my diaries of Renfield's case that I fully realised the extent to which I was crippled by residual fear. I am embarrassed to admit that, having opened the safe and seen the bound transcripts of our talks and my old dictagraph recessed therein, I found myself physically unable to reach inside and pull them out into the light of day. I had read four different accounts of those days over the previous two nights, including my own, but something inside me was not yet prepared to read or actually to hear the wretchedness of Renfield's long-dead voice, preserved on the two or three cylinders that happened to survive Dracula's destructive rampage. Cursing my weakness, I slammed the door and spun the combination dial.

The more I resisted my duty of re-examining those materials, the more the remembered sound of Renfield's voice came back of its own volition to haunt me. He could be addle-brained and grovelling, but he could also rise from such pathetic displays to attain a towering hauteur and menace; he was sometimes disabled under the weight of a terrible mental strain that made him seem quite simple, but there were other times when he was nearly as poised and articulate as an Oxford don. One might think that, instead of small animals, Renfield had eaten many different men and mastered all their tongues, using whichever of them was most useful and conniving at any given moment. He sometimes addressed me with sheepish formality, but there was in his subservience the underlying sarcasm of a dog patiently awaiting an opportunity to bite—as he did on one occasion. (I still bear the scar that proves it.) His laughter was like the jagged sobbing of a pigeon or beaten child. It was not always easy to know when Renfield had lured small animals into his cell because of the noises he seemed to produce involuntarily even when he was alone. *No!—I did not look forward to hearing that voice again!*

But perhaps my greatest dread about consulting those papers and recordings again was that—knowing now what I did not know then—I might make retrospective sense of some furtive hint or prophecy of Renfield, buried in those May sessions prior to Dracula's arrival at Whitby, whose early detection and comprehension might have helped to save lives so precious to me. But before Dracula's arrival, how was I to know that Renfield was no ordinary lunatic?

5.

The trip from Purfleet to the Harkers' beautiful home in Exeter occupied the greater part of an afternoon and required me to book a room for that evening at one of the local hotels. Accompanied by a change of clothes, I left the asylum early Saturday morning and took the local train to London, followed by the express from Paddington to the West Country. Travelling the same distance Jonathan had covered to re-new our acquaintance gave me a more vivid appreciation of how far his open hand had reached in friendship.

Some hours after arriving in Exeter, I re-dressed in clothes that were elegant if not quite formal and hired a hansom cab to take me to their door-step. During the ride, my sense of anticipation re-kindled such unwelcome turns of thought that I nearly ordered the coachman to turn around. Long-suppressed images began to burst through the settled earth of memory: Lucy, as she appeared to us in the Hampstead churchyard where we believed she had been laid to eternal rest, her former sweetness corrupted to a spitting animal ferocity; the pained resolve I read in the face of my rival Arthur Holmwood as he took hammer and stake in hand and brought an end to she whom he and I had loved most in life; Professor Van Helsing and I, alone in the crypt, reaching into the vat of cold blood that was her coffin and sealing her sanctity by sawing off the protruding shaft of the stake and decapitating her tiny corpse, its luxuriant strawberry-blonde hair soiled and matted with scarlet chill, and stuffing cloves of garlic inside the mouth where Arthur, to my agony—and, I now admit, also my envy—had planted a farewell kiss. And I remembered Mina's voice, more plainly than I had heard it in years, shattering a stunned silence with the words "Unclean! Unclean!" It occurred to me, as I listened to the coach's wheels turning over the cobblestones, that one of the two diaries in my possession had been carried by Jonathan during the coach-rides that took him to the Borgo Pass, and then beyond. Dracula's own hand may have once held his diary as my hand was gripping it at that moment.

But when Mina greeted me at the door, her expectant radiance banished all morbid thoughts at once. We did not embrace for as long as I would have wished, but the sight of her happy tears was sweet compensation.

I half expected the Harkers might surprise me by inviting Arthur to dinner as well, but when I enquired after him during our splendid meal, Jonathan admitted that an invitation had indeed been extended to Lord Godalming, who had sent his sincere regrets.

"I do not believe poor Arthur has been able to move on since the death of Lucy," Mina offered.

"He is seldom seen in public anymore," Jonathan added.

"An introspective man who doesn't keep a diary consigns himself to a special hell," I observed, as one who knew Art well enough to make such a statement. "As we have all discovered this past week—magically and quite independently of one another—to express one's feelings to oneself on a daily basis can help to ease, even cure, the pains we hide from the world." I raised my glass: "To Mina and Jonathan—my dearest friends!"

After dinner, they led me to their parlour, where our diaries lay arranged on a table. Shortly after we had seated ourselves around this display, Jonathan announced: "Jack, Mina has something important she would like to discuss with you."

I smiled at this pronouncement, suspecting that they were about to request that I be godfather to their child. "I'm all ears," I said.

Mina began, "I must own that we had this idea, Jonathan and I, before reading your diary in full, but now that we have seen what it contributes to the overall design, we feel more strongly than ever about this. These accounts must be collected and published."

I suppose I said nothing because the notion exploded in my head all at once like a supreme inevitability. Indeed, the fact of their eventual publication almost seemed to pre-exist and pre-determine the extensive notes we had, each of us, kept. Nothing could have made more sense.

The Harkers, however, interpreted my silence as confusion or resistance and pressed on with more detailed reasoning.

"While reading our diaries, Jack, did you not find pages where your own diary was in a position to observe or explain something that ours could not?" asked Jonathan.

Indeed I had, I gestured.

"We had the same impression while reading yours," he continued. "Furthermore, Mina—"

"I found letters," Mina interrupted with excitement, "letters that Lucy wrote to me, unopened letters sent to Lucy, letters exchanged by Professor Van Helsing and myself . . ."

"I also have such letters," I offered. "And telegrams."

"And I have found newspaper stories at the library—back numbers of *The Pall Mall* and *Westminster Gazette*, dating from that period—which provide additional comment," Mina effused. "You know how I am about researching things!"

"When you arrange all of the documents in chronological sequence . . ." Jonathan interjected. "Well, it's uncanny. You can almost read the pattern of that Hellspawn's movements between the lines!"

"Yes," I said, in words that felt to me almost pre-scripted. "I imagine that you can."

"We thought we were doing the right thing at the time, but now we can see how selfish and wrong we were to suppress the story of what happened to us," Mina declared. "If I can admit now what happened to me . . . candour should pose no problem for the rest of you! Certainly, it will require some time and effort to compile our journals and all the other materials into their correct order, but I am willing to undertake it, with Jonathan's help—and with your blessing, Jack. Circumstance has left us stricken, and robbed our lives of so very much, but it has also given us this collective testament, which we are in a position to give to the new century, as our gift . . . and as a gift from those no longer among us . . . as a safeguard against future visitations of Evil."

Without question, I gave the Harkers my blessing to use my personal diaries of this period for their compilation, as they saw fit.

I had devoted much of that day to preparing myself, mentally and sartorially, for our reunion, and so, after spending a few hours in the warmth and joy of renewed friendship, I made my apologies and reluctantly rose from my seat, explaining that I would be needed back at the asylum at the earliest possible hour of the following day.

After my return to Purfleet, before announcing my return to my staff, I went directly to my home study. There, fortified by the experience of the previous evening, I opened my floor safe and reached inside, pulling out my dictagraph case by its grip and placing it on my desk. I could not have felt prouder had I delivered a baby. I unlatched the lid and removed it from the apparatus, revealing the device itself, centered in a velvet-lined tray which displayed only four intact recording cylinders on twelve upright spools. I did not permit myself any pause in my actions, selecting a cylinder at random and securing it on the dictagraph. I settled back in my chair as its needle skated into the groove, reproducing the crackle and hiss of the not-so-distant past:

. . . and in his face there was such wisdom! His wee eyes were so proud and brave and yet so defenseless as they looked at you, so very trusting, very trusting he was. He well knew how big the world is, he well knew how stacked the odds were against one of his diminutive stature, and he knew perfectly well . . .

You're repeating yourself now, Mr. Renfield. We know by now that repetitions in your speech tend to upset you.

Oh! Was I? Repetitions open doors, you know. Well, I meant only to say that he also knew . . . perfectly well that I loved him more than anything else in this world,

Doctor. But that's the way he was, dear thing. Always curious to a fault, always putting the brave foot forward, was Jolly.

At Renfield's first mention of that forgotten, perhaps deliberately suppressed name, I reached over and halted the playing of the cylinder.

But it was too late.

Jolly was already under my skin.

6.

It took some time, but with the help of an established novelist, Mina cobbled our journals (as well as some documents belonging to Lord Godalming, who in time rejoined our circle) into one giant work. She was prevented from performing this task more punctually by the needs of one Quincey Harker (born 7 November 1892—seven years and a day following the death of his namesake). When the manuscript was completed and accepted by a prominent Westminster publishing house in the summer of 1896, young Quincey's mother and father commemorated the occasion by re-visiting Transylvania, where they brought themselves lasting peace by challenging the empty ruins of Castle Dracula with their own eyes.

Dracula, as Mina's book was called (in proud defiance of the name she had learned to speak aloud once again), was first published in 1897—and, by general agreement, credited solely to her collaborator, and presented to the world in the only manner it could be presented: as a work of fiction. As Mina later explained to me, her original suggested title for the manuscript was *The Un-Dead*, but Mr. Bram Stoker, who understood and was sensitive to her motivations, persuaded her that openly proclaiming the name of the vampire might help her to cope with her residual fears.

That book had its own particular tale to tell, and its own particular reason to exist. It is generally what happened, but due to certain literary flourishes and editorial decisions, it does not record the whole literal truth. And because the authors did not have access to certain of my documents, it offered only a modest account of Renfield's story, portraying him as little more than an interpreter of the Unspeakable, a gibbering shadow cast by his Un-Dead Lord and Master, and focussing exclusively on the final months of his wretched existence.

Mina's remarkable bravery during the preparation of *Dracula* was an inspiration to us all. Speaking for myself, I was—shall I say, *surreptitiously*—inspired to meet her example by embarking on the work you are about to read: the story of R. M. Renfield, as I knew him—a chronological compendium of his scattered (and sometimes suspect) reminiscences, his ranting citations of Scripture, and his arcane charts, accompanied by my own reminiscences and annotations about his case, now so long ago as to be presentable.

What I discovered in the process of assembling this manuscript is that Renfield's story—in some ways—is also my own story, but I fear it is a story that may sully, rather than elevate, the human spirit. For this reason, because of the volatile times which have befallen our new century, I have elected to suppress this work until after my death, when the matter of its eventual publication will be left to—I hope—

more dependable and trustworthy hands. I pray the time shall come when the general public will recover the moral strength of character necessary to read such a document without succumbing to its base influence. The fact that you are reading these words may indicate that such a time has finally arrived.

Believe me when I say that I take no pride in having so well maintained the secrecy of this project. Had the end result of my efforts been the companion gospel I had intended, I would have gladly circulated its unpublished pages amongst my friends, but this was not the case. Unlike *Dracula, The Book of Renfield* received no daily encouragement from others during its gestation, and there was neither celebration nor sojourn to mark its quiet completion. For years, I masked the reasons for my preoccupation and erratic, brooding behaviour with lies. When I finished the manuscript, there was nothing to do save explain to all concerned that the cause of my long distraction—the professional idea of a lifetime—had ultimately come to nothing.

I write this Foreword in the autumn of my life, while feeling intimations that winter is imminent. The manuscript that follows was undertaken in the spirit of a cautionary tale: to explain the tragic circumstances of Renfield's life which made him the perfect pawn for Count Dracula, a broken bridge which the Lord of the Un-Dead could ride into the teeming veins of Western civilisation. It was my belief that such a story could shed light on the dark strategems of Evil, making it more predictable and less destructive in its future incarnations; I did not expect that its preparation would become an agent of my own moral decay.

The clandestine labours which I have invested in the preparation of this work have caused me to live untruthfully in relation to everyone I've ever loved. I can now also freely admit that the spell cast by this book led me back, for some time, to my indulgences in morphine—the only respite I could find from the otherwise constant sensations of rodents scrambling through the pipeworks of my bones, of soft-bodied insects slipping though the bands of my sinews. As for the furious kicking I sometimes feel in the chambers of my heart, this—I am all too certain—is Jolly, whom Renfield loved more than anything in all the world.

Renfield went to his grave with all of his Lord and Master's promises of immortality broken. There are indeed "glad tidings" (to use Jonathan's words) in this simple fact; it confirms what we know of Evil. And yet, by resurrecting Renfield's pathetic life and words in this book—by preserving him as I have, like an insect in a jar—one question haunts me: Have I not inadvertently kept Dracula's word?

What is left for me to say?

"God's will be done!"

John L. Seward, M.D.
Director, Carfax Asylum,
3 October 1939

33

CHAPTER I

Dr. Seward's Diary.

21 MARCH 1885.—I was apprehensive about attending to-night's dinner party at the home of Lord and Lady Remington, but one does not reject such an invitation out of hand. After much trepidation (doubtless brought on by overwork) and cajoling by Art, I made up my mind to attend—if only for a short time.

The evening began much as I expected, as I found myself standing with Art and our host in the company of some other men of their social station, who were discussing the usual rot: business, politics, the colonisation of West Africa—subjects which hold not the slightest interest for me. Such conversations, which one gets trapped into simply by virtue of one's sex, are one reason why I have long since ceased to look forward to such gatherings as doorways to opportunity and adventure, yet this is precisely what the evening became.

As it happens, my seating assignment at the dinner table placed me next to Mrs. Lillian Westenra, a convivial, dove-like woman whose eyes sparkled with intrigue as I was introduced to her as the founder and chief superintendent of Carfax Asylum. Many are the women who would turn to their other nearest dining companion by reflex, at the mere mention of an asylum, but Mrs. Westenra was refreshingly curious and open-minded, asking about my work with interest and sensitivity. Not once did her fascination abate long enough for me to balance our conversation with polite enquiries about herself, nor did she try to coax "colourful" gossip from me about my most tragic patients. As a result, a delicious meal went down very well, and with a slight immoderation of red wine.

As I rose to join the other gentlemen in attendance for the usual amenities in Lord Remington's spacious den, Mrs. Westenra gently took me by the arm and guided me to an adjoining room, where I was introduced to her charming daughter Lucy, who had been seated elsewhere at table, unbeknownst to me, in conversation with Art. The poor fellow was himself dragged away to the smoking room, but the combined charms of Mrs. Westenra and her daughter persuaded me to forgo my brandy and cigar in favour of their continued good company.

In the course of our conversation, we discovered many acquaintances in common and Mrs. Westenra began to speak of me to her daughter with an enthusiasm I might have found embarrassing in any other circumstance. However, the more glances I stole at this young woman, I felt a peculiar gratitude at receiving such endorsements of my good works and character. Miss Westenra listened with a most becoming placidity and sly humour; it was my observation that the natural and quite charming effusiveness of Mrs. Westenra has taken a good deal of demonstrativeness out of her daughter. Miss Westenra spoke very little when her mother was near, but once her mother excused herself to converse with our hostess, the daughter's manner transformed, blooming in a most beguiling way.

From the moment we two were first left alone in facing chairs in a corner of the drawing room, Miss Westenra became more forthcoming.

"Tell me, do you *always* look at young women that way, Doctor Seward?" she enquired with a wry smile.

"And which way is that, Miss Westenra?"

"You have been looking at me with an expression of great resolution. Your gaze has been most direct."

I felt quite disarmed. "Please accept my apologies," I stammered. "To be perfectly candid, I have been working much too hard of late, and I'm so accustomed to speaking only to my patients, probing their faces for answers to questions they cannot or will not articulate . . . Well, I am well to be reminded that not everyone I meet is a riddle to be solved."

"Oh, I'll bet you couldn't solve the riddle of a face like mine," she challenged.

A woman takes a terrible risk when inviting a man to drink as deeply of her beauty as he dares—and a man dares to risk all, should he accept. Indeed, Miss Lucy Westenra presented to me a most inscrutable face. She has a sweet, bubbly character and a vivacious hauteur that is at once knowing and yet utterly naïve. This combination of opposites has the uncanny effect of making her look as candid as she is mysterious. This is a conundrum that would take even a husband a lifetime of happy effort to solve—but foolishly, I accepted her dare.

It was rather like the blinking contest which children play. She presented her face to me, and I leaned forward, granted permission to peer as deep as I dare through the windows of her soul. What I beheld there made me jittery in its unflinching candour, and I began to finger the lancet chain—I believe that's what it's called—that secures my grandfather's pocket watch to the fob pocket of my waistcoat, to steady my nerves. Several moments passed in which the room and world around us ceased to exist.

One of us had to bow to the other first, and Miss Westenra wasn't about to give me the satisfaction of flinching, so finally I did the gallant thing and broke our silence.

"You afford me a most curious psychological study, Miss Westenra," was my unfortunate choice of words.

She giggled and shot back, "Oh, I should be quite certain of that, Doctor Seward!" (Would she have spoken so provocatively had she not intended to encourage me, wished me to remember her?)

With this episode in mind, I am retiring early in full expectation of pleasant dreams.

22 MARCH.—My first thoughts as I rose this morning were of last evening. Must focus on work.

29 MARCH.—As if in answer to my prayers for something to occupy me, this has proved a most eventful Saturday evening—Sunday morning, rather!

A new patient has been installed here at the asylum,

quite a bizarre and interesting case. He was brought to our care by two police constables who chanced to spy, in the light of the Moon, his shadow moving about in the rubble of the Carfax estate. This festering property, formerly an abbey, has long been for sale, but no one will go near it. There is something foreboding and worrisome, almost supernaturally so, about a holy place that has fallen to ruin. It stands there in the midst of our street like the Devil's triumph.

Approaching the vagrant stealthfully from behind, the constables initially thought he must be deep in prayer, as he was kneeling and in a bowing posture, but as one of them signalled their presence by stumbling over a stray bottle, he whipped around to face them and they saw his mouth bespattered with fresh, wet blood.

Hanging from his hands were the limp remains of a rat—its abdomen scooped out by a single bite. The constables, perhaps weakened by their revulsion, found the man's resistance unexpectedly strong. They said it was not their counter-action of strength that finally subdued him, but rather that the remains of the rodent slipped from his hands during their struggle, which broke his concentration. To be separated from this unspeakable rag of hair and flesh seemed to bring him the most unbearable, inconsolable sorrow. He pleaded with the constables for the carcass, promising them his co-operation, but when it was denied him, he shrieked, "Give it back to me! It was promised me! *It is mine!*"

The constables assumed him to be one of my patients, gone over the wall, and they brought him here. They turned him over to the strong arms of my ready attendants, but even they could control his violence only with the greatest difficulty—and these are big, burly men! Soon enough he was packed into a strait-waistcoat, which made him easier to manage. My initial impression was that this hellion should be assigned one of our isolated cells below-stairs, if not the padded one. However, as we were guiding him in that general direction, the fellow happened to catch sight of an open room on our main floor whose window looked out upon the ruins where he was apprehended. I was standing in a position to see what he saw; the abbey was like a black moonscape whose pock marks were stencilled against a blue-black sky. It is a regrettable view, unwholesome and hardly a tonic for the morbid of mind, which is why that particular room was un-occupied. But as we passed that open door, his behaviour changed so dramatically that we all took notice. He was becalmed like the sea after a great storm, so suddenly that the attendants later told me they thought it might be a trick to get them to loosen their grips, that he might scurry away. To me, his transformation seemed to be perfectly sincere.

"No, here!" he exclaimed. "I must stay here!" He looked inside the un-occupied room with all the joy and surprise of a child looking into a room where a birthday cake with all its burning candles awaits. He turned to me, sensing that I was in charge, and showed me the more reasonable and conciliatory sides of his nature. "*Please*, Doctor," he begged, hissing slightly through teeth still stained with the disgusting remnants of his last meal. "I beg you—I beseech you—I promise you, sir, that your kind indulgence will be greatly rewarded!"

It was a bit over-done, but his very peace of mind seemed

to depend on this accommodation, so I granted his wish—on the condition that he remain chained to the wall nearest the room's cot, in his strait-waistcoat, throughout the initial observation period of twenty-four hours.

As he was being introduced to his quarters, I stood by to take stock of our new resident. He is a husky, middle-aged man, pear-shaped though not quite stout, with a great mop of unkempt grey hair on his head, tiny white hairs sprouting along the edges of his fleshy ears. He wears narrow spectacles, which were not broken, despite the scuffle. These may offer a clue to his past as they are the kind worn by people associated with close—perhaps clerical—work; they were not very clean, and he looks over the top of them more than through them. He is a nail-biter, but so meticulous in this fixation that his attentions rather improved the look of his stubby, dirty hands, which are dimpled along the knuckle line like a child's. He was given to my care in a shabby suit, stained with dirt and dust and dried blood and semen. The latter may have derived naturally from nocturnal emission, as he exhibits no signs of satyriasis or inclination to self-abuse. No further clues to his identity were found on his person, though in one of his pockets a handkerchief was found in unspeakable condition; it was monogrammed RMR and wrapped like a burial shroud around the skeleton of a large rodent.

As his arms were led into the sleeves of the strait-waistcoat, the patient recited a passage of biblical scripture, which one of the attendants later identified for me as coming from the Book of Revelation: "*Do not fear what you are about to suffer. Behold, the Devil is about to throw some of you into prison, that you may be tested, and for ten days you will have tribulation. Be faithful unto death, and I will give you the crown of life."*

My first religious fanatic!

30 MARCH.—Our new guest's first night passed peacefully enough, which caused me to think he might be removed from his irons. However, with the sunrise, angry moans—which rose into yells and finally screams as the sun reached its noon peak—were heard coming from his room. Worried that he had somehow used his chains to deal himself a serious injury, the attendants raced there and found him cowering from the sunlight that was streaming through his window. When the men tried to intervene, the patient leaped at them like some kind of rabid animal, but was held firm to the wall by his shackles. His wails were most disruptive to the serenity of our house and disturbing to the other patients.

I was looking forward to our initial interview, but this being quite impossible under the circumstances, I decided to take an extended walk around the gardens to soothe my ears and clear my head . . . during which my thoughts returned once again to Miss Westenra—to Lucy—as they now tend to do, however much I ought to be concentrating on my professional duties.

Returning in-doors one and a quarter hours later, I recorded some letters, treated myself to a small cordial and a short nap on the leather sofa here in my office, then rose again to conduct my evening tour of the patients' cells. I was met by [the attendant Carlton] Watkins, who apprised me as usual of his observations while standing guard. He reported that the vociferous agonies of the new patient, which had no physiological impetus, had subsided as the sun began to go down. His exact, amused words: "His spirits went bright as the sky got dark." (Possible allergy to light? Unfortunately, it is not possible to appease these anxieties by curtaining the window, as any material could be taken down and tied together to form a noose.) I instructed Watkins, for the sake of experiment, to have the strait-waistcoat removed from the patient for the balance of the evening, that he might enjoy a comfortable night's sleep, but to make absolutely certain he was returned to full safeguards by cock-crow.

Before recording this entry, I looked in on the poor fellow, who had been thoroughly washed and dressed in a pair of clean, loose-fitting pajamas; he was kneeling on his cot and looking out the window of his room, his hands folded in front of him. He appeared to be deep in prayer. I did not wish to disrupt his moment of peace with the questions I was burning to ask, or with a simple hello—so I withdrew, saying nothing.

CHAPTER II

Dr. Seward's Diary.

1 APRIL.—It appears our new patient doesn't approve of the food produced by our kitchen. [Wilfrid] Hardy—another of our attendants, who shares the guard duties with Watkins— told me this morning that the food delivered to his room is either ignored or thrown at the wall.

As he was being re-dressed in his strait-waistcoat before sunrise, our fanatic asked to be given a Bible. I authorised his request to be granted immediately, as I knew it could lead to further violence if not satisfied; I also hoped that this request signified that he might settle down and become a contented reader . . . but once again, as the sun began its slow ascent to noon, our main floor was back to sounding like a hell of cats.

This man's voluble suffering is frightening our other patients, and his offensive language is driving everyone else outside. Fortunately, the weather is not presently adverse to this, and the schedule of the patient's madness—I shall call him R. M. R. until more exact identification is made—is making itself known.

At one o'clock, R. M. R. was of explosive disposition, roaring, cursing volubly, and making bizarre ululations so indecipherable that he might be speaking in tongues. As Watkins showed me later, he very nearly tore himself free of his restraints. But by seven o'clock, he had rid himself of his devils and was seen once again to be quiet and content, absorbed in his reading with his back turned to the door. I looked in myself and the only sound to be heard was that of his licking the tips of his fingers as he turned the pages of his Bible.

10:10 P.M.—At last I have conducted my introductory interrogation of the patient in his quarters. He was of calm disposition, but not knowing how my questions might affect his moods, I insisted that he be placed in his strait-waistcoat for our interview. I was accompanied by Watkins for protection, and by Ralph Morrison, who kept a record of our meeting in shorthand, to which I refer now and shall embellish as need be.

"Good evening," I greeted him. "I am sorry that we could not make our proper introductions before now, but let us take this opportunity to put things right. I am Doctor John Seward, the chief superintendent of Carfax Asylum, which is the name of this institution. Could I please have the pleasure of knowing your name?"

The patient was sitting on the floor, half facing his wall. He seemed to occupy his own world rather than the one we shared, and gave me nothing by way of an answer.

I produced his handkerchief from the side pocket of my white work coat.

"You were found in possession of this soiled handkerchief, bearing the monogram R. M. R.," I noted. "May I presume that these are your initials?"

The introduction of the handkerchief excited him. He turned toward me more directly, scrambling from his sitting position onto his knees. His expression, sullen but a moment before, became positively child-like.

"Who gave you that? It's mine, give it back to me!" Then, in case his bullying had no truck with me, he added in an altogether meeker voice, "Please, Doctor, it belongs to me. May I have it back?"

"Perhaps, but first—the initials?"

Now the patient brooded, like a petulant child or grumpy pet who was required to perform a trivial task before receiving a reward.

"They are the initials of a stranger who took me into his home and raised me. He gave me his name . . . and he gave me that handkerchief. May I—?"

"You may have it back, when we finish here," I told him sternly. As I returned the folded handkerchief to my pocket, his expression darkened, as if silently cursing me behind pursed lips. "The initials R. M. R. . . . ." I pressed on. "They stand for . . . ?"

"Renfield. I cannot tell you what the R. or the M. stood for, as my benefactor was always known, to me and everyone else in our village, as the Reverend Mr. R. M. Renfield."

"A priest?"

"A vicar."

"I see. . . . And where was his vicarage?"

The question seemed to inflame the patient. He leaped to his feet, exclaiming, his consonants hissing, his vowels gasping: "Do I look like a Judas to you? I cannot tell you that! A vanguard does not reveal his trail. . . ."

"And what do you mean by that?"

At first, Mr. Renfield said nothing, but looked upon me with an expression that could be described only as abominable. "To you," he said, "such indiscretions may mean nothing . . . but to those of a higher calling . . ." He did not complete his sentence, but what little he did express caused him to stand taller, more erect. He gestured with his head towards the bonds that strapped his arms to his person. "What right have you to handle me in this disrespectful manner?"

"Mr. Renfield, you were found in the abbey ruins of the Carfax estate, which adjoins these grounds. I admit the grounds appear to be wide open to the public, but they are, in fact, private property—albeit no longer in any condition to keep people out. Therefore, you are guilty of criminal trespass. Also, at the time of your discovery, you exhibited signs of being dangerous and irresponsible of your actions, so it was assumed that you belonged to us. We are holding you for observation."

"Observe all you want," he smirked, re-seating himself on the floor with an air of smug superiority.

"We have observed, Mr. Renfield, that you suffer terrible agonies during the daylight hours. We can practically tell time by you. What can you tell us about these episodes?"

"Agonies—yes!" he agreed, hissing and snapping at the very air in agreement. "You see . . . when the sun rises, my soul ceases to exist. In the place of that void, I begin to hear a buzzing sound—not a single buzz as you might hear if a bee or a fly was in the room, oh no—but a vast chorus! And, as the sun continues to rise, this buzzing grows louder and louder, until I could swear my head was encircled by a halo of

47

flies. But there is nothing to be done for it, save count the days until my tribulations have ended."

"Only to resume the next morning," I noted.

"Our Lord's suffering is eternal," Renfield countered. "If He would have me suffer, He must have a most excellent reason."

"Mr. Renfield," I asked him directly, "what were you doing in Carfax Abbey?"

"Seeking shelter."

"You're lucky to have been pulled out of there alive, you know," I told him. "That place is a death trap waiting to happen, full of dodgy floor-boards, weak walls, and areas of ceiling that look straight up to the stars at night. It hardly qualifies as shelter."

"It called to me with a voice I knew. It looked familiar to me . . . like home."

"Because you were raised in a vicarage," I reasoned. "Is there anyone from your family you wish us to contact?"

"I have no family."

"You mentioned a vicar."

"Today, the Reverend Mr. R. M. Renfield may be contacted only by means of prayer."

"So you have no one?"

"None but those I carry inside me . . . here," he said, gesturing to his heart but missing that target and pointing closer to his stomach.

"That is most regrettable," I said. "You have my deepest sympathies, Mr. Renfield."

"And you have mine, Doctor Seward," he said, without even turning to witness my reaction.

I was confused, and perhaps somewhat defensive: "Excuse me—I have *your* sympathies?"

The patient looked at me now and moved forward slightly onto his knees. Watkins prepared himself to intercede in the event of a lunge, but I tacitly gestured for him to remain seated.

"Oh, indeed you have!" Renfield exulted. "I may be many things, Doctor, but I am nobody's fool. Fools are to be pitied as lambs to the slaughter."

"You fancy me a fool?"

"Perhaps not as you occupy this room, not at this moment, but . . . *imminently.*" The man Renfield narrowed his eyes at me, as though I could be seen and fully sized up through even so narrow an aperture.

I can only assume—no, *I can only admit* that he touched a nerve. What I said next was highly unprofessional, to say the least, and I already regret it: "Tell me this, Mr. Renfield. Does the likelihood that you were born a bastard cause you any undue remorse?"

He replied as matter-of-factly as if I had asked him to prophesy the morning weather: "If you ask my opinion, the knowledge of one's origins is greatly over-rated. What is important is not where one has been, but where one is going—what one is becoming, be it sage or fool. I am far more interested in the person I am becoming. Aren't you?"

I could feel my face turning slowly red, and so, with that remark, I nodded to my associates that the interview was at an end. Watkins stayed inside the room to remove Renfield's strait-waistcoat. The moment he was free of it, Renfield surged towards the door, then caught himself like a player of cards who fears that he has tipped his hand too far. He turned his most entreating eyes on me.

"You have perhaps forgotten . . . my handkerchief, Doctor Seward?"

"Oh, yes." I reached into my pocket and passed it to Watkins, who passed it to Renfield. We all watched in fascination as he unfolded the linen, as if searching for something therein—and delicately, as if that something might break. I remembered the skeleton. Then, not finding it, the patient turned to me with an incandescent hatred.

"Where is it?" he demanded, spitting through clenched teeth. Watkins barred him from coming any nearer to me. "What have you *done* with it?"

I tried my best not to appear startled, but the size of his anger appeared literally to transcend the size of his being. "The handkerchief was badly soiled and had to be laundered," I explained. "As for the animal remains, they were . . . unsanitary, Mr. Renfield. Naturally, we disposed of them."

As I spoke, Watkins slipped outside and threw the bolt on the patient's door. We watched through the observation trap, saw Renfield collapse to the floor, where he contracted into a fœtal position, shrinking into himself like crumpled paper consumed by flame.

"You monsters," he wept. "You heartless bloody monsters! Have you never loved anything? Have you never loved *anything?*"

9 APRIL.—Interesting lunch today with Lord Remington and his friend Peter Hawkins, a solicitor. Hawkins wanted to meet the doctor whose asylum adjoins the Carfax estate—a property for which he may have found a buyer! Evidently his firm was approached by letter, bearing the seal and signature of a Romanian Count of ancient family, who is presently seeking a suitable property for his London base. He understood London to be a modern city, yet hoped to find somewhere in its vicinity something like his castle in Transylvania. Condition and money were no object.

One of Hawkins's young employees, who happens to live near our by-street, thought of Carfax right away and suggested they reply to the Count with full details of the property and its deplorable condition, but Hawkins rightly felt that to trust such a delicate purchase to correspondence might grant the Count sufficient pause to change his mind. He therefore insisted that this younger solicitor—Harker by name—travel to the Count's castle in the Carpathians with contracts in hand and conclude the deal while the iron is still hot. Arrangements have been made for the end of the month, when Mr. Harker will journey to Munich by train, then travel by coach for the remaining distance. It sounds like quite an adventure!

He confided to us that young Harker is exhilarated by the prospect of this mission, and a sale that stands to make his career, but also torn as this trip shall necessitate his first lengthy separation from his new fiancée. Both Remington and Hawkins, being men of the world, had a merciless chuckle over this, but my heart went out to the poor chap, as I know exactly how he must feel. That said, I have every confidence that their love shall survive it.

I must admit to indulging in daydreams of being a neighbour to a distinguished Romanian nobleman with deep pockets and seeing the decadent eyesore that is Carfax renovated to its original splendour. I look forward with great excitement to this gentleman's future residence here and the changes that his presence is likely to affect in stodgy old Purfleet!

To my utter surprise and relief, and that of my staff and our other patients, the daylight fits of Mr. Renfield did not recur to-day. After ten days of our hospitality, the buzzing void in his head has diminished to bearable proportions, it seems. I hope I do not speak pre-maturely.

11 APRIL.—No further change in Renfield's behaviour. He now spends his daylight hours in relative and most welcome docility. We have released him from his chain and strait-waistcoat, and he appears to be rewarding that trust. His case interests me; there is nothing like him in the current literature of mental aberration. I find myself wondering if he might be the patient I always hoped would find his way into my care, someone whose unique distress I might explore, delineate, and perhaps cure for later presentation in the form of a published study. I have accrued a certain standing in the community as the founder and head of this asylum, but this is not enough. Not nearly enough accomplishment for the man who may someday decide to ask for a certain lady's hand in marriage. . . .

12 APRIL.—Unable to resist temptation any longer, I decided to put this Sunday to the use of informing Miss Lucy Westenra that she has found an admirer in Jack Seward. I had no address for her, so I was obliged to question Art, whom I knew to be acquainted with her family. I found him not so willing to surrender the information.

"Really now, Jack—I was there first," he reasoned childishly.

"Come now, Art," I shot back, "surely you aren't afraid that your gentlemanly charms can't stand up to a little friendly competition?"

"It's just that this one is . . . special to me, Jack. More than my eyes, this time, my heart is involved."

I could say nothing to this, but I daresay the cast of my expression showed him that my heart was no less of a participant.

"Very well," he said grudgingly. "I will give you her address, but for one reason and one reason only: because I trust her to know what we mean to each other, although I have yet to actually declare my feelings and intentions."

And so it was that I went, today, hat in hand, to Hillingham at 17 Chatham Street, where Lucy lives with her widowed mother. The servant let me in, and I was promptly met by Mrs. Westenra. She was mildly cross with my impulsiveness, as it caught her and her daughter unprepared for company at teatime. Lucy, on the other hand, seemed quietly pleased and impressed by my spontaneity and she insisted, by turning all of her charm on her mother, that I remain for tea. Clearly, Mrs. Westenra can deny her daughter nothing—and who can blame her?

It turned out to be the most delightful tea imaginable— they served oolong, which they called "the champagne of teas," and almond scones frosted with orange glaze—but I recollect these mean details only out of my determination to

retain every aspect of this afternoon; I hardly partook of anything, which I am certain was noticed by both mother and
daughter. My appetite was submerged throughout in a dark
turbulence, a heaviness of the stomach and vitals utterly new
to my experience. I did much of my talking with Mrs. Westenra, and most of my gazing at her beautiful daughter, whom
I am convinced was feeling—or at least physically aware of—
all that I was experiencing, to judge from the tenderly stu-
dious gaze she returned over the golden rim of her teacup.

So thoroughly has this woman invaded my waking
thoughts and dreams that to sit beside her once again was a
trifle disorienting. I cannot even relate the topics of which
we spoke, so little attention did I pay to the surface details of
our meeting. I can only wonder if I didn't leave their home
with Mrs. Westenra thinking me a babbling, incoherent fool
worthy of locking up in my own asylum. Though I ate and
drank very little, when I came home, I was so overcome with
emotion that I vomited voluminously.

16 APRIL.—Rather than pour my heart into this journal, as
would be the wise and circumspect thing to do, I have been
foolish enough to bare my heart to others. I have put my confused feelings into words and released them into the world
like the contents of Pandora's box. Such indiscretion may
lead to evil, but according to the legend, even in the most
horrid depths of some Pandora's box there was also hope.

Yesterday I accepted a dinner invitation from Lord Remington and agreed to meet with him at Boodle's, his club on
St. James's Street, which is available to guests of the mem-
bership. Remington is old enough to be my father yet as ap-

proachable as a corruptor; he is aware of the imbalance that exists between his confessions and my own, but he has always joked that I shall have adventures of my own someday, and then he will recoup his investments.

After our meal, over a tawny port, I listened to his rollicking account of the problems he was having with a young woman who did not agree that their brief but highly satisfying acquaintance had served its purpose. He sensed my distraction.

"What's got into you, Jack? You look as I imagine I look myself when contemplating a plunge." The last of his words tumbled out over a deep, throaty laugh. His light-heartedness made me wince, for I was feeling a most serious young man.

"That dinner party of yours may prove to be a great turning point in my life," I told him. "I am feeling . . . an unease, whether divine or profane, I cannot say."

Remington held up a hand in warning. "Do not confide her name to me, I warn you, as I am likely to know either the lady or her parents. For your sake, let us hope it is her *parents* that I know!"

"You scoundrel," I grinned. The port was very emboldening.

"Seriously, Jack: you spoke those words with a gravity that is most unlike the Jack I know. This worries me. I won't be so indiscreet as to ask you whether or not this is the first wound you have suffered from Cupid's bow, but I shall take this opportunity to extend some . . . avuncular advice, if I may?"

"Please do."

"Speak of your feelings *to no one*—to no one other than the object of your affections, if affections they truly are. When I was your age, there was a young woman . . . not the first, I admit, but this one was special. She aroused a shyness in me that was most unlike me. I rushed myself to the conclusion that this shyness must be the difference between a jolly good time and true love. I spoke of my true love to the rascals who were my confidants at that time. Not a man of them offered any counsel worth hearing, but my inexhaustible desire to ponder my feelings through conversation was, as I can now appreciate, a perversity. It became a substitute for the natural relationship I might have had with this young woman. I spoke of my feelings to everyone—everyone but her, ordering my confused emotions into the certainty of love by the simple act of stating and restating them to any fool who would listen. I persuaded myself that I had fallen in love, when it might have remained no more than a passing fancy without my worrying it into something gigantic. I missed my moment and doomed myself to months—years, if truth be told—of pain and recrimination that there was never any real need to endure. It was all self-mesmerism, a mouthful of air. Words are dangerous things, and words of love are the most damned and dangerous of all."

"Hardly the words I would expect to hear from a man I know to be an incorrigible *amator*."

"Well," he allowed, "I can say them because I have been around the course, so to speak. Anyway, heed my advice: If words of this nature must be spoken, keep them to yourself until this young woman, whoever she is, lets you know, through a gaze or a touch, that she is ready to hear them."

23 APRIL.—Too distracted to record anything of a personal character. My self-absorption is leading to long afternoons of

absence and patients entrusted to the more responsible hands of the good Doctor Hennessey.

Have listened once again to the details of my previous diary recording. I remember our tea and the way Lucy looked at me, and I cannot help but ask myself:

Have I not already been given that gaze?

30 APRIL.—After a month of residency, Mr. Renfield continues to snub our menu and occasionally has to be restrained and fed by force. (Is there perhaps some religious foundation for his fasting, of which I am not aware?) On those occasions when we introduce unwelcome foods into his system, he purges himself—so it is mysterious to us how he manages to sustain such a well-fed figure.

Earlier tonight, I happened to look in on him, which led to an odd exchange. I saw him seated in the middle of his floor, arms held limply at his sides, with his eyes pointed up as if to Heaven, as one sees in paintings of the saints dating from the Renaissance. He looked so transfixed, so intent upon an ideal known only to his innermost soul, that I believed he took no notice of me—but then his eyes sharply fell and met mine with unnerving directness.

I flinched and spoke before I could think: "What are you looking at?"

"A fool," he answered simply.

"We are back to that, are we?"

"We never left," he observed.

"And why do you consider me a fool?"

"Because everything is now in motion. I have been in your house for a whole month now, and you have ignored me, while mooning over meaningless things. The day shall come when you will rue this missed opportunity."

"I underestimated you, Renfield," I told him. "I did not think you the sort who makes threats."

"Threats? I offer you prophesies, not threats."

"I have better things to do than to listen to you," I said, preparing to shut his trap.

"Your folly," he said, raising his eyes once again to celestia only the mad can imagine.

12 MAY.—I have fallen so much out of the habit of keeping this diary that the use of this dictagraph is no longer second nature; in order to record this unspirited entry, I had to consult the operational instructions that were included with it. I see that it is actually called a "phonograph"! It is hardly worth the bother. There has been nothing to record these last weeks but thoughtless work. "Work" hardly seems an appropriate word for such fetid preoccupation.

24 MAY.—Though more than three hours have passed since the events I am about to record, my skin remains cold and clammy over a searing core of mortal embarrassment. My proposal of marriage was not received as I had hoped.

She loves another. She loves another.

I did not trust to spontaneity, but like the fool Mr. Renfield knows me to be, I went back to Chatham Street with every word and motion rehearsed, like an actor on the stage. As Lucy invited me into her parlour, I nearly sat on my hat, and when she spoke, I was so intent upon remembering everything that I wanted to say that I could not listen or take note of the wonderful privilege of her company. I became so nervous that I could not keep myself from fumbling with what I stupidly, in my state, referred to as the "lancet" chain of my pocket watch. This isn't what you call it at all. She reached out not once, but twice to still my hand. I cannot relate much of what she said, save that it was not what I had hoped to hear.

I began by confessing how dear she had become to me, despite the brevity of our acquaintance. Then I proceeded to tell her how wonderful my life would be, how dedicated I would be, were I given the boon of her love and support. She absorbed this information with a beatific expression, saying nothing, so I advanced to the emotional blackmail of a desperate man, enumerating the ways in which I would be most unhappy if my offer of marriage was rejected! The preamble of this reprehensible litany brought tears to those beautiful eyes. Immediately I apologised, damning myself as a brute, promising that I would say no more. And then, to make myself a perfect fool, I said more.

I must admit to breaking that promise once again in parting, because I had to know if my proposal had simply been pre-mature and that she found the haste of my courtship unseemly, or if she might learn to love me in time. As I saw the gleam in her eyes retract, as if swallowed by dark reply, I understood that Art had not been mistaken in trusting his heart to her care.

I apologised to Lucy for disturbing her and wished her all happiness, knowing that I could never be a part of that happiness, though I did remind her that my friendship would be there if ever she had need of it.

Oh, dearest one! I have lost you completely!

CHAPTER III

Dr. Seward's Diary.

25 *MAY*.—Ebb tide in appetite to-day. Cannot eat, cannot rest, so diary instead. Since my rebuff of yesterday I have a sort of empty feeling; nothing in the world seems of sufficient importance to be worth the doing . . . As I knew that the only cure for this sort of thing was work, I went down amongst the patients.

I paid short visits to each of them and realised, to my dismay, that none was exactly unhappy in their insanity; it seemed to me that they had all, to a greater or lesser degree, achieved a form of perfection in their madness. If these individuals were stories, they had all reached their happy endings—the only tragedy involved is that the stories were brief but the curtain, such as it is, will last a lifetime—like an infinitely sustained note from a cello. The exception to this rule is Renfield, whose seeming ability to see into my heart of hearts has made me keep my distance of late. **He is so quaint in his ideas and so unlike the normal lunatic, that I have determined to** stop evading him and **understand him as well** as I can. To-day I seemed to get nearer than ever before to the heart of this mystery.

I questioned him more fully than I had ever done, with a view to making myself master of the facts of his hallucination. In my manner of doing it there was, I now see, something of cruelty. This aspect was already present in our relationship, of course, and mutual. I wished to keep him to the point of his madness—a thing which I normally avoid with the patients as I would the mouth of Hell. (Under what circumstances would I *not* avoid the mouth of Hell?) *Omnia Romæ venalia sunt. Hell has its price! If there be anything behind this instinct it will be valuable to trace it afterwards accurately,* so I had better commence to do so, therefore—

R. M. Renfield, approximate age fifty-nine. Sanguine temperament; great physical strength; morbidly excitable; periods of gloom ending in some fixed idea which I cannot make out. I presume that the sanguine temperament itself and the disturbing influence end in a mentally-accomplished finish; a possibly dangerous man, probably dangerous if unselfish. In selfish men, caution is as secure an armour for their foes as for themselves. What I think of on this point is, when self is the fixed point, the centripedal force is balanced with the centrifugal; when duty, cause, etc., is the fixed point, the latter force is paramount, and only accident or a series of accidents can balance it.

I knocked and entered his room, where I found him once again at his window. His eyes were narrowed, and he seemed to be inhaling information carried to his nostrils on the spring breezes.

I offer our conversation as it has been preserved in my ad-mittedly distraught memory. There was no apparatus in place to record it, nor was I accompanied by Morrison to transcribe our conversation, as I was motivated by forces more personal than professional.

Before turning to face me, Renfield recited aloud a non-sensical couplet:

"If a call to war is what you choose, the wisdom is to march in twos . . . If harsh defeat is as you please, the wisdom is to march in threes."

"If that is a quotation, Mr. Renfield, I fail to recognise it," I admitted.

"The couplet is mine, but I shall not publish it . . . per-haps someday it shall appear under the name of some other fool," he said obliquely.

"You once described me as a fool."

"Was I mistaken?"

"Well . . . let us just say that, if I be a fool, I have the com-fort of knowing that I made a fool of myself. That is certainly better than to be *made* a fool."

Renfield twisted towards me, away from the window, on his knees, his eyes quite horrible with suspicion. *"What . . . do you . . . know?"*

"Nothing!" I exclaimed in all candour, removing my empty hands from my pockets to show them. "That is why I have come to you. I am not here to talk, Mr. Renfield, but to listen. You are hearing voices that I cannot hear. I want you to help me to hear them. Bring them to my ears. I wish only to listen. I can help you only by listening."

As I regarded him in open appeal, I saw his mask of

seething suspicion slowly melt away from an expression nearly as candid as my own. He looked anxious and concerned, but there was something decidedly behind his emotions, like the presence of a trickster who might allow these admissions in the short term, but who, in the final tally, would permit only himself to be satisfied.

"Do you know what you ask, Doctor Seward?" he asked, stressing his s's. "What you *risk?*"

I took two tentative steps towards him, and he scurried away from his window, climbing onto the pillow at the head of his cot. I looked outside his window at the barren landscape, the disaster area, that was Carfax Abbey—but the image that hovered before me in transparency was the proffered face of Lucy Westenra, a placid mask with eyes closed, indulging my wish to admire it for as long as I wished—for the rest of my life, if I so desired—or so I thought.

"I am of a humour to go a little mad," I told my patient. "I have nothing else."

"You will be damned," he cautioned me, almost singing the words.

"Then damn me, Mr. Renfield—I implore you. But if my soul is to be at stake, we need to do this properly."

I thought of having Renfield escorted to my office, where I could record his voice directly to a wax cylinder, but I intended to extract much more from him than the few minutes allowed by Mr. Edison's new and still-limited invention. So I sent for Morrison to record our conversation in short-hand as it took place. The wonderful thing about Morrison, which makes him the ideal secretary, is that his personality exudes very little force; he is the type who can fade into the wallpaper. Renfield and I would feel free to speak completely openly to each other, as though only the two of us were present to hear him.

"Now, Mr. Renfield . . ." I said, once we were all properly assembled in the patient's room. "I want to know your story, what has brought you here and now. Take me on your journey."

"Where shall I begin?" he asked.

"I think . . . where you are most afraid to begin."

Patient's Oral History.

My earliest memory is terror of the dark. I must have been pulled screaming from my mother's womb, mortified of the darkness inside her, and crying all the more as strange hands tore me out under a moonless sky on a night when high winds let no candle or lantern stay alight. My mother must have been so exhausted by my never-ending cries of hunger and terror that she cast me away.

As the story of my life goes, I suppose it began when the vicar found me. Unlike me, the Reverend Mr. Renfield was quite enamoured of the dark. As the story was first told to me, when I was of an age to appreciate it, the vicar first set eyes on me as he was stepping outside to take a stroll in the moonlight. He found me crying, alone, frightened to death of the dark. You may not believe this, but although I was only a year or two old at the time, I have a very clear picture in my mind of my saviour as he first saw me; he knelt before me with his face bathed in blue-grey moonlight, and spread his cape to gather me. The lining of his cloak was of a pale, grey-white silk—the colour of pigeons—and its luminance offered bright refuge from the night. I stopped my weeping as he took hold of me, and that was that. He became my guardian.

The vicar was a very tall, thin man with grey and white hair, piercing blue eyes, mutton chop side-whiskers, and avian features. He did not wear eye-glasses, as I later did, being one of those rare people of his age who are gifted with perfect eye-sight. I daresay he was in his early fifties at the time he took me in—younger than I am now. He did not seem so old to me because he was my whole world, as I was first becoming aware of it, and the women who cooked and cleaned for him at the vicarage were a bit older still.

When I became old enough to question my identity, Father—I always addressed him as "Father," though the vicar accepted me as his ward rather than as an adopted son—he explained that he had made every attempt to locate my birth-parents, in the weeks and months following my discovery, but had been unable to discover anything about my origins. All of the local children, going back several years, could be accounted for, and he found no reports of tragedy amongst the daughters of the townspeople. I accepted this—a child, at the age I was then, doesn't push where such things are concerned.

To the townsfolk, Father was seen as a stern figure, commanding of all the respect and obedience due his office, but to me he was always warm and kind, with an eye for the magic of creation and a mind that took pleasure in thinking thoughts free of earthly gravity. He was, as they say, young at heart. Not all of his ideas were popular, including the one about accepting a foundling into the vicarage, but they were his and could not be changed. He was often quite exasperated by the townsfolk, who were a superstitious lot, and he did not conceal his opinion of them; nevertheless, ours was a small and isolated village near the sea, and there was no other place for them to worship, so they forgave him anything and everything. He sometimes made demands of private families that would have been unthinkable in a more populous village—including some where I was later concerned—and they were met without a moment's delay. People presumed that his demands were the demands of the Anglican Church.

Even before I arrived, various local women took turns coming to the vicarage to care for Father's domestic needs. These same women were also expected to look after me, but none of them took to the task of nannying me with any pleasure. Their faces and figures changed, but their attitude was always the same as they met me; they made me feel like a contagious disease, like something unwholesome that must be kept at arm's length. Yes, they would bathe me, dress me, and prepare my meals, but it was all done out of obligation—to please Father, to serve the church, or perhaps to make amends to God for their various sins, never out of love. Any attempt I made to show my appreciation or express my affection for these ladies was rebuffed with alarm. You would have thought a rat had gone up their dress. My touch was not welcome.

I remember one of them particularly well. She was quite fat, you see, and there was something about her corpulence that I found most inviting. I imagined that she must be equally plump in warmth and heart. Most children follow their impulses without a second thought of their propriety, but with me, it was different—I had somehow been cowed from following my affectionate impulses, perhaps because no one had ever accepted them, not even my mother. One day, after days of rigourous self-control, I could not resist the temptation any longer and threw my arms around this cook, burying my face in the folds of her fat, wanting to burrow into her so deeply that I could close her behind me. She squealed and grabbed me, thrust me back out and slapped my face; she called me "a little devil" and crossed herself. Perhaps this chastening had befallen me once before, which would explain why I felt so reticent to do what I finally did. . . . But not again did I repeat that performance, I can tell you that much. This woman had words with Father, I suppose, and never returned to his service after that episode, except to attend the Sunday sermons with her family. Even as I stood in her presence, she would not deign again to set eyes on me.

Father's helpers tended to be strange women, cold and dutiful creatures drawn to his cloak. As an older child, I asked Father why these pious women, so devoted to serving the church, seemed to regard me with such contempt. He explained to me that, for most people, their Church is the only source of unconditional love they ever know in their lifetime—in simpler language, of course. He added that, though the relationship between a man or woman and their church was most sacred, it was a love based on faith—and therefore was not a love that begat love or a desire to understand anything or anyone outside that faith. Doubtless this would have been another of Father's unpopular ideas, had he ever pronounced it from his pulpit, but it was typical of the candour he showed to me as his ward. Thus, I began to understand that being a good Christian did not necessarily make one a good person.

Our vicarage was a stone house adjacent to the church and the churchyard where past generations of townsfolk were buried. When I arrived, the main rooms were already claimed, except for one room which was maintained for the convenience of the house-keepers. I was posited there, in a crib, until I was old enough to require a room of my own. At that time, Father prevailed on some strong men from the village to extend the shaft of the kitchen's bread oven into the cellar, that I might sleep there and be warmed by a hearth that Father would set blazing behind a protective grating on cold winter evenings—the same protective grating that you have shielding the glass of my room here, Doctor. This became my haven, and as I lay there in my bed at night, I would spend long periods gazing at those friendly flames and sometimes looking away from them to marvel at the living shadows they cast on the stone walls. My fondness for that hearth led to some confusion in my early religious instruction when Father tried to instill a fear of Hell in me; it was hard for me to understand a roaring fire as being anything but benign.

There was a little bed with a used mattress, a bedside table, a lantern that was kept alight for me throughout the night, and a chest of drawers that held my clothes—which were handed down to me when the other children in our village had out-grown them. On the wall of my room hung a painting of an Angel appearing before two children who were walking in the forest; it was the last thing I looked upon every night before sleeping. Not having anyone to hold and rock me at night, I learned to use the muscles of my body to rock myself to sleep.

It was Father who weaned me from my fear of the dark. One night, at the dinner hour, Father summoned me to his side, bemoaned the state of my fingernails—which I could never keep out of my mouth for very long—and told me that, if I ate all of my parsnips, there would be a most wonderful surprise for me afterwards. Naturally, I did as I was bidden. Then, straightaway after dinner, Father took me by the hand and led me to a stone bench in the garden.

Night was beginning to fall, and I started to fuss, began to cry. I didn't like to be there, when it was turning dark, but Father opened his brightly lined cape and draped it around me, as he had done upon finding me. He sat on the bench as I stood between his knees (which rose to my shoulders), enfolding me in his cape to keep brightness available for me and to keep the evening chill off my bones. He spake of many things, but only one lesson seems to have stuck with me.

He told me that day is separated from the night by four shades of blue. "The first shade," he said, "is *azure*, the colour of the ocean that rolls between the white countries of the clouds. The second is *cyan*, the colour of that ocean as it grows still and motionless in its sleep. The third is *beryl*, the darkening—and the fourth is *sapphire*, in which all of God's jewels are revealed."

We had the garden all to ourselves during the first phase. In the second phase, we were joined by the Moon and, under cover of the third—one becoming two becoming twenty— the sky above us began to fill with bats. I became quite upset, because I knew that bats were creatures of the dark that frightened me so; it was their element, and I didn't like to look very closely at their flitting, darting shadows. *"But watch,"* Father said. "You're missing the whole show!" With his encouragement, I poked my head out of the folds of his cloak and looked. Above us, under sapphire skies, the heavens exploded with stars and the number of bats became legion, emerging from the nearby woods and from our bell tower, forming a fantastic, massive whorl in the clearing over-head.

"And the four living creatures," whispered Father into my ear, *"each of them with six wings, are full of eyes all around and within, and day and night they never cease to say, 'Holy, holy, holy is the Lord God Almighty, who was and is and is to come!'* That is a quotation from the Book of Revelation, chapter four, verse eight."

It was a breath-taking display, better than acrobats in any circus! This was the beginning of a little tradition with us. We followed our supper each night with a visit to the garden, where Father helped me to work through my fears of the dark and its creatures, and to recognise the signature of God in all things. He taught me to appreciate the beauty of frightening things. He taught me not to flinch, or to show signs of anything but wonderment, as the bats swooped so low and close that I could almost hear the tiny hearts drumming beneath their fur. Of one bat in particular, I remember catching a glimpse of two tiny, red, dumbstruck eyes, ever so close to my face, before it soared high above our up-turned faces once again, to rejoin a flurried congregation that appeared chaotic and without design—but, as Father pointed out, was in fact a natural mandala, a nebula of Divinity in which collision was simply not possible.

At times, I found the beauty of their cyclical formations so dizzy-making that I had to hide my eyes from the miraculous designs they etched against the evening sky. If anything, my cowering was a prayerful gesture, but seeing me do this, Father whispered warm reassurance into my ear, interpreting for my other senses that which sight would have them deprived. He spake to me admiringly about all types of bat . . . from the unrefined, pug-faces that squeaked to the sleek red ones, beautiful as foxes, that cronked like geese.

This is where the story of my love of animals begins. A child who feels unloved, you see, brings love into his life by giving love to smaller, less fortunate creatures than himself. Some animals give love of their own accord, and others love us in the way a mirror loves us on a good day; they reflect the love they receive from us. I began to identify with the bats because Father called them "the children of the night," adding "just like you—you were a child of the night when I first saw you and took you in."

Standing in the folds of Father's cape, I once asked him, "Are these your wings, Father?"

"No, lad," he corrected me. "My wings will come later—as will yours—when our Lord and Master comes to collect us. Hear the babies?"

Indeed, coming from somewhere nearby, I could hear the barking of rodent young—a sound like the scooting of wet fingers on glass.

"They want their mothers," Father explained—and he was being sly, Father was, knowing that I would not be able to resist opening my heart to other babies abandoned by their parents. As a foundling, the only emotion more developed in me than my primitive fears was my need to be loved, and to give love—and only in Nature was that hunger more abounding than in my own breast.

As I lay in my bed at night, rocking myself to sleep—I would hear a loving voice, a woman's voice, murmuring the sorts of words that no woman had ever said or sighed or sung to me. It may be that I invented that voice; it may also be that it was genuine. I can only tell you the words it whispered to me in solemn promise:

I will not leave you comfortless; I will come to you.

I later discovered these words, after I learned to read, in the pages of Holy Scripture. To our Lord and Master, any emptiness in any heart is as a room bidding Him to enter. All we need do is accept Him as our Shepherd, and we shall not want.

Commentary.

There was indeed damnation for me in Renfield's words, in that—given my self-destructive state of mind—I could glimpse reflections of myself in his autobiographic ramblings and musings. To wit, both of us were alone, both of us were unloved, both of us had mortally embarrassed ourselves by flinging ourselves at women not ready to accept us, and we both stood on opposite sides of the same bars. Yet Renfield could speak his heart and mind aloud to another human being, while I spoke of such things only to posterity, so which of us was the most healthy, the most free?

I had the escape of my private residence in back of the

asylum, which offered the additional escapes of my home study, my favourite chair, as well as my pipes and libations. Having retreated from my interview with Renfield, it was my immediate intention to surround myself with all of these creature comforts, and to indulge in them while watching the sky outside my window darken from azure to cyan to beryl to sapphire.

The deeper I withdrew, my thoughts occasionally reverted to Renfield and the pathetic options for escape at his disposal, which involved crouching into smaller and smaller balls in the isolation of his cell and hugging his ragged Bible. But—and this is my lasting damnation—I mostly thought of myself and the devastation wrought by rejection, a wasteland which no God was vast enough to fill. I tortured myself with thoughts of Lucy's beauty, her daring, and the fantasy of her laughing in other people's company, also of her submission to another's lips and husbandly embrace. These fantasies became so vivid to me that I could imagine her reality in ways I had never been so fortunate to experience. For one sweet, flashing instant, I saw her naked and freckled, laughing and complicit beneath the weight of me; I could feel the playful, bucking energy she put into her hips. . . . As the hours passed, I would repeat to my anguish the same imagistic patterns, accelerated shufflings of her brave face, her submissive face, her assertive face, and her laughing complicit one, until I began to chuckle mirthlessly at the pain I was causing myself with their steady and measured infliction.

To this brink of despair was as far as Bell's whisky would take me; to get beyond it, to the more Elysian side of pain, I would need to take the more wanton step of availing myself of the dispensary. And so it was that I first consigned myself to the arms of Morpheus.

It was with these arms that Lucy ceased to taunt me and merely held me, held me for as long as I wished, toying with a lock of my hair as I dozed against her. In my heart of hearts, I knew that she was gone, that I must try to think of her as dead, but it was rapture to pretend otherwise as she whispered, warm and loving:

I will not leave you comfortless; I will come to you.

CHAPTER IV

Dr. Seward's Diary.

26 MAY.—This asylum has always been the locus of my existence—the platform of my professional pursuits, where I have studied the varieties of mental illness and strived to lessen the burdens of those who suffer from it—until to-day. This morning, as I crossed from my private rooms into the asylum proper to execute my first duties of the day, I found myself moving from room to room in a place that was infinitely less like a mental hospital and infinitely more like a Hall of Mirrors.

Mrs. Cornelia Willet, a woman who has been weeping inconsolably through every waking hour since she lost a daughter in childbirth more than fifteen years ago, seemed to be weeping for me; Mr. Philip Abingdon, whom we dare not release from his strait-waistcoat without sedation, appeared an unkind illustration of my own internal bucking against circumstance, so incriminating that I felt reluctant to look at his face; Mr. Florian Keller, who has not spoken a word since he was a young man yet presents a face to the world of supreme knowledge, seemed to know every answer for which I was blindly scrambling, and his smugness so annoyed me that, when the two of us were alone together, I actually broke from my professional decorum and cursed him, making him smile all the wider and more wicked; and then there was Miss Evelyne Cushman, not yet twenty-five but hopelessly addicted to drink. Rather than walking as one apart from these and other pathetic creatures and clinically charting their day-to-day progress (or, most commonly, stasis), I felt the status quo had been flayed and pulled inside out, so that I was now under their observation, encircled by crazed eyes in a nest of conspirators.

As for Mr. Renfield, I found him asleep on the floor of his room, shunning a perfectly good cot and using his Bible for a pillow. I was grateful for small mercies, as I was feeling too vulnerable after my indulgences of last night to face him. Pat Hennessey, who was making his own rounds, caught me observing him through the trap.

"Dead to the world," he chuckled. "It would seem that our Mr. Renfield has stayed awake once again through the night."

"A strange case," I offered—rather unimaginatively. "He used to fear the night dreadfully, but now it is the only time when he feels contented."

"Contented?" Hennessey questioned. "Cows are contented. The look I've seen on his face at night I should describe as 'rapturous.' More than once have I opened that trap at night and seen eyes so sparkling, a face so radiant you would think it had been shown all the promises of Heaven."

"You're a poet, Hennessey."

"Alas, it doesn't pay very well." He smiled.

I could appreciate the distinction Doctor Hennessey had made, having seen it in action myself. The tides of Renfield's disposition would appear to be mysteriously chained to the arcs of the sun and the Moon. Things have changed or settled since the initial agonies he suffered here under the influence of the sun—that "buzzing void" he described has evidently released its hold over him. He is no longer assailed by the light of day as one tortured; when the sun is at its brightest, Renfield now becomes increasingly withdrawn, quiet and still, almost a void himself. But as night approaches, he becomes more out-going to the point of intoxication. His energy becomes more manic; his movements become less restrained, more theatrical; his attitude more confident, more arrogant, sneeringly so. His topics of conversation become less focussed on the immediate and more on the eternal; his speech becomes rather more serpentine, with a tendency to exaggerate his s's into hisses of menace. The dichotomy of Renfield is that, while he may well be happiest after dark, that is also when he is most mad and most dangerous.

As we stood there, I could feel Hennessey's clinical eye on me, weighing evidence. "Are you feeling well, Jack?" he asked. "You seem a bit sluggish, and you're perspiring a bit."

I explained that I haven't been sleeping well or eating regularly, and was probably smoking too much. All this seemed to satisfy him—at least I thought it had, until he pressed on, mentioning constipation. I could tell from this question which trail he was following, so I denied any retention with emphatic good nature.

In future I must remember that not everyone within these walls is mad or dissociated, so I had best be more careful about what I do to ease my distress, lest I parade my symptoms.

LATER.—Throughout our initial conversation, I found Renfield susceptible to malefic expressions of smug superiority, implying that I—who should have been in control—was somehow at a disadvantage. Therefore, for our second interview this afternoon, I made the decision to have Renfield brought to my office instead.

Though it was afternoon, which guaranteed Renfield would be somewhat docile, I deemed it wise to restrict his movements in some way, without resorting to the full security measure of putting him into a strait-waistcoat. I settled on a strong leather belt which could be connected by a strong chain to an iron link on my office wall. This kept him within easy reach of the comfortable wing chair across from my desk, yet at more than arm's distance from my throat. Morrison was present, seated in a chair behind Renfield, to record everything that was said. The placement of Morrison's chair enabled the patient to lose sight of the fact that there was a third person in the room.

I remember Renfield's eyes as he entered my office for the first time . . . how they darted about with alacrity as he noted the disparities of scenery—the stark difference between his humble quarters with its plain table and stool, its cot and slop bucket, and my leather chairs and walls of polished cherrywood; the ruin visible from his window and the verdant boughs of the trees visible from mine. Of my displayed me-

mentos, he showed particular affinity for a small, decorative bronze casting of Michelangelo's *Pietà* positioned to the side of the centrally placed clock on my mantel. He asked to handle it, but considering its weight and sharp edges, I could not allow this, owing to the ease with which it could be deployed as a weapon. He understood and politely withdrew his request. I invited him to sit and make himself as comfortable as his restraint would allow.

"Your office is as different to my room as your fine suit is to this potato sack you would have me wear," he said, referring to the clothing we assign to the patients who do not have their own. The springs of his chair squeaked under his weight as he sat, reminding me that his heft was remarkably well sustained for a patient who, to all outward appearances, was bent on starving himself.

I started by explaining that Mr. Morrison would be joining us, as before, to record his statement—but should be paid no heed. I also showed and demonstrated briefly my Edison phonograph, which I explained might also be operated at times of my choosing to record actual samplings of his voice. As I began to relate in some detail how the apparatus works, I sensed that the patient's attention was divided . . . Perhaps he was merely taking the size of my unfamiliar quarters, or it could be that, like any prisoner, he was scrutinising the four walls for weak joinings, possible paths to escape should an unguarded moment ever present itself?

Upon seating myself across from Renfield—at a distance suitable to maintaining my safety—I determined that his attention was held with craven intensity by something in the vicinity above my head. I followed the line of his fixed gaze but saw nothing but the overhead electrical lamp suspended from the ceiling. I assumed that Renfield—a provincial, after all—had never seen Mr. Edison's other wonderful invention adapted to everyday use; indeed, he would not be the first of my office guests to express wonderment of it. However, his object of fascination was unwavering, so it is possible that he was not admiring the lamp at all, but focussed on some idea that loomed only in the fracas of his own shattered mind.

As he had already told me about his known origins and his early years in the care of the vicar, I proposed—rather than continue on with the chronology of his life at this time—that we change the subject of his monologue to his religious fanaticism, which I put to him as his "religious devotion," as it seemed so central to his thinking. Was it merely a trait which he had inherited from the environment where he was raised? Was it the product of his own untended imagination? Or might it be the out-sized reaction to some undisclosed personal trauma, a protective barrier he had rallied around himself in defence against his inner demons?

Patient's Oral History.

My religious devotion is a devotion to life, Doctor; it is as simple as that. Our Lord promises all of us who accept Him that we will someday walk beside Him through an everlasting life. That's for me! The dark no longer holds any terrors for me, but death has always disturbed me; I have always found it . . . unacceptable, a grievous error in the design of an otherwise splendiferous creation.

I will tell you a story. One day, when I was a child of perhaps three years, I felt that Father was ignoring me. I no longer remember the reason; it may have been that he was involved in the problems of some member of his congregation, or engrossed in the writing of one of his sermons. Whatever the cause, I made the decision to absent myself from the vicarage in the hope he would notice I was missing and come looking for me. Is there any more wonderful feeling than to be sought out by someone who has missed you, and found?

I was feeling quite angry—I went stomping along the edge of our property with a sling-shot I had made, firing little rocks hither and yon. As I made my way past the churchyard, I was drawn to a tree by a commotion of birds. The sound was coming from a high branch. As I turned my gaze down from on high, I was startled to find a dead bird at my feet—a swallow, to be precise. It must have fallen from its nest, distressing its family. I dropped my toy and lay down on the grass, on my stomach, for a closer look at this animal which, when alive, is too quick to be studied, too quick to be touched.

Never before had I beheld a dead thing; it lay perfectly straight and stiff, its wings at its sides and its chest pushed proudly forward, with an expression on its face that I can only describe as noble. It would have looked no different had it been standing in a queue in Heaven, listening to a litany of praises while awaiting a medal to be pinned to its breast. It looked like a perfectly dressed, serious, little man—with a beak, of course.

Nature was abundant around the vicarage, and I had seen birds of many colours and countenances even in my short time. I never thought much about birds, really, because they have no outward personality; even in life, they all look stuffed when they stand still. But it was only as I reached out and gathered this dead bird in my hand that I began to appreciate that birds do have personality, but a personality which moves at a different speed than people can see; it can only be seen in the stillness of death. Perhaps a bird's living movements are too quick, too fleeting for slow, human eyes to appreciate, but as this swallow lay in my hand, the size of a small carrot and just as rigid, I felt I knew it as well as I had known anyone of my own species. He was a bit pompous . . . we might have our differences . . . but he was essentially kind and giving. In the first ten minutes in which I held his feathered form, this bird became my friend, and in the next ten or twenty, he became my close friend. I became possessed of the strange conviction that, as long as I continued to hold him, there was a chance that my warmth might reach him and bring him back. I sat at the base of that tree for hours, cradling this dead creature in my hand, and listening to the frantic tweeting of his uncomprehending family on the branch far above my head. I stayed there, my hand filled to brimming with death, until that tweeting subsided into meek acceptance and night began to fall. It is true that Father introduced me to the night and to the aerial dance of the bats, but it was only then—as I held death by the hand, whilst night fell—that I truly overcame my fear of the dark. I understood that there was something bigger, darker still to fear.

As the sky's cyan edged into beryl, true to my hopes, I saw Father's caped figure silhouetted against the coming night in the distance. There was something resolute in his stride that made his shadow look stern and bespoke of certain punishment . . . but, as it drew closer, it spoke more clearly of patience and benevolence and love.

"I've been looking everywhere for you, child," Father said, in a vexed mixture of the cross and the warm. He knelt beside me and frowned at the dead bird in my hand, telling me to put it down, that it might be diseased, but I refused. I also refused when he asked me to give it him, and by so refusing—which would have been unthinkable in any other situation—I conveyed to Father what a distraught state I was in. He began to talk to me about the dead bird and the ideas racing through my mind.

Father told me that, while my love and sympathy for animals was most commendable, and though animals were among God's most marvellous creations, it was important for me to understand that they were *without soul*. "Animals were meant as an adornment to Man's world, companions before the arrival of Woman, nothing more. They are without soul or consciousness or hope of Heaven—where we shall need no more of companionship than is given by our Lord."

I began to cry. The little bird, who looked so proud and presentable to our Lord, could not have known that he would be kept waiting indefinitely.

I pointed out to Father the personality that I felt was so evident in the dead bird's little face, and he humoured me. "Well, what do you know?" he said. "He does look like a little man, at that. A little soldier. Perhaps this was an exceptionally good bird, brave and a good provider to his family, and he is to be rewarded—by being re-born as a man, by which course he may yet ascend to the glories of Heaven."

"Can it not be so for all animals, Father?" I pleaded.

"Perhaps it could, but according to the Book of God's Word, it is not," he answered. "Most animals one sees, when

83

divested of spirit like this, are indistinguishable from a plank of wood—as you will eventually discover for yourself, if you continue to poke your nose into woods and forests and churchyards. Put it down, child."

"But, Father . . . If I put it down, the story of his life will be over."

"It *is* over, child. Put it down."

But I refused to put it down, just as I refused to accept the Bible's view on this unknowable matter. I knew that, in some people's eyes, my stubbornness would be tantamount to blasphemy, but I trusted in Father's forgiving heart—I was still, after all, just a child. He had the word of the Lord God on his side; on my side was only righteous indignation and the belief in a still more loving and sympathetic Lord and Master. After all, Doctor Seward, if animals are truly born without souls, why have they such a capacity for love, the most human of emotions? Animals are so loving, and so unparticular as to whom they show their love, that I believe—contrary to Holy Scripture—they have an *abundance* of soul.

In his piety, Father presumed to know all the secrets of the animal kingdom, and he told me one hundred times if only once that the purpose of religion was to expunge the lowly animal from capitalised Man. He told me that animals lived only to breed and feed upon one another, that they were born damned as they were not able to read the Word of our Lord and therefore could not venerate Him—even that they could not see colours. But what else is any man to tell himself, when the Bible expounds that animals are unreasoning creatures born of instinct, that "whoever kills an animal shall make it good," while whoever kills a person shall be put to death?

Father and I sat there together, under that tree at the edge of the churchyard, until the sky had turned sapphire. Then, under its jewels, we returned to the vicarage, the dead bird still clutched tightly in my hand. At the door-step, Father instructed me to go straight down to my room and prepare myself for bed, telling me that he would look after the bird, seeing that it was given a proper burial. Reluctantly, I released it and blessed it, but—instead to going downstairs to my room as I was told—I ran upstairs to the room where Father slept. There, I found a suitable window from which I could attend the funeral service from above—a bird-like vantage.

Without so much as a look at the feathered husk in his hand, Father sent the dead swallow into the overgrown grass on the other side of the churchyard wall with an underhanded toss.

"Food for the earth," he muttered, as he turned on his heel.

As I numbly descended the stairs to my room, I swore to myself that I would belong no more to Victoria's England, that I would now shun its hypocrisies by denying the soul of my own kind and becoming a most fervently loyal subject of the animal kingdom. So tenaciously did I cling to this oath that it was not until after several hours—of lying there in my bed, absolutely still with my chest puffed out and my tiny feet erect—that I finally fell asleep.

In my dream, I felt gentle currents of air bussing my face and my arms. I opened my eyes and saw that I was far above the ground, riding the winds with out-stretched arms. By changing the position of my arms from parallel with my shoulders to, say, twenty of two, I could career sharply to my left and see the world beneath me spin like a top, but I never became dizzy. Although my eyes took in the entirety of the ground below me, they were less focussed on the whole than on the particular. The world below me was careening counter-clockwise in one mad swirl, yet my eyes could be attuned to the squiggling of a single earthworm. By inclining my head and moving my arms to twenty of four, I was able to swoop down and capture it as feed, and I felt such pride I thought my chest would burst. With this worm-meal in my mouth, I flew to that branch in the tree above the church-yard, proud to carry sustenance to that poor family of birds which had lost their father and husband. They were quick to accept me in his place, and I experienced a sense of belonging that was unlike anything I had ever known. I dropped the worm-meal into the nest, and the mother bird took it into her beak, chewing it thoroughly before sharing it with her off-spring—*our* off-spring.

I knew the joy of being in a place where I belonged, doing what I was born to do—and then there was a sharp pain—perhaps my heart had burst with pride!—and I fell from the branch and everything that I loved. I saw myself tumble all the way to the ground. I saw my family far above me, chirping in a chorus of despair, losing me now and forever, while on the ground, not far away, a young boy approached me, enormous, towering over me. He was carrying a toy he had made with his own small hands. *He had used it to take my life away—why?* And with this question on my beak, I awoke—on the floor beside my humble bed—and broke into the most terrible tears. I never played with my sling-shot again.

I prayed that morning more fervently than I had ever prayed before. I do not know to whom I prayed, but it was not to Father's God—I addressed my prayers to the open air, where they might be intercepted by any spirit sensitive to the animal soul. I prayed for forgiveness and forsook everything about myself that was mean and human and disrespectful of animals. And do you know, Doctor Seward? From the moment I opened my eyes, after that prayer—from that moment to this—I have dwelled in a world in which all of the picture-book colours were erased, re-painted top to bottom in greater or lesser degrees of shadows and ashes and milk. So deeply offended was I by the wrong I had done, and so repentant, that I actually willed myself to become colour-blind. And the world of animals, sensing this transformation, embraced me as one of their own.

So doubt not my authority when I speak to you of animals, of clean animals, and of animals that are not clean, and of birds, and of everything that creeps on the ground. I know all the birds of the hills, and all that moves in the field is mine.

Notes on Transcript.

Morrison's transcript does not encompass a brief exchange that took place between the patient and myself immediately after the recording. On the subject of the dead bird, Renfield remembered some further instruction from the vicar: "You must remember, boy: If you should ever find a young bird that has fallen from its nest and survived, do not touch it. If you should pick it up, mend its wing, and later return it to its nest, the mother bird will smell you on it and will no longer accept it as one of its own. She will feed her other babies, but the one that has been touched will be bumped from the nest yet again, or left to starve."

To this, Renfield added: "I spent years wondering if this was what happened to me. Could this be why my family did not want me? Because I was touched?"

Dr. Seward's Diary.

6:00 P.M.—This afternoon's meeting with Mr. Renfield produced some very positive results. He spoke to me at length about animals and the role they play in his spiritual philosophy. His ideas are certainly un-orthodox but wayward, not at all what I would call "mad." He has clearly given the subject a life-time of thought. He was not at all abusive towards me to-day, and I thought that perhaps the change of scene, as we moved from his room to my office, had put him at a sense of disadvantage. But now, in retrospect, I think his comparative courtesy was encouraged by the fact that I was willing to listen to, and respectfully ponder, his theories and philosophies.

What I find most interesting about Renfield's latest addition to his oral history are the inconsistencies that exist (quite obviously, in fact) between what he says and what he is. There are times when he impresses me as a virtual caricature of a Christian zealot; he fasts, sleeps with his Bible, is clearly something of a Bible scholar to judge from his ability to quote and cite Scripture—yet he claims to have turned his back on Mother Church, because it denies the existence of the animal soul.

He never did—and perhaps could not—explicitly confess to me that he was responsible for killing that bird with his sling-shot, but this truth was unmistakably there in the details of the dream he related, in which he assumed the role of the bird and experienced its death. This irrevocable event was traumatical and clearly altered the very fabric of his reality. He has striven to make amends, becoming assertive in his love of animals (indeed, he imagines himself to be an honourary animal), which is plausible to the extent that the patient has been disregarding the poultry and beef apportioned on his dinner plates. Yet he was brought here after orally eviscerating a rat which he had caught with his own bare hands! (Must pay close attention to future sessions for references to colour, in the event that his boast of having willed himself colour-blind may also be proven false or self-delusional.)

Question: If Renfield successfully willed himself to be colour-blind, in his oath of fraternity to the animal world, did he also will himself to become without soul?

CHAPTER V

Dr. Seward's Diary.

27 MAY.—Dined last evening in solitude at Simpson's restaurant, near the Savoy. I timed my meal for the final curtain, thinking that the excitement generated by an audience fresh from seeing the latest Gilbert and Sullivan (*The Mikado*) might be good for a lift.

I was thinking about Lucy as I sat at my riverside table, casting my eyes soulfully out over the dull glitter of the Thames—when, without warning, my thoughts were disrupted by a bold and humorous American voice: "Good sir, that hang-dog face of yours can mean only one thing—you and I share the secret shame of being denied the hand of Miss Lucy Westenra in marriage!"

Quincey P. Morris! We first met in North America, when I was tagging along with Arthur on one of our trips to distant lands. We were two Londoners trying to act rugged by pitching our tents on the American prairie, and Quincey, who was doing the same as a simple fact of life, took great humour in us. We resented his amusement at first, but before long, the three of us were laughing as one. We grew to like his company, his refreshingly out-going nature, and spent some delightful hours together listening to the stories he told over campfires in his Texan accent—some of them were rather raw—but when it was time for us to move on, we did not exchange addresses. Imagine our surprise when, the following year, while travelling in South America, whom should we discover there but Quincey, admiring the sights on the shore at Titicaca! Well, after a coincidence of such proportion, you simply must exchange addresses, and after raising many a happy glass—and some hell—in Bolivia, we certainly did.

I stopped travelling with Arthur after founding this asylum, but I continued to see Quincey on occasion when he came to London. And now here he was again, in the most astonishing coincidence of them all. It seems he was the third man, besides Arthur and myself, to propose marriage to Lucy—not just to the same woman, but on the same afternoon! It was simply too absurd . . . enough to leave you wondering if such a coincidence was proof of God or the Devil himself. I wasn't even aware that they knew one another! Arthur must have introduced them, as well.

It was wonderful to see Quincey, but to be reminded of Lucy as boldly as that, without warning, and especially in an attitude of mocking humour—and to discover that he, of all people, had been another player for the fair lady's hand—came as rather a concentrated shock. Quincey evidently saw some shade of these violent thoughts flash across my face; I saw him teeter for an instant, wondering whether he had done the right thing by approaching me, and as I was witness to this indecision, I experienced a moment of profound insight—profound enough to look both ways, as it were—and could suddenly see through all the nonsense to the sort of decent, gallant—and humorous—man I would be a fool to call anything but friend.

We embraced, and he took a seat at my table, snapping his fingers at the waiter for service. "Your man Pat Hennessey told me I would find you here." He smiled, looking around. "Fancy place! Not at all like that place where the three of us used to . . . What was it called?"

"The Korea," I said, adding nothing more until after the waiter had come with an opened bottle of red wine and a second glass, and then gone; even then, it was Quincey who broke the silence.

"Well, Jack, I guess the best man won."

"Yes," I moaned, salting my wounds. "The best man, not the proper groom."

Quincey frowned as he raised his glass, tipping it slightly in my direction, in salute. "Now, correct me if I'm wrong, but I gather you aren't taking Miss Lucy's decision very well."

"Correct *me* if *I'm* wrong, Quincey," I countered, "but I cannot see how you could have invested your own proposal with very much feeling if you can."

He chewed on this comment for a moment or two. "I do admire and adore the lady," he finally said with American courtliness, as he replaced his glass on the table and folded his hands, "but I have seen enough of this world to know that admirable and adorable ladies are not exactly in short supply. Maybe not so nice, maybe not nearly so pretty—but maybe a better match for me."

"I've seen far less of this world than you, so I can feel only devastation."

Bolstered by another gulp of his wine, Quincey took command of the situation. "Now listen up, Jack," he said, "our buddy Art has a right to expect better of you. We should behave under these circumstances as he would want us to behave, in his place. He's just been given the best reason to celebrate that he's ever going to have in his entire life, and he needs someone to help him commemorate the occasion—to give him an evening he won't ever forget. And that, right there, boils it down to you and me."

"Two green peas in a pod," I said, drinking.

"Aw, don't look so plum miserable!" I was reprimanded.

"I'm sorry, Quincey," I apologised. "It's been a rough time, and I'm just rotten company."

"I know what you need, old bean," he said, summoning up a silly endearment from our past. "You need gaiety. I'll tell you what I'm going to do. I am going to order another bottle of this most excellent product. When we drain it dry, I am going to pack you into a coach and go back to my hotel room. If my hand is still steady enough to hold a fountain pen, I will dash off a slushy note of congratulations to Lord Godalming's boy and sign both our names to it, telling him that you and I have made the Devil's own plans and have quite an evening of revels in store for him."

After more talk and more wine, we finally agreed upon Saturday evening. Thought I'd had enough to drink to forget my cares, but I tossed and turned in bed, knowing that something far more soothing than wine was available to me.

I have notified the staff that I am feeling under the weather and will not be leaving my private quarters to-day. It is important that I take charge of myself and solve this problem before it becomes more visible to Hennessey, or—God help me—even to Renfield.

"Physician, heal thyself."

28 MAY.—Insomnia last night. As I lay in bed, thinking of Renfield's proud dead bird in its righteous *rigor mortis*, my thoughts turned to the methods I have been using to ameliorate my disappointments. I tell myself that I am gold-plating my problems rather than solving them; that however successful an escape narcotics may provide in the short run, they are now compounding, rather than easing, the upsets assailing my peace of mind. I am also aware that my normal state is turning more demanding, short-tempered, and easily upset. Any little annoyance or disappointment—the need to deal with one's monthly bills, the piling up of tedious but necessary work that one does not wish to do, a waiter in a restaurant apologising to me because the dessert I have ordered and anticipated throughout my meal isn't available—can also trigger the appetite for oblivion. There are also the burdens of guilt and secrecy to consider, which complicate one's life beyond description and make one less available to spontaneities like unannounced visits from old friends, who know all too well how one is supposed to be.

My professional focus on Renfield is a far preferable, more constructive, and indeed promising diversion—and yet this is a diversion that, through involuted process, seems to bring me back to the very thoughts I seek to elude! His story, which is only just beginning to be told, has already reminded me of how crucial is a balance of love and affection in one's life to keep one on the straight and narrow. Untended human beings—like weeds—grow wild and proliferate, strangling. But perhaps

Renfield's story will help me to uncover certain valuable secrets, revelations of roads untaken, that may lead me to my own salvation.

Good God! Listen to me! What kind of doctor am I? There is a man, here in my asylum, in a terrible mental state. It is my sworn duty to apply my knowledge to his curing, but all I can think about is how he might help me! If truth be told— and if I cannot tell the truth here, where can I tell it?—this is not the first time I have taken note of this tendency of mine. It is for this reason, in fact, that I am staying at home this weekend, behind closed doors, away from all my patients, as I struggle to get hold of myself and stand on my own two feet.

Must try to cut back.

No—*must* cut back. *Est modus in rebus.*

Speaking of Renfield—an interesting development in my absence, as told to me by a letter that I found slipped under my door this morning . . .

Letter from Patrick Hennessey, M.D., M.R.C.S.L.K., Q.C.P.I., etc., to John Seward, M.D.

28 May.

My dear Sir—
Please forgive this intrusion, but there has been a development concerning Mr. R. M. Renfield of which I feel you need be informed.

This morning, as I was making my rounds, and yours in your stead, the patient fell to his knees before me and begged to be given another book. He requests a plain note-

book in which he may write down his thoughts in your absence. Though it was quite early in the day, the more he appealed to me, quite frankly, the more anger and resentment he expressed towards you. He is most upset by your absence, though I explained you are ill and principally concerned with not infecting the patients. But he would have none of it. His exact words: "What kind of doctor invites these stories, summons these images from the past, then flees just as the dam is about to break! Please, Doctor Hennessey—before I explode, I must have a little book. Help me to purge these memories from my head!"

I consulted Renfield's chart and found no annotations portraying him as a suicide risk, so I trust I have done nothing wrong by presenting him with a small pocket-sized notebook and pencil. He was writing in it quite eagerly as I left him, under guard. With your permission, I will administer a sedative to him later in the day, so that we may ascertain what he has written with such urgency.

Yours faithfully,
Patrick Hennessey.

From Renfield's Notebook.

FIRST ENTRY, UNDATED.—A dark figure stands in the distance, beckoning me to follow. The place we inhabit is equally dark, so I cannot discern his features—only an occasional glimmer of moving skin, stretching and adjusting with his changes of expression; that much catches the light. He beckons me to follow; and I do follow, because although he is a fearsome figure, there is something quite familiar about him. Anything familiar is both mysterious and a wonderment to me, and I cannot resist the tug of it.

The figure leads me into deeper darkness, but I understand somehow that, beneath the black, enriching its lustre, is a layer of the most beautiful blue—and this is a comfort to me. This blue-in-black is at the heart of the atmosphere inside an enormous ruin, and it is here, to the heart of this fantastic ruin, that I have been beckoned. It is a cold and dead place, to be sure, yet there is something about it that bespeaks of great warmth and glory. I want badly to bask in it.

The figure beckons me to follow him deeper still into the ruin, and I do follow. He leads me to a place where the blue shines through the black in such an intensive way as to take my very breath away. Then he beckons me to look more closely at the black—no, into the black—and I do. And I discover that, as the black derives its radiance from the blue beneath it, the blue derives its beauty from yet another colour beneath it, which is of the most astounding gold. He beckons me to follow the urge which comes naturally, which is to plunge my two hands into those colours that reside deepest within the dark. I do—I plunge my hands into those colours, and I feel wetness—not a disconcerting wetness, but a pleasing, cleansing wetness. The blue, I realise, is the blueness of a pool. My hands thrash about in the pool and find shapes to grab on to, hard and solid shapes, and when I pull my hands out of the pool, I see that my hands are filled with shining objects of tremendous value—*indeed, a treasure!* But once I have plucked from the blue pool its last source of gold, the blue is weakened and the black loses its lustre. I find that my greed has plunged me, and the beckoning figure as well, into the deepest possible darkness—a darkness without light. Then, in the distance, visible through the breaks in the walls of this ruin, the orb of the sun can be seen rising up behind the curving horizon—and its scattering rays strike the golden treasure in my arms. The light bounces off my treasure and is reflected onto the face of the other in my company—*I can see his face!* I am horrified to see that this shadowy figure is not a man at all, but rather hundreds—no, *thousands* of flies . . . standing before me in the shape and the height of a man! It was the movement of the living flies, moving yet holding his shape, that I had mistaken for the movement of living flesh!

His hand of living flies gestures to me, trying to convey a thought to me, and I notice that such pantomime is necessary, for this thing of horror has no mouth with which to speak. The fly-man suddenly looks vulnerable, in need of me. He repulses me, but I feel as much pity for him as revulsion, and he has taken such pains to lead me, past my fears, to a place where I have found great wealth. I reach out for his tragic hand in great sympathy, which causes me to drop some of my treasure with a clang, and the flies that give his hand shape scatter at the noise and at the bump of my touch.

As I withdraw my hand, and as the clang ceases to echo through the ruin, the flies return and resume the shape of a hand—a hand that continues to reach out to me. Then, in a moment of inspiration, the hand rises, gesturing to where the figure's mouth should be, for it has no mouth. I understand that he is asking for my kiss. It is repugnant to me, the idea of kissing this face of living flies, but I am grateful for all that this figure has done for me and so I lean closer—but with a distaste I cannot disguise. My lips touch the surface of living flies.

They feel like the bubbles in a glass of champagne. Yes, the kiss tickles, and as I pull back, some flies remain stuck to my lips and are slow to scatter—but they do. I blow at them and wave them away like thistle-down. I see that my kiss has left a hole in the mass of insects that lend form to the fly-man's head. The kiss worked: I have given him a mouth. The mouth spreads wide and begins to laugh. The laugh has no sound, but I have a feeling in my blood that this laughter is mocking me.

The sun has filled the ruin with light, and I can see that what I thought was a treasure is nothing but glistening weeds plucked from the pool. I feel as though I have been tricked, and, in my frustration, I lash out at the fly-man. The flies do not scatter this time, but hold their shape as the figure topples to the ground, trailing a cape of flies behind him. He lies there inert. The mouth I have given him remains open and slack. Have I killed him?

I kneel beside the fly-man and peer into the chasm of his mouth, the mouth I have made, as if it is the opening of a deep cave or bottomless pit. The dark there is inviting, familiar, with all the pull of the familiar. Then it surprises me by moving, articulating words—as a familiar voice says, with its dying breath:

"But don't you want to know who you really are?"

I am aghast at what I have done because yes, yes, I do so want to know . . . but, as I watch in horror, the flies that give shape to the mouth that gave shape to that question begin to move closer to one another, to converge on all sides, causing the mouth to shrink before my eyes, to shrink until it is sealed like a tomb—and no kiss no kiss no kiss on earth can bring it back.

CHAPTER VI

Dr. Seward's Diary.

29 MAY.—I returned to the asylum to-day—very late in the day—after my first night of unassisted sleep in three or four. I do not know if I am quite ready, I do not know what Hennessey or Renfield will see when they see me, but the entry in Renfield's notebook has persuaded me that, if anything can command my attention away from the things that would haunt me, it is the altogether bigger things that haunt him.

LATER.—When Renfield was brought to my office earlier this evening, he made no attempt to disguise his displeasure over my sudden disappearance. He showed me naked contempt in the presence of the attendants, and it was not until I had apologised and pleaded a personal emergency that he relented and agreed to carry on. Even then, there was a ring of rebuke in his words as he stressed to me that his story was of the greatest importance, and, though it would take days for the full story to be told, I must not confuse its urgency with a luxury.

Watkins chained the patient's belt to the iron link on my wall, gave the chain a couple of test tugs, and tipped his white cap to me as he and Hardy left the two of us alone.

"You may not—indeed, you *do not* realise this, Doctor," Renfield stressed to me, at the very moment that the door was closed, "but you are on a time-table. Strategic maps and battle lines have been drawn. Make no mistake, war is coming! Such a war as the world has never seen! I can afford to take my time, but I caution you: You are in no position to be taking vacations—least of all from me!"

"I see," I told him—though I didn't, really.

The patient narrowed his eyes, as though he understood as much. And then, as I seated myself and saw the direction of his gaze, I perceived that his vision was once again trained on the electric lamp hanging overhead. The last time he saw it, it was afternoon, thus it was no more distinctive than a chandelier; but now it was evening, and it was illuminated. I decided to bring the matter out into the open: "I see that you are interested in our modern electrical lighting."

Renfield said nothing, as his attitude darkened to morbid brooding.

"We cannot afford to have the entire sanatorium re-done as yet," I explained, brightly. "For now, it is a convenience reserved for the private offices of the staff. Mr. Edison of America will soon change the face of old London. Before long, our gas-lights will be nothing but a bittersweet memory of a world that no longer exists."

"I don't give a *damn* for your lights," Renfield growled, making a complete turn-about. "But yes, all of this"—he paused as he peered around the room, encompassing every detail of my daily reality in his statement—"will be naught but a memory before very long."

"Why do you say that?"

"Because the four walls of this office are but a square on a chess-board," he explained, casting a glance at my checkered floor tiles. "A chess-board of history, if you will—indeed, a chess-board of destiny. The game is being played by a Master, who knows His every move and is well on His way to victory before His opponents are even aware the game has begun. It is a game worthy of one who has commanded armies! Every piece is in place for His inevitable triumph!"

"As this Master's personal adjective wields a capital aitch, the war you perceive as imminent must be a religious war."

"Finally—he *listens*!" Renfield exclaimed, hissing. "Yes, of the highest order!"

"Very well," I allowed. "And who are you on this chess-board, may I ask?"

"Merely a pawn," he said, "until you came along. Now I shall walk with the Lord, for I am the Word! I am His Gospel!"

"The Book of Renfield?" I said, sarcastically entitling his fantasy.

"Yes!" he exclaimed, saliva firing through the gaps in his teeth. *"My soul shall live because of thee!"*

"Does that make me also a pawn?"

"In fact, Doctor, I am not at all certain if you are any longer in play. The Queen struck you from the game at your first advance, did she not?"

I knew he meant Lucy . . . but how the devil did he know about her? Especially with my nerves a bit frayed by the stress of a perhaps pre-mature return to work, it took all my will-power not to strike him. I bade him to continue with his story, anything to shut him up about current events.

I nodded to Morrison to begin his transcription, and he looked at me sympathetically, as one who knew my problems from transcribing my diary cylinders and, out of either devotion or solid professionalism, held his tongue.

Patient's Oral History.

For the first several years of my life, the vicar shared his home and time and affection with me, ensuring that I was fed and taught right from wrong and acquainted with the teachings of our Lord. I considered him wondrous and wise in many ways, but after the incident involving the dead bird, I came to understand that he was not wise in all things. I began to withdraw from him. Despite his blind spots, Father was a sensitive and kindly man, and he noticed that a subtle change had taken place in our relationship. His interpretation of this change was that I was reacting to a lack of the balance in my life that only a true family can provide. And so it was decided—when I was of the age to be starting school—that I should live away from the vicarage for a while, perhaps somewhere closer to the school-house, in the home of a real family with room for an extra child.

It was during one of his Sunday sermons that Father appealed to his congregation for the patriarch of one such family to step forward, out of Christian charity, and give his foundling the environment that is the bedrock of all good and God-fearing people. The family that stepped forward that day had the name of Griggs.

Mr. Griggs, a tall and beefy-looking man, came to collect me one Sunday after church. I made such a fuss that he walked me to his house with his big hand tight about the nape of my neck, pushing me insistently forward the entire way. Besides that, and the bruise it left, all I can remember of leaving the vicarage is crying, feeling that Father no longer loved me, and thinking that the only thing in the entire world smaller than myself was the little suit-case in which I carried my clothes and the one or two items I could truly call my own belongings. I cried because the room that Father had built for me, whose hearth was at the centre of all my notions of sanctuary, was being taken away from me—at least for five nights of the week—along with all the little things I had found to decorate it and make it all the more mine . . . beautiful feathers and rocks that contained the calcified remains of ancient fish and mammals. I could have taken these with me, but I was afraid that I would never find my way back to the vicarage had I done so. I was so beside myself with anxiety that I would have forsaken my beliefs in the animal soul, or claimed to, just to appease Father that I might stay where I belonged.

The Griggses had been married long enough that they had become, as the Bible says, as one flesh; they resembled each other so much that one might imagine them to be brother and sister. Mr. Griggs was a hard-working farmer, and Mrs. Griggs was a good wife who kept her husband's meals on the table and his home and clothing clean. She was the only woman in our village who ever had a kind word to say to me. I often pondered the mystery of why that should be; perhaps it was because they had raised their own children to adulthood and lamented their empty nest. I lived with them for two years, filling that familial void between the ages of five and seven.

During the two years I spent under their roof, I never saw Mr. Griggs kiss his wife or show her any affection, but at times in the evening, when Mrs. Griggs thought I wasn't looking, I observed her stealing pinches of her husband, on his face and his arms, with an energy of fun and excitement, that reminded me of children my own age when they play tag. (I had seen other children play such games but was never invited to participate.) In the night, as I lay in the sagging bed that had once belonged to one of their heavy children, under a threadbare quilt that had once warmed them and taken all the punishments their childhoods had meted out, I heard incomprehensible noises coming from the Griggses' room—animal noises.

The next day, I looked about their farmhouse for animals who might have wandered inside, but I could find none—nor any other explanation of what had occurred in the night. But the missus's furtive touching and poking and pinching of her mister, like a toothsome piece of meat, continued unabated.

A gradual but alarming change took place in the midst of all these pinchings and gruntings. Week by week, Mr. Griggs began to lose weight, and his wife—who was just a little bit of a thing—began to grow fat. He became so . . . I didn't know the word then, but . . . *desiccated*. He became so *desiccated* that he ceased to perspire, walking in-doors from a day spent under the sun with his skin as dry as driftwood. Yet his wife, who seldom ventured out-of-doors, perspired all the time from her layers and skirtings of newly accrued flesh, as if she spent her entire days over a steaming wash-tub. She began to walk about with difficulty, as though she was carrying the bodily fluids of two; I could sometimes hear them slosh about inside her as she waddled past me.

There were some subjects I understood, instinctively, which I should no longer discuss with Father on those occasions when we were together—as the Book of Timothy tells us, *"Have nothing to do with foolish, ignorant controversies; you know that they breed quarrels."* However, I knew that Father was wise in certain ways of the world, and so—as I continued to do from time to time, when I needed advice—I walked to the vicarage one day to confide in him. I told him about the inexplicable changes I had observed taking place in the Griggses' house, as well as some of the peculiar noises I had heard.

"Father," I told him earnestly, "I believe Mrs. Griggs is eating her husband."

He frowned at me in bemusement: "Whatever do you mean, child?"

"Mr. Griggs is wasting away. And Mrs. Griggs is fattening up with all the fat he used to have. I think she eats him a little each night."

Father shook with a very quiet laughter and then, musingly, quoted scripture from the Book of Genesis: *"Bone of my bones and flesh of my flesh; she shall be called Woman, because she was taken out of Man."*

I was confused. "Do you mean to tell me," I asked, "that Woman . . . *continues* to take out of Man?"

I could tell from Father's face, and his hesitation, that he was wondering how best to answer my question truthfully without resorting to absolute candour.

"Married women, yes," he allowed.

I imagined, in my youth, that I understood his meaning

and continued to illustrate the situation with further examples and evidence. "You know, Father," I told him, "when their bedroom door closes at night, I hear the most frightening sounds. I don't know what she's doing to him in there, but I don't think he likes it very much. I'm afraid that, one day, he won't come out, and she will walk out instead as fat as two people!"

"It may be that Mrs. Griggs is with child."

I gave this a moment's thought before answering, "No. I don't think so."

"Why not?"

"They don't need one. They have me."

However, some months later, Father's insights were proven correct. On a dark and stormy night, after nearly two full days of howling pain, a mid-wife pulled a new and screaming life out of an incomprehensible thatchwork of blood and black hair that resided like a terrible secret in the middle of Mrs. Griggs. The farmhouse we all lived in together was small, and I could not help but be exposed to what was happening. The birth was considered quite miraculous, due to Mrs. Griggs's age, and their house was descended upon presently by neighbours and well-wishers, bearing warm food and linens, all flocking like sheep to see the miracle infant born of their unwaning love. It was a boy . . . like the baby Jesus . . . like me. They named him Royle.

If my life has taught me anything about people, it is that all little boys are hateful, and Royle was no exception. I had been raised by Father to keep my personal needs in check—never to scream, never to demand, never even to make them known—yet little Royle made absolutely certain that his every passing whim was satisfied through the exertion of his strong lungs and toothless maw. Young as I was, I was appalled, but as I sat there and watched in our close quarters, Mrs. Griggs would sit by the fire, rocking the little monster in her arms, as I had learned to rock myself. And if that didn't appease him—and it never did—she would open her blouse and fetch out a plump sack of flesh which she called a boobie to silence the little monster. The peace that fell over the house as the baby fed was mysterious and sublime. Mrs. Griggs never discouraged me from watching, but she never offered me the other boobie. I was too much the gentleman to ask for it, much less to scream out my demands as bloody Royle did, but that does not mean I did not covet it—savagely—either out of hunger (because my own supper was always withheld until the infant was sated) or a simple yearning to be that close to someone who loved me enough to nourish me from their own body. There were numerous feedings throughout the day and night, and I attended most of them longingly, though they became increasingly stinging—like a damnation, a banishment.

Once, when no one was looking, I took a chance and bent over Royle's crib, truffling over his mouth for a whiff of what a mother's love smelled like. Once, when he was put down after a feeding, I swabbed out his mouth with my pinky; it came out coated in a thick and only faintly milky glaze. Quick as a bee, I slipped that guilty finger inside my own mouth, but I could taste naught but Royle's sticky saliva.

In my sagging bed at night, I would lie with eyes open, peering into the shadows until I saw, in the absolute black, motes of all colours floating there, unrecognised and invisible to the unconcentrated eye. My young mind instructed me that I might find anything were I to peer long enough into the right void, and, over time, an image began to coalesce. I began to envision the woman who had been my mother, who was my mother, like the women of exalted beauty you see in paintings but seldom if ever in life; I told myself, as I rocked myself, that she would someday come for me and claim me as her own, accept me and nourish me, care for me and teach me things that would lead me to my special destiny.

Rocking myself was a saddening and humiliating ritual, as you can imagine. It served to relax me, but it also made me more aware of what was lacking in my life and sapping the life from my heart. It was more than once that I cried myself to sleep—and, one night, I was heard.

"There, child," came the voice. It belonged to Mrs. Griggs, who leaned over me, her hay-coloured hair dangling down in long rope-like braids that she always wore up, save at bed-time. "Hush now, Rennie," she whispered. "You'll wake the baby." She sat down on the bed beside me, studying me as she had never studied me before, to my knowledge. "Here, what's the matter now?"

Being only a child, I could not put my yearnings into language as I can now. "I don't know," I told her, honestly. "I feel lost here. I keep hoping someone'll come looking for me and find me."

Mrs. Griggs looked exasperated, but not exasperated at me. "Poor thing," she sympathised. "God punish the stupid woman who could leave you to the world's tender mercies when so many women cry in the night, as you do, for want of a baby."

"They do?"

"Some do most bitter, I promise you."

"Why won't they take me?"

"I suppose because they love their suffering more. Hush up now, we can't have you waking the baby. You'd better come in with us."

She took me by the hand and led me through small rooms that felt like falling panels of destiny until she took me behind the door of the room from where the awful sounds had come. There was the same darkness as in my own room, but more things, and the smells were unfamiliar—smells of stale tobacco and bare feet. I heard her tell her husband—not ask—that I was to spend the night with them, as I needed comforting, and being mostly sleepy, he mumbled his lack of interest.

I got into their large bed, followed by Mrs. Griggs, and my feet recoiled as they brushed against her husband's long and hairy stick-legs, which stuck out the bottom of his night-shirt. Surrounded by their bigger breathing, I thought of myself as a tiny valley between vast mountains and, before long, drifted into sleep.

As morning broke, I was awakened as light poured through a window and warmed my face. Mr. Griggs was still sleeping deeply, his lungs sawing steadily at a cord of dream lumber. His wife lay beside me, close enough for me smell her breath. I did not mind the touch of her legs against my feet, though they were hairy too—hers was more of a downy hair—nor did she flinch from me. I saw a fly on the arm of her nightdress. I watched with interest as it sat hunched on its legs and sawed its foremost ones, one against the other, like men sharpen their knives before digging into a much-belated meal. My eyes followed it as it walked higher up the arm of her night-dress . . . That's when I lost all interest in the fly because, somehow during the night, Mrs. Griggs's night-dress had come open, allowing her right bosom to loll free. For once, Royle's little head was not blocking my view and the missus's eyes were closed, granting me complete freedom to study and admire this strange and beautiful thing. It was like naught I had ever seen before; I would have thought its opulence artificial had I not been close enough to it to see it shift with her breathing, the heavy flesh of it trembling ever so slightly with her heart's beating.

Make no mistake, Doctor Seward: my young veins were screaming at the sight of that pap as if it were my birth-right, but I might have been content merely to stare at it in secrecy, had not Nature intervened. As I lay there, marshalling my excited breathing so as not to awaken her, though everything within and without my universe seemed to be exploding, I watched in awe as a bead of milk appeared at the dark, engorged tip of her swelling gland. The bead became a tear that spilled along the full curve of that fleshy minaret, followed by another and another—all of that love going to waste! Inborn reflexes, far more powerful than any learned thing of the mind, compelled me to clamp my mouth over the leak and, as right as rain, I began to take nourishment from her.

My ears went warm, so warm I wouldn't have been surprised had they sprouted fur and grown as long as a rabbit's. My very brain seemed to dissolve; so defined was my brain, do you see, by its anxieties and frustrations, that to experience such fulfillment was almost like ceasing to exist! I was stealing a mother's love, but it was a mother's love nonetheless, running thick and sweet as dappled nectar. I kept taking and taking, but she was fighting me now, trying to pry me from it, but I held firm; the more she fought, the harder I sucked, wanting to gulp more and more before this liquid gold that was rightfully mine was taken away.

One moment, I was doing what God had designed all mammals to do, feeling perfectly requited and whole and normal—but the next, I was standing in the corner of that room with all eyes on me, and the room was screaming that I had crossed a line that could never be uncrossed. Mrs. Griggs was standing too, on the other side of the room, in tears and covering herself up and quite upset with me.

"You!" she shouted, making me feel ever so small. "You would steal the food from my own child's mouth?"

Mr. Griggs was sitting up slowly in bed, rubbing his eyes and stubbly face. When he got his bearings and looked at me, I knew there was a beating in this for me, no getting around it. But I could not understand the wrong I had done. I could not understand her indignant stance, her accusations, her denial of my simple human need, why I needed to be beaten—and the lack of sense in that moment charged me head to toe with the blackest, crackling hate.

Mr. Griggs's skeletal form climbed out of bed and into his trousers, which he put on only so that he could make a more threatening show of removing his belt, and I was chased around that small house and whipped. I ran close to the walls, to the floorboards, as mice do when caught in-doors, dodging each lash of that leather strap. The outburst woke little Royle, who cried and was spitefully consoled.

Need I tell you, Doctor, that I did not spend another night in that house?

CHAPTER VII

Patient's Oral History (cont).

Two years after they had taken me in, I was returned by the Griggses to the vicarage. Father was not yet prepared to accept me back for good, and not once during that homecoming was I allowed to think that the situation would be permanent. He received me rather coldly, I must say, so I imagine the Griggses explained the reason for my expellment from their happy home in a way that put an hysterical slant on the truth.

It took months for Father to find other lodgings for me. I do not know whether the members of his congregation spoke amongst themselves of what I had done, but I presume so, for no other family was eager to adopt me. They taught me hate, those people did, standing in tall circles above me, looking down on me, refusing or denying me what every one of them had as their own from the time of their first day on earth.

Being warned, almost daily, by Father that I mustn't get attached to living at the vicarage—and, in my own child's way, I suspected that he was pushing me away because his flock wanted no part of me—I began to spend more time out-of-doors, as it was the only home that no one could ever steal away from me. I came inside only for meals and baths and to go to bed, though I would not have minded much to sleep under the stars. Assiduously, I prepared myself for the next upset by divesting my cellar room of the few little things of mine which gave it the shades of my personality; I moved these things to hiding places outside—which was appropriate, as this was where I had found all of these pretty stones and skulls and feathers.

Eventually, Father had to look outside his own congregation for a solution to my housing problem. And so it was that I came to stay with a family by the name of Craddick. This might have been a happy arrangement if not for their two boys. Mr. Craddick had a deeply etched face and long black moustaches. He worked in the tin mines and was beset by a leg injury. Whilst he was on the mend, Mrs. Craddick had begun to accept laundry and other outside cleaning chores, in addition to her own housekeeping, to make ends meet. Their eldest son had died some months before after a long illness, so they decided to take in a roomer. Father, who did not bully them from his pulpit, agreed to pay the couple a weekly stipend, pooled from his collection plate, for my care-taking.

The Craddicks were decent people, but their two surviving boys, nine and ten to my seven, were not. It was a predicament in which I would find myself more than once, and so I know it to be universal: Children are murderously jealous of their parents' attention. In the wake of their older brother's death, the Craddick boys must have been heavily doted on by their mother, and when I came to stay with them—occupying the room of the absentee brother, whose share of mother love had been divided between them—I became the focus of her attention, which they greatly resented. As I was introduced to them—this is Colin, this is Christopher—the Craddick boys impressed me as being ever so cordial and polite . . . but from the moment their mother left our presence, that we might become better acquainted, it was made plain to me that I was unwelcome, out-numbered, and among the bitterest of enemies.

I came to live with the Craddicks in the summer-time, when there was no school. We three boys were encouraged to spend our days out-of-doors, so as not to disturb Mr. Craddick and to let his wife get on with her duties. I would have been content to stay indoors and read the Bible—one of the only books the Craddicks had, and my favourite reading during those years I was banished from the vicarage—and I daresay the boys would have preferred not to have me along, but we were always being sent out of the house as a gang.

On one of these days, the three of us embarked on a walking trip that took us quite a distance away from home. It was, without a doubt, the farthest I had ever walked on foot. Collie and Kit, being older and more experienced, had more energy and stamina than myself, and I suffered throughout the entire walk a fear of not keeping up and being left behind in unfamiliar surroundings—because I knew they would like nothing better. After walking for quite some time, the boys brought me to the edge of a woods that, they said, would take us back to our home in much shorter time. I became quite frightened because it was a local legend that these woods were haunted, and all the adults in our village—including

Father—had warned us many a time not to linger there. But Collie and Kit told me that, if I did not follow them and take this short way, I would have to return home by myself, by taking the long way around which we had just taken, albeit in reverse. I had not paid attention to every twist and turn, so I had no recourse but to follow them through what ever dangers lay ahead.

The path we walked took us into the heart of a lush wooded area, which opened onto a sort of ledge. It was a natural drop, which had been given additional definition and safety by a short stone wall. This wall was scarcely broader than my own two feet, set side by side. On the right side of this wall was a short drop onto a pebbly road, which they told me led out of the woods; on the left, there was a drop that seemed to plummet down forever into a thin, silvery ribbon of water, far below.

Kit and Collie had obviously been there many times before, and had led me there on purpose. They bounded onto the ledge without fear and walked four or five steps across, just far enough to get around the shrub that grew there and jump off to the right, onto the pebbly road. But I was terrified of the height—too frightened to take that first step onto the ledge. They chided me mercilessly, and I tried very hard not to cry, which would only have made things worse for me and better for them. I protested that I couldn't follow, that I would surely fall over the wrong side and be killed. They grew bored with my haggling rather quickly and started walking away, along that pebbly road, calling out their farewells with great amusement. That's when I knew I would have to walk the ledge—and quickly—or be left behind in that haunted woods. I suppose my fear of abandonment overcame my other fears, because after a few seconds, I swallowed my trepidations and walked the ledge, surrounded in all directions by the sound of wind and the sounds of animals, both of them infinitely vaster than the life-and-death drama in which I found myself involved. After five or six carefully placed steps, I jumped off the ledge onto the pebbly road and ran after Collie and Kit. I did not take a moment to congratulate myself on having cheated death.

As I ran towards them, I saw Kit and Collie spin around to face the ledge we had successfully crossed, and they ran past me as though I wasn't there, to peer over the side. Collie screamed my name into the abyss. He was joined by Kit, who did the same and then turned around, looking as though he was about to be sick.

"Poor little bastard," he said. "I didn't think he would actually . . . Tell me it didn't happen, Collie! Tell me it didn't happen!"

I was confused, as you might imagine. And then I heard Collie say, "I can't tell you it didn't happen . . . because it did! Rennie fell—fell to his death!"

Kit's eyes bulged like two great eggs as he took another look over the side of the ledge, as did Collie. Then Kit hooked his forearm over the bridge of his nose, so as not to see anymore.

"Oh, Collie," he cried, "don't look! It's horrible! His head . . . it broke when he hit the ground! I saw his brains slide out of his skull . . . I saw them rushing down the river!"

Then Collie screamed, still looking into the depths beyond the ledge: "It's too late, brother! I saw it! I saw it too!"

I had not fallen at all, of course—I was standing right be-side them!—but Kit's knees began to shake, and he fell to the ground, his back against the ledge. Collie rushed to comfort him in his distress. The two boys were greatly upset—too upset to cry, but quite so. The next to speak was Collie, who wondered: "Dear Lord, Kit . . . Whatever are we going to tell Mother and Father?"

Kit said, "I don't know . . . we're going to be in a lot of trouble . . . but we'll have to tell them the truth. Eventually, I mean. For to-night, perhaps they won't notice he is missing if we don't set a place for him at the dinner table . . . if we hide his chair at table so there won't be an empty one . . . and you and I could eat his share of supper, so there wouldn't be an extra helping sitting there un-eaten? If we're careful—I mean, very very careful—there is a good chance that no one will notice he's gone missing!"

"They will too notice!" I yelled. But the two Craddick boys took no notice of any voice other than their own.

"Yes," Collie stammered. "It might work . . . Oh, poor, poor Rennie! We were rough on the little bastard sometimes, but he wasn't so bad, really. And now we'll never hear his voice again . . ."

I stood there, watching in horror, calling out to them that I was all-right and standing right beside them, and that I was not a bastard, but they didn't seem to hear me, even when I was screaming that I was alive at the top of my lungs! They did not react to my presence there in the slightest. Nor did not react to my small-fisted punches—until Collie finally flinched. I had made contact; he knew it and I knew it.

"Ouch!"

"What's wrong, Collie?" Kit asked.

"It's nothing," he replied. "I didn't think losing the little monster would hurt so much." Before I could strike him again, Collie exclaimed: "Wait! Did you hear that?"

I stopped my futile punching, the better to listen.

"You heard it too?" Kit asked, with a spooky inflection. "But, Collie, how could it be? How could we hear . . . Rennie's voice—when he's dead? When his poor little pink brains are gliding down-river?"

"Yes!" I shouted, louder than before, more desperate than ever to bridge the gulf between life and lonely death. *"It was me! You heard me!"*

"Do you think it could be . . . ? No!" Collie trailed off, refusing to believe.

"Do you mean . . ." began Kit, unable to complete his own fantastic question.

"Yes," Collie confirmed, about to finish the thought. *"Renfield's ghost!"*

"But I am not dead!" I insisted.

The two of them looked at each other as though they had finally heard me. They crossed themselves like two poor souls who had felt the very breath of the Grim Reaper hot on their necks, too close for comfort.

"Oh, Kit," Collie shuddered, "please tell me I didn't hear that!"

"I wish I could," Kit replied, getting very upset, "but I don't want to lie! I don't ever want to tell another lie! I take back every lie I've ever told in my whole life! Yes! I did hear a voice—oh, who am I fooling? It was Rennie! And he was saying . . . Oh, I can't say it!"

He couldn't, but Collie could. He said: "He was say-ing . . . *that he wasn't dead!*"

"Then there's only one explanation," said Kit with great seriousness. "Rennie's ghost doesn't *know* it's a ghost. He doesn't know he's dead! He must be trapped . . . between two worlds! He'll never get to Heaven now, the poor little bas-tard . . ."

"I am not a bastard!" I yelled. "I am not dead!"

"This is terrible," Collie shuddered. "He's going to spend eternity locked out of Heaven . . . hanging high above the fires of Hell!"

I tell you, Doctor Seward, they had me believing it! When Collie painted this horrible picture of my fate, I shrieked almost to the point of fainting. I fell onto the peb-bles, screaming and crying, burying my sobbing face in my hands, praying for release, and I stopped only long enough to watch as my two companions fled from that place in a state of absolute horror, screaming and running, as though it was as haunted as everyone said. I sat there in tears, striking the rocks with my little fists until they bruised and bled, the pain I felt not quite enough to convince me that I was not as dead as they said I was.

It took me hours to find my way back to the Craddick house, alone and long after dark. I understood what had hap-pened only after I entered the house and saw the entire fam-ily seated around the dinner table—Kit and Collie exchanging furtive looks of triumph, as their parents ob-served my tardy arrival with dismay and disapproval. Mrs. Craddick looked at my dirty face and knees and hands and told me to wash up quickly before my supper got any colder.

"The boys told us what you did, Rennie," she said, once I had seated myself at table. "They know they are not allowed to go into those woods—and they are certainly not allowed to go anywhere near the high wall—but they told us how you ran across it, making them come after you! And we also know all about the rocks you threw, and how you hit them, and all about the bad language you used!"

"But, missus, I didn't!" I objected.

"Don't you contradict me, child," she insisted. "I cannot tell you how disappointed I am—and you the foundling of a vicar!"

Before I could fork a single mouthful of food to my lips, Mr. Craddick—despite his bad leg—got up from his chair and grabbed me by the arm. I was afraid he might remove his belt, but he only dragged me to a corner of the room and ordered me to stand there in silence until I was spoken to. I stood there for hours, denied my dinner, listening to the sounds of the family's eating and Kit and Collie's exaggerated yum-yumming over their desserts and the clearing away of the dishes. Through it all, I stared ahead through my tears at the point where the two walls of the room converged. In time, I felt a dark heaviness under my stomach . . . I wanted to bring to someone's attention that I needed to relieve myself, but when I spoke the name of Mr. Craddick, he barked back at me that I had not yet been released from my punishment, that I needed to stand there quietly and think about all the wrong I had done. And so I continued to stand there, feeling the heaviness accumulate and accumulate, listening to Mr. and Mrs. Craddick wondering if the extra money I represented was so important, compared to the bad example I was setting for their two good sons.

A decent, God-fearing family this, Doctor Seward! Can you imagine—punishing a poor child by making him stand in a corner, forbidding him to speak, to beg, to signal his needs, until the seat of his trousers are soiled with shite? I was too embarrassed and frightened to speak, but my condition made itself known by the smell of it, and I can still remember those two evil boys laughing at me as I was marched upstairs. With every climbing step, I could feel it there, stopped as it was coming out of me and pressing against the seat of my breeches like a tent-pole, and hearing Kit and Collie down below, laughing that it looked like a donkey's tail trying to burst out of my pants.

CHAPTER VIII

Patient's Oral History (cont).

The real devil of the two Craddick boys was Collie—no, "devil" is too flattering to him. He was no fallen angel; he was a little hob-goblin. Collie had a pattern of befriending me as an older brother so that he could get a bit closer and then sink the knife in a bit deeper—and I was eager to have someone to look up to.

That summer, I awoke one day, and, not knowing what to do, I decided to tag along with Collie, who was going to see what he could do about getting stinking rich. I thought I might make some money, if only by walking behind Collie and picking up what pieces of his fortune he was likely to drop. Kit didn't come with us, not being very interested in working for money. But Collie and I resolved to earn as much money as we possibly could by accepting odd jobs around the town. After a number of disappointments from our immediate neighbours, we heard that our old school-teacher, Miss Hamish, might need some work done or some errands run for her, so we went round and knocked on her door.

She seemed surprised by our offer, and, after thinking about it for a few minutes, she suggested that we might dig out the weeds which were sprouting up between the bricks of her courtyard. Collie and I exchanged looks of triumph; this was the sort of job we wouldn't even think to do, or propose doing. Miss Hamish didn't have any tools, so we ran back to the Craddick place and got some gardening tools from the shed and rushed back, feeling absolutely certain that days of great wealth were upon us.

We toiled in the hot sun for the better part of two hours, which is a lot of time when you're a child, as we were. When we had torn out all the weeds and made nice, neat grooves between the bricks and swept away all the loose dirt, Miss Hamish's courtyard gave me a sense of pride and accomplishment. We called her outside and watched in suspense as our school-teacher surveyed our efforts with a wan face. Then she produced a small black coin purse and withdrew two coins of the smallest denomination you can imagine. The bleeding crone!

We had embarked on that day anticipating the fortune we would doubtless make, but we had spent so much time on Miss Hamish's courtyard that there were not enough hours left of daylight for us to add to our pockets elsewhere! We were also tired and dejected, and the last thing we wanted to do was to waste more of our day and sweat for so little compensation. So we sat on a knoll to cast about for ideas of what we could buy with our meagre earnings.

After a few torturously quiet minutes, Collie announced that he was going to add his coins to his piggy bank and forget about it. But I had no piggy bank, nor had I ever held a coin that was entirely my own, so I was determined to spend it on something, hopefully of greater value to me, that I could cherish. Alas, my coin was not enough to buy a toy, nor a book, nor even a piece of penny candy. But Collie had a suggestion.

"I know something you could buy, Rennie," he said, smiling.

"What?"

"You love animals so much, why not buy a pet?"

"It's not enough to buy a pet," I scowled at the coin in my open palm.

"I'll bet it is!"

"Puppies cost more," I protested, showing the coin. "Kittens cost more. Tweeties cost more." I was so upset, I could have almost thrown the damned coin away to cure my mind.

"You could buy a mouse," Collie suggested.

Collie took me to a neighbouring farm owned by a family called Jenkins who had a son of Collie's age who sold me a mouse. He didn't breed them, of course, though this was the image I had in mind as we walked there . . . He simply walked into a barn, shook up a haystack, and caught a nice one as it came sprinting out. He carried it to me by its tail and passed it over to me as he took my coin. It was a real champion!

I couldn't carry my pet home by its tail, so I was given a small box to keep it in, with a lid poked full of holes so it could breathe. When the Jenkins boy handed me the box, I felt ever so special. I peeked inside the box, and, the way my mouse looked up at me with its wee black eyes, I had the sense that it had already had learned to love and depend on me. I looked back at him and said, "I know just what I'm going to call you. I'm going to call you Jolly."

Jolly . . . I could not tell you why I named him so; there are simply times when you look into a face and know. He was so funny and rotund, yet so vigourous in his kicking and his whisker-bristling, and in his face there was such wisdom! His wee eyes were so proud and brave and yet so defenceless as they looked at you, so very trusting he was. He well knew how big the world is, he well knew how stacked the odds were against one of his diminutive stature, and he knew perfectly well that he mattered to me more than anything else in this world, Doctor. But that's the way he was, dear thing. Always curious to a fault, always putting the brave foot forward, was Jolly.

I beamed at the thought of him, in that box under my arm, for the length of our entire walk back to the Craddick cottage. Collie could see how happy I was, too—almost happy enough to skip—and he added to my pleasure by saying, "Oh, won't *Mother* be pleased to meet Jolly!"

By the time we returned home, Collie had stoked my anticipation to the point where I couldn't wait to share Jolly with Mrs. Craddick. I thrust the box at her, telling her there was a most wondrous surprise inside. As she peered under the lid, her wary expression contorted into one of extreme revulsion; she screamed and actually flung the box across the room. Jolly got free and then a bad scene became all chaos and screaming and worse, with Mrs. Craddick dancing on top of a chair until I scooped the wee frightened thing back into his box.

Mrs. Craddick cursed me for playing such a trick and told me to get that—what she called a "rat"—out of her house. I argued that Jolly was a mouse, not a rat, but truth and sense were no weapon to be wielded in this particular war. Remembering Jolly's eyes and how they had looked at me with such trust, I cried and fell on my knees in front of Mrs. Craddick, begging her to let me have this one thing, this one thing to love and call my own, which already loved and depended on me.

Collie stood there watching with Satan's own grin on his freckled face. "I'll get rid of it for you, Mum," he said. "I told Rennie not to go buying *rats*, but he never listens! He does whatever he likes, and when you warn him not to do things, he makes sure no one is around . . . and then he uses bad words!"

Collie tried to wrest the box from me, but I refused to relinquish it. I knew that I was to be blamed for bad language that I had not used, nor had I ever used, but as I knew that punishment would be coming anyway, I opened my mouth and let those words fly, as I struggled to keep hold of Jolly—one word after another after another, reaching the limit of my knowledge of such words, then doubling back to use them all again in different combinations.

Mrs. Craddick came off her chair to slap my face, causing me to drop the box to the floor. Jolly got free again and darted in terror along the sides of the walls, boxed into imminent death as it were by the house. I saw Collie begin to stalk him, stomping his foot down harder and harder whenever he thought he had a chance. I was so . . . attuned to Jolly, so sympathetic with his plight, it was like I could feel those stomps falling near me, heavy and straight as the columns of a Roman temple, as they sent horrible tremors of doom through the wooden floor.

"Stop it, Colin!" his mother cried, but Collie had already raised his boot and thought he might just as well bring it down, as hard as he could, one last time, for good measure—fortunately, missing his quarry once again.

I got down on all fours, like my poor Jolly, and began to look for him under the furniture. It did not take long for me to tempt him back into the protection of his little box, because Jolly knew my intentions and trusted me. I felt as though I had found my own heart and got it successfully back into my chest. I stood up again, calmly, and looked bravely at Mrs. Craddick, the shape of whose hand continued to throb on one side of my face, feeling redder than red.

"I am sorry to have frightened you, Mrs. Craddick," I said, politely. "May I keep Jolly outside, then?"

"Things like that *belong* outside, boy," she told me with a groan. "Take it out of here this instant!"

"But I *can* keep him?" I pressed.

"Outside!" she clarified.

I thanked her, making a little gentleman's bow, and carried the box out-of-doors. I looked around for a safe place to put Jolly's little hole-punched house, stopping here and there to collect handfuls of grass and vegetation for him to eat. In the yard there was an old, hollow tree that had an opening level with the ground; it looked the perfect place for Jolly to live and was just deep enough to accept the entire box. Before putting him inside the tree for the night, I opened the box to put his dinner inside. Right away, Jolly began to nibble and look up at me with satisfaction; I was keeping my part of the bargain in keeping him safe and fat.

"Now listen to me most carefully, Jolly," I told him. "I

will bring you food at least three times a day. I will visit you even more often than that. But you must take care to stay inside your box. Inside this tree, if possible. If you come out, you might get lost—or worse. And whatever you do, even though the house is just over there, don't come inside looking for me. Whenever you need me, just send me your thoughts, and I won't be long."

Jolly looked at me, nibbling, like he understood and was agreeable to this arrangement.

I put the lid back on and stood up. While smacking the dirt off my bare knees, which I knew Mrs. Craddick would not countenance in her clean house, any more than she would countenance Jolly being in it, I saw Collie standing not far away, his arms folded. "Going to keep it there, are you? In the tree?" he asked.

"Is that all-right?" I asked with concern.

"As long as it stays there," he said, smiling.

That night, as I lay in my bed, I thought of Jolly and how unfair it was that we could not sleep together, and of how meagrely protected he was from all the dangers of the dark by his little box, at the foot of that open tree. I knew that I would have to find him a safer place, perhaps under the porch of the Craddick house. I worried, hardly sleeping a wink, and was up and dressed for the new day at cock-crow. I collected some things for Jolly to eat, from the kitchen and from the yard, knowing that he depended upon me for his care, and I felt satisfaction in the keeping of my promise.

He gobbled up his breakfast ever so gratefully—not all of it, as he also saved a portion for later, being such a wise and prudent little man. I kept him company until he snuggled into a corner of his box and began to sleep, flat on his back with his big belly and little toes in the air. Perhaps he had also not slept well during the night, for fear of the dark, but now—with me watching over him—he felt safe enough to risk it. In time, I closed the lid and slipped it back inside the tree trunk—and then ran off, as children will, to enjoy the summer's day.

It was hours later, when I began to feel hungry and knew that Jolly would be feeling the same way, that I returned to the Craddick house. To my great and happy surprise, I saw Father's carriage, and Father sitting on their covered porch, dressed in his usual blacks and cape. No one else wore black, least of all in summer, so he could be seen from far away. I thought that, perhaps, he had missed me and come to take me back to the vicarage—but, as I drew closer, I saw that his expression was serious, even grave. I surmised that Mrs. Craddick had spoken to him about my unseemly language.

But his first words to me, as he pulled himself back from my embrace, were, "I'm so very sorry, child."

I asked what he was sorry about, and he told me that my mouse was dead.

"But Jolly isn't dead!" I laughed. "He's safe in his box, out there in one of those trees. I was just going to feed him."

The box was indeed there, inside the tree trunk, where I had left it, and I fetched it out to show Father, with my own two hands. I started to remove the lid, but Father placed his own larger hand over the top, holding it down. Then—with an air of regret that seemed to accept that everyone must discover everything for themselves and that no one can be absolutely shielded from the darkness in life—Father relented . . . and withdrew his hand.

I raised the lid in full expectation that Jolly's dark yet bright little eyes would be there, ready to return my gaze of unconditional love . . . but I found him lying there on his bed of grass and newspaper . . . still asleep, I thought . . . but then, with the lid fully removed and the sunlight streaming in, I saw his eyes not only shut but scrunched . . . his little mouth open, his little pink tongue lolling out on one side and his poor little body looking like it had been stamped on, hard enough to crush and mush it all up, but not enough to bleed, at least not outside, just enough to mash its wee bones to a jelly.

It wasn't the sight of Jolly dead that made me cry, but *the sight of me dead*, I suppose . . . Like me, he was a trusting orphan taken into a strange home, where all its capacity for love had been stomped out of it with its life. He lay there as I knew, one day, I would lie there, like a lost soul in the void, his lifeless husk curled into a corner as if seeking one last sweet measure of comfort in an inhospitable world. Inside that little box with the holes punched in was the essence of all the mystery which has confounded me from then till now: Jolly was there, but Jolly was gone.

I looked up and saw Mrs. Craddick and her smiling sons assembled to watch the scene from a window, and I knew from the look on Collie's face—a face of deep, smug satisfaction—that poor Jolly had not died a natural death. And then I felt my face begin to stretch, as though involuntarily, in different directions . . . my expression was pulled into a deeply fixed grimace . . . and my head began to wobble on my neck . . . and from my fixed grimace, from behind teeth clenched tight as prison doors, came a small, frightening sound that grew into a deep, guttural, animal growl. I wanted to stop, but I could not; the sound had to come out. I stood there, embarrassed to be seen like this and not wishing to be seen like this, so I turned and ran from that house as fast as my legs would carry me, barking and crowing.

I ran in no particular direction—only away. I fled across yards of high grass, over streets of cobblestone, over dirt roads, and finally into the large open field bordering our haunted woods. The field was full of tall stalks of cat's tail grass—used to make hay for the animals—and it reached all the way to land's end. I came to the edge of a precipice and saw the crashing sea below and could run no farther—but I had to continue running, I had to, so I turned and ran through the field again, this time in circles. My circles started out large, then drew me nearer and nearer to the centre, and as I ran, I thought back to the bats Father had shown me, executing their mad parabolas against the sapphire sky and never crashing into one another; I felt as though I had become one of them. As I kept on running, I began to feel a centre of gravity in my circles, and I feared that I was being sucked down a great sink-hole; I couldn't stop myself, I was like a fish being reeled in, cutting a spiral pattern into the cat's tails I was trampling, until, somewhere in the centre of that field, I fell down on all fours . . . and I continued to run until the palms of my hands were raw and the flesh of my knees was torn. Then I stopped, feeling pressed against the nape of my neck the benediction of a soft and gentle hand.

This hand, and its mate, took hold of me and helped me to stand up. I could not take my eyes off of these hands, they came as such a surprise. They were slender, graceful—a woman's hands, gloved in the most delicate black lace but with the fingers exposed and their nails painted—not covered, just a little daub of red on each. I know what you are thinking, Doctor Seward, but I was just as surprised as yourself to be confronted with a colour I could see! These hands took hold of me firmly, warmly—sending waves of compassion through me—and before I could raise my eyes to her face, she turned me so that I stood with my back against her skirts, with the flat of her hand pressed against my chest. There was something in the position we held that made me feel, without a single word being exchanged between us, that it was the two of us against the entire village—and that these were most excellent odds.

Only then did I begin to feel my fixed grimace relax and the guttural animal growls leaving my very sore throat. My face was covered in tears, which her free gloved hand rose to brush from my cheeks; her touch made them feel like a blessing.

Then this female presence lowered herself to match my height. "No more running," she spake into my ear in the most unusual voice. "Now they have given you power."

Having said this, she rose once again to her full height. She released me and I turned around to look up into her face. But I could not see the Lady's features because she wore a dark veil, of the same black colour as her long and fashionable dress, which looked ever so cultured in its hour-glass proportions and out of character with what we country folk wore. It was my first impression that everything she wore, with the exception of a stately signet ring, was black—but the more I looked at it, I began to see that it was in fact a nearly black blue . . . a shade beyond sapphire . . . a shade I told myself was "moony blue." I had willed myself colour-blind, but in this Lady's presence, I was not only aware of the colours she wore but *exquisitely* aware.

Though I could not see her face through the lacy patterns of her veil, there was something familiar about her, as if I had known her always. I asked myself, Could she be the woman to whom I sent my thoughts each night, as I rocked myself in strange beds and awaited the coming of my dreams?

"Mother?" I asked.

She did not lower her eyes to meet my question, but rather kept her vision level, looking out over the field to vistas that lay beyond it. I got the sense that she was surveying land as far as she could see it, mapping every acre in her thoughts and making strategic plans for its conquest. I turned away from her, to follow her gaze, and once again, she held me close to her, her hand firmly pressed to my heart.

"They killed him!" I sobbed. "They killed Jolly!"

"You will have yours back," she promised.

"I don't want to go back," I said.

"You must," she said simply. "Trust in me."

I felt that returning to the Craddick house would demand less courage of me than to wilfully separate myself from the safe harbour of this stranger, in whose presence my whole mad slanted world was levelled. I took a few tentative steps, then turned back to face her.

"Will I see you again?" I asked, fearing the answer.

The Lady reached out to my face with one hand, which curved as it slid across my face in a friendly caress. Then she lightly pinched my nose and, giving it a playful wiggle, spoke as if from the very core of me:

"I will not leave you comfortless; I will come to you."

With that, she turned on her heel and walked away, opening above her head a parasol of the same moony colour, its fabric and ribbing flexing taut like a bat's wing. I watched in amazement as she receded from me, through the cat's tails, shrinking towards the horizon until she was naught but a black speck. Then I realised, to my amazement, that she had strolled towards land's end! Concerned for her safety, I called after her and ran through the trampled path she left in her wake—and after covering less than a quarter of the distance she had travelled, found myself poised at the brink of a cliff. There was no fallen body on the rocks below . . . It was as if she had strolled off into the clouds.

Then—as the Lady had predicted by opening her parasol—it began to rain. It was the last rain we were to see in our village for some time.

Dazed, I walked unconcernedly through the rain back to the Craddicks' house, where Father sat on the covered porch with my packed bag beside him—holding on his lap my dead Jolly in his tiny hole-punched coffin, the better for him to breathe in death. Without a word of farewell to the Craddicks, he helped me aboard his carriage, and we began the long ride back to the vicarage. When we were perhaps half-way there, with still not a homeward word spoken between us, the rain stopped and the air turned so dry that it felt crisp—much like the stinging eyes of a young boy who has promised himself, "I will cry no more, I will cry no more . . ."

As we arrived at the vicarage, Father left my bag on the door-step, then placed a consoling hand on my shoulder and walked across the yard with me to the tool-shed. There, he handed Jolly's box to me and took up a spade in his own two hands. We continued across the yard to the low stone wall that encircled the churchyard. Father found a spot just inside the entrance, one that I could easily find again if ever I wanted to visit, and he made a place for Jolly. Neither of us had yet said a single word to the other, but we seemed in perfect, fated accord.

Once the hole was dug, Father reached into his pocket and gave me one of his handkerchiefs, embroidered with his initials, and I reached inside the box and took what was left of Jolly in my trembling hand and placed him in the midst of it, wrapping him up like a great Pharaoh. Then I stashed him back inside the box, which was placed inside the hole and covered with earth.

When it was all over, Father embraced me and said his first words of home-coming: "Forgive me, child, but it had to be done. You were beginning to doubt me, to question me, to see Evil in me—and, for the sake of your own sense of right and wrong, I felt you needed to leave this haven I have made, to be amongst other people, and discover for yourself what the world is really like. But now you know . . . and now you are home—for good."

It was good to be home again, but I missed Jolly, who had been taken from me much too soon. Father explained to me that we could never lose anyone whom we had truly loved, because we keep the memory of them alive in our hearts. With this in mind, as I took it to be very wise counsel, I invited Jolly's wandering spirit into my heart. I became his accommodation. From that moment on, I no longer felt my own heart-beat; I felt Jolly's fat little legs kicking around in my chest. We were as one, and I was back where I belonged, with the world of my hopes and dreams confirmed.

Dr. Seward's Diary.

LATER.—A marathon meeting to-day with Mr. Renfield, portions of which I recorded on cylinder by way of experiment. He arrived for our interview in a foul temper, inflamed with bravado and intimations of secret knowledge. His boastful manner may have made him less careful in his secrecy, as he began to introduce proper names into his recollections, and described enough of the countryside of his childhood for me to peg it as Cornwall. I shall say nothing to bring my awareness of these details to his notice.

Just as Renfield is becoming less careful (or more candid) in his revelations, his story has taken a turn towards the mysterious, with vaguely Super-natural elements now introduced to tempt my disbelief . . . But, as Professor Van Helsing used to tell us at university, the greatest defense of the Super-natural is its ability to inspire disbelief. Renfield speaks of a veiled apparition in "moony blue" . . . She may be a fantasy figure summoned in answer to his maternal desires—or, as my old professor would caution me to consider, perhaps something more. Time and patience will tell, and the limited use I made to-day of phonographic recording will grant me the ability to study his inflections as well as his words.

Reliable narrator or not, Renfield himself affords my only compass in this study of his inner mind. I have no choice but to follow, wherever he leads me. Therefore I shall disregard no detail; whatever is real enough to be accepted by my patient is relevant to his treatment and therefore of value to me.

CHAPTER IX

Dr. Seward's Diary.

30 MAY.—It is Saturday, and to-night is the evening Quincey arranged for the three of us to band together and celebrate Arthur's good fortune.

The plan is to meet at the Korea, for old times' sake, have a goodly number of drinks, amuse them with my penchant for impressions, and see where the evening takes us. (I trust that Quincey has not arranged anything that will make it too uncomfortable to look into the shaving mirror to-morrow.) Since I shall have to make my toilet early and be ready to join my fellow rogues for dinner, I decided to make the most of my time by not lingering abed and coming into the asylum early.

As I walked into my office, perhaps half an hour ago, I was taken aback by the unexpected sight of a step-ladder, unfolded like a letter A, to the side of my desk. Standing on the second rung from the top, balancing herself there precariously, was one of the young women from the domestic service I employ to keep the house tidy. She was wiping out the interior of the glass bowl covering of the hanging electric lamp—

the one that holds such fascination for Mr. Renfield—but was just as startled as I when she heard me enter.

"Good heavens!" I said in reaction to her, and she cut loose a short yell of surprise. She bumped the hanging lamp, which sent it swaying from side to side, and seeing the ladder wobble under her, I reached out and grabbed it and—accidentally—her ankle. When steadiness was restored, I released her, and she descended with caution and a face flushed with embarrassment.

"I'm ever sa sorry, sir," she said in a northern accent. "I was s'posed to be finished with me work bafore you coom in."

"That's quite all-right," I assured her. "It is a bit early for me to be here, but it's better to be here at this hour than still in bed, trying to sleep. You know, you really should avoid using a step-ladder unless you have someone to anchor it for you. You could take a nasty tumble."

"I'll remember tha, sir." She looked at me tenderly before catching herself and suddenly becoming very interested in her shoes.

"What exactly was the problem with my lamp?" I asked her. "Was it flickering?"

"Naw that I knoo of, sir—but it's too arly for the lights to be on, so I wouldna really knoo."

"Then what required the use of this ladder?"

She explained by opening for my inspection a white linen cleaning cloth that was folded, handkerchief-like, in her hand. As she folded back the last page of the soft, white fabric, exposing the contents she had collected from the lamp, she underlined what I saw with a brief verbal account: "Flies, sir."

"Flies?"

"Tha 'lectric light attracts 'em, y'see? Like moths to the flame, I'm guessin'."

"Well, I'll be dashed—I never noticed!"

"It's expected a busy doctor like you wouldna notice, but you doon't want your guests t' be visitin' ya here and takin' notice fer ya!" Her eyes widened at what she had said before the words were quite out of her Cupid's bow mouth, which she covered meekly as she made hasty amends for her unintended criticism. "I'm ever sa sorry, sir; I didna mean tha the way it sounded."

"That's quite all-right . . ." I trailed off, mutely requesting her name.

"Beryl," she said, as if somewhat ashamed of the name her parents had chosen for her.

"Beryl," I repeated, somewhat more melodically.

She smiled shyly and ventured, "It soonds summat prettier win you say it."

"So . . . Are you finished here, then?"

"Yeh, sir," she said.

"And next time?"

"If I should neet t' use the step-ladder," she promised, "I'll get t'other girl to coom and stan' down below."

"The other girl?" I asked—while thinking, *If she says "Lucy," I shall surely lose my mind.*

"Yeh, sir—Michelle. She's t' other girl who coomes t' do the cleanin' w' me," she explained. "She's workin' down the 'all . . . Do ya want I should call 'er?"

"No, Beryl," I sighed with relief, "that won't be necessary."

There followed an odd moment of silence between us—perhaps a fleeting social discomfort engendered by our difference in station and my term of familiarity, which could not be withdrawn. The last words she muttered, as she prepared to make her exit: "I'll jus' take me flies and me ladder an' goo, then."

I held the door open for her as she did just that. I must own to sitting behind my desk for some time after she left, smiling at her funny ways and her shy farewell, and musing on the curious coincidence of her name and an adjective that figured so prominently in Renfield's world.

LATER.—At the agreed-upon time, Watkins arrived with Renfield and carried out the usual preliminaries. It was early afternoon. He entered my office with an attitude of watchful, furtive calm. He nodded in greeting to Morrison, which I thought unusually kindly of him . . . but from the moment he took notice of the freshly wiped light fixture, his temper turned sanguinary once again. Nothing was said, but the dark clouds of vexation introduced into the room were unmistakable. It was then, and only then, that I understood: The object of his fascination had not been the lamp or the novelty of electrical lighting at all, but rather the black, confetti-like accumulation of dead flies in the bottom of its opaque bowl covering. It was then that I made the mental connexion to the baleful fly-man about whom he had written in his notebook.

"You seem rather discontented to-day, Renfield," I observed. "Are we not treating you to your satisfaction?"

"The food you serve in this gaol is inedible," he groused.

I could tell that he was, in effect, changing the subject to keep me and the flies well apart.

"I am sorry," I smiled. "But the other patients might feel otherwise if we started serving dead rodents just to please you."

"Why, I have never eaten anything dead in my life!" he announced, taking deep and terrible offence at my comment . . . but the inference of his objection was even more offensive, an irony that seemed to elude him.

"Never mind these clever diversionary tactics, Renfield," I admonished him, deciding to lay my cards on the table. "I know the real reason for your . . . contumeliousness. It's the light fixture, is it not? It has been cleaned. Observe! The flies are gone."

Renfield's eyes dropped at once from the lamp and locked with mine.

"All-right, if you're so smart! Where did they go?"

"Where do you think they have gone? Do you suppose they woke from their death-sleep and flew off to Heaven?"

"Don't toy with me, Seward. You may think yourself superior as you . . . lay your cards on the table? But I hold the winning hand."

His choice of words and expression were disarming, as I had considered the "cards on the table" simile before addressing him so frankly. I immediately dismissed the idea, but the notion did cross my mind that this rascal might actually have the ability to read my thoughts.

"If that is so," I dared him, "why not tell *me* where the flies went?"

Renfield fumed from his chair as one thwarted, as one who yearned to leap at my throat but was curbed by the chain that held him close by the wall. As I watched his anger simmer, he seemed to settle down, his fidgeting face suddenly finding calm, as if in response to a comforting whisper from within. He closed his eyes, as if to listen closer, and I could almost believe that he was in the act of receiving information. Then a smile spread across his face in a manner that was frankly upsetting to behold, and his eyes sprang open.

"There are four stages of the dark," he announced in portentous, theatrical fashion. "The first is *azure*, the ocean that rolls between the white countries of the sky. The second is *cyan*, the colour of that ocean as it grows still and motionless in sleep. And the third is *Beryl . . . the cleaning girl!*" he closed in triumph, collapsing in a shambles of laughter.

Yes, to my complete astonishment, Renfield had deduced that the cleaning girl had swept them up—and her name, as well!

"So my office has been cleaned and you deduce that the cleaning girl must have done it," I recounted in an attempt to save face. "Congratulations, Renfield—but any sane person could have arrived at that deduction."

"Sane? Does that mean I am free to go?" he asked, all but batting his eyes in feigned innocence.

"No, you are much too dangerous," I said—and then, catching myself and not wishing to add fuel to his arrogance, added, "More to yourself than to others, of course."

"Of course," he mocked me, settling down. "It is just as well. Had you said yes, Doctor Seward, I would have been required to do something drastic to remain your guest. There is only One who has the power to release me from this place and, believe you me, that One is not you."

"That One," I surmised, "is He whom you address as your Master?"

At this, Renfield seemed, behind pursed lips, to bite his tongue. His head trembled slightly, and he averted his face away from mine. He seemed suddenly replenished with fear, frightened nearly to the point of tears. I followed the line of his vision to the small bronze casting of the *Pietà* adorning my mantel and felt a sorrowful shade of what this rendering of the crucified Christ in his mother's arms must represent to him, because I knew him better now than when he first took notice of it.

Patient's Oral History.

Doctor, does that beautiful object ever give you pause to wonder how the hands of the artist were able to distill such feeling from unyielding stone? Was it his love of God or his fervour for the subject? Might he have been using this scene from the Bible as a means to express the tragedy of his own relationship with his own mother? Or was he perhaps no more than the pawn of a disembodied force that guided his hands towards the working of that minor miracle . . . ? Even if this was so, it is *his* work and name that is remembered, isn't it—not the name of the force! The force is unspeakable. We cannot speak of the force. We cannot see the force for the trees. But where were we?

Oh yes, we were returning to the vicarage. At the time of which I am about to speak, I was seven or eight years old. Do you know, Doctor, that a child makes its most important bonds, and learns how to give and accept affection, between the ages of three and eight? I spent those particular years of my life being passed from one pair of stranger's hands to another—smacking, punishing, torturing hands! Hands wielding belts and switches, stomping feet! Yet so many evil stories about me had been told, as it were, over backyard fences, that there was no other family in our village, or in the neighbouring village, that would have me; and after I returned to the vicarage, there was no woman in our village willing to attend to Father's housekeeping. There was not a woman in his entire congregation who would prepare food for us—good, decent, God-fearing people, these!—and Father's services began to suffer in attendance.

Being the man that he was, Father welcomed me back not only as his ward, but as his cause. From his pulpit, he shamed the absentees from his services to the ears of their neighbours. He called them old goats, he called them swine; he called them dogs and mules, lice and jackasses—insulting them with the noble names which Adam had coined for the animals. And as I may have mentioned in passing during our last talk, it was during this period that the skies began to deny us rain for days, weeks, and eventually months on end. Father scolded his flock, telling them that the clouds had gone dry as their divine comeuppance for having denied the wretched of the earth in need. More than ever did our neighbours regard me with suspicion, their idiot superstitions investing me with diabolic powers not yet mine. All children yearn to be accepted, and there is no question that I suffered from being the object of so much inexplicable fear and contempt.

One evening, Father came to me . . . it was wonderful to be back in my room . . . to furnish it anew from new treasures found abounding in Nature . . . rocks, bones, shells, bird's nests, feathers . . . and, as the breezes turned cooler, to watch the blazing hearth which Father taught me how to light myself. I was very happy to have my room back, but on this particular evening, Father came in response to my weeping, which had become quite voluble—perhaps because, needing consolation but uncertain of how to ask for it, I wished for my sobbing to be heard. He sat with me and expressed to me, in quieter and more vulnerable terms than he spoke from his pulpit, his bitter disappointment in his fellow man. He wanted to make it up to me and told me that he considered it his first and foremost responsibility to find another housekeeper to take care of us as soon as possible—someone who would share our home (quite respectably, of course) and be there always to cook our meals, and to provide warmth and stability and, above all, continuity.

"What kind of lady will she be, Father?" I asked.

"What kind of lady would you like?" he asked in kind. "As you lay there, waiting for sleep to come, why not give some thought to the matter. Tell God what sort of lady you would wish to come and care for us, and perhaps your prayers shall be heard."

At Father's invitation, I did exactly this. I tried very hard to remember the Lady of the cat's tails in her every detail, so that the Lord would make no mistake whilst filling my order. As I rocked myself to sleep, I thought of her and stroked a pet phrase in my thoughts over and over, as lovingly as if it were my poor, sweet Jolly:

I will not leave you comfortless; I will come to you.

Months—even years—had passed without the Lady

keeping her promise that she would come to me and not leave me comfortless—so much time that I began to accept that I had lost consciousness that day, while running through the cat's tails, and dreamed the entire episode.

In the meantime, I spent my days with the books in Father's library. His tastes shunned the popular novels of the day—the Jane Austens, the *Tristram Shandies* and *Vanity Fairs*—but he had quite a good collection of theological texts, collected sermons, non-Romantic poetry (including Mr. Milton's *Paradise Lost*), and also fables, which he impressed upon me for their moral values. He had taught me to read long before I entered the little school-house in our village, so that I came there already familiar with most every lesson Miss Hamish proposed to teach. Thus her most promising pupil quickly learned to stop listening to her and her room-full of nose-pickers and listen instead to the words that ran like a river through my own head, anything remembered or half remembered from the Bible or some other book of Father's . . . *Her eyes are wild, her head is bare, | The sun has burnt her coal-black hair, | Her eyebrows have a rusty stain, | And she came far from over the main. | She has a baby on her arm, | Or else she were alone: | And underneath the hay-stack warm, | And on the greenwood stone. | She talked and sung the woods among, | And it was in the English tongue.* That's from Wordsworth—the only Romantic poet Father could tolerate. As you might expect, most of the tomes at the vicarage were religious in nature, so after reading as much of Wordsworth or John Bunyan or Mary Shelley as I cared to do, I had no recourse but to test those deeper waters. Father had been concerned about me and my spiritual well-being, so when he saw

me opening books on theological subjects, he was warmly encouraging and took this as a sign that his prayers on my be-
half were being heard.

Not every book I opened was written to be grasped by a
young person's mind, but just as I had willed my senses to be
possessed of an animal keenness, so it followed with my reading; the meaning of words I did not know, words I could not
pronounce and would not encounter in the course of my
school education until much later . . . all of these were conveyed to me with perfect comprehension—simply by running my eyes over them. I fancied that my eyes were like a
pair of shaving razors, able to cut through the symbols and
abstractions of things to get straight to the juice of them.

I read as wolves eat: voraciously. I also ate as many
wolves eat: any garbage that was put in front of me . . . because during this period when no one was caring for us, Father prepared our meals himself. He enjoyed a bit of company
and conversation as he went about his work in the kitchen,
so I would stay with him and sometimes read aloud to occupy
our time. He would ask me questions about what I was reading and what I was deriving from his books, to ensure that my
food for thought had been, shall we say, fully masticated.
During our meals, or at tea, he would quiz me about my subjects, asserting, for example, that no one who knew only
basic history—names and dates and places—could be considered a true historian; it was also necessary to have a knowledge of what went on above, below, and next to a fact.

As Father once told me: "Sometimes, people will admire
a beautiful top-soil and credit it to the farmer who tills it, not
taking into account that it is being nourished, far below the

surface, by the bonemeal of armies fallen centuries before. That is why it is not enough to know a little about everything, child. It is infinitely more valuable, in a world like ours, to know everything about a little."

The more I read, it slowly dawned on me that so-called academia—on any subject—is so much I-see-green-where-you-see-brown, where-I-see-F-you-see-K. And nowhere is this truer than in the annals of biblical scholarship. As I made my way through the dusty books filling Father's shelves, I discovered countless inconsistencies—even in the most basic interpretations of the master text. For example, in Deuteronomy 6:13, we are told, *"It is the Lord your God you shall fear. Him you shall serve and by his name you shall swear,"* and yet one of the commandments instructs that we must not take the name of the Lord God in vain! I believe that every single line of the Holy Bible has been contested—its meaning, its essence, its translation, its application to our daily living. I, for one, find a great truth in these discrepancies: a suggestion that God . . . the promise of Heaven . . . all these things may assume different shapes and substances for each of us, each of them equally valid. But people cannot accept such breadth and fairness or complexity of truth, least of all where God's Own Truth is concerned. They insist that God be reconfigured as narrowly as they can imagine Him.

These things troubled my mind, and I would sometimes discuss them with Father, confronting him with my findings and pointing out how one scholar disagreed with another, or with something he had pronounced in one of his own sermons. It was Father's tendency to respond in one of two ways: he might explain to me some fine theological point which had eluded my grasp, or if he found he could say nothing in defence of the scholars' stances, he might mention them by name and say "So-and-so means well," or "So-and-so is a good, God-fearing man."

This phrase "God-fearing" has always been a bane of mine. The Old Testament depicts a fearsome God, angry and jealous; "You shall fear your God," as Leviticus instructs us. Moses deflected his gaze so as not to look upon the Lord, and after that encounter, it is said that the skin of his face literally shone from being so close to the fact of the Lord. And yet, as the Bible flows from the Old Testament into the New, God becomes re-configured. He walks the earth in the form of a Son who is gentle, articulate, and persuasive. There has always been debate about whether Jesus Christ was the Son, or a manifestation of the Father, but they are fundamentally different, are they not? People like to be thought of as "God-fearing," but all of them to a man prefer the more approachable Son. They would rather embrace their Lord than prostrate themselves before Him. They want to by-pass the vengeful, smiting warrior God of the Old Testament by sneaking into Heaven through the back door offered them by gentle Jesus.

Father listened patiently to me as I voiced my confusion about the two distinctly different Gods of the Holy Bible and that one horrid phrase in particular, "God-fearing." When I had finished, he turned to me and asked, "Child, do you remember how frightened you used to be of the dark?"

"Oh, yes," I said.

"You were afraid because the dark was the embodiment of everything that was unknown to you. It was like a mirror held up to your own imagination. Well, the Holy Mystery of Our Lord is like that. We are wretched creatures; we fear the things we do not know, especially when the sum of our ignorance is so much greater than us, so much more profound, shapeless, and infinite—and there is nothing greater, or more profound, than our Lord and His Divine Mystery. When your Day of Judgement comes, child . . . on the blessed day that you finally meet your Maker, it is only right that you should feel an infinitely greater terror than you ever felt shivering in the dark. A terror so great, a fear so immense, so complete, that your only possible response will be . . . to bow to It, to fall to your knees before It, to grovel for Its infinite mercy. When that day comes, when you feel something that powerful, so shall ye know Him."

With these words resonating in my mind, I continued my extra-curricular reading . . . and the more I read—and, more importantly, the more I learned from my direct experiences of people, made in their God's Own Image—the more I came to believe most of all in the smiting God of plagues and tempests—a warrior God. But the average person doesn't want a God like that, a God who can see them for what they are, who could make them cease to exist with less than a simple, side-ways glance. It would make them too afraid to die. But I can believe in a God like that—indeed, I *serve* a God like that because I have no intention of dying. My belief, you see, guarantees me ever-lasting life.

Which brings us to another fault with people's thinking: if you talk with most people about such subjects, by which I mean religious subjects, their pathetic points of reference are Above and Below—their precious Heaven and abhorrent

Hell. I reject such fairy tales! What I know to exist—absolutely and without question—is Without and Within. Neither of them exist to the naked eye, but each is given form and definition by the barrier that separates one from the other: our own bodies of flesh and blood. The Without is eternal, the Within is eternal—only the body, created by lust in the image of our parents, is temporary . . . should we choose to accept this. Should we choose to accept *them*.

Father was very good for me, but I was also very good for Father. As our conversations about my reading became more and more the essence of our evenings together, in the kitchen and over the dining room table, the subjects we discussed began to materialise in Father's week-end sermons. At first, I was quite impressed by this: that Father thought enough of my questions and insights to subject them to further worrying from his pulpit. However, in time, as I found myself supplying more and more grist for Father's mill, I became resentful of his leeching. I prayed to my warrior God to grant me the power to speak for myself.

I would try my own hand at writing a sermon.

CHAPTER X

Patient's Oral History

As you might have guessed, the theme of my first sermon was the question of the animal soul.

My thoughts had been drawn back to this subject by the death of Mr. Griggs, which I had fully expected. Neither Father nor any of the other adults in the village would give a name to the disease behind his sudden and pre-mature debilitation, but I well knew the cause. On the day of his passing, before the hour had come, I followed Father to the Griggses' farmhouse—against his wishes, if truth be told—and saw Mrs. Griggs from afar, positively rotund with the life she had absorbed from her mate.

I walked back inside that place that had no want of me only after all eyes were turned to the skin and bones of the patriarch as he lay on his death-bed—the bed where Mrs. Griggs would sleep alone that night. Father entered the room and seated himself with a flourish that pronounced him a master of such situations. Mr. Griggs's appearance was quite shocking: his skin was already dry as parchment, stretched like thin canvas across the clutching bones of his hand, which held tightly on to Father's priestly raiments, refusing to unhand them. There was a palpable desire in that room, emanating from everyone save Father, that nothing go wrong—though, as I saw it, this event could conclude in but one way, though Mr. Griggs would doubtless experience it differently than the rest of us.

When I saw how comfortable he was in his role, I wondered how many dying faces Father must have looked upon in his day—how many desperate hands he had let squeeze his cloak into the countenance of their own wrinkles, as he helped them to find life's secret egress and squeeze through. How many must there have been, for him to smile upon that face, always with one aspect in common, the aspect of coming death, and call that aspect "friend"? And I wondered: Has he been led to that secret egress often enough to find his way there by himself?

Abruptly, my curiosities were curbed as Father's consoling voice cut through the jagged sounds of Mr. Griggs's wheezing: "There, there, John . . . Fight not against the flow of what must be. You are a farmer. You know that there is seed, there is a moment of ripeness, and then there is the harvest. So it is with Man. You have had your youth, your maturity, and now you must bend to the harvest for which we are all bound, the harvesting of Heaven. Of course, there is a natural desire to cling to what we know, to all that is familiar, but once you cross over, from pain into Paradise, you will be delighted to tumble down into the true familiar place: a place of youth and energy and colours as bold as when you first saw them as a child. All that you have known—the learning, the struggle, the matrimony, the harmony, the pain, and the discord, even the monotony—have been but rungs in a ladder to help you ascend to this moment, the fruition of your spiritual fibre. You are as a strong cord of wood, dependable and burnished with tens of years of experience. Not so tight, John. Only now, with a long, full life behind you, can you appreciate what is now to come, and your family—your wife and your children—they will surely weep to be separated from you, yet there will come a time for much greater rejoicing when our Lord extends his great arms to embrace all whom we have known, the living and the dead, as one, and present this to us as our due as good, God-fearing Christians. It is time now to let go. Let go, John."

Then Father leaned closer to Mr. Griggs: "Here is the secret to crossing over . . . Open your mouth as you did as an infant. Let your mouth be filled with nourishing air, drink it in harder and harder, drink of life to its very dregs, until you feel yourself sated . . . until you feel yourself . . . restored unto God."

Mr. Griggs was the first human being whose death I witnessed—and, to be honest about it, I was vastly disappointed. I felt absolutely nothing as his spirit fled the room; there was neither the drama, or the acceptance of the process, or the tragic dimension of loss that I had experienced when witnessing the deaths of animals. Of course, with Mr. Griggs, I felt absolutely nothing when his spirit was *in* the room; as a living breathing man, Mr. Griggs was singularly lacking in soul.

To look upon Mr. Griggs in death was not very different than looking upon him in life; he looked like the empty trouser pocket you turn inside out as you fish for a farthing. But the sight of him lying there with his mouth agape grieved everyone else in the room, which slowly erupted into the un-suppressed sounds of mourning—by which I mean sobbing, whining, wheezing, shuddering . . . *animal noises*. The area surrounding Mr. Griggs's death-bed became a veritable barn-yard, with the sounds of his family and relations neigh-ing . . . mooing . . . bleating . . . oinking into sopping handkerchiefs. Mr. Griggs's death had no effect on me, but I found this response—the instinctual return of everyone as-sembled to their animal roots—I found this metamorphosis quite poignant. It moved me . . . in fact, it moved me to join their chorus:

"*Baaaah . . . squeak . . . neigh . . . moooo . . . oink!*"

I started out low, not wishing to be seen because I knew that I was not welcome, but the sounds of their mourning made the Griggs house more like a home, a world to which I belonged! It felt so fulfilling to become an animal in the midst of that common herd that I let my cries grow to sing as one with the others, until our braying sadness shook the room. That was when Father silenced everyone by rising to his feet abruptly, leaving the bedside and crossing the room to where I stood. There and then, in front of all the other an-imals, he slapped my face. It was the first and only time he ever raised his hand to me.

"You will show respect in the presence of Death, child!" he admonished.

I thought I *was* showing respect for Death. For me to come across an animal dying, or already dead, as I was walk-ing along a road or through a field, always came as a terrible slam in the guts, a shock to all my senses; it made me feel a dimension of tragedy that seemed to encompass the entire world and all the horrible sadness in it. To become an animal in the face of Death . . . why was this considered less respectful and more defiant than being so arrogant and presumptuous to stand face-to-face with it like a man?

Have you ever looked into an animal's eyes as it is about to breathe its last, Doctor Seward? A pet cat, perhaps? As you sought to comfort it by stroking its still-warm fur and squeezing its paws in reassurance, did you look into the depths of its eyes to show it, without the abstraction of language, the depths of your own affection? Did you happen to spy there what they have to give you back? You might spend your entire life with the same animal, you might speak the same nonsense words to it, time and again over years, and then when this time comes, when your eyes form a bridge, as it were, from heart to heart, you offer it the last of your lies . . . You say, "It's all-right . . . it's all-right . . ." And you know, in that awful instant as they look back at you, that they know infinitely more about death and dying than you ever shall. It's as though they have been through it all before, and remember every bitter detail of the process. What you see there in their eyes isn't wisdom, nor is it bravery, but *awareness* . . . a numb awareness that your words of comfort are a *deception*, that the brave face you're wearing for this holy occasion is a *farce*. Yet, in the eternal spiritual beauty of their kind, they blink their sweet forgiveness at you and accept your mortal failings with their special capacity for selflessness and love . . . They remember that, for all the difficulties they have made you suffer—the furniture they've torn up with their claws, the rugs they've soiled in their illness, the sleep you have lost from their crying and running around at night—you have somehow looked past it all and continued to care for them, to provide them with shelter and safe lands in which to roam. And, as you acknowledge all this in your silence, looking into their eyes, into the deep pools of their souls, their gaze admits an additional respect and you tell yourself that, now—now it is too late! You have finally learned how to communicate with this creature who has been your companion in times of play, a comfort in times of tears, a keeper of your secrets, an accessory to all the departments of your disordered life! And then they close their eyes . . . upon a life of obedience, as if bowing their heads to the ultimate submission—meekly, ever so meekly—and the room you both occupy becomes the room you occupy alone . . . an instantaneous re-definition of space that is nothing short of miraculous and astonishing. It is a moment so all-powerful that makes you want to bow down, to prostrate yourself before it, to grovel for its mercy—and by this do you know that your Lord and Master has laid His almighty Hand upon the very room in which you stand, and have been left standing. This, the moment of an animal's passing, is so great that it trivialises all words, all language . . . It awes you, embarrasses you, humiliates you . . . yet the animals, in their simplicity, accept it with such grace it makes you love them all the more. Then someone—a doctor, a farmer—comes along and picks them up like trash to be disposed of . . . *and it's a sin.*

Genesis tells us that God made His covenant not only with Man but with every living creature of all flesh. The very windows of Father's church, fashioned from mosaics of stained glass, were illumined with the likenesses of men and women *and their animal companions.*

I took care to mention all of this in the first little sermon that I wrote. Father was impressed by the initiative I had shown by attempting a sermon, at an age when most boys find it difficult to put five sentences together. It was only a page or two in length, but there was the seed of a mature sermon there—something Father could use, and he did.

"Perhaps someday I can bring consolation to the dying, as I have seen you do, Father," I speculated—and he allowed that, if I were to follow in his footsteps someday, and keep the vicarage going, this would make him as happy and proud as any natural father could be of his son.

I made a present of my sermon to Father, who dressed up my simple thoughts in fancier language, softened some of my more harsher and most unforgiving questions, padded it out with biblical quotations—and then read what was essentially my work to his parishioners the following Sunday. I was witness to the emotions it aroused among those who heard it. When he finished, Father announced to his flock that he had a confession to make—and acknowledged that I had been the true author of the thoughts and words placed before them that morning. I felt every pair of eyes in the church turn towards me. There was surprise, perhaps a few were impressed by my talent, but most were resentful, as though Father's respected office had knowingly tricked them into heeding the babblings of a child with piety. As seconds passed, I felt the eyes of the adults turn away, leaving only the eyes of the other children in attendance to burn on me, blazing with green hatred. I had made them all as common as they were, you see.

Later that same day, I was going outside to empty the slops when I discovered a special reply to my sermon which someone had left on the back steps of our vicarage: a dead squirrel. I sat down the buckets and knelt to examine the poor thing more closely. Squirrels being very quick creatures, I comforted myself with the thought that it must have died a natural death before its brains had been dashed out by a heavy rock gripped in a small and resentful hand; this brought me the small consolation that what lay before me was an act of profanation rather than torture.

But you may be sure that I wept for it—this animal so sleek and so beautifully made by the Hand that made us, and the rhythmic sound of my controlled weeping was like the churning of an orchestra whose violins were strung with dog whiskers and cat gut. It was an elegy, I suppose, composed of the strangled screeches of cats garotted by bored children in search of amusement; the whimperings of dogs whose care-less owners allow them to run free until they expire in cold weather; the panicking of small birds who are buried alive under repairments made to thatched roofs; the whispering souls of pets, both canine and feline, who were made to look up the barrel of a shotgun for breaking a lamp or dirtying a rug; and, intertwined, the yelps of animals giving birth in the wild, with no shelter to cover them or their offspring, or to warm them, and the first newborn peeps and mews of the tens of thousands that were being brought into this world every day, each of them knowing with an animal's terrible knowledge of all the lives it has lived, all the pain it has known, exactly . . . what it was in for. . . .

Notes on Transcript.

I was certain at the time that our session had reached its end, as poor Renfield collapsed in tears after reliving this upsetting moment. I excused Morrison and granted the patient some time in which to collect himself, which took a little while. Once this was accomplished, Renfield was of a mind to continue, but I told him that it wasn't possible for me to carry on due to a prior commitment, and that it would be best if he returned to his quarters.

In the months I had known Renfield, I had observed that, whenever he wanted to get his own way, he became overly entreating—at first charming and cajoling, and when all else failed, pleading, begging, grovelling. This time was different—alarmingly so. This time—I remember that my office darkened, as though the sun had passed behind a bank of clouds, as though Renfield himself had willed it!—and as the room darkened with his mood, he stood up sharply, rattling the chain at his waist, and showed me a scarlet mask of such smouldering anger that I would not have been in the least surprised had he started frothing like a rabid dog. Yet there was no lunging, no arm swinging as he stood there perfectly erect and perfectly still.

"Yes," he hissed. "Time *is* running out—out of the hourglass! Whatever your foolish plans may be, they can wait! I need to talk, damn you—and you need to listen! This is not just my story—*it's your story, too!*" As the cloud passed, so did his flash of dark temper, and his demeanor became fretful, worrisome. "Without my words to guide you, you won't take notice of the warnings! You'll be marching into peril blind!"

Dr. Seward's Diary.

4:45 P.M.—Shortly after returning Renfield to his room, Dr. Hennessey observed an unauthorised communication between the patient and Beryl, our cleaning girl. During the period of our interview, she had taken the opportunity to tidy his quarters. Hennessey saw nothing pass between them, but once the girl had gone, he looked through the observation trap and found Renfield seated, cradling a neatly folded piece of linen in his hands.

Perhaps overzealously, Hennessey appropriated the cloth and brought it to me. He told me that the patient surrendered it freely, explaining that he was desperate for distraction and thought he might dust his room. Renfield is indeed a fastidious sort who likes to keep himself physically occupied. If you were to place a stack of randomly chosen books on his table, within ten minutes, he would rearrange the stack into either alphabetical or chronological order, based on the date of copyright.

The idea crossed my mind that the folded linen might be the same one Beryl had used to sweep the dead flies from my lamp, because Renfield had been so intent upon the filth . . . coveting it . . . but to what end? But, as I opened the neat folds of the linen, I saw that it was without content either living or dead.

CHAPTER XI

Dr. Seward's Diary.

31 MAY.—It is quite late, or early, as I record this entry, so I imagine that today will be "shot"—to borrow one of Quincey's colourful American phrases. I am hesitant to record the events of this evening, but I am feeling more disoriented than sleepy and know that, were I to go to bed now, I would undoubtedly suffer with sleeplessness for hours, running through these same thoughts without the benefit of recording them for future study, reflection, or purposes of blackmail.

A little after the hour of seven, last evening, I met Quincey and Arthur at the Korea, the adventurer's club where we used to meet and show the rest of London that we were the city's new, young lions. I was always their guest . . . True, I had managed to see my share of the world, thanks to Arthur's generosity, but my own background was middle-class; I never had the advantages of blue—or, in Quincey's case, black blood (as seems to be the magic colour of his family's fortune, first with Angus cattle and now with oil)—so the part I tended to play in our "good old days" was listening to the two of them reminiscing about their great encounters with fellow adventurers and, of course, women—women of all ports and tongues and colours. I imagined this evening would be more of the same, although with a new, bittersweet emphasis on the fact that we are now, all of us, either rapidly approaching or just past the age of thirty and know all too well the exact dimensions of the worldly experience we can in future ascribe to our reckless youth. The emphasis would be most unfavourable to me because, instead of pursuing women and adventure—as I seldom had coin or the personal confidence to do—I had pursued a career. Here I am, seventeen years shy of the average life expectancy for an Englishman of to-day, in my own way regarded as a pillar of Purfleet society, yet inwardly as emotionally crippled as one of my own patients because the woman I love has rejected me—the same woman who said yes to the man I embraced this evening in good brotherhood.

Quincey was there, gregarious as always, and Arthur too, of course . . . He was quite dapper-looking and juggling—most heroically—the mixed emotions of seeing his wedding and his ailing father's inevitable death (and thus his own lordship) approaching, all seemingly hand in hand, as well as the equally gravid billiards of two crestfallen beaux. Had either Quincey or I been in Arthur's shoes . . . that is, if either Quincey or I had been the lucky man rather than he, I know that neither of us could have shown half as much grace as Arthur Holmwood, in showing more concern for our disappointments than delight in his own good fortune. His compassion alone, I told myself, could have sold him to Lucy. Within a few minutes of being back in his company, it was really quite impossible to be resentful of him, especially as I had him laughing so hard I thought he might die with my impersonation of two of my Cockney attendants, Huntley and Black.

After the hilarity had subsided, there came a time when Quincey excused himself to answer the call of nature, and Arthur turned to me with an expression willing itself towards a speedy sobriety. "Listen, Jack," he said, "while we have the table to ourselves, I am going to speak to you frankly, because I feel I have the right."

"A man of my station should not do coarse impressions in public," I said, anticipating him. "You may well be correct about that."

"Look, I know you well enough to know, despite the very amusing front you're putting up, how very disappointed and distraught you really are about all of this. Your man Morrison is quite worried about you, you know. I want to impress upon you the following. First of all, knowing as I did your interest in Lucy, I would not have proceeded with my proposal if I had any doubts about my own feelings for her, or about her feelings for me. I care enough for your happiness, and hers, that I would almost relinquish my claim on Lucy, if I thought you could make her any happier . . ."

"Almost," I said, pouncing on his safeguard.

"Yes, *of course* 'almost,' Jack," he reasoned, half laughing. "I'm a man in love, not a bloody fool. I know that I'm un-likely to find what I've found with Lucy with any other woman, for as long as I live—and since my feelings are recip-rocated, I daren't deny them. What I mean to say, in all can-dour, is that I have discussed you with Lucy, and she told me of your attentions—and I hasten to add that she was quite,

quite flattered by them and has the utmost respect for you. But I am quite certain that Lucy herself would be astonished and very likely mystified, were she to witness—as I can, knowing you as well as I do—the full extent of your feelings."

"You may be right," I managed.

"You will find much greater comfort, if you will simply allow that I am," he advised me wisely. "Quincey is coming back now," he added, adjusting his look of concern to one of the affable and slightly tipsy club man. "Try to at least *look* a little gay, won't you?"

Quincey returned to the table and seated himself heavily, looking about at the leather-bound books and mounted animal heads and tusks and pelts lining the walls. "I think I remember now why I stopped coming to this club," he said, draining his glass.

"Oh?" the other two of us said in concert.

"Don't misunderstand me," he cautioned. "The atmosphere here is a boon to my good spirits. I'm a Texan, and proud of it; I like to feel like a man. And I have found few places in London more manly than this, but nothing . . . and I mean nothing . . . makes me feel more like a man than to be . . . in a room full of women!"

"Now, Quincey," said Arthur, wagging a finger, "I hope you haven't taken it upon yourself to arrange such a panorama, especially with me as the centre-piece, because I take my engagement very seriously."

"Don't you worry, Art old bean," Quincey laughed, slapping his back. "I would not expect you to do anything that would compromise your holy bond to the beautiful Miss Lucy . . . However, should we, your sorrowfully unattached compatriots, find *ourselves* in the midst of some-such opportunity, we may require an extra pair of hands to—"

"To?" Arthur asked, archly.

"To hold our hats!" Quincey laughed, so loudly that every white walrus moustache in the club must have popped out from behind the evening *Times* to cast a stern look in our direction.

After another round of whiskies, we tumbled out of the Korea into the coolth of a sparkling spring evening. We walked aimlessly for several blocks, looking casually about for promises of local adventure, at which point we became intrigued by a distant music of festivity. We followed the sounds to Coram Fields, adjacent to St. George's Garden, where hundreds of people—mostly young working-class men and women—were flowing in and out of a garishly lighted facility of obscure intent. Out front, dozens and dozens of people—including some children—were being entertained by a Punch and Judy show, in which a figure in black was stalking a woman in white. Puffing on the short cigars we had fired up back at the club, we pushed past the puppet show like men who had done with their childhood pleasures and were bent on sampling as many flavours of new adult experience as we could manage in one evening, knowing it would be our last chance to do so together.

Past the puppet booth, we rolled through a turnstile and found ourselves inside an arcade, the most ambitious example that any of us had ever seen.

"What place is this?" Arthur asked, mystified.

Quincey held up his hands as if to stop time itself: "Just look at the signs, Art—a palm reader! The bearded lady! The crocodile man! The Siamese sisters! Clearly, we have some-how found our way—back to *Carfax Asylum!*"

Arthur and Quincey roared with amusement, and damned if I did not do the same.

Quincey grabbed poor Arthur by the collar and dragged him towards the sign billing the palm reader, insisting that his fortune be told. The palmist, who wore a veil of lime green, was an older woman in her fifties, I suppose, with coils of grey hair framing a pair of striking, violet eyes, deep enough in their potent wine colour to persuade most fools, I suppose, of her oracular gifts. Throughout the reading, which was the usual nonsense, our American friend took pernicious delight in guying poor Arthur, asking questions of the divine seer such as "Did Miss Lucy Westenra choose the right hus-band?" "How long will this marriage last?" and "Once the wise girl has had her fill of this roué, which of the two of us will be next in line?"

We sampled some of the other exhibits on the main floor, testing our strength and gawking at the weird and strange, pausing now and again to "down a few brews" (Quincey again). Then, while we still had some starch left in our wobbly legs, we pushed on into a waxworks. Here, we found ourselves held in particular thrall by an assemblage of the great military minds of ancient times, those great strategists of lore whose prophetic comprehension of human psychology was such that they could anticipate the reactionary moves of any and all en-emies, several steps ahead on the chess-board of history. Attila, Genghis Khan, and history's other paragons of bloodthirst.

"This is cheery!" Arthur exclaimed, rolling his eyes. "But I thought we were looking for sex, not violence!"

"*We* were, Arthur," I teased, "but I thought you weren't having any!"

"There will be plenty of time for not having sex after you're married, old bean!" Quincey japed.

The subject of sex having been introduced, we pressed on in search of more provocative exhibits. Surely, we felt, there would be waxen harem girls or belly-dancers or at least a revealing Cleopatra diorama on display somewhere. But the next department of the exhibit was dedicated to a different kind of violence—specifically, the usual horror clichés. We wandered amidst the most vicious deeds of the great murderers and criminals of history, which led us to another section of exhibits devoted to likenesses of Britain's great statesmen of the moment—a transition which I alone found humourous. Quincey, being an American, did not get the joke, and Arthur, being the son of a lord, refused to.

When we did finally locate the area of the waxworks which catered to the public's more erotic interests, it left us feeling less victorious than desperate. There were the usual immortal beauties—Cleopatra, Helen of Troy, and so forth—but each of them had been modelled by women whose beauty was, I am sorry to say, anything but eternal; the contrast between their faces and the names etched onto plaques at their feet was so extreme as to be laughable.

When Quincey expressed his disappointment at the meagre pulchritude arrayed there, Arthur patted his shoulder and said, "There, there, Quincey—if you find these bodies boring, imagine how they must seem to a doctor like Jack!"

He laughed heartily, and I, in my sombreness, started to make a comment—about how much more appropriate it would be to immortalise Lucy's beauty in wax—but was cut short as we were joined, out of the shadows, by a fourth man.

The noun flatters him; he was of mature age, I don't doubt, but there was much more of a boy about him, the experienced sort of enterprising boy one sees all too regularly on the streets of London. He was freckled and not particularly clean and wore what I am sure, within his means, was a better-than-average suit with a bowler hat.

He broke in with a series of *tsks*. "Those ain't too ginch, eh wot?" he asked, offering his question to the general assembly. I am sure that we all felt we had been estimated most poorly. "Loondon 'as mooch better 'n thot aroound, as I seen w' me own eyes," he continued. "I knoows all the top 'ouses in town! See there, like she's got 'em? Fancy summat like that, oonly bigga? Summat like to melt in yer mouf? Like booter oonly sweeta, so's they tell me."

The three of us first looked away from one another, because his intrusion was coarse and his choice of topic so deucedly awkward, but as he kept on, we exchanged a series of covert glances, glances that grew more amused, steadier and bolder, and more probing as we silently asked one another if we were game to go wherever this human oddity might lead us, for the sake of one last adventure. I believe that Arthur and I were undecided at best—my own heart was, ridiculously, so invested that even I felt I should be committing an infidelity by going . . . but it is one of the interesting facts of human behaviour: in groups of odd numbers, the minority vote sometimes turns the tide.

I can understand why Quincey wanted to go, and I suppose I can understand Arthur's motivations as well, but my own curiosity was limited to whether this charmer would lead us to a palace worthy of our station and attire or down a hillslope to shadows beneath a bridge. I had my doubts about the former, as no clean house would cast such an unclean sort in the role of solicitor. We expressed our interest in as non-committal a fashion as possible, and the fellow presented us with a card, tastefully lettered in script on a light blue stock, bearing a certain West End address and the name of Mother Nature.

"A card?" Arthur questioned. "Surely, you don't expect us to give you money in exchange for a card that might lead us to—God knows where?"

"I'll no' be wantin' yer mooney," the boy protested, showing us all ten fingers of his two hands. "Noo noo noo—take this card t' where it says right there and, don't you worry 'bout Collie, sirs—Colin's me naime—I'll get me commission fast as rabbits. I 'as the blue cards, y'see!"

I stood there, already dazzled by the hectic environment and now further disoriented by the boy's unexpected utterance of that familiar name, and looked to my friends to anchor me in the moment. I am not denying responsibility for the direction our evening took when I say that I was content to follow them wherever they decided to go or do. Telling ourselves that we might at the very least come away from the experience with stories to tell, we hired a coach and took our blue card to an unassuming address off Leicester Square. We were not permitted inside until after the foyer of the building was cleared of the gentlemen callers immediately preceding us. Once we had gained full admittance, our card was taken from us by a door-man, formally attired, who marked it with a three and laid it inside a tray, which was littered with similar cards printed on pink, green, purple, and yellow stocks, as well as a few other blue ones. From a glance, I surmised that the unnumbered cards had been brought there by single visitors.

After a few moments, a darkly attractive woman appeared—Italian or Greek would be my guess, and, fortunately, of a much higher class than her solicitor had been. She escorted the three of us to a private room, which thoughtfully assured us that there would be no opportunity for accidental encounters with other clientele. We were seated on a comfortable sofa and told by our guide that the available ladies of the house would soon join us so that we could make our selections.

Quincey broke the silence after she had gone by saying, in continued expansive good cheer, "It looks like each of us three brothers is about to find out what the other two brothers like!"

Arthur turned to him with a mock-sour expression and said, "I already know what *my* two brothers like!"

Those words were like a needle-prick to whatever lingering tensions were still amongst us at this late hour, and they popped with a huge laugh, leaving us all tremendously relaxed. We were soon rejoined by our guide and six of her ladies, each of a distinctly different type. There was a saucy redhead, an exotic negress with green eyes, a buxom blonde, and a motherly type standing next to a type one would not wish one's mother to meet. There was also a girl who re-introduced a certain discomfiture into the room because she bore a vague resemblance to Lucy. The moment we saw her, I could tell (as I am certain Quincey could tell, also) that Arthur felt something proprietary about her, and that for either of us to choose her might re-introduce tensions, if not a more complex problem. It was not that Arthur felt entitled to choose her—he clearly had no intention of doing so—but that he was aware, as were we, that the only reason either of us might choose this girl would be to fulfill a fantasy involving the woman to whom he was betrothed. To my surprise, because it would be impossible to imagine a man further from the crib, Quincey chose the one I had pegged as "the motherly type"—chestnut hair, doe eyes, bountiful of bosom, unattractive hands you could more readily imagine scrubbing a floor than bringing a man to pleasure; Arthur selected the saucy redhead ("purely for companionship, of course," he winked, as they left the room together), leaving me alone in the presence of five watchful women intent upon my voicing of my predilections. I found that, even in the presence of dispassionate professionals, I could not quite bring myself to make them known. I could have gone with the Lucy-ish girl, I suppose, but half of me knew that it would mean betraying Arthur, as the other half knew it would mean betraying Lucy—so I did not give her a . . . fifteenth look.

"Are you Mother Nature?" I asked the raven-haired woman who had paraded the others into the room.

"No, sir," she answered. "Mother Nature is not available at present."

"Well, I am in no hurry," I said, thinking quickly, "and I am certainly interested to meet Mother Nature, whose charms are so prominently billed by your establishment. Why not show me to a room, where I can pass the time with a cigar and some heady libation, and show the good lady to my door when she becomes available?"

"Are you sure, sir? You would make your selection sight unseen?"

"Yes," I said, "I am quite sure. After all, we can leave it at a handshake, if I wish—correct?"

"Well, yes, sir—so long as you pay for the handshake." The other girls giggled at this, and letting her authority to flare, the dark-haired one sent them all packing. I was shown upstairs to a medium-sized room with a working fire-place, where I was free to smoke and toss back brandies while sitting in contemplation of the canopied bed, dressed in dark blue, which dominated the space. The flames behind the grating sent shadows of provocation shuddering from one wall to another, never in the same consecutive sequence, maddening shadows cast by the bed and its ruffles and its plump pillows and polished wooden posts. The shining of the flames was caught in points of reflection that stretched lengthwise up and down the long stems of those posts, where it gleamed as red as the flesh of figs. The walls were papered in a profuse, leafy pattern, crimson velvet on white—very nice—with a thick border along the top, depicting cherubs gathered and peering with wry expressions over the edge of a heavenly mezzanine—a scene that was repeated every twelve inches or so, until the entire room was thus encircled. The carpet and the bedding were green as grass.

There came a knock at the door, and I bid my visitor to enter. Stepping inside was a tall woman wearing a robe and hood of the most profound blue. In a single, fluid movement, she managed to slip inside the room and bolt the door while keeping her face averted in a shy courtesan fashion that reminded me of stories Arthur had told me about his foray into the Far East. The garment she wore was riddled with holes; these were not made by wear, but were rather a deliberate pattern intended to be revealing and alluring, as they certainly were. Then she looked over her shoulder at me and, though I could not as yet see the face recessed within that hood, I could see that it was smiling.

"Mother Nature?" I asked.

"I could be," she said, stepping forward and peeling back her hood. Exposed to the shuddering light of the room, her hair was grey, but not an ageing grey; it was an immensely unusual and attractive shade, an enhancement rather than a diminishment, as though she had deliberately coloured it so. It was also provocatively styled; she wore bangs trimmed at mid-brow, from which her hair fell straight to her shoulders on either side, but when viewed in profile, the hem of her coiffure rose in back to expose the nape of her neck almost fully. The face framed by those tresses was, in contrast to their colour, in the prime of youth—yet there was nothing young about the sophistication of her facial expressions, which belonged to a very experienced soul indeed, the master or mistress of all those things she knew. Her facial characteristics were patrician, suggesting aristocracy in her lineage; she looked down her nose at me, but it was quite an elegant nose, and her eyes sparkled with possibilities both sweet and illicit, which neither of us was crude enough to articulate. I told myself that she might be the offspring of a streetwalker's blind tryst with a member of the royal family on the night of a *bal masqué*. On one side of her face there was a beauty mark—not a natural one, but the sort of small, round appliqué that women used to carry about in patch boxes in centuries past. It provided a titillating, antiquarian touch. "I could be—anything you wish," she finished.

"I'll bet you could," I said approvingly.

"So . . . you *do* wish?"

"Oh, yes indeed," I repeated, already losing my self-control, my words shuddering in echoes around the room like the flickerings of Hell.

"So, will it be *with* the beauty mark . . . or *without* the beauty mark?" she asked. The question was put to me with a certain inflection, as one might hear if the question were "So, will it be with the revolver *loaded* . . . or *unloaded?*"

"That depends," I stammered hoarsely, feeling as though I could not possibly shed my clothes fast enough. "Are you more beautiful with the mark . . . or without it?"

"Different men are of different views," she answered with a certain hauteur. "But, sometimes"—she qualified her statement with a feigned dolorousness—"the men who have me with the beauty mark . . . they forget me. But"—she added while slowly revealing the fullness of a most wicked smile— "the men who have me *without* the beauty mark . . . They *never* forget me!"

"Then off with it," I laughed. "Off with everything!"

Looking back on all of this, I cannot help but wonder if the brandy decanted in that room was drugged; this would at least offer a rational explanation for what I was about to experience. This stylish whore stood there, taunting me, removing the articles of my clothing, until I stood before her as Nature had made me. Then she goaded me with her starry eyes until I fell flat below her blue canopy. She approached the bed and, wearing an expression more sober than flirtatious, peeled the beauty mark from its resting place to the left of her chin and placed it inside a tiny silver receptacle on the bedside table for safe-keeping. As she did this, the shuddering light in the room began to diminish, as though the log on the fire had spent its last. Declaring her dominion with a sweeping gesture, Mother Nature spread wide her dark robe, which seemed to fly away from her, evolving into something vast and elemental, becoming the very sky above us; indeed, this star-pocked sky she had flung away seemed to become our entire, enveloping reality, as I was no longer aware of the bed I occupied or the room I occupied or, indeed, the world I occupied. I was in her world now.

I heard her voice say "I will come to you," and as she moved towards me on all fours, the wings of her hair hanging low like the ears of some animal, I thought to myself that we might be giants embarking on the act for which a constellation was named, or the players in some other legend of equal magnitude that happened to be played out beneath man's reckoning on the level of the infinitesimal. In the starry darkness, I could not see the details of her naked body, only the way the available light adhered to the curves of her, accentuating her physical tone and musculature, which was prominent but without detracting from her lithe femininity. I lay there, floating beside her, knowing that the clutch was coming—inevitable, destined, legendary—my thoughts racing with the excitement that her touch would either heal, anneal, or flay me.

She did not fall upon me with sinking teeth and nails, nor with kisses of sweet redemption; rather, she rolled into my waiting arms with strength and agility, like the Angel who wrestled with Jacob till the break of dawn. There were no met or reciprocated kisses; there were scratches and laughter, a laughter of delight and shocked sensibilities. What the palms of my hands felt as they roamed over her body in the dark was—I was astonished to discover—hair, sparse in some areas while dense enough in others to feel like fur. The short, feathered hair I had seen at the nape of her neck extended down the length of her spine to a point between her sacral dimples; her legs were bristly at the calves and I took the greatest pleasure in rubbing the fine down covering her warm thighs. Her breasts were covered in the same gentle down, which seemed to make the flesh below it glow ever warmer, and below her nipples were other nipples and other nipples, six in all, each set of dugs growing smaller as they neared her lap. Whenever she felt me becoming too languid in my attentions, she would spur me with her nails, her eyes flashing encouragement, and we would fight like two happy cats in a bag, like two sibling creatures in their mother's womb.

I am almost certain that I did not give her my name, but she called me Jonathan and then—oh, I realise this is all so strange as to be unbelievable, the most unbelievable night of anyone's life!—but, as our climax drew close, I seemed to occupy—for mere glimpses at a time—the rooms and the beds and, indeed, the very bodies of my two friends. To be more precise, in a series of successive yet staggered moments, I found myself taken out of myself, away from Mother Nature, and put in with the saucy redhead whom Arthur had chosen and the maternal whore of Quincey's choosing; I could feel their teasing, I could feel different urges driving my body, dif-

ferent areas of my body responding as they pressed their bodies against me like whispers, breathing on my neck, licking
their lips and, again, calling me Jonathan—though John is,
in fact, my full given name.

Sitting here now and looking back, I have no memory of
disengaging from the woman who called herself Mother Nature or seeing her leave the room. I awoke alone in that
canopied bed feeling wasted, depleted . . . my last strength
taking the form of a desperate need to escape the premises
with my last shred of sanity intact. Had I found the door
locked, I would have surely used the window to effect my escape—but thank God! it was open.

As I stepped into the outer corridor, looking down at my
sad shoes on the crimson carpet, two other doors of nearby
rooms opened and my friends—my brothers—joined me, also
looking rather more cowed than exhilarated by their respective experiences. We stood there, hats in hand, for what
seemed a long moment, and then we walked quietly to the
exit, where we paid handsomely for our pleasures. Then the
three of us stepped outside, where we were met by the cab
that would take us home.

Climbing aboard, I looked back at the house from which
we had emerged and thought it looked almost indistinguishable from a vacant premises. As the sun rose on this new day,
denying the existence of the evening we had shared, we kept
our eyes trained on the passing sights, the passing houses, the
passing barges, the passing moments—everything but one
another's face.

Deep in our coats, we said not a word.

CHAPTER XII

Dr. Seward's Diary.

31 MAY, 2:30 P.M.—Rose today after only a few hours of sleep and, feeling penitent, attended the Sunday morning service in our chapel with the patients.

Mr. Renfield was persuaded to join us for the first time. I was seated within view of him and observed his misbehaviour. He listened with something like reverence for the first half of the sermon, but as time drew on, as the hour drew closer to high noon, I could see him becoming more bottled up, more constipated with rage. Shortly thereafter, he began to disrupt the service—bedevilling Father Reville by quoting contradictory Scripture aloud with the jeering tone of a heckler and, at other times, by breaking wind as loudly as possible. I quickly had enough of his bullying, and signalled to the attendants to escort Renfield back to his room—only to find *myself* suddenly beset with the inconvenience of gas, which I was at least successful in suppressing from the hearing of others in attendance. The involuntary, animal noises made by the physical body, as the ear strains higher, towards the spiritual plane described from the pulpit—there, I reckon, is the entire human drama in a nut-shell.

So determined did I feel to put a new foot resolutely forward that I resolved to break my habit of Sunday rest and ask that Mr. Renfield join me to continue the recording of his oral history. Naturally, I do not intend to reveal that I have been eavesdropping on the fantasies he records in his notebook.

LATER.—To-day's meeting with Renfield took place this morning, immediately after our Sunday services. I would have preferred to wait until a later hour when his mood was less sanguine, but his closing words to me yesterday were so full of urgency, I had him brought to my office in his strait-waistcoat. As Hardy was attaching his coat to the iron link in my wall, the patient surprised me by asking, with perfect politeness, if it would be possible for us to conduct our meeting to-day without restraint.

"But, Mr. Renfield," I said, sincerely surprised by such an appeal, "the last time we met, we ended with your mood taking a most volatile turn . . . and earlier this morning, I was witness to you conducting yourself in a most deplorable manner."

"That clergyman you have pontificating in your chapel is a fatuous fool," he declared. "He is likely nothing more than an errant curate who was sent to this looney bin by his vicar to punish him for some mis-deed, or to teach him a lesson. He makes the miracles of our Lord sound like the delusions of madness. Does he not realise that, in a place such as this, he is preaching to the converted? A man like that deserves the worst criticism my arse can summon."

I noticed Hardy looking at me, awaiting my decision of

whether Renfield was to be chained or not. I gestured for him to stay a moment.

"Let us say, for the sake of argument, that what you say is reasonable," I presented to Renfield. "What does that have to do with the way you intend to conduct yourself here, in this room, for the next hour, or however long it takes? Why should I trust you to behave any differently here?"

"For one thing," he said simply, "it is time. Do you not re-alise that, as of today, I have been your guest for two whole months? Am I not entitled to some special consideration, in token of our little anniversary?"

"Well, well." I smiled. "Happy *little* anniversary. But the answer to your question, I'm afraid, is no. Understand that I am not dismissing your plea out of hand; on the contrary, I should like very much for you to bring me around to your way of thinking."

Renfield smiled at me as though I had given him all the cash on my person, all the keys of my asylum.

"Doctor Seward," he asked, "what makes you think that you are any different than I? Because you sit in this office in a coat with that little chain on your watch-fob? I sit in this of-fice in a coat with a little chain. Do we not speak of the same subjects? Do we not suffer from the same cravings? By sum-moning me here, to your office, on a Sunday . . . by insisting on working on the Lord's day of rest . . . are you not also thumbing your nose at the Sabbath?"

"Not at all," I said, mildly offended. "If I owned all the water in town and a house caught fire, would I refuse to douse the flames because it happened to be Sunday? I have asked you to join me here to-day, Mr. Renfield, because you expressed to me yesterday that there was some urgency attached to my understanding of you."

"I am pleased and honoured and deeply relieved that you remember," he said.

"If I insist upon working on Sunday, I am not 'thumbing my nose at the Sabbath,' as you put it, but rather placing a higher value on truth than on tradition."

"The same here," Renfield declared, making the word *here* extend in time for a good five seconds. "We understand each other perfectly, Doctor Seward—as the worm understands the apple. You being the apple, of course. We are like two green peas in a pod."

Once again, the patient impressed me with a sly insinuation that he knew more of me and my internal workings than I had or would share with him. This time, he had used a specific phrase which I remembered using recently in private conversation with Quincey Morris. Had Renfield indeed become, to use his simile, the worm in my apple?

"I'll tell you what," I proposed. "We will try it your way this time—and see if you earn another."

At my signal, Hardy warily unfastened the strait-waistcoat binding the patient's arms to his torso—and looked at me like he was tempted to strap me into it. I instructed him, as he pulled the garment away, to stand guard outside my closed office door—and I instructed Renfield to take his usual seat, warning him that, if he made any attempt to stand, to pace, to approach my desk, I would call Hardy back at once and have him forcefully subdued.

"You could not have expressed my own wishes more perfectly," he said, lowering himself into his chair.

As Morrison was arriving, Hardy made his exit and I explained to my startled secretary why the patient was not under duress. I insisted that he move his chair from its usual place to a safer distance, and this was done without question. Renfield crossed his legs and laced his fingers, clearly revelling in the freedom to do so. He looked at me, then at Morrison—rather like an orchestra conductor asking his brass and woodwinds sections with a glance if they were ready to blend into music—and then, as I nodded and Morrison pressed his pencil to the top sheet on his lapboard—Renfield launched into the latest twist of his reminiscence.

Patient's Oral History.

"Return to me, says the Lord of hosts, and I will return to you, says the Lord of hosts."

This passage from the Book of Zechariah was referenced in one of Father's sermons that summer, written in response to the many dry weeks that were on the point of becoming the worst drought of my life-time. He was making the point that if those still-stray members of his flock returned to our church, the Lord might return to them in the form of the rain they so desperately needed for their crops. But being a line of Scripture and thus open to interpretation, it gave rise in me to an altogether different idea: to return to the field where the cat's tails grew. If I returned to that place of magic where I had my encounter with the mysterious Lady, perhaps she would return as well!

Our village had not seen a drop of rain since the day I last saw the Lady, when she had walked off into the clouds. The cat's tails had turned stiff and brittle under the brunt of an unforgiving sun, so much so that they snapped under my passing touch, whereas they used to gently bend, crunching under my shoes. I looked and looked, but the Lady was nowhere to be found. It seemed that my little world was starved not for water, but for her.

Day followed day, hope diminished with hope. Father had assured me that it would be his first priority to find a house-keeper who could take care of us, which gave me the hope that the Lady would use that opening to return into my life, but I never saw him do anything to bring us nearer to that end. He was always distracted by the needs of his flock, the text of his next sermon, but mostly, he took the matter into his heart as a prayer and left it to the Lord to send the right woman in response to our prayers.

And so came that blackest of days, that darkest of disappointments. I was coming inside from a long summer's day spent in hope among the cat's tails when I passed thoughtlessly by the kitchen and found a strange girl there, sitting at table, skinning carrots.

She wore her black hair pulled into a bun as though it had been yanked back by a powerful hand. She had no bosom and sat with her legs wide apart beneath her skirt. The dress she wore was hand-made and looked as though it had spent at least half of its days in scalding water, its pattern dimming like something better forgotten. I looked at her fingers, knobby and calloused from a lifetime of washtubs and hot water, broomsticks and rakes; her thumbs were gnomish, like the round ends of the carrots she was scraping. Never had I seen a skinnier woman and there was something also flinty about her, utterly bereft of the softness of youth. When her quick, black eyes flashed in my direction, something about her empty glance—in combination with her black hair and her hard surface quality—made me think of her as a bug, as a black armoured beetle. I told myself that if she spat at me, which from her nasty look was not at all out of the question, she would spit tobacco juice, as grasshoppers do. Her shoes were worn and mannish, like the hand-me-downs of a brother who didn't care what he walked in, or walked through. Not far from her feet lay an old carpetbag, faded and threadbare, stuffed with enough of her possessions to let everyone know that she intended to stay a good while.

She continued scraping, saying not a word to me and, other than that disdainful glance, gave no notice of me whatsoever. She was without question the lowest living creature I had ever seen, yet she acted towards me as though *I* was beneath *her*. I returned the discourtesy.

Most upset by what this stranger portended, I marched straight back to Father's office, where I found him in conference with a man from the village, who was sitting across from his desk—much as I am sitting across from you now, Doctor. He was holding his hat in his hands, by the brim, turning it clockwise a little at a time as he spoke in soft words I could not hear. Father responded to my arrival with a harsh look that gave me no possibility of misunderstanding that he could not speak with me just then. So I withdrew, passing the stranger in the kitchen once again on the way back outside. I did not look at her a second time, telling myself that once was quite more than enough. I was also playing a little game in my mind, to be perfectly honest—I told myself that, if I could succeed in seeing her only once that day, she would not be staying with us—as I feared was the case, and would seal the iron door between the Lady of the cat's tails and me.

I left the vicarage and went to sit amongst the headstones in the churchyard. Often, when I felt the need to get away from everything, I would retreat amongst the unmarked headstones in the northwestern quarter, where at least a score of nameless beggars and itinerants had been buried since the time of its founding in the fifteenth century. No one ever visited those graves, so I was guaranteed my sullen privacy; these plots were also positioned to present me with a view of the windows of Father's office. Sometimes, when those windows were open to admit warm breezes, I could hear him composing his weekly sermons, practising his lines aloud, or reading from his Bible the most fabulous descriptions of miracles and redemptions and things in which I would have liked to believe.

It was also a wonderful vantage from which to observe the gradual and resplendent greening of the area each year, the return of birds from warmer winter climates, the surfacing of the ants from their subterranean slumbers, the eruptions of bees from hives secreted in the trunks of dead trees. I saw sparrows nurturing their hatchlings with worms, owls regurgitating nutritious ropey pastes of carrion for their young, pink hairless barn mice welcomed to the pink hairless nubs on their mother's belly, drones honouring their queen. As much as I considered myself a member of the animal kingdom, I observed these annual miracles in admiration of their miraculous predictability and damned myself for having been born human, with a human life subject to irrational shocks and instabilities. I sat there on browned and brittle grass, under a barren cloudless sky, and fretted over the way in which my homelife was about to change, once again, for the worse.

After the troubled gentleman with the clockwise hat took his leave of Father's office, I saw Father himself move some papers, sigh, rise to his full height, and exit the room. I knew that his first challenge would be to find me, so I kept especially quiet—to make my discovery all the more difficult, to test his love that much more, and to punish him for choosing this woman without my approval. A minute or so later, I saw him step outside the vicarage. He walked to the dirt road, looked to the left and right, then walked down the road for a length of perhaps twenty steps before he stopped and turned instinctively and walked directly to my hiding place without the slightest uncertainty. Wishing to keep my hiding place a secret, I quickly scrambled over to the nearest graves with names etched on their headstones, keeping low as I moved, and settled down while trying to look as though I had been there and nowhere else all the while.

"Oh, there you are, child!" he said in greeting. "I thought you might be—I don't know—over there somewhere."

"No," I fibbed. "I was here all the time."

Father, who could be quite uncanny, seemed to see through my fib, yet it was he who stood above me, shifting from one foot to the other, generally looking like someone who had been caught in a lie. I squinted my eyes at him, and he bolstered his manner with the stiff pride of an adult who knows he has done something wrong but intends to stand firm on his seniority, that his mistake might pass into law without comment.

"I suppose you have met our Moira?" he asked.

"I saw a stranger in our kitchen," I said. "I suppose her name could be Moira, but she's certainly not mine!"

"I am sorry that I wasn't available to introduce her to you properly, child, but I have faith in her and think she could make a home for us."

"But she is not the one I wished for, Father! You promised me the one I wished for!"

"Now I did nothing of the sort, lad," he said sternly. "I told you to send a prayer to our Lord, to describe to Him the sort of house-keeper you would like to have come and stay with us. But the decision of whom to send is ultimately His, and it is not for us to argue with His selection."

"How do you know that she is His selection?" I asked.

"Because I left the matter entirely in God's Hands," Father replied. "I did not go looking for someone to take care of the house. *Moira found us*—as I knew someone would— much as I found you, should that make it any easier for you to understand. The poor thing . . . my heart went out to her. I found her hesitating outside the vicarage like a beggar, as if she was afraid of knocking. She had nowhere else to turn, you see, and a hard life has made her very untrusting of others, fearful of new acquaintances and experience. I took her in and began to make her some toast and tea, but in the end, she made me the toast and tea. She is a nervous sort, always has to keep her hands busy. In time, she began to talk. She talks with her hands. I got the impression that her life has been so full of strife and misery that she might well succumb to despair without a safe harbour at this particular point in time. I could not turn her away. I grant you, she is not quite the house-keeper I envisioned the Lord sending to us, but He

189

doth work in mysterious ways. Moira is not a very bright woman, but I can tell by her energy that she is hard-working, not a shirker. She is also a pious, God-fearing woman, so the seed of goodness is planted somewhere in her; but she needs the right companionship to help her cultivate it. She will be good for us, and we will be good to her. Is that understood?"

I had little choice but to accept. Father took my hand and walked me back to the vicarage, where I was to be properly introduced to this grim and coltish girl whose awful life had won out over the rights of mine. We found her in the kitchen, still quite absorbed in her duties, and Father announced us by saying her name:

"Moira?"

She was so alarmed by this gentle intrusion into her private thoughts that she dropped the pot she was holding, which was full of an uncooked soup she was concocting. It spilled in a kind of exclamation point across the kitchen floor. I looked down at the dense broth, the chopped vegetables emerging as the spreading broth thinned, and thought to myself: *This is vomit.*

She muttered some exclamation, crossed herself, and set about containing and cleaning the mess as Father continued: "Dear me! I'm terribly sorry, my dear! It didn't mean to alarm you!"

"'Twere me own fault, Rever'nd," she said.

Father forced a smile to mask his concern and forged ahead: "Moira, I would like to introduce you to my young ward, a foundling to whom I have given my family name of Renfield. The child is gifted in many ways"—believe me, Doctor, I am not embellishing Father's words in the least!—

"but has always suffered from the unfortunate lack of a woman's guiding hand. It is my fondest hope that the two of you will become fast friends and take comfort from each other's company."

She raised her face from the rowing movements of her scrubbing, and her eyes followed the upwards movement of her head slowly, like the head of a doll with articulated eyes that was broken somewhere, deep inside. She was in so many ways still a girl yet already haggard, benumbed to life, and she looked at me with her black eyes as one might regard the mistake of someone for whom they have absolutely no respect. I knew at that moment that there would never be, could never be any affection between us. I knew instantly that Moira was a terrible mistake Father had made, out of his boundless Christian charity, and one that would only grow worse and more painful with time. Time would only confirm that knowledge.

"A'll do me best, Rever'nd," she said flatly, wringing the soapy soup water from a glutted rag into a bucket. It made the sound of someone being sick.

Father could not quit the scene of our mutual discomfort fast enough. With our introductions now made, he patted my shoulder and, beaming with the self-satisfaction of one who has done his duty, traversed the length of the house in long strides, closing his office door firmly behind him. I remained standing there in the kitchen doorway, curiously transfixed by the sights of this stranger at her unpleasant toil—the large round veins popping off the backs of her hands, her mannish shoes buckled in labour, the soap and the soup.

Some moments later, while wiping some briney sweat

from her brow, she cast another hard glance at me and said sharply: "If you're wantin' ta feel a wooman's guidin' hand, boy, sure and you're goin' about it the right way."

Those words—the first she spoke directly to me—established a pattern that would remain consistent throughout all our communications, more or less. The only words Moira spoke to me, and to most other people apart from Father, were deflating. When she talked, it was only to hear herself babble; she was not inquisitive about other people and had no interest in letting them have their say, cutting them off with abrupt changes of subject. Her only care was for the echoes bouncing around inside her own empty head. She may have been a pious woman, as Father claimed, but hers was a selfish piety; she seemed to make a misery of her life on earth as part of a crooked scheme to suffer her way unto a free berth in Heaven. She could talk your ears numb about Jesus and the Holy Mother, but not once in the years I knew her did I ever see her open a Bible, and not once did she act in accordance with its teachings. It is possible, I suppose, that she was illiterate, didn't know how to read, and blindly believed in a God shaped in vague accordance with her own needs, but she concealed her ignorance with craft and wiles. She talked of how she looked forward to dying and lived in daily anticipation of her heavenly reward while spending her days at no worthier task than whispering to her neighbours about what vile rubbish she knew everyone else in town to be.

"All they does," she would tell her rare confidants while pinning Father's and my clothes to an outdoor laundry line, lowering her voice as one of those others passed by, "is talk about ye b'hind yer back . . ."

She made tentative friendships with some of the women in Father's flock, and with others who lived nearby, but couldn't maintain any of these relationships. People soon saw her for the mean-minded, ungenerous soul that she was. She regarded anyone and everyone who visited Father with suspicion, speaking nonsense about them as they left. I can remember a day when a gypsy family passed through our village, pulling their belongings behind them in a ramshackle wagon, looking for charity—but, preferably, work. Father never knew about their coming, because Moira chased them from the vicarage in short order with her abuse, calling them names with her black eyes shining hard. Dear me, the way she spoke of people—any people who weren't exactly like her—ways in which I would never speak of those people who abused me, though they had given me every right!

Her contempt extended beyond people, to the things found in Nature. To anyone who could stand to listen for more than a minute to her selfish natterings, she would express her complete and utter boredom with the first to last of God's miracles. This amazed me, even as a child, that this most joyless of creatures could consider herself a religious or spiritual woman and find naught of holy manufacture worth a second look!

After finally queering herself with the entire village, Moira took to spending her empty days in our kitchen, friendless and alone, looking out a small square window and muttering to herself that all those turned backs out there were all the proof she ever needed that people were "just no damn' good."

Our own relationship never improved. The only times

Moira ever touched me were to grab me by the wrist, to curb me in some way, to slap my hand for picking my nose, to march me to the wash-basin when I fought against washing up before dinner. It started out as simple antipathy, but my feelings matured into literal revulsion—a revulsion I felt, above all, for her flashing black eyes. Sometimes I would be minding my own interests and feel something like a spider crawling along the nape of my neck; there would be no spider there, but I would find Moira sitting nearby and regarding me with a pinched look of hate and curiosity, as if she was using me as a tool to sharpen the cutting edge of her own hatchet face.

My loathing of Moira made me aware of something about myself which I had never quite articulated before. To look at Moira was to look at someone utterly devoid of promise or prospects. I knew that, when Father found me and took me in, I must have looked even less promising, but as far back as I can remember, I was aware of something inside me—a spark, if you like—that raised me above much of mankind's dust. Even as I felt this inexplicable sense of privilege, I could wonder how someone like myself—an ordinary foundling, after all—could be the seat of such blue-blooded sensitivities. I began to wonder if I mightn't have been abandoned as a baby because I was the unwanted off-spring of royalty, perhaps the son of a queen who had given herself to the king of a rival country, a forbidden love which robbed me of the exalted life that was rightfully mine, and singing in my veins, a life of castles and kings, of thrones and finery, of armour and victory.

Seen through my imperial eyes, Moira was less than

human; she was something low and dirty and uncivilised. There was an absence of soul in her eyes, a void as black as ink; Father's were an earthy brown, but mine—as you can plainly see—were green, England's green, as green as God's own world. There was something about Moira that was an offence to my blood, something that made me swear to myself that I would never fall so low; that I would ascend far above her and her kind, or die and be damned in the attempt. And so, through my instinctive contempt for this intruder—who had usurped the place reserved in my life for the mentor I truly deserved—I began to inculcate in myself a self-respect, a sense of noble purpose to which the known facts of my life, if truth be told, had given me no particular right. But I told myself nonetheless that I was destined for great things, that I would someday soar high above the likes of scabby Moira, that I had been chosen from the moment of my mysterious birth to know a calling far greater even than the one Father had answered.

CHAPTER XIII

Patient's Oral History (cont).

Around the time of Moira's unbidden introduction into my life, I had a terrifying dream that I immediately recognised as one I had dreamed before—and with some frequency. I could tell that the images brought forth by this nightmare had been part of my mortal fabric throughout my entire life; indeed, the images were so forceful, so indelible that I can see the dream's final image before me now, as I close my eyes. It remains as vivid as though I was standing there at the very scene . . . but the image no longer makes me tremble. The dream and I are now as one, indivisible.

The dream had no narrative. It was instead in the nature of a slow, irrevocable movement towards a climactic image. It began with a view of the woods—the same haunted woods I described to you in our previous meetings. The scene appeared to be an entrance into the woods, where the trees stood tall and well apart, their branches interlacing high overhead to form a natural archway—a veinwork like the bluish traceries I could remember underlying the ripe skin of

Mrs. Griggs's dugs—and there was a path discernible between them, boring deep into the darkness beyond. Out of
nowhere, the scene was illumined by bold flashes of light—of
a terrible bright blue, as one might see just before the outbreak of a terrible storm—and this affected the entire variety
of colours one saw when looking at this setting. Yes, I could
see these colours of the forest: the greens of the leaves, the
browns of the wood, the purples of the wildflowers seemed to
flicker with another set of colours, a more unnatural set of
blues and whites . . . and there was a distinct orangeing of the
air. An unsettling magic was abounding.

As all this happened, I felt myself drawing closer—but to
what end, I could not tell. In time, I felt my forward momen-
tum come to a halt, and I had the intuition that the purpose
of my dream had been revealed, but that it would not be fed
to me on a spoon. I would have to discern that purpose myself, in my own time, were I to prove myself worthy of it.

Then came another flickering of the light, as though the
real was alternating with the un-real, and I saw something
different—something new had been added to the image,
something at rest at the foot of the most prominent tree. It
was a *carpetbag*. Seeing it there, I felt something like a great
orchestra crescendo in the depths of my soul and woke in a
cold sweat.

As I lay in my bed, fearful of going back to sleep, I thought
back at once to the carpetbag which I saw near Moira's feet
the very first time I saw her in the kitchen. It was not the
same carpetbag; Moira's was worn and full of holes, a poor
country cousin to the carpetbag in my dream, which was more
regal and grand. Had my feelings turned against Moira from

the moment I saw that bag, because it was not the one from my dream . . . ? If so, why would I prefer the carpetbag that I could remember only as the centre-piece of a nightmare?

My instinctive dislike of Moira may have been rooted in my dreams, in her absolute lack of polish, or in her contemptible cooking, but there came a day when it exploded into full-blaze hatred—not owing to something that she was, but to something she had done.

I was out-of-doors, playing on the outskirts of the haunted woods—taking care not to get too close—when I chanced to hear a violent thrashing sound. I say "chanced," Doctor, but I believe that I was *destined* to hear it, so crucial would this episode be in the future direction my life would take. My curiosity overcame my fear, and I followed the sound into the woods until it became sounds—not just a thrashing, but a thrashing and a dull clanking. The nearer I came to the source of those sounds, the more there was to hear, all of it awful. Soon I came upon a heart-rending sight: a poor hare had got its leg caught in a poacher's trap. It was horrible to look upon, as there was a great deal of blood and damage, but its eyes, terrified as they were with mortality, seemed to reach out to me, pleading for my assistance. I was frightened but took courage and released the poor creature from the teeth of the device. It made no attempt to get away, as it was no longer able to run, so I gathered it into my arms, never minding the blood, and ran with it back to the vicarage, calling out for assistance as soon as it came into view.

"Help me!" I cried hoarsely, upon coming through the door. "Somebody please help me!"

Moira, as usual, was working in the kitchen. She stepped

out, wiping her sweaty hands on her apron, her teeth clenched on the stem of a small corn-cob pipe she sometimes smoked. She wrinkled her face in disgust and complained, "Cor, what're ya bringin' that mess in 'ere fer?"

"Help me!" I demanded through my tears. "It's poor leg got near torn off by a trap!"

"Whur did y'ever find such a thing?"

"In the woods!"

"The vicar'll tear off'n one o'yer oon legs if'n 'e finds out ye bin goin' thar," she warned me. "Ye li'l scamp."

"Please, Moira," I begged her, "can you stop the bleeding?"

"I knows 'ow," she said roughly. "Bring 'im in 'ere."

Having set her pipe on the edge of the basin, Moira placed a towel against her apron, as a safeguard against the gushing blood, and told me in a strong voice to give her the animal. I did as she bade me. The hare was jittery in her arms, not knowing her and not knowing what to expect, and she surprised me by soothing it with soft caresses and soft words—"There . . . there now"—gaining its trust. I had never seen her comforting, caring side before and was quite impressed. But then, while smoothing the fur on its face, she took charge of the relaxed animal and, with a firm twist, snapped its neck. The creature went limp in her arms, all the twitching of its pain over in an instant. Its suffering was ended, but the suddenness of it was somehow more atrocious, more horrible. I was speechless with horror.

Moira saw how I was looking at her. "That's 'ow you stop the bleedin'," she explained brutally. "Ye stop the 'eart beatin'."

"You . . . *murdered* it!"

"I *'elped* it, boy. Can ye not see that?"

"Like you help *us*," I accused her. "Like you help *me*."

"Don't go testin' me patience, child—the wretched thing was on the point o' dyin' anyweh," she reasoned. "You'll be feelin' mooch different aboot it once ye taste 'er in a stew."

She slammed the carcass on the kitchen's wooden cutting block. As its dead weight struck there without any reaction, my hand jerked to my mouth in a sharp reflex and I backed away, fearfully, as though that black-eyed harridan might snap my neck next. She stood there, fitting her pipe back between discoloured teeth, regarding me without any feeling whatsoever.

"Begone now, 'efore I raise me 'and to ye!" she scolded me, doing just that as a warning.

I turned and ran—never wanting to stop, not ever—until I found myself back amongst the cat's tails. In my highly emotional state, I ran straight through the middle of the field; I wanted to continue running, for ever and ever, so as I remembered doing before, I enlarged the field by running in circles—in circles within circles—wishing to fully abdicate, once and for all, from the hateful human race into which I was born, by becoming as one with the other creatures who lived there in the fields, in the wild. I prayed that I might sprout fur, gallop on four feet, lap fresh water from running springs, tear at wild rain-washed vegetation with my teeth, sleep in the trunks of trees or the walls of people's houses in warm, close, heart-beaty huddles with others of my own kind. As I changed from a run into an animal's gallop, I tripped over a rock and went flying, landing on my face.

Looking up, a bit stunned, I saw at ground level an entire netherworld of wildlife in the field that could not be seen from above the cat's tails proliferating there. They were funny little things, rodents of a sort, all darting past me with tremendous energy, bolting blurs of fur and thunder, all surging toward a common goal in the woods beyond. My hands sank into the dusty earth beneath the cat's tails, and, as I pulled them out, they looked so clotted with dried soil as to look like paws. My heart-beat was now accelerating madly, and I could see ever so much better; I did not know how poor my vision had been before that. I found myself transformed and part of a family I could never have imagined, one amongst us all the time yet invisible to the human eye above the level of those bending weeds.

I could feel the centre of my being shift from my hips to my spine, my arms beginning to feel like legs. My brain was brimming with all these details, and yet, at the same time, it seemed to contract with every rapid thump of my heart, shrinking until everything that had been pounded into me by life and school was blissfully shed—religion, phonics, mathematics, love, hate, even need—until I was wholly defined by my capacity to attend to a single impulse: *to follow*.

Now I could stop running in circles and move, as it were, in a straight line. The field, as I now saw it, was like a golden arrow pointing to the woods in the distance; once I had raced as far as the trees, the land that lay beyond them seemed to form a second arrow, leading to a path deeply recessed within the woods; and once I got that far, the path also appeared as an arrow whose direction I followed until I found myself in a clearing where the ground was teeming with wildlife, small and inconspicuous, yet a family to which I truly belonged. I had a sense not only of belonging, but of being the entire reason for the gathering, the very centre of the ceremony that was about to take place, with all the other creatures present merely as witnesses. Some of the animals were familiar, and others were of a kind you might never know were all around you in a million years—things that come out only in the dark, with the oddest sort of eyes that can pierce the deepest dark as though it were daylight. As I looked around me, every creature I saw had a kind of anticipatory terror etched in its face, the sort of terror I imagine can come only from knowing all there is to know; it exuded from their eyes, their faces, their musk. I imagined I must look very stupid indeed to those others, because I didn't have the common sense to be scared, only to be mystified by the nature of the threshold upon which we were all crouched together, in giddy expectation.

The woods were a place of many shadows, especially when the sun pierced through the boughs in the hours preceding and following noon. There, we creatures of the forest watched in thrall as the shadows before us moved in a quiet dance, passing, converging, and finally combining in a single, hour-glass shape. Taking my breath away, the Lady of the cat's tails stood before me once again, collapsing the dark wing of her parasol. Every other pair of eyes in that clearing, I am certain, saw her too and felt that her attentions were focussed solely on them. It made me wonder if the squirrels and chipmunks and cats and vermin assembled in community around me were not animals at all but, like me, the animal forms of people who lived for miles around, who knew, on some deep level of themselves, the same things I knew to be true but dared not speak aloud.

The Lady stepped forward, wearing the same veil and fashionable garment of moony blue as before, moving in my specific direction. I had the distinct impression that every other creature in that clearing had a similar impression of her, that she had come solely to confer with them—that she was somehow meeting with all of us, speaking to all of us, and giving each of us her complete attention. This was a being as faceted as a jewel.

As she advanced towards me, she raised her right hand and, using the other—which bore a marvellous, rubescent signet ring—she gently tugged at its fingers of fine moony blue lace, to remove her glove. Obediently, I raised a forepaw from the ground, which came to rest on her palm in the usual configuration of five fingers. But the hand which the Lady extracted from her dainty glove was covered in whorls of greyish hair, with black leathery pads at her palm and along the backs of her elegantly tapering fingers.

She lowered herself to my height—her long skirts spreading out beneath her like a pool—and, releasing my hand, raised both hands to lift back her veil. Thus revealed to me was the face of a magnificent animal, near like that of a timber wolf, but possessed of a truly imperial beauty. I began to see through the surface layer of her beauty to the levels beneath; she had airs of extreme sophistication—well beyond the capability of one who had yet to live a single life-time—and of a wisdom instilled in her by centuries of suffering. I knew that this astonishing creature could not be the mother of my body, but she might well be the mother of my soul. As

I crouched before her, I could easily believe that she had given birth to the entire world's secret soul.

She raised a pince-nez to her furry nose and peered at me appraisingly. "Your tragedy, Renfield," she observed, calling me by name, "is that you do not have the first idea of what you are capable of achieving. So much magic inside you, and not a glimmer of how to bring it out. No idea even of how to reach within yourself to touch it, to stroke it, to pet it, to culture it."

"Yes, Milady."

"And this is because your mind is too raucous with questions, your heart too raucous with hunger, to let you ruminate on more important matters—not even the matters most crucial to your destiny."

"Yes, Milady."

"If you cannot ponder your future, the chances become more likely that you shall not have one."

"Yes, Milady."

"I promise you, my pet, as sure as I stand here, that your questions shall be answered . . . your hungers shall be fed . . . and I *shall* come to you. I promise you all of these things. And when these promises are kept, make no mistake—you *will* be beholden to me. Are we agreed?"

"Yes, Milady."

"Then prepare yourself for my coming," she ordered me, rising to her full height. "I have watched over you; I know that you like to read. This is good: read all that you can. Only by improving yourself can you be of any use to me. Disregard the external; concentrate on the internal—that is where the eternal begins. No city, no work, no army, no being ever had its origin outside the brain and seed of mortal man." Here she paused, cocking her head at me strangely. "How many faces do I have?" she asked—a most curious question, which she posed in the manner of a teacher who asks, "How many battles were actually fought on British soil?"

"Why—just the one I can see, Milady!" I exclaimed in confusion.

She smiled teasingly. "Today you see one. When next we meet, you shall see two."

"Are there still more?" I wondered.

The question seemed to delight her. "I have four faces in all. The third you will see when you are ready to receive and fulfill your destiny. The fourth is reserved for . . . *special occasions*." She rolled her lace glove once again over her bared hand. "Now scoot—they summon you."

"I don't hear anything, Milady," I told her.

The Lady smiled at me in a most curious manner: by curling one side of her mouth under a wry brow. It was the sort of complex expression one could never see on the face of a young person or young soul; in that single expression were woven irony, vexation, amusement, and—I like to believe— a little love. She placed one finger beneath my chin and bowed towards me; I met her half-way by standing on the tips of my toes. She placed her muzzle to my lips, softly and warmly. It wasn't a peck, as I had seen some mothers kiss their children as they sent them out the door to school in the mornings; nor was it all licky and lingering and disgusting like the kisses I had seen exchanged by grown-ups who weren't supposed to know each other when they thought no one was looking. I do not know how exactly to describe what it was, but all of a sudden, as the black lips showing from the midst of her fine grey fur touched mine, I could hear every conversation in the woods, the industry of every ant, the clicking of every beetle, the bristling of every nested bird as it shook the rain from its feathers—to describe it all makes it sound a cacophony, I know, but it was actually very musical, like a grand symphony in which one's own biological sounds were an essential component note of the musical score. And, in the midst of all that noise, I could hear, as clear as a bell, Moira's caterwaul, calling me to dinner.

Back at the vicarage, Father awaited me at the dinner table. I washed my dirty hands at the kitchen basin and took my seat beside him, bowing my head in thankful prayer for the meal we were about to receive. Behind my closed eyes, I could hear our meal being placed before us; when the prayer was ended, I opened my eyes to see Moira ladling into the bowl in front of me rabbit stew.

"I'm not going to eat this, Father," I announced, looking at the lumps of skinned meat in the broth.

"You can and you certainly shall," the vicar corrected me. "On this most joyous day, of all days, you must. We do not turn up our noses at the food which the Lord provides for us—nor at Moira's home cooking."

"Didn't she tell you? I brought this rabbit home to mend! It trusted me . . . it needed me . . . and she took it from me, won its trust, and then she broke its neck! She killed it!"

"It was an *animal*, child—not a person made in the image of our Lord! *Whoever kills an animal shall make it good*," he added, quoting the Book of Leviticus. "Now I won't tell you twice, child! You will eat that stew, every last spoon-full, or go to your room with nothing!"

Then I heard the Lady's voice, as near to me as my own heart-beat, and it advised me, *"For now, do as they bid you. It will not always be this way."*

Having placed my complete trust in the Lady, I did as she instructed: I remained in my chair, dipped my spoon into the broth, and raised it brimming to my lips. Father and Moira watched me intently as I accepted it into my mouth.

As I swallowed and lowered my spoon, Father said, "You see? That wasn't so bad."

I raised my eyes to Moira—her black eyes crisp with spitefulness—and, to her private annoyance, pronounced her hateful stew "delicious."

Indeed, I could not taste the stew. Instead, like a secret between myself and an unseen witness in the room, in every spoon-full I raised from that bowl, I could taste Milady's parting kiss. I spooned it to my lips again and again until my bowl was bare, scraped of every last ounce of her love—and also the love of that trusting hare, in its self-sacrifice. Unlike Moira, whose eyes—averted from Father's—had flamed at me before she turned on her heel and took refuge in her kitchen, Father was heartened by my show of appetite.

As he saw me mopping up the dregs of my stew with bits of bread, he quoted to me from the Book of John: *"And when they had eaten their fill, he told his disciples, 'Gather up the left-over fragments, that nothing may be lost.'"*

Father and I were curiously of one mind. For my part, I was also thinking of the Book of John, but an altogether different passage held meaning for me: *"But he said to them, 'I have food to eat that you do not know about.'"*

Dr. Seward's Diary.

31 MAY, 5:30 P.M.—To-day's disclosures from Renfield were his most disturbing and fantastical to date. I was left feeling quite unsettled by his closing words of Scripture, which he seemed to direct not only at those who surrounded him in the past but those of us who attend him to-day, in the present.

After sending him back to his quarters, Morrison and I sat together in silence for several minutes. Finally, more to smash the silence than out of actual curiosity, I asked Morrison what he made of all this.

"I am not here to express an opinion, sir," he said.

"I'm aware of that," I told him, "but perhaps you might humour me by venturing one?"

Morrison pursed his lips in an inward chuckle and offered, "It rather strikes me as a Perrault fairy tale that got left in the drawer."

"Accidentally or by design?" I rejoined. "These stories have festered in Renfield's memory for the last fifty years. Doubtless he has embroidered them with fantasy to some extent, but to his way of thinking, everything he is telling us is absolutely true; I have no doubt of that. He also insists that these stories have some bearing—some urgent bearing—on the present, but in what regard, he has yet to say."

"If I may say so, sir," Morrison ventured, "urgent bearing not only on the present, but on the facts of your own life. He has framed these stories he is telling as a personal warning to you."

"That may be nothing more than an artful strategy to command my fullest attention," I supposed. "But he would have had that, anyway. He is a Narcissist, yet he sees himself as some kind of Cassandra figure, a prophet of imminent catastrophe. Perhaps it is the only form of self-respect available to him, after having fallen so low."

"An interesting parallel," Morrison smiled. "Cassandra lived her life imprisoned and was cursed, as a prophetess, to tell only the truth, but only truths that were doomed never to be believed."

"I'm a bit rusty on my Greek history," I confessed. "What did the old girl do to deserve such a curse?"

"She was given the gift of prophecy by Apollo, who adored her," Morrison explained. "But in the end, Cassandra shunned the god who had given her this gift, so He turned it against her. Cassandra's father, King Priam, locked her up for her own safety as their city of Troy was besieged by Greek invaders, who found her boxed into her cell and raped her . . . repeatedly and without mercy."

"At least we know Renfield's story will not end *that* way," I smiled.

I asked Morrison if I might have the transcript of to-day's meeting by the end of the day, that I might look it over again to-night at home—and standing to leave, he promised to do his best.

LATER.—Morrison did not disappoint me; I had the transcript of to-day's oral history in hand well before I was ready to leave my office.

Not long after I dictated my previous entry, I was surprised to receive a most unexpected visit from Arthur and his new fiancée. I have not seen or spoken with Lucy since the day she turned down my proposal of marriage, so our reunion might have been deucedly awkward—but they both greeted me with the utmost warmth of solicitation.

In point of fact, I was scolded by Lucy with mock-petulance for having made myself so scarce since the announcement of her engagement—"and after pledging to me your eternal friendship!" she chided. I explained that I had not been intentionally neglectful, but was working very closely with a particularly demanding patient.

I took them back to my private quarters, where we seated ourselves in three intimately arranged and comfortable chairs. When I offered a cigarette to Arthur, Lucy startled me by reaching over the box and asking, "May I?" There was no way I could refuse her, or would, but I must admit to being mildly perturbed by the sight of her perfect face drawing tobacco, the smoke of her exhalations dimming the glow of her cascading strawberry-blonde hair. Arthur himself was embarrassed enough to apologise, after a fashion, explaining that his own smoking habits were responsible for corrupting her. "She asked if she might try one of my cigarettes, and what was I to say? No? How can anyone say no to a face like that, to such a perfect pout?"

I knew exactly what he meant.

"My husband-to-be smells like tobacco and tastes like tobacco," she reasoned most persuasively. "So why should I not smoke tobacco, especially when he is not to be around and I get so very lonely?"

Arthur patted the hand on the arm that was interlaced with his own, and explained that he and Lucy were going to be parted for some weeks—their first separation. Lucy and her mother were making plans to leave town for their annual vacation at their summer-house in Whitby, leaving Arthur behind to tend to the business affairs of his father, Lord Godalming, whose illness seems to be nearing its inevitable close.

Perhaps it was due to their impending separation, but as they sat there, side by side, there was an undeniable unity of spirit about them; if I was not entertaining a single entity, I was playing host to two entities inclining very much towards becoming one. Lucy looked somewhat less of an individual than she had been as I was courting her so miserably. Despite myself, I found myself reflecting back on that couple from Renfield's past, the Griggses, the farmer who wasted away as his wife grew plump with child and possibly more than her husband's seed—but in this case, it was Lucy who was lessened and Arthur who was looking hale and prosperous. I spent most of our visit deliberately focussed on Arthur, not wishing to weaken my own resolves by gazing too much at Lucy, and if she is half the girl I knew, she must have noticed this. They invited me to join them for dinner in town, but I begged off, explaining that I had need to return to my patients.

As I walked with them to the main gate of the asylum, Arthur shook my hand warmly and said, "You're a successful man, Jack . . . You need to find some good doctors who can teach you to relinquish control of this place, at least for a few hours each day, so you can get a decent meal into you."

Lucy, still smelling of tobacco, exchanged a little look with her fiancé—seeking permission perhaps—and then raised herself on her toes to kiss my cheek. I hope someday to write an entire thesis on that kiss, but—to offer a quick abstract—it was soft, relaxed, and cherry-sweet—and a bit more than a peck.

"Lucy will be returning from Whitby at the end of August," Arthur informed me. "Though we haven't announced it yet, we have chosen the twenty-eighth of September as the date for the wedding. It's a Monday . . . because my bride is so very fair of face. Jack, would you do us the honour of standing up for me as my best man?"

"Naturally," I said without thinking. Fortunately, at that moment, one of the attendants came running to summon me for some reason, and I took advantage of this interruption to excuse myself. As soon as my visitors were gone, I pushed the attendant out of my way and went back to my private quarters, where I sat down and smoked one, two, three cigarettes.

PART TWO

Do you not know that friendship with the world is enmity with God? Therefore whoever wishes to be a friend of the world makes himself an enemy of God.

—James 4:4

CHAPTER XIV

Dr. Seward's Diary.

1 JUNE.—Renfield is usually eager to co-operate, but to-day he has refused to continue with his oral history. When Hardy came to my office accompanied only by this message and a shrug of his shoulders, I decided to go directly to Renfield's room myself and enquire what was the matter. I thought, perhaps, he had somehow become aware that I had been surreptitiously reading his notebook, but I received neither accusation nor reprimand. He remained seated throughout my visit and would not turn to face me; he would not give a reason for his obstinacy and spoke to me only tersely, with his back turned to me. If I did not know better, I would have sworn he was nibbling at something—eating of his own volition! I angled myself for a better look and could see only his dog-eared Bible open in front of him. Perhaps he was reading aloud at a low whisper, and cross with me for interfering with his concentration?

Such a confounding case! His personality would appear to be trapped between two compulsions: the compulsion to boast and the compulsion to keep secret the particular maps and governors of his madness. The former sometimes gets the better of him, yet the latter clearly exerts the greater force—but irregularly, as if only during certain times of day or phases of the Moon.

LATER.—When I visited Renfield at his cell earlier to-day, I saw a man who was making every endeavour not to be seen. But, within the hour, Hardy knocked at my door, announcing that my reluctant patient was now *demanding* immediate audience with me! "You should see him with his proud gestures, sir," Hardy said with perverse merriment. "You would think 'e was 'Enry Irvin' playin' 'amlet, you would!"

This I had to see . . . and so I followed Hardy back to Renfield's room, where we found the patient standing very much as though a spotlight was shining down upon him at centre stage!

"Mr. Hardy tells me that you have changed your mind and you now want to keep our appointment?" I asked the patient.

"Hardy is not reliable in many ways, but he does manage to tell the truth," Renfield replied imperiously.

"Renfield, I came to you not an hour ago, but you would not even turn to face me. What has changed in so short a time?"

"Then you wanted to talk with me . . . now I want to talk to you," he answered quite reasonably.

"Very well," I said, "but on one condition: given the extreme shifts of mood and temperament you have shown this morning, I must insist that you be brought to to-day's interview in your strait-waistcoat."

Renfield's response was delivered with a flourish worthy

of the great actor cited by Hardy: "I give you my assurance that, between you and me, good doctor, nothing shall pass but the time, and that very quickly, as I hold you in thrall. I give you my word as your patient, and I give you my word as a gentleman!"

Indeed he did. As he spoke to me of amazing things, incredible events which (if even remotely within the realm of the possible) would have had irreparable impact on the steadiest young mind, Renfield spoke today as though he was the pet crony of all the dark forces abounding. Utterly mad, of course, but the deluded world in which he exists—and his distorted, delusional past, in which he also seems actively to dwell—is one of the most disturbing yet inviting mental cases I have ever examined.

I rather thank God for the distraction.

Patient's Oral History.

You will forgive me for keeping you waiting, Doctor, but before I could proceed with my story, it was essential that I summon the nerve, the courage—the audacity, if you will—to frame what is to come in words.

Have you given any real thought as to what you are asking me to do, whether it be for your information, your curiosity, your distraction? I daresay none of the other pathetic souls in this prison would consent to re-visit the scenes that laid waste to the weak barricades of their sanity. Of course, I am a different sort of patient . . . I am not a guest of your asylum because you think I am crazy. I am your guest because . . . *no* . . . *no! I shouldn't say!* Because you don't really *know* why I am here yourself, do you?

217

I am sorry, dear fellow—dreadfully sorry—but you will have to remain without a clue until the time comes—very soon—when I can tell you everything, every horrible detail! But even sooner, given all your soppy mooning and distraction, it will be too late! Yet I will tell you this much, and mark my words: You have the honour of being in the presence of the ring on the hand that will fall so heavily, it will obliterate everything that you know: this house, this life, this England.

This hand that will take from you has given to me—oh, so very generously! I can remember a time—I must have been ten or eleven years old—lying abed and reading with great interest a story in a book of fables which Father had given me for Christmas. In one of the fables, a character happened to mention that the light of a new Moon had the power to grant one's dearest wish. As I continued reading, even as I continued on into different stories, this intriguing thought stayed with me.

When Father poked his head into my room, later that night, to say hello, I put the question to him: "Father, a story in this book of fables says that the light of the new Moon has the power to grant one's dearest wish. What does it mean, 'a new Moon'? Isn't it always the same old Moon?"

Father laughed gently and took a seat beside me. "Of course it is," he murmured. "Same old Moon, the same Moon people saw who are now long dead and who hammered out of air the very languages we speak. However, there are different stages of the Moon—'phases,' they call them. For example, there is the full Moon. You know what that is?"

I thought I did, and answered: "Yes. That is when the

whole of the Moon is lit up by the sun, and is made to shine like a great coin in the sky."

"Indeed not!" he said, catching me in a trick question. "You see, a full Moon is when only *half* of the moon is illumined by the sun. There is an entire side, one half, of the Moon that we never see! It's a round Moon, child—not flat, like a coin."

"I see!"

"Another phase is the half Moon," Father continued. "Do you know what *that* is?"

"A half Moon," I supposed, adopting his logic, "would be when we can see . . . *one quarter of the Moon in the sky?*"

"Now, child, was that a question . . . or a declaration of fact?"

"A declaration of fact," I lied.

"Clever boy," he praised me, winking. "You catch on fast! Now the new Moon—which is the phase preying on your mind this very night—is a very interesting subject, a very interesting subject indeed. Would you care to venture a guess as to the nature of the new Moon?"

"Is it when the sun shines especially bright and makes the Moon look especially bright and new?"

"I never thought of that!" Father said in mock-amazement—then adding, "Probably because it couldn't be any further from the truth of the matter." He mussed my hair. "All-right, now listen closely, child, because this is a tricky one. The new Moon occurs when the half of the Moon we never see—the so-called dark side of the Moon—receives *its* share of the sun and is illuminated."

"So what do we see?"

"Not a thing, child," Father explained. "The new Moon is when we see no Moon at all."

"Then how can anybody wish on the light of the new Moon?" I wailed.

"Now that is a very good question, for which I do not have a ready answer," Father admitted. "But do you know what I think? I think your fable sounds very much to me like a parable about the mystery of faith."

"Faith? That's what you talk about in church."

"Indeed it is," he said. "Faith is the act of believing in things without having, or even requiring, proof that they exist." Father then placed a warm hand on my shoulder and asked, "I take it, from all this talk and curiosity, that you have a dear wish in your heart of hearts, which you were planning to entrust to the light of a new Moon?"

"Yes, Father," I confessed.

"I see. Well, child, I can well remember the impatience of my own boyhood, so you will be pleased to know that the next new Moon is only a few nights away." He patted me and rose, pausing on his way out to turn back and offer a parting suggestion: "I should be disappointing my office," he said, "were I not to suggest that—should you tire of waiting—you might try your chances by bending a knee and presenting your request to Our Lord in the form of a prayer." With that suggestion, Father bade me good-night and left me to my book.

That night, for the first night in many years—indeed, for as long as I could remember—I did not wait for sleep to come while thinking of the Lady and the promises she had made to me; a project, a special experiment, was taking shape in my mind. I thought back to something I had witnessed earlier in the day, while returning home from school: Collie Craddick had somehow obtained a magnification glass and was using it to train beams of sunlight on tiny insects, causing them great pain and suffering. There was a crowd of other school-children around him, and, as I broke through them for a look, I saw him torturing the loveliest butterfly with this device—torturing it till its church-window wing began to smoke—and then he collected it in a pinch and chased one of the girls, trying to give her a whiff of it. I thought of that and began to wonder: *If a concentrated beam of sunlight could have such a physical effect, what magic might a concentrated beam of new moonlight unleash?* Collie's sunlight experiment had re-quired the use of a magnification glass and a tangible ele-ment, such as the butterfly's wing had been. How was I to lend material form to a wish?

By the time the day of the new Moon had arrived, I had formulated an answer. How else? I wrote my wishes on scraps of paper—and another and another and another. After all, no child has a shortage of wishes, and I had more than most. At some point during this process, Father discovered me in the midst of my mad scribbling.

"So!" he exclaimed. "To-night is the night of the new Moon, is it?"

Knowing that no known wish can be granted, I reached out with both arms and gathered my scraps of paper to me—and confirmed to Father that it was.

"Never fear, child," he blurted out in response to my shielding of the scraps. "I did not mean to intrude, and you have my word, I will steal no look at your wishes." Then he told me that, seeing as how the new Moon would not be visible, I might like to know in which portion of our sky it would be hiding. I accepted this mysterious information gratefully, and Father withdrew with tongue in cheek.

When I felt that I had expressed every last one of my wishes onto paper, I looked long and hard at the lot of them, knowing I could select only one. Each was etched with its own hope—I WISH FOR MORE BOOKS, I WISH ANIMALS RULED THE WORLD, I WISH FOR NO MORE SCHOOL, I WISH COLLIE WAS DEAD, I WISH TO KNOW WHO I AM, and so forth. I judged their individual values as I prayed the new Moon, in its great wisdom, might and selected one and only one—my most fervent wish of all—as the centre-piece of my Moonbeam Experiment.

I had very little appetite at dinner, which put Moira's nose out of joint, but Father understood my excitement. He offered to accompany me outside during my mission, but I insisted on going about it alone. I did as he advised and wore my coat out-of-doors—not because it was cold that night, but because it gave me pockets in which to carry my chosen wish and also the magnification glass I had borrowed from Father's office.

Outside, true to Father's word, there was no visible Moon in the sky, but a certain moony quality of light did appear to be everywhere. My experiment required a convenient clearing, someplace where the boughs of trees would not interfere with the moonbeam that needed to be channeled to my experiment, so I chose the most obvious spot nearest the vicarage: the churchyard. I found a place there where I could sit and look up into the exact area of the sky which Father had specified—it happened to be the very spot where Father and I had buried Jolly, years before—and I waited there through the sky's evening phases of azure, cyan, and beryl, until it achieved ultimate sapphire—in which all of God's jewels were revealed. I no longer saw these colours anymore, other than as deepening, star-shot gradations of grey and black; but because they were abounding that night, I knew Milady must be watching over me.

I knelt on this spot where Jolly had been planted—grassy now—and took my hand-written wish from my pocket, unfolded it, and pressed it to the earth, trying to flatten its folds with the palms of both hands. In the sapphire light, my hand-printed words stood out starkly against the shiny white paper, upon which I had written the words I WISH FOR A FREND—"ef ar ee en dee."

There was nothing left to do but to do it. I took Father's magnification glass from my other coat pocket and held it over the paper, angling the surface of its thick lens this way and that until—to my utter surprise and amazement and pleasure—it caught an invisible beam of moony light—light that would never have been caught or trained, had I not the faith that it would be there! That narrow shaft of moonlight focussed specifically, of its own accord, on the all-important word FREND.

I waited. Nothing happened, and there was a gentle breeze that kept rocking the paper and blowing it out of the light's range. Finally, I had the idea to fold the paper into a compact square, whose edge I pressed down through the soft earth until it was completely buried. Then I trained the moonlight beam on the slit left in the ground. Taking a word of Father's advice, I steadied myself on one respectful knee, before swearing to myself that I would not move—not a muscle!—until something happened. I waited and I waited, holding the glass so still that the beam of light from above was absolutely unwavering.

I know that you are a man of sound reasoning, Doctor, so I do not expect you to believe what I am about to tell you, but I give you my solemn word that I make no exaggeration. In time, the very ground beneath my knees began to tremble—not as in an earthquake, mind you, but rather as if some living force from below was bent on pushing itself upwards and out! The vibrations became so intense that I nearly surrendered to my fears and ran away, but before I could, the grassy soil around the slit where I had inserted my folded wish pushed up and split open, releasing a gleaming froth of black beetles, all running amok as though maddened by the new Moon's light! And then, following in their wake, he stepped forward . . . his dark eyes twinkling with nervous curiosity, his whiskers bristling, still putting a brave foot forward.

How I laughed when he pushed his way out of the hole completely and I first saw the whole of him! My Jolly had been just a small yellow mouse, but here was a grand golden rat! He was a grand one—a treasure, trundling along like a man on all fours, moving about inside a baggy suit. My heart rushed right out to him; I gathered him up in my hands and he did not bite me when I cradled him and brought him closer to my face, the better to see him in the dark. I looked into his eyes and found his soul, the very one I remembered, right there—not deep down inside like it is in people, like something afraid to venture out of its burrow or its hates or its Bible—and I laughed for joy through my grateful tears because I knew at once that my wish had been granted! I was no longer alone; this pudgy little man had been sent back to me from the dark side of the Moon to be my one and only friend—my one and only Jolly!

Just as the ground had trembled, I was shaken by my direct experience of all the magic that is truly available to those in this world, if only they know how to avail themselves of it. But I was getting older now, and understood that keeping my friend would require me to accept responsibility for him. There was a woman in the vicarage now, Moira, and, having learned how women felt about fat little fellows like Jolly, I knew that my friend had to be a secret one, a secret kept even from Father. So I carried Jolly into the vicarage in one of the deep side pockets of my coat. I told him to remain perfectly quiet as I returned indoors and took the magnification glass back to Father's library and answered his inevitable questions about how the experiment went. He knew the rules of such things better than to ask precisely what I had wished for. When I got Jolly back to my room, we embarked on the first of many happy conversations that lasted deep into the night.

The first night we spent together, Jolly slept snug in the breast-pocket of my night-shirt, and I was very careful—even when deep in my sleep—not to roll over on him. In the days that followed, I found a suitable box, which I lined with hunks of grass and the scraps of paper on which I had written my other wishes, and kept it hidden under my bed. That is where Jolly slept through the day, when I was away at school or running errands for Father or Moira, as the case may be. By the time I returned to my room, Jolly would be rising to keep me company as I read my books and thought about things. I would feed him vegetable scraps and crumbs of other different things sneaked away from the kitchen or the dining table and watch him nibble at them, with fierce concentration, bristling with gratitude. I would stroke his wee ears and his golden fur, and put him back into his box only when I could stay awake no longer, lowering the lid each night with regret and always stealing one last peek at his beady eyes. They seemed to look at me in a manner as bonding as a contract: *Yes, I will be yours. If you care for me, I will give you all the love I have to give.*

I could blabber to Jolly about any old thing, anything—and he would listen with the keenest interest. Before I had you, Doctor, I had Jolly. Those were the first nights in my short life when I cried myself to sleep not out of longing or regret, but because there was no other way to express such uncontainable joy.

CHAPTER XV

Patient's Oral History (cont).

Why do you look upon me with such scepticism, Doctor? Do you believe my happiness a sham? Do you think me, at heart, a tragic figure?

It is true that I was an unhappy soul for much of my childhood—the orphaned years, the foster parent years, the years of waiting for the Lady's return—but, with Jolly back in my pocket, my out-look brightened. It is true that the Lady remained off-stage, as it were, but I had felt her presence governing the magic that brought Jolly back into my life—what other explanation could there be?—and every blessed time I looked at that little fat man, I received an intimation of the Lady's existence, like a kiss upon my heart. She was not *in* my life, perhaps, yet she seemed to surround it, and everything in it, like a halo of the most profound blue.

Now that I had a friend, a secret that was all mine and to be kept from the entire world, Jolly became the absolute focus of my affections. I also had affection for Father, of course, but in our relationship, respect always came before affection. And there was no one else—certainly not Moira!—so Jolly, very quickly, became my entire world. We were inseparable, and, to spare us the pain of being apart, I wanted to take him everywhere with me.

Once I had impressed upon Jolly how very important it was that he remain absolutely quiet whilst in my pocket, I was able to take him with me almost anywhere I went: to church, to the dinner table (where I would sneak him little scraps off my plate when Father was not looking), even to school—though I did this only once.

Almost from the moment we arrived at the school-house, I knew that I had made a terrible mistake in bringing him along. My school-mates—Collie in particular—had an uncanny knack for sniffing out my vulnerabilities, and throughout that day, he kept trying to separate me from my coat, suggesting that it was terribly warm. "Why not take off your coat, Rennie?" he would say. "Are you too fat to take it off? Go ahead and take it off, Rennie; we won't laugh at your fat. Don't you worry, I'll hold your coat for you . . ." That was Jolly's first and only day at school.

In the evenings, if I happened to be reading a book in Father's library, Jolly would be snug in my pocket, as snug as you would be in a hammock. If I was reading in my room, Jolly would sit beside me on my bed, mostly covered up by a quilt so as not to be seen should someone come visiting—or he might rest upon my shoulder, on the side of my neck that could not be seen from the door. Moira never came into my room except to call me to supper, which I learned to anticipate to keep her away as much as possible, and Father was absorbed in his own work, so I seldom saw him in the evenings except at table or when he came to light a fire in my hearth on cold nights. Once Father had gone to bed, Jolly and I would be left alone in the crackling glow of our fire-place. When I closed my book, I would put him back into his box, which I kept near my pillow, lowering his lid as I lay my head down. Sometimes, after some minutes had passed, I would raise the lid again, just a little—just enough to steal one more peek, and find him still awake . . . sometimes squatting on all fours and wiggling his pink nose . . . sometimes lying on his back and presenting his furry white belly to the world and looking at me in witless exclamation, like I had caught him in the bath-tub! Sometimes his expressions would make me laugh so hard that I had to press my pillow into my mouth, so as not to waken Father. Then I would say good-night once again and lower his lid, and now my earth-bound thoughts were free to wander, to drift back to the Lady and the special destiny I knew she must be preparing for me—and for which I was preparing myself, with my constant reading.

As I immersed myself in the world of Father's books, the world around me seemed to soften, to recede into a state of fuzziness. I paid little mind to this and continued squinting for long hours over different texts, until there came a day when the world around me was not fully restored to its rightful focus when I put my book of the moment away. I worried that my attention to my reading—my greater belief in the world of books, so to speak—had dealt my real world a permanent damage, brought on by my own neglect of it. Was I beginning to cease to exist in the world in which I lived, and beginning to live in the world about which I read?

I shared my worries with Father, and he clucked his

tongue and arranged for my eyes to be examined. That is when it was first discovered that I needed spectacles, which I have worn to this day. I am near-sighted, so I never need them to read, only to move about within the world that exists physically around me. On the day I returned home to the vicarage from my eye doctor, wearing my first pair of spectacles, Father walked me into the kitchen to present me—the new me—to Moira.

What happened next was most unexpected. At the mere sight of me, Moira seemed to shorten by two inches. Her knees bent involuntarily, and she thrust out an arm, all five of her fingers stiffly fanned, like this . . . Her other hand—balled into a fist, which she shoved into her open mouth to stifle a sob, which rocked her forward as though I had punched her in the stomach with all my mature strength.

She started gibbering, muttering words so small that only ants could have made sense of them, but they grew louder by the word, by each disbelieving word: *"He looks jus' like 'im . . . You bastard . . . Take that face o' yourn back t' Hell!"* Her voice had by then become a scream which she could bring to an end only by slapping me across the face and knocking my glasses askew.

"Moira!" Father shouted, stilling her hand—but it was too late.

As the side of my face rang with violence, Moira sank onto bowed knees, hiding her face and screaming: *"God forgi' me . . . it weren't my doin'!"* With curled fists, she began to strike herself on the sides of her head, her temples, wailing and hitting herself.

I was probably twelve years of age, or close to it, at this

time—maturing but still too young, too involved in my own thoughts, to fully grasp the implications of Moira's sudden break-down. I was given no time to linger; after re-fitting me with my glasses and confirming they had not been broken, Father firmly instructed me to go to my room and stay there until I was summoned back. I was happy to do so, because more than wanting to see what Moira's stupid problem was about, I wanted to show my new eye-glasses to Jolly and get him used to them.

As the two of us had our happy time together, with me fitting my glasses on the bridge of Jolly's twitchy pink nose, we heard unclear voices coming from upstairs, rising and falling in volume, anger, and acquiescence. After some time had passed, I heard Father's footsteps move in the direction of his office, where he remained in contemplative silence for the better part of an hour, never summoning me. In the meantime, I heard the usual preparatory clanks and clatters coming from the kitchen, so I surmised that whatever had passed between Moira and Father had not been enough to prompt her dismissal. *Too bad*, I thought.

Then I heard Father rise to his feet and start walking in the direction of my room. I was reading the memoirs of Saint Thérèse. Jolly was watching me from beneath a hillock of quilt, looking like Our Holy Bewhiskered Mother of Patch-work. I signalled for him to keep quiet by drawing a finger to my lips, and he complied by pedalling backwards under the blanket.

Father soon knocked and leaned into my room. "Might I have a word with you?" he asked.

"Of course, Father," I told him.

He sat down beside me on the edge of my bed and, holding my jaw and tilting my face this way and that, scrutinised me. "Moira didn't hurt you, did she, lad?"

"Moira could *never* hurt *me*, Father," I assured him.

He sat with his hands folded in front of him, his face rather remarkable in the tenderness of its casting. "I am at a complete loss for words, my boy. All of this comes as a complete surprise to me, as it comes to you, I am sure . . ."

Father at no time stated explicitly the nature of this surprise, and my own attentions were divided by my worry that Jolly might somehow be sat upon or otherwise discovered.

"The Lord indeed works in mysterious ways," he continued. "It would appear that I have opened this vicarage not only to a child but to a family, incomplete though it is. Moira denies any wrong-doing, denies that she ever abandoned you . . . and she has no wish to leave the vicarage, because her life here, with us, is all she has in the world. She has told me her story, lad . . . and while I do not believe everything she has told me, if only a portion of what she says is true, she has led a life of unthinkable misery and tragedy."

"I hate her," I said.

"She is not to be hated, my boy, but pitied. You must try to find it in your heart to forgive her. She's a simple creature, and I do not think she ever had it in her to cope with the responsibility of a child. She tells me that she was herself raised in an orphanage . . . Necessary places, of course, but terrible in many cases. I sometimes wonder if God's own wilderness would not serve just as well, if not better. The poor thing told me of a night when she, as a child, had wet her bed and was punished by being stripped of her soiled bed-clothes and put naked into a cellar . . . It was a stormy night, and as the light-ning flashed, she found that it was swarming with rats. One of them stood on its hind legs, peering at her with its own black eyes . . . That could have been your lot in life, too, I suppose, had I not discovered you and brought you here. That, or much worse . . ."

Father fell silent, lost in his thoughts. He appeared to be quite distressed, so I remained respectfully silent—but inside I was laughing because here I was, under Father's very nose, also in a cellar and being peered at by the black eyes of a rat under my bed-clothes! Moira's horror was my delight—how appropriate! But then, unbidden by me, Jolly took the silence that had fallen between us as his invitation to pop back out into open view—and Father caught sight of him.

Father looked up with a comically monstrous expression, and, knowing that my entire happiness was suddenly at risk, I began to sob. Father laid a large, warm hand on my leg as he bent over to peer beneath the quilt. "Now, now—what on earth have we here?" he asked with gentle awe.

"Father," I beseeched him, "please don't take him away! He's all I've got in the world! He's my only friend in the world!"

Father extracted Jolly, who was happy to be held in a pair of larger and more accommodating hands, and turned a seri-ous eye on me. "Your only friend in the world? Is that so? Pray, what am I to you, then?"

I could not answer . . . I could only sob, sob as though each streaming tear was an exquisite distillation of pain and tragedy, and hell to part with.

"There now, lad," he comforted me. "Quiet. It's not all as bad as that, is it? Secrets are fine things, but it is much finer still to share with them with someone you trust. Am I some-one you trust?"

I nodded in the affirmative, mostly as an entreaty.

"I take it you already know how to care for this fine, fat fellow?"

Again, I nodded.

"Well, then . . . I have no intention of coming between such a very happy fellowship as you and . . . What name have we given him?"

"Jolly."

"Another Jolly, eh? Well, then! If that isn't the most per-fect name for this little man I could possibly imagine!" Father returned Jolly to my care, and I seized him back so desper-ately that I might easily have harmed him. "Careful!" Father cautioned. "He's a fat thing, but he's also a wee thing—and wee things have wee bones."

He watched me shed my tears of love over Jolly for some moments, quietly and respectfully. Then he stood and, in readiness for his leave-taking, looked down upon the two of us with warm consideration.

"One word of advice, my boy," he cautioned me. "Should you ever leave your little friend in this room unattended, make certain that you leave him in a place where he will not be discovered by chance. I am sure you think that your room stays clean like this by some magic process, but Moira comes in here every day to tidy up after you. With the memories she carries around, we would not wish her to be on the receiving end of any unwelcome surprises—would we?"

"No, Father."

"Love is the reason we are put on this earth, my lad. To

learn it, to give it, to receive it, to share it. It is the essence of Our Lord, the essence of the Lord which we are given to share with others. It warms my heart to know that Nature has provided you with something—*someone*—who might teach you these most valuable lessons. I wonder how much Jolly has taught you already?"

"Oh, quite a lot, Father! I love Jolly so!"

"That's good, laddie. Very good. Do you think, then, that you might find it in your heart to forgive her?"

"Who?"

"Why, your . . . *Moira*, of course."

"I suppose so," I said, without much reflection. "I don't have to like her, though, do I?"

"I suppose not," he replied after a moment's thought. "But as the Bible says, you must forgive their sin—but if not, blot them out of the book you have written."

"I haven't written any book, Father!" I said in amazement. It had frankly never occurred to me, before that moment, that books were actually written by living men and women who put pens to paper. I suppose, in not giving the matter much thought, I thought that Father had plucked his books from trees, much as I had plucked them down from his shelves.

"Reading as much as you do, lad, some day you may," he said, wishing Jolly and me a good-night and withdrawing down the hall.

The true nature of my relationship to Moira, which must now be obvious to you, was still beyond my ken; I suppose I may have been denying the truth which had been revealed, refusing that any blood bond existed. In fact, I can remember thinking, perhaps even chanting to myself in my own inner-most thoughts, that she and I were different species, made of entirely different stuff. Everything I had seen of my own small share of the world and read of the world and its people at large made this skinny, mean-spirited, provincial woman only more alien and inconceivable to me. Alas, I was not in-conceivable to her.

The next morning, Moira prepared runny eggs and burned potatoes. As she scraped the garbage onto our plates, I peered at her through my new spectacles, which made her physical flaws all the plainer to see. She was acting unlike herself, somehow; she moved about as ineptly as ever, though with more than the usual caution. The way she used to look at me, as though she might spit or snap her fingers at me, was different; I caught her stealing looks at me, timid looks that became more brazen. I tasted her flaccid eggs, undercooked even to a child's palate, and took the shakers of pepper and salt and shook them and shook them—I knew I wasn't about to eat them, so I might as well insult them—until I felt Father's eyes fall upon me in a silent but stony reprimand. Relenting, I forked a mouthful of egg into me, closing my teeth around it and finding that there was now only season-ing to taste—no substance, only spice and a horrible slimi-ness. I spat it onto my plate, the swill tumbling from my maw like something aborted.

I sensed that Moira was observing all this. I could feel her tensing, becoming slowly infused with tremor when, all of a sudden, she raised and shattered a china plate on the table with a loud exclamation, unfamiliar to me, but which I took to be a curse.

"*Moira!*" Father exclaimed, chastening her.

"*You're not 'im!*" she yelled at me. "*You couldn't be 'im! They took 'im away! They took 'im away, I tell ya!*" she shrieked.

"*Moira! You are excused!*" Father insisted.

"*Canno' you see 'ow he looks at me, sittin' there? Look at 'im glowerin' a' me—like God's own judgement!*"

She looked upon me with what I can only describe as horror and began to babble, incoherently, "*They took ya from me . . . they took ya from me . . .*" as she backed away from me, from Father, out of the dining room. Then, on the word *took*, she began coughing on her words, coughing until she spat something into the bowl of her two hands. She looked into them with revulsion and let spill what she had caught. It was blood—black as tobacco juice. She tried to scream, but her throat was too clotted with the stuff, and it came out rasping. She looked up at us, incredulously, and the flow ran over her chin, so thick and black that it coated her teeth and made her look old and toothless. Moira had been stricken with consumption.

I cannot point to an exact moment in time when I first fully understood that Moira—this harridan, this black bug in the kitchen, this murderess—had brought me into this world of magic and misery. "My natural mother"—how I detest this expression, because everything I knew of that woman went against the grain of my love of Nature! I loathed her as people loathe what they consider to be the lower forms of life, the creatures they despoil, to whom they feed their refuse, even those which they themselves take as food.

I believe that Moira—I could never call her "Mother," a

name to which she held no right—told Father the exact circumstances of how I came to be abandoned, but as he suggested to me that he did not entirely believe her account, I asked for no further information. I accepted this mystery into my heart as another of her offences—perhaps the greatest of them all. As I grew older and became somewhat better versed in the subject, I assumed that I had been unwelcomely conceived, perhaps through an act of rape or incest—sins of which I would be absolved of any personal guilt, of course—and abandoned as an unwelcome reminder of a past event my mother would prefer to rewrite.

Moira's illness advanced rapidly over the course of the next year. She was soon so debilitated of energy that she took to her bed in her private room at the vicarage. With the coming of her disease, our roles were reversed: Father and I began to look after her. No one else in the village cared to wait on her, as she had burned her bridges with every last one of them; they knew her for the snooper she was, prying into people's private business, gossiping behind their backs. I hated every second of my servitude, because how had she earned such devotion—from me, of all people? No matter how many bowls of soup or cups of tea I brought to her throughout the day, she never spoke another word to me—but I could always see the wincing torture underlying her black gaze as she looked upon me: *I looked exactly like him.* Whoever my father may have been, whatever sort of scoundrel or devil, she made me feel eternally grateful that I favoured his side of the family. Much as I detested catering to her, I entered Moira's room often, just to sit there beside her and glory in the revenge of being seen. Father told me he had never seen such devotion as I showed to Moira, that he had never seen such a moving example of human compassion!

Months passed, then there came a day when Father was called away from the vicarage on official business, leaving Moira entirely in my care. This opportunity I seized as my recompense for all that I had suffered as a result of her incapacity for love. I sat beside her bed and took note of the glassiness of her eyes, a fear of ultimate consequence that you will never see in the eyes of an animal who feels the end is near. Animals are always accepting of the end, grateful for all they have had in this life; you also see this in the eyes of dying children—I can tell you this as one who, in Father's company, was privileged to be present at such sombre occasions. But in the eyes of men and women, people who have lived full lives, you always see at least a glint of uncertainty and terror—terror that the crimes they have quietly committed against their fellow men are all too evident to the all-seeing eyes of the Higher Powers. That's it—terror of the final judgement. Terror of the face of God in all its facets. Terror of the dark.

As I saw this terror in Moira's eyes, I leaned forward. I took her inelegant hand in mine and spoke to her, after the fashion in which I had seen Father speak to other dying parishioners, taking it upon myself to guide her towards life's secret egress as best I could.

"I can tell by the look in your eyes, Moira, that Death's hand is perched on your shoulder, pale as bone. I have often thought—as I know it to be Father's fondest wish—that I might someday become vicar here, when his time is done.

With this dream in mind, I have often wondered what words of comfort I might share with a dying parishioner when her time was near. And now, as we sit here together, you and I are about to find out . . .

"Who exactly are you, Moira? Who are you to have spent your life regarding all of our Lord's creation with such boredom and contempt? How many days, rich with possibility, were given to you by our Lord so that you might sit in your little kitchen and stare out the window and declare yourself to be uninterested? On how many occasions did God bring new acquaintances into your life—old and venerable people, young and trusting people—only to see you shrink from them, withholding your mean spirit, telling yourself that they were hateful and suspicious of you, because you, in fact, were hateful and suspicious of them?

"I do not speak of myself, for I wanted nothing of you, not even the sight of you. No, I think of the needy creatures who bleated at your kitchen door, bleating for love and sustenance . . . the way you responded to the needs of hungry cats with saucers of cow's milk laced with poison. I watched your charity with revulsion . . . the way you made sport of the growls coming from their hungry stomachs—and the way you pushed them away as they sought to repay your generosity with affection, rubbing against your legs, pushing their furry faces into your hands—denying them a love you did not have it in you to spare. And, if I really care to torture myself, I think of that scared rabbit . . . how its bones must have snapped as you wrenched its neck . . . and how you forced me—your own flesh and blood, so they tell me—to sit down to a dinner where it was served as a meal, filling with that animal's death the mouth you denied nourishment from your own pap. So many nights I awoke in fright, dreaming of the expression on that hare's face as you twisted the life out of it . . . And now here we sit, your own moment of truth fast approaching, and I ask myself, 'What shall be the look on Moira's face when she finally sheds her mask of servitude and piety . . . when God reaches gigantically down to her *and twists her neck?*' The answer will soon be known to me, and I shall be satisfied, but it will never be known to you.

"But know this, Moira—you are on the point of going where every person . . . every animal . . . every thing that has ever died before you has gone. You will pass through the door through which everyone, from the oldest sage to the stupidest infant, has passed, soiling itself in sheer terror. You are moving towards it even now, floating on a gentle stream away from the familiar, towards something bigger and more infinite and more terrible than you have ever known. The movement you feel, Moira, is due to the fact that you are being sucked irrevocably towards the very sink-hole of existence. Every person, every prince and every pauper . . . every saint and every murderer . . . every animal from the noble horse to the wretched leech . . . every rat, every bat, every mouse that ever affrighted you . . . every insect . . . every cockroach that spat mustard under the murderous weight of your shoe. This sink-hole is a dreadful portal indeed, rank and thick with the nasty mattings of all their spent blood and hair, all their blistered skin and rancid pus . . . and now you'll go spinning down that same sink-hole, tongue first, to wherever their souls have gone, to meet the same judgement . . . *no better than they . . . no better than they . . . no better than they!*

"That is my final wish for you, Moira. Not eternity in a void, but an eternal darkness spent in the very close company of every one and every thing you've ever judged, everything you've ever spoiled, everything you've ever smashed or snapped or stepped on, or stepped in; every child you ever shat out and walked away from—like the other whelps you probably had before me, who died sobbing out of sheer need of a loving touch. May the heap of their fallen carcasses cushion your fall and envelop you as you sink through the layers of their rot. May their rank wastes become an eternal womb for you, and may you starve in that womb of their pressing flesh and panting breaths until you cannot do otherwise but open the very mouth of your soul and gorge yourself on all the damage you have done in your life of damnable selfishness.

"Once you make a feast of all that, perhaps your penance will be paid in full. But know this: *Not even then will I begin to forgive you.* I wonder . . . would God even recognise you as one of His own if He saw you, you God-fearing louse? Do black bugs like yourself truly fear God? You do? Perhaps it is with good reason. Or might it be because you do not know Him? If that is the case, allow me to introduce you . . .

"Lord and Master, hear the voice of your humble servant, Renfield. I hearby consign into Your hands, for her *eternal* recompense for deeds done in this life, one of your own. I know her as Moira . . . but you know her . . . as *my mother.*"

With those last words dead on my lips, I reached deep into my coat pocket and pulled out Jolly, placing him at the foot of Moira's bed. He stood up on his hind legs for a better look at her. I heard Moira draw in her breath sharply, which in itself was enough to kill her.

"Look, Jolly," I said in time, picking him up and stroking him. "My mummy's dead."

There was a sense in that small room that something of enormity had just occurred—but what, in fact, had changed? I had no mother, then as ever. I felt no love lost, no sorrow gained, nor even anger—only a raging and insatiable hunger.

Even in death, the bitch gave me nothing.

CHAPTER XVI

Notes on Transcript.

1 JUNE, 11:00 P.M.—Earlier to-day, Renfield gave me his word "as a gentleman" that he would keep a tight grip on the reins of his emotions throughout our session. He then proceeded to tell me a set of incredible stories—one about the return of his pet rat from the dead, another about his discovery that the woman he detested most in the world was in fact his own mother, and, finally, another about her early death, to which he was witness and quite possibly a catalyst. Whatever else I might think, he kept his word.

I sincerely doubt that, as a youth, he spoke with such control and sophistication as he depicted himself presiding over the scene of his mother's death-bed. He related to-day's stories with such icy self-possession one might have thought he was relating the facts of a scene observed through the lens of a micro-scope or the wrong end of a spy-glass, a tragedy observed at great distance that actually befell someone else. Indeed, although the topics of the oral history he recorded to-day were exceedingly personal, when his heart and mind should be most present, to-day—of all days—he often seemed quite distracted, as though his brain sought to be in two places at once. He also gave me cause to consider whether the "chosen" Lord to whom he refers as his Master might be one other than the Lord God.

To-night I looked in on Renfield and found him mooning through his window at the ruins of the Carfax estate. He might have been gazing at a beautiful woman; he looked as I must look when I am thinking of Lucy.

"Good evening, Doctor Seward," he said, without turning around, as though he had two eyes in the back of his head. "Was our conversation this afternoon not enough for you? It was quite enough for me, I assure you."

"I would describe your mood today as 'elated,' Renfield," I explained, "and I know, from my past associations with other patients, that moods of elation sometimes portend a swing towards an opposite extreme. I wanted to check on you and ascertain that you are feeling quite all-right this evening."

"I feel . . . perfectly marvellous, Doctor," he said, still not turning.

I made a comment to the effect that he looked like he could actually see something out there in all that pitch. Without tearing his eyes away from whatever he thought he saw, Renfield spoke to me in a terse and edgy whisper I might have supposed to be confidential, were we not the only two people within range of his voice.

"You may think I see only darkness," he hissed, as though exercising tremendous self-control, "but as I peer beyond these bars, the night is no wall. It opens before me, like a flower, and I am sucked into its darkness as though by a powerful absorbing force. It does not wish to consume me, only to bring me closer, to confide things in me—to carry the news, as it were. Would it interest you to know, Doctor, that Carfax Abbey is no longer orphaned? It is true. I know this to be true as I know that the rubble of Carfax Abbey will soon be sown with seeds of dead souls and watered with living, scarlet nourishment. When you look at those adjoining grounds, you can see only what men and time have made of them, but I have the eyes of eternity. I can see what a palace of indescribable splendour shall arise from those ruins! The abbey was not a blind purchase at all—*no!* The Master . . ."

As he said this, he twisted round almost angrily, but caught himself. "Damn you, Seward! Never you mind!" Then, after a few moments addressed to calming himself, he continued to speak, but with an increasingly reverent tone: "*I* toured those premises through my own eyes, heard the sounds of the tiny creatures living there amongst the rocks and rotting timbers through my own ears. When I walked there, it was as though I walked with our Lord—yes, mark my words, as Enoch once did! Everything you and I have ever known, Doctor, will cease to exist, perhaps sooner than you think; it will all be ground to mulch, mulch to cradle and nourish the seed of His kingdom's red flower. All that we know will disappear . . . every eye that beholds the tentativeness of life with tenderness will rot . . . all the Moiras of this world will be dashed and damned, but I . . . I shall live on. Because *I am chosen! I am the Lord's Gospel! My immortality is assured!*"

CHAPTER XVII

Dr. Seward's Diary.

2 JUNE.—Having awakened with the sound of Renfield's closing words of last night still ringing in my ears, I decided to
pay a visit to-day to the grounds of the Carfax estate.

Any property owner despises neighbouring properties
which have been allowed, by deliberate or unavoidable neglect, to fall into disrepair; one rotten apple is enough to
de-value an entire bushel, and regardless of the work and expense my team and I had invested in raising the standards of
our asylum, with regular appliances of fresh paint, mindful
gardening, and what-not, the appearance it presented could
never rise above a certain standard given its unhappy proximity to the leprous wen which had once been Carfax Abbey.

I did not wish to trespass or vault over the wall like a
common vandal, so I resolved to gain proper authorisation to
tour the premises from the solicitor in charge of its sale—
Peter Hawkins, whom I had met through our uncommon,
common friend, Lord Remington. I went over to London,
where Mr. Hawkins keeps his offices, and explained to him

the reasons behind my request. He seemed quite happy to see me again, apologised profusely that his colleague Mr. Harker was still away conducting his business related to the estate's sale and thus not available to show me around, and then volunteered to do this himself. Frankly speaking, Hawkins's ebullient personality is not reflected in his physical being, and one imagines he does not care to walk unless absolutely necessary, so I was surprised by his offer and grateful for his outgoing company in such gloomy environs.

During the ride back to Purfleet, I mentioned to Mr. Hawkins how pleased I was about the prospective sale of Carfax, given that the untended and oppressive look of the property had made it increasingly difficult for me to project a positive image for my asylum. He chuckled warmly and observed that the proximity of a lunatic asylum had not exactly been an attractive selling point for the Carfax property, either. I must admit, the obverse view had never occurred to me before, and coming from so amiable a soul as Mr. Hawkins, I could not take offence at it.

He then enquired why, feeling as I did about the estate, I had retained the name of Carfax for my asylum, rather than calling it something like Purfleet Asylum or the Seward Sanatorium. I confessed that I had no more specific reason than that I preferred the clenching, affirmative sound of "Carfax" to the feline prissiness of "Purfleet"—he had quite a laugh at this. I added that there was never any serious consideration of lending my family name to my place of business which, considering its serious nature, would appear showman-like at worst and, considering that I am still in my twenties, also presumptuous. This was a more sobering thing to say, and Mr. Hawkins seemed quite satisfied with my explanation, though I could have taken it soberer still. If there is any definitive reason why this place is not called the Seward Sanatorium, it is because founding this asylum was achieved through my own hard work and without any particular support or approval from my parents or broader family, who had no understanding or sympathy for those who suffer from mental ailments. I felt I could neither honour their lack of support or mock their prejudices with such a herald.

"You're not inaccurate in calling your haven Carfax Asylum, in that your grounds do in fact adjoin the estate and were once included in its acreage," Hawkins informed me. "The stone wall that now divides the two properties was erected sometime in the late eighteenth century, when the landowner relinquished the grounds outside a twenty-acre radius. The story goes," he continued expansively, "that the name Carfax is a corruption of the French *quatre face*, meaning four-faced. It is young Harker's theory that it was so called because the abbey itself has four sides, or faces, which stand in perfect alignment with the cardinal points of the compass. It is my own theory that those walls were so built to stand in representation of the Angels described in the Old Testament's Book of Ezekial, and again in the New Testament's Book of Revelation. These celestial creatures were also possessed of four faces—man, lion, ox, and eagle—each one corresponding to the four cardinal points of the compass, and each perhaps also corresponding to the four Gospels attributed to Matthew, Mark, Luke, and John."

I was taken aback by the perspicacity of Hawkins's biblical scholarship and told him so. He chuckled amiably and confessed, "If you're a businessman—and a garrulous one, as I am—it behooves one to know a bit about everything."

As we arrived and dismounted from our carriage, Hawkins took a solemn look at the derelict place—beyond the rusted iron gates and oaken framework where the worn and dilapidated "Property for Sale" sign was displayed—and sighed, "Dear, dear me . . . How our Angels have fallen!"

Hawkins produced a large and ancient key to unlock the gates, which were set inside the stone wall encircling the property. They opened with an unaccustomed groan that gave the grounds the personality of a giant roused from long slumber with little energy but a sullen disposition. "Unfortunately, these gates are not the only means of entry," I noted. "There are at least a couple of collapsed portions of wall along its circumference, and the wall's general condition is so pitted from wear and neglect that any portion at all offers convenient hand- and foot-holds for climbing."

From the moment we advanced onto the property, all of the colour in the world seemed to disappear; even the greens were stale, beaten down as though by some noxious, invisible oppression. Further along inside the grounds were tangles of trees and other flora, untended for decades and thus free to go mad; weedy grasses that had grown until, like hair, they had ceased to flourish of their own accord; paths made of heavy fitted stones which had cracked under the accumulated stress of eons of contracting winter cold and expanding summer heat, and also dirt paths where the riotous impressions of human and animal feet blended in and out of one another in the furtive act of trespass. There were smells of moss and decay and fæces, and a preponderance of flies. And there, be-

yond the stone wall to the right of the path we walked, was
Renfield, keeping an eye on us from his window.

He saw me catch sight of him, and once he was certain
that his look was being returned, his mouth began to move in
a fury—but the sound of his voice was unable at that distance
to reach my ears. He might have been having another of his
early morning fits or cautioning me with great urgency
against what I was doing, I could not tell, but his antic demeanour added to my trepidation.

I informed Mr. Hawkins that we were being watched, but
he made no comment other than to mention to me that, when
writing to the Count who was interested in purchasing the
property, his employee Jonathan Harker felt it necessary to report that my asylum was not visible from the estate grounds.

"Ironic, isn't it?" Hawkins smiled, while lighting a cigar.
"That someone might spend tens of thousands of pounds on
all this mess without a second's hesitation, yet might be dis-
suaded because it borders a place like yours, tidy and bustling,
which is consecrated to restoring peace of mind to poor, be-
devilled souls."

I suggested to Mr. Hawkins that we follow the path to the
side of the abbey that could not be viewed from my own
grounds, so that we might proceed unobserved. The property
is more immense than it appears from here—some twenty
acres, according to Hawkins—and we continued our conversation at a relaxed pace until we got to the point we wished
to reach.

"Here we are, then," he grandly announced as we finally
turned the corner to the side I had never seen, "your dark
side of the Moon!"

It was, as we anticipated, more of the same but with one significant point of exception. At the foot of one of the high-rising, cratered walls of the long-forsaken abbey, there was a cluster of stones and a ganglia of thorny vines, from which had sprouted a single, perfect rose. In the midst of so much deathly colourlessness, it stood out against the general achromasia like a single drop of blood. It was so peculiar in that environment that it held my gaze as Hawkins, unimpressed, walked on. He disappeared behind a jutting section of the façade and then called out, "Seward, look here! This may interest you!"

Startled out of my reverie, I followed the sound of his voice and the profusion of the thorn-bush which seemed to halo the abbey until I, too, stood on the other side of the adjutment. There, growing wild, were *several dozen red roses in full bloom* . . . A sight to enrapture any romantic, but in this gloomy setting, they stood out like the difference between a speck of blood and a violent arterial splash.

Naturally, the sight of those roses recalled to me Renfield's phrase of last evening, as he promised that the abbey's rubble would "soon be sown with seeds of dead souls and watered with living, scarlet nourishment." My world seems inexplicably entwined with Renfield's phraseology . . . His metaphor was so potent a match for what I had seen that I could almost bring myself to believe that he had somehow seen those uncanny blooms, but he could not see them from the vantage of his room, and they could not have sprouted before he was placed in my care . . .

I went directly to Renfield's room upon returning here to the asylum. I found him sitting on a wooden stool and reading his Bible, whose covers he slammed shut as I knocked and entered. He turned to me with a smile that I judged to be false.

"You have been paying a visit to our Lord's house, as have I—as best one can, under duress," he said, gripping his Bible tightly.

I smiled back: "The Carfax estate hasn't been a house of God in several hundred years, Mr. Renfield."

"*Everything is beautiful in its time, yet eternity exists in the hearts of men, who cannot know what God has done from the beginning to the end.*"

"Meaning?"

"Ecclesiastes 3:11, more or less. Meaning that several hundred years may represent an eternity for some, but to others, it might be less than the blink of an eye. No dog knows the measure of a man's life, no spider knows the measure of a dog's life, no fly knows the measure of a spider's life, nor could a mortal such as yourself possibly know the measure of mine. Unlike yours, my own life is no longer shortened by each beat of my heart. I no longer take blood from there."

"You stopped taking blood from your heart?" I repeated, taken aback by the preposterous claim.

"Yes!" he confirmed. "My heart continues to beat, as you would doubtless remind me, but I no longer rely on its blood for my life. It does not matter that I tell you this, because knowing it will do you no good. Knowing it is not enough!"

"And what blood is it, then, which sustains your life?" I queried, humouring the poor, deluded man.

"Why, the blood of my Lord and Master, of course!" hissed Renfield. "His blood alone flows through these veins."

He stroked and caressed his two arms as though they were valuable things, turning them this way and that under my eyes, modelling them.

"Oh? And how does it get there? In your veins, I mean?"

"Through the act of Holy Communion, of course."

"That sounds very Catholic for one who was raised as an Anglican," I remarked, but my observation attracted no answer. Besides, I was not at all satisfied by this explanation, as Renfield had made no request to any member of my staff that he receive Holy Communion, but I kept my doubts to myself and allowed him to continue.

"With His regal blood flowing through me—through my eyes, through my brain—I have the privilege to see everything in a new light, as He sees them, through senses that know the meaning of eternity. Oh, I could tell you many things . . . ! I know how the story began . . . on ancient battlefields washed in the blood of a conquered people . . . and I also know how the story will end—long, infinitely long after you and the rest are dust!"

I thought this quite an extraordinary thing to say, so I baited him to reveal more: "Very well, Renfield—how *does* the story end?"

Renfield bared his teeth and inclined towards me, halting only a hair shy of a proximity that would have felt threatening. Then he pulled back, as though remembering his supposed superiority to base impulses towards violence or intimidation, and replied with chilling calm:

"Much the same as it began, but on an altogether vaster scale . . . Death will fall like thunder from the skies, and men will defend their territories from open graves . . . There will be graves filled by the thousands, and the skies will catch fire . . . Huge shafts of steel and glass rising to the sky will topple, and His triumphant mists will reign over great cities like a vast, inescapable Colossus. Worse still will occur, but would you care to know the ultimate horror?"

I nodded, feeling a great expansion of pity for the poor fellow's state of mind.

"The ultimate horror is that the story itself *will never end*," Renfield continued. "It's the people in the story who come to an end, as they have always done. Stories have endings, happy or otherwise, and they teach us to expect endings from life, but life goes on without end. And so the story of this world shall go on and on and on . . . as it has always done . . . as long as there is at least one man left alive to tell the tale. And I shall *always* be here to tell the tale."

CHAPTER XVIII

Patient's Oral History.

2 JUNE.—Moira was buried in our churchyard in a plain grave, her resting site marked by a simple stone bearing her Christian name (the only one we knew) and the date of her death. A pittance of acknowledgement, perhaps, but more than she deserved. I felt no remorse for the death of that scapegrace, who—as fate would have it—had brought me into this world, only an interior giggle of delight that Jolly and I had helped put her there.

I must own, however, that there was one aspect of Moira's death that unsettled me. Many times over the years, in the course of his sermons and eulogies, I had heard Father describe the Afterlife as a promise of great reunion, our ascent into Heaven as a spiritual flowing back into our bloodline, where all the faces of our family would be assembled to greet us when our life was done. For some, this may be their idea of Heaven, but I could not imagine a more searing, flagellating, unforgiving Hell than to rise into the snakery of Moira's negligent arms! Yet the way things are set up in

Heaven, or so the leading theologians seem to concur, such a reunion is unavoidable. The more I thought about this in the days after Moira's passing, the more bad dreams I suffered by night—and so I prayed, prayed as hard as I have ever prayed for anything, that I might discover some alternative to dying, some means of living other than by accepting the blood that pumps from my heart. This is why achieving immortality became so important to me: given the worthlessness of my bloodline, I have no chance of Heaven—only a choosing between the Hell up there and the one down below.

Father observed during this period that I became more sullen and prone to tears, which he judged a natural reaction to a boy's loss of his mother. When he questioned me about this, I was quick to set him straight. Yes, I confessed my real concerns to him; unfortunately, he was in no position to settle them. He sought to comfort me with the promise that Heaven was a positive realm in which nothing negative could exist—that, once ascended to Heaven, Moira would no longer be the woman she had been on Earth, no longer selfish and mean-spirited and simple-minded but a spirit free of the earthly encumberments which had maimed and twisted her human visitation upon this earth. In Heaven, he said, she would blossom, achieving the absolute summit of her spirit's potential; I would be greeted at the moment of my death not by Moira, but by the ideal of Moira, my own maternal ideal. He went on to assure me that my death would involve a deep-cleansing and ever-lasting obliteration of all my troubled feelings, the blessed absolving of all my earthly problems, and I would find no obstacle to embracing my mother at the moment of our reunion with complete love . . . not because she had given birth to me in the life which had passed, but because my birth and life, however painful to the person I had been, were necessary to experience before achieving this ultimate bliss.

I listened to Father with all the respect he was due, and I wanted very much to believe what he said, but—I asked myself—how could he possibly know any of this? As I listened, though I wanted so desperately to believe, every fibre of my being was shouting NO! It was wonderful that Father had faith that the Afterlife would be as he described it, but I could not be expected to put aside my own feelings on the basis of *his* faith. I needed an answer that would speak with immediacy to my own faith and ameliorate the lot of my terrible misgivings.

I continued to bury my disappointments under large helpings of food and got to be quite as fat as Jolly. To be fat and a probable bastard made me popular with other children in ways no one wants to be popular, so the older I got, the closer I stayed to the vicarage, where Father entrusted me with more adult responsibilities, including transcribing his scribbled notes into readable sermons and tending the churchyard.

A life that has neither hate nor hope, and nothing to look forward to, soon grows monotonous, and, as young people often do, I began to rebel against my lot in life—and perhaps my lot in death. My methods of rebellion were quite secretive, so much so that I doubt anyone ever noticed it, even at the height of its raging. For example, in order to have mine back at the expense of the children who taunted me for having no legitimate family, I sometimes used my time in the churchyard to re-arrange as many headstones as I had the muscles to move. I pruned many a family tree in my day, and re-arranged still more. Hatefully, I exchanged the identities of men with those of women, strangers with strangers, and adults with children. I put married men in the ground next to women who were not their wives, and if I really hated their descendants, as I detested Collie Craddick, I would wed them to their own grandmothers.

Mind you, not all of my re-arrangements were destructive in nature. There was one little dead girl, who had perished in 1812 after a life-span of only two days . . . I favoured her with a taste of the full life she never enjoyed by dragging to her earthen crib—with great effort, walking it along by tilting one corner onto another—a larger, heavier monument from the gravesite of the Higgins family patriarch Joseph William, who had died that same year, although at the remarkable age of 101 years.

Whenever Father became overly absorbed in his work or was otherwise ignoring of me, I would revenge myself by re-arranging the humble cruciform markers designating the plots of his predecessors. I exchanged the monuments of mayors with the driftwood markers of drifters. Each time I moved a headstone to a new location, I used the churchyard's access to Father's office window to ensure that his plot ledger reflected each of my covert adjustments. I also kept a secret ledger of my own, in which I recorded all of the true names and locations of the people buried there, less for posterity than to heighten my own sense of glee. But as the years passed, it was my own ledger that began to resemble a work of fiction. Fancy that—I had erased the order of the world God made and not been struck dead! What a discovery to make for a child of my age!

The drought which had befallen our countryside still

reigned during this period; I cannot tell you exactly how long it lasted, but our village was without rain long enough for everyone's crops to wither and for the grass everywhere to have been burned yellow by the unrelenting sun. It was not uncommon to find animals in the grass, or along the roads—birds, cats, squirrels, and other wildlife of the woods—which had expired from lack of that which Nature most often gives freely. It was a trying period for everyone, not least of all Father, who was forever being bullied by his parishioners to explain God's motive in denying them rain and profits from their farming. Most of his sermons during this period, as I recall, originated from the Book of Job.

One Sunday afternoon, following a particularly difficult sermon, I happened to see Father sitting alone in one of our church's pews, his arched back quaking as he wept into the palms of his own two hands. I did not disturb him, but I was moved by his distress to take the few coins which had been dropped into the collection plate that day, walk to land's end, and cast them from a bluff into the sea as an appeasement—praying to the God Neptune, whom I had seen in one of my books of fables—that He might share some of His bountiful water to quench our people's thirst.

As I stood there at the end of the field of cat's tails, on the lip of the precipice, overlooking the sea, my thoughts returned to the Lady. I had flung those coins into the roiling brine with the thought of ending the drought everyone in my village was suffering, but as my thoughts returned to the Lady, I rescinded that wish in favour of a more personal plea, that my personal drought, my own thirst, might be quenched.

As I raised my eyes from the churning sea to the sky

above, you can imagine my surprise when I saw, floating out there over the waters—originating from exactly the same spot on the horizon where the Lady had disappeared at the end of our first meeting—a single cloud! As I stared at the miracle of it, it grew larger in its steady approach, followed by others in proud formation, like dark-clad soldiers on the march across the sky! They were not only moving, but rushing towards land! Neptune had accepted my bribe!

Before I could race back to the vicarage with my wonderful news, not only were the first clouds already overhead, but the first droplets of rain were already falling—plummeting from the purple sky as large as grapes! I yelled and yipped as I ran, and my cries drew the townsfolk from their thirsting houses: I saw farmers—the most stoic of men—running outside, trailed by their wives and children, dancing in their barren, brittle fields, embracing one another and falling to their knees in humble gratitude. Dancing! Praying! Awed and grateful to a magic I had unleashed! My shirt was soaked through before I was half-way home; I nearly paused to take shelter in the woods, but an uneasy feeling fell over me as I ran past a particular ingress into the wilderness, of which I took note as lightning came close and shattered the orange-ing light with a burst of the mooniest blue. Yes, Doctor, I saw colours—proof of the marauding magic in the air . . .

I must have passed that spot on countless occasions in my dozen years, but only now, under these conditions, did it make itself known to me as the exact setting of the dream I described to you the other day, about the carpetbag. I looked away just as quickly, fearing that if my eyes happened to catch sight of the foot of the most prominent tree in that gathering, the carpetbag would be there and I would find myself back in the un-beating heart of my most forbidding dream. So I averted my eyes and continued running, still safe but now incontrovertibly aware that a place existed, not so far from my home, where my nightmare occupied the plane of reality.

As the vicarage came into view, I saw Father outside on the front steps, jubilant of face, standing ready with a heavy towel to dry me. He caught me with the towel, but I threw myself past it into his arms, embracing him as I had never embraced him before—not even as a child.

"Hold me, Father," I said, trembling, "I'm afraid."

"Wretched child," he said. "I have never known a time when you were not afraid of something!"

Father pulled me indoors and disengaged himself, the better to frisk the rain from my hair. Once this task was done, he led me to the window at the front of the house and put his arm around me, reassuringly. Father loved storms, you see—from the time I was very small, he always stopped whatever he was doing to watch the rain, which he saw as happy proof of a benign Creator mindful of watering His plants—and this was the most magnificent storm he had ever seen. I could feel only terror, because I felt responsible for its magnificence; I was fretful that I had inducted forces I would be unable to control.

"Look at this!" Father marvelled. "Look at this welcome splendour! Isn't it marvellous? Doesn't it make you feel small? Doesn't it take you completely outside of yourself? All this is so much greater than we are . . . Try not to cheapen the gift of life you have been given with fear, lad. A display such as this . . . deserves to be witnessed on bended knee. Not out of fear or cowardice, but out of a boundless respect." Heeding the good advice of his own words, Father seized the opportunity to lower himself onto one knee, genuflecting before this demonstration of the All-Powerful.

The windows and shutters rattled with such fury, we did not recognise at first that the pommelling at the front door was in fact the patient knocking of a caller. Father suddenly sprang back onto both feet and answered the summons. I stood behind Father, watchfully, as he opened the door—just a crack—onto an afternoon that looked the third stage of night. A visitor was indeed standing outside on our doorstep, a silhouette barely discernible against the bruised light.

"Good heavens!" Father exclaimed. "What a time to come calling! Come in fast, my dear, before you catch your death!"

Despite the outer raging of the elements, the figure hesitated.

"I am welcome to enter?" asked a woman's voice, through the elements.

"But of course, my dear!" Father chuckled, ushering our visitor indoors. "All are welcome here, and this is no weather to be standing on ceremony. We would welcome a stray cat on a day like this, if one came scratching!"

Once inside the house, the shadow collapsed her parasol. She stood before us tall and imperious, dressed at the height of fashion, though entirely in mourning black, with gloves and veil of the finest lace. I was convinced that she must be someone other than the Lady—after all, my offering to the sea had been rewarded with rain, and I had been waiting so long for the Lady's promised advent into my life that I daren't hope for more.

"The weather is inconvenient," admitted the shapely

shadow, "but when there is need, it is best not to wait. You are the vicar—the Reverend Mr. Renfield—and in need . . . of help, yes?"

Father looked at her in some perplexity: "Do I know you, my dear?"

"You do, I think, but not by name—and, it would seem, not by sight," came the weirdly melodious voice from behind the veil.

"Please don't stand on ceremony, dear," Father chuckled. "Put down your things."

The visitor complied by resting on the floor her folded parasol—and a large carpetbag. Her lace-gloved hands freed of their burden, she fanned her fingers artfully and raised her veil. I felt all the little white hairs on my arms, along the edges of my ears and the nape of my neck stand erect, as the skin on my legs thickened with gooseflesh.

There was no face of foxy fur behind that raised veil, but then I remembered her words from our previous meeting: "Today you see one. When next we meet, you shall see two."

So this was her second face! She was an older woman—not old enough to be elderly, but old enough for someone of Father's generation to regard her without the slightest suspicion—old enough to be, as they say, respectable. Her skin was luminous—only mildly wrinkled, a minor blow to what must have been an astonishing beauty in her youth and was now seasoned to an almost regal stateliness. Her hair was silvery grey and gleaming, arranged about her countenance like clouds streaked with pearl. She had a definite aristocratic bearing—with poise and flashing eyes knowing and sophisticated—and there was a beauty mark to the left of her chin.

"Permit me to introduce myself," she said, her words perfectly timed with the diminishment of the storm to a gentle rain, which made it easier for us to hear. The room began to brighten, bringing out the under-shades of blue in her dark dress. "I am . . . Madame Vulpes." She pronounced it *Vulpesh*.

"Oh, of course, of course!" Father smiled—though I knew he was now more confused than ever, but determined to fuddle through, gratefully accepting of the Heaven-sent coincidence.

"It is true you are in need of someone to cook and to teach?" she asked.

"Well . . . yes," Father stammered. "That is, only recently—"

"And you," she said, turning her eyes on me, "are the young man whose need has summoned me from so very far away?"

"This is Master Renfield," Father introduced us. "Renfield, say hello to . . . ?" He had either already forgotten her name, or was unsure of it given the Lady's exotic accent.

"Madame Vulpes," I finished for him, while making a courtly bow.

"*Very good*, my pet!" the Lady praised me, the edge of her mouth curling in a wry smile that I now know to be peculiar to the Balkan regions of Europe. "Look at him," she praised me, stroking the line of my jaw with her finger and pinching my cheek, "like clay, eager to be moulded. I can give this boy all that he will need to meet his future."

"Of course, Renfield attends the local school," Father offered awkwardly.

"That is good," the Lady allowed, "if you want him to

know what only farmers need to know. But you want more for him—yes? Not to be a farmer?"

Father did not reply to the specifics of that question, but he was obviously deeply gratified that this stranger brought to us by Providence seemed to want the same things for me that he had always wished for, in his own way.

"I must say," he chuckled, "you certainly say all the right things, my dear! But now that we know what you can do for us . . . what could we possibly do for you?"

"What I do, I do at the bidding of my Lord and Master. He sends me here, and so it pleases me to be here."

"Indeed," Father beamed, placing all of his weight briefly on his toes.

"For myself," the Lady continued, "my needs are few and nothing that need concern you. I am a foreigner, as you must plainly hear. The English that I know, I have learned through the reading of books. I feel . . . too much like a book; I wish to feel liberated into flesh and blood. I wish to learn English by actively using it, in my daily discourse, and this position would grant me such an opportunity."

"My dear!" Father enthused. "But you speak our language with remarkable eloquence!"

"Perhaps," the Lady allowed, "but not with true ease. The people of your country are distrustful of strangers, no? And I wish to erase from my language anything that might arouse . . . suspicion. You understand."

I did not turn to look at him, but I could feel on the side of my face that Father had turned to look at me and was smiling upon the absolutely pure adoration I felt for the Lady, which I showed unashamed.

"It's funny," Father chuckled, musing. "Only minutes ago, I was standing here in awe of the most impressive storm I have ever witnessed. I was moved to drop to one knee, as a gesture of my respect for the miracles of our Creator. Now, I feel myself similarly moved by the fact of your arrival—a perfectly simple occurrence, yet also a most fantastic happenstance. I have no idea how our needs were conveyed to you, my dear, but I am ever so grateful for the mysterious ways in which our Lord moves."

"They *are* mysterious, are they not?" the Lady purred in agreement.

"I do not recall ever seeing you at my services, my dear," Father mentioned discreetly. "Do you live nearby?"

"I have . . . a place to go, if that is what you mean?"

"Yes," Father explained. "Your husband . . . Mister . . . he allows you to work?"

"I am . . . the word in English escapes me," she faltered. "How do you say . . . married to a dead man?"

"A *widow*," said Father, providing the word. "I am most sorry, my dear."

"Life goes on," the Lady philosophised.

"Yes, indeed," Father agreed. "But I—"

"Do not concern yourself with my comforts, Vicar," she hushed him with a broad and wonderful gesture of both hands, which seemed to paint an invisible circle between them. "Neither your house nor habits need accommodate me. You will never want of hunger. I will keep your house clean—as though time stands still. And I accept it as part of my duty that you will never be made unduly aware of my presence, of my comings or my goings."

"Why, dear lady, that is most considerate of you!" Father enthused, his eyes nearly spinning with disbelief. "Well then, it is agreed. I hereby entrust into your care this vicarage and my young ward, Missus . . .?"

Again, I repeated her name for Father, both annoyed and mystified by the difficulty it posed for him.

The Lady laughed and stroked me again: "Ah! He is a natural, eh? Master Renfield, let us make matters easier for the vicar, shall we? You may both refer to me as . . ."

"Milady?" I suggested.

She laughed gaily and responded, "Why not?"

I closed my eyes, took in a deep and delicious breath and replied, "Very good, Milady."

"That should make things a good deal easier, thank you, my dear," Father smiled, looking a bit perplexed by the difficulty he had experienced with such a simple name. His downcast eyes then raised slightly, as he regarded me with open affection. "I care a great deal for this young man, Milady," he said. "He is like a sparrow fallen from its nest. I have mended his broken wings as best I could, with a firm hand and the rugged staff of God's Word. It is my hope that you can take the . . . clay I have readied for you and make something of it. Teach this little bird to fly."

Milady listened patiently to his words, which made me feel embarrassed, but my feelings of self-worth rose to meet them, even to surpass them, as she turned her eyes on me, glimmering with mystery and merriment.

"Fly he shall," she promised.

CHAPTER XIX

Patient's Oral History (cont).

Milady thus became in fact what she had always been in theory: the great love of my life. Needless to say, our mutual affection remained perfectly chaste; when my body began to sprout hair and know the carnal urges of young adulthood, I suppressed them—or, rather, I took care of them, much as one takes care to void one's bladder and bowels.

I recall the period of my life when Milady took care of Father and me as this old world, if it remembers things, must remember the Renaissance. A lifetime of torturous, unhappy constrictions, which I might well equate with the strait-waistcoat you sometimes require me to wear, was suddenly flung away, and anything was possible! Father withdrew me from the public school, and Milady's home instruction became the exclusive source of my education from that point . . . well, from that point until the end. My removal from school resulted in some unhappy feelings between Father and the local citizenry, who felt that he was placing me too conspicuously above their cat-strangling, snot-nosed off-spring. The people of my village had always been distrusting and resentful of me, and now they were distrusting and resentful of Milady, who never made any attempt to mingle with them, or to acknowledge them in any way—and their hatred of us made us all the closer. Father continued to address a dwindling number of worshippers on Sundays. It took the disappearance of a local infant to fill the townsfolk with the fear of God once again, and eventually, back they came in larger numbers.

Much of my educational process under Milady's tutelage was listening in complete rapture as she told me tales about her past, about her long life and many travels and the strange things she had seen. She told me that she had come to England from Romania, where she had been the bride of a great nobleman and soldier, much honoured in his time. She spoke of episodes from her country's ancient history as though she had been a living witness to them all, speaking with familiarity not only of names and dates, but of the personalities behind the names and the verities behind the dates. (I would ask her, and she would smile. "No, I was not alive then . . .") Yet she knew well the smell of history, the heavy hooves of the battlefield, and she conveyed her love of country so vividly that she had me wanting to go to war in its defence myself.

She gave me to feel that I could speak to her about almost anything—I stress the "almost"—so I asked her why she had continued to wear her widow's weeds so long, I presumed, after her husband's passing.

"He is not dead for me," she answered, "or for many others still in my country. When God turned His back on my people, my husband arose from the smoke of the battlefield as our new God, filling our men with the inspiration and blood-lust needed to repel the invader. He was revered in our time of plenty, after the last battle had been fought. I wear this colour—not black but the deepest blue, the colour of the sky at mid-night—because it was the time when he said he felt most alive, the time of his greatest triumph on the battlefield. Do you see the blue?"

"Yes, Milady."

"Very good. Most people cannot."

"I don't see colours at all, usually," I told her. "But I can see them all around you."

"My pet." She smiled. "This blue is also the blue of the blue flames—something else most people cannot see. You have heard of the blue flames?"

"No, Milady!" But I certainly wanted to.

"The blue flames are a legend of my country," she explained. "They are also known as the friar's lantern, or the will o' the wisp."

"I've heard of that," I said. "I always thought it was a kind of tree."

"No, my pet," she corrected me. "A will-o'-the-wisp is a blue flame that becomes visible above the earth only one night in each year, on the night of Saint George. The earth is a graveyard of many buried treasures, as you must know from all the books you have read, and on the night of Saint George, these treasures burn with a blue flame. Only those people who are favoured by the powers that be can see such a shade of blue. You, Master Renfield, are so favoured."

"Can you see it, Milady?" I asked.

"But of course!" she exclaimed, as though scandalised that I had to ask. "It is also known as the fool's fire, by those idiots who believe not in magic."

I was determined that, someday, I too would see the blue flames of the will-o-the-wisp.

True to her initial promise, in all the time Milady was with us, I never saw her come and only once saw her go. She arrived before cock-crow and left well after dark—sometimes after I had gone to bed—to return to another life, another dimension whose secrets Father and I never knew or questioned. To escort her home after dark would have been the gentlemanly thing to do, but the one time I suggested this, she stroked the side of my face and looked at me almost lamentingly, as though I should have known better than to ask. There was an unspoken understanding between Milady and me, you see, that she had come to the vicarage to oversee an important process involving me—to enable a destiny that would remain otherwise unfulfilled without her personal guidance. I understood implicitly that it would be crude to openly acknowledge this purpose, that to do so might burst the bubble and bring a sudden end to the whole adventure.

Milady always withdrew unobserved. Father might be lighting a cigar at table following dinner, patting his full stomach and whimpering that it was a pity to have to swallow food such as Milady had prepared, so deliciously did it dwell upon the palate—and, suddenly, Milady would be gone. She came and went like sudden death, exciting my imagination as much in her absence as in her presence.

I well remember my own first exposure to Milady's propensity for magic. I was sitting in Father's library one morning, reading a book. The library had a window facing east, and strong sunlight always poured through that window onto a wall of shelved books in the early morning hours. Father, who could be very particular, often fretted over the condition of the spines of the books on that wall, which, alone out of his entire collection, had become so terribly sunned that he couldn't tell anymore by looking at them who had written what. Milady did not see me sitting there as she strode into the room, and I watched in awe as she walked right up to those books, pressed her laced-gloved hands flat upon the glow warming their leather spines, and *physically moved the light to another wall*.

She could not have moved the position of the sun in the sky . . . this I knew, but without a doubt, I saw her *bend* the direction of the light entering that room through its window. I gasped despite myself, and she spun around in surprise, turning on me with her most disarming smile.

"Master Renfield!" she said brightly—and then said nothing else for a long, awkward silence. "You saw? The sun is not good for books, like it is not good for people—not if we want to live to a ripe old age. Our little secret, yes?"

"Yes, Milady."

She tilted her head to one side and narrowed her eyes appraisingly, before rustling in her skirts to my side and taking a close seat. "There was always a sadness in you," she noted, "but since I have come to you, I now also see . . . dread. What is this dread that is giving you a little wrinkle here?" she asked, touching my forehead.

I told Milady of the concerns about the Afterlife which were secretly troubling me. I did not have to worry about concocting a metaphor for what I was thinking, or otherwise condescend to her in any way; I could tell her exactly what was on my mind, and she could respond to me in an equally comfortable way.

"So your problem," she summarised, "is that you wish neither to go to Hell or to Heaven. Do I understand this correctly?"

"Yes, Milady."

"Then your course is set, Master Renfield. *You must not die.*"

"But Milady . . . everybody dies!"

She twisted her lips in her Romanian way of smiling, perched a hand on my shoulder, then leaned close and said to me in a warm, confidential voice: "This is what the churches tell you—and do you know why? So that churches can remain standing long after you are gone. I am your teacher, Master Renfield, and if I can teach you only one thing in the time we have together, let it be this: Never trust authority."

Ottority, she pronounced it.

I had seen this woman bend the path of sunlight, but I did not know if I dared accept as fact what she was telling me: "Do you mean I have the choice not to die?"

"But of course," she said simply.

"How is this possible?" I asked.

"Let me try to explain," she prefaced herself. "Everyone is born into a cage that is their own, unique prison. This prison is defined, before we are born, by our fellow men and the cage of ideas they have chosen amongst themselves to accept as fact. Everyone is likewise born on fire with questions, and in most people this fire is quickly extinguished. It still burns inside you; this I can see. To fulfill yourself, your potential, you must find the way to break out of this cage—the human cage—to find the answers to those questions—answers that no man born of woman can give to you. You hate your fellow men, Master Renfield; I know this. You recognise and love Nature—I know this, too. *Bravo!* It's a good beginning."

"Just a beginning, Milady?"

"You are still young, so everything is a beginning, no?" she reasoned. "There is Nature, which is what men call the parts of the world they know—and then there is the Supernatural, which is what men call the parts of Nature they cannot acknowledge because they do not understand them. But you love all of Nature, don't you? The part you do not understand, perhaps most of all, eh?"

"Yes! How am I to break free of my cage, Milady?

"I cannot tell you how to go about it," she answered, disappointing me. "Don't look sad—listen. If I were to tell you this, to hand over the answer like it was nothing, it would be nothing. Do you see? But if you find your own way to the point where you can break free, where your questions can *be* answered, you will make that moment important by the long path you walked to get there. Do you follow me?"

"I follow you, Milady."

"My pet!" she beamed proudly. "Then this I shall promise you," she added, turning very serious: "one day, when your life is in tatters . . . when you discover the true meaning of horror, so terrible in its truth that you cannot even admit it to yourself . . . subject yourself to one more burden of *unimaginable horror*—and you shall be freed of your human prison. At that moment, you will learn everything I could ever teach you, including my own secret—a secret that has allowed me to witness the passing of centuries."

I was astonished: *"Centuries?"*

"Centuries," she confirmed. "You must pay for this privilege, with pain torn from your own life, but the glories far exceed the cost. I speak to you now as I would not speak to a child—you know this?"

"Yes, Milady."

"Very good," she praised me. "Now I ask you: Is that not something wonderful to anticipate—even if the waiting should last for many, many years?"

"Oh yes, Milady," I agreed.

And with that, she reached out and pinched my cheek and resumed her house-cleaning.

I was perfectly sincere as I agreed with Milady, Doctor, but you know how children are. Children have much longer days and months and years than adults, and are impatient by nature. I felt that I had already suffered enough in my twelve or thirteen years to be shown the way directly to whatever answers might await me; that whatever path one might be required to walk before reaching that oracle of wisdom was already well travelled, in my case. It is the curse of every brain to think it knows everything, even before it is fully formed, and it should be obvious to you, even now, that I had no real notion at that time of the ultimate price I must pay.

In the wake of Milady's talk—perhaps because of the ultimate horror she declared I must experience before breaking free of the threat of inevitable death—my nightmares persisted, growing stranger and ever more vivid. In one of these, I found myself as naked as the day I was born, floating in a vast and terrifying void that evoked my earliest memories of fear of the dark. To affirm my existence in this void, I screamed—numerous times, each time louder than before— and my cries sounded back, confirming for me that there were walls enclosing me out there in the nothingness that enveloped me. Just as my lungs were on the point of needing more air for a renewed outburst, the darkness above me suddenly opened like the mouth of a purse . . . and I saw Milady's face smiling down upon me from without, as radiant of face as a Madonna in a Renaissance painting.

At once, I stopped crying, shocked out of myself by the surprise of her immeasurable beauty. Then she held out her two hands and reached deep into the darkness to pull me out, to rescue me! As she raised me up and out, I could see—as the skies were scored with jagged arcs of lightning—that she was removing me from *a carpetbag!* Yes, I was back at the scene of my earlier, recurring nightmare . . . but now I was being lifted out of the carpetbag at the foot of that tall tree by Milady!

I felt such contentment, such gratitude as she saved me from the darkness and pulled me out into the brighter world, where I felt no fear, but as my eyes adjusted to the light, I could see that I was being cradled in the half-human paws of something more animal than human . . . and from the edge of Milady's wry smile broke a long and glassy strand of heavy drool, wetting me—and then she turned her head swiftly as she became aware of another presence . . . It was a tall male shadow in a long black cloak that reached all the way down to the mossy ground. As I looked upon that figure, a pair of red eyes emerged from the darkness above its collar, as fiercely luminous as two blazing coals! Again I screamed—awakening in my room, where the black-cloaked figure still loomed over me, leaning over my bed!

It was Father! I had awakened him with my screams, and he had rushed to my room in answer to my calls. He lighted the lantern on my bed-side table, and my eyes darted all around my room, taking in every detail of my environment as reassurance, reassurance that I was safe and indoors. I took comfort from the blazing hearth and its companionable crackling, and also from wonderful Jolly, who scampered out of his box as the light came up, running across my chest on his little short legs and into the breast-pocket of my nightshirt—always my valiant protector in times of danger.

"Dear me, child," Father said in a low voice. "Don't tell me the nightmares are upon you again?"

"Yes, Father," I said, wiping my tears, "worse than ever."

When I made this confession, Father allowed me to see a particular shade of his expression that I had never been permitted to see before—not the usual face of a man in love with the sheer wondrousness of the world in all its variety, but that of a mature and well-rounded man who understood that every human experience, however positive, also had its dark side. He gripped my hand compassionately and spoke to me not as a youngster, but as another person—much as Milady had also recently done. I had the intimation, from the way people were starting to talk to me, as an adult, that the tenor of my entire life was about to change, was about to become more challenging somehow.

Father explained to me that the images haunting our worst dreams can sometimes be dispelled simply by talking about them—or, in the event of images which we cannot share with others due to their personal import, by writing them down. He proceeded to tell me that, when he lived as a child in the vicarage, he had been tormented by a series of bad dreams about a black demonic face that lurked in the deepest recesses of his bedroom closet. He never had any waking fears about his closet, had no particular feelings about his closet at all, but when this demon appeared to him in his dreams, it reminded him that behind this mundane reality lurked his most persistent adversary. He did not know that this dream was a recurring nightmare until each time he found it starting up again, when his foreknowledge of his footsteps and his passage through that dream environment reminded him that he had played this same role in this nightmare many times before.

"The face of this . . . thing in my closet was so black that it shone in the darkness," he explained, reaching over to stroke the back of Jolly's head as it poked out of my night-shirt pocket. "It had a radiance that was absolutely unholy. What was most frightening about it was not the way that it scowled at me . . . or the way it spoke to me in a voice as deep as Hell itself . . . It was the way it *smiled* at me . . . as though it wanted to slide a knife into me . . . as though it could wait for that opportunity for ever . . . and would."

At this point in his story, Father folded his arms and rubbed his upper arms vigourously, as though warding off a chill. "The last time I had this nightmare," he continued, "I had started keeping a journal . . . writing down the things I read and the things I ate . . . and I woke from my bad dream and—purely by instinct—I wrote it all down, in every detail exactly as I remembered it, swearing to this demon all the while that I would never let him enter my dreams again, that I denied his power over me. And do you know what, lad? *I never had that dream again!* It was a bad thing that ran out of my brain, down my arm, through the fingers of my hand, and died in a pool of ink."

"I wish I could do that," I said, trembling. "I don't want to dream about the woods anymore."

"Very well," Father said. "I shall get you a notebook, if you like."

"Yes, please, Father."

"Since I cannot offer you one at the moment," he said, "perhaps you would like to share your dream with me, let me share its burden with you?"

I hesitated, not wishing to go over it all again.

He persisted: "I guarantee you that, after you confide to me all those details that seem so horrible to you now, you will begin to see them as the foolishness they are, and that those things you dream could not possibly be further removed from the truth."

Trusting in Father, and wanting badly to divest myself of the dream's terrible power over me, I let all of the details Father wanted to come pouring out of me, out of my mouth. I told him everything—except that the woman who found me was Milady. I felt an internal imperative to keep everything I knew about Milady an absolute secret. When I mentioned the carpetbag, Father turned to me sharply, as though I had spoken a profanity. He stood up abruptly and turned his back to me.

"Has someone been talking to you?" he demanded—

speaking to me for the first time in his life, in my life, without the least trace of warmth or humour. "Is that it? Have children been talking, perhaps?"

"Father . . . ?" I managed, speaking from a place of complete bewilderment.

"Or was this *truly* a dream?" he asked with sudden wonderment, turning towards me again, his tone implying that there might also be divine reasons for such unbidden knowledge to come. "Very well, then—after all, I always meant to tell you, when the time was right . . . when you were old enough to understand it all properly . . . You are a young man now."

"Tell me what, Father?" I asked, sitting up in bed.

"Listen to me, Renfield . . . and try to find it in your heart to forgive me when I confess to you that . . . well, that you and I did not meet under the circumstances I have always described to you."

"But I was left on your door-step, Father!" I argued, as this is what I had always believed. "Of course I was! I can remember it! *That woman* left me . . ."

"No, my boy," he insisted, drawing nearer. "You remember what you were told had happened. The mind can play such tricks."

"But I can remember the terror I felt!" I argued. "My terror of the dark!"

"*That* is a perfectly legitimate memory—yes. Yes, you remember the terror, the darkness—but not the dark. It was not the night that frightened you. As in your dream, it was the darkness inside . . . a carpetbag."

"A *carpetbag?*"

Father took a solemn stance and lowered his head, looking not at me, but rather deeply inward.

"I was out for a stroll that night," he told me. "I always took pleasure in taking solitary walks by the light of the Moon, but there was a time when I felt it a duty of my office as vicar to take such walks—as a gesture of my determination, as an ambassador of God, to reclaim the night from Evil, if you will. The people of this village were crippled with superstitious fear. They were all too frightened to leave their homes after dark, so I took my nightly walks—knocking on every door in the village as I went about—to show them all that such pleasures were possible to have without something terrible happening.

"This particular night, the Moon was very large and full and I took uncommon pleasure in its companionship. Without meaning to, I kept walking until I found myself . . . well, at the very vantage point you described in your dream . . . at the entrance to the woods, the woods those stupid fools claim is haunted, near the field of the cat's tails. It is usually quite dark there at that hour, but as I say, the Moon was so bright that evening, that the air was—as you mentioned—an almost uncanny blue. And all of a sudden, I heard a sound that I thought might be an owl or some other nightbird. I followed the sound to a dark, lumpen shape resting at the foot of a tree, which looked from a distance as though it might be an injured animal of some kind. But as I drew closer, I saw that it was a carpetbag. Then I saw its covering move and heard the sound again. Then, to my horror, I knew all too well what I was looking at—but I cannot tell you how I dreaded the confirmation of my fears were I to open that bag and look inside it. But it was my duty as vicar to look inside, and so I did . . . and there you were."

"You *feared* me, Father?" That part made no sense to me, but I jumped past that question and hurled another at Father, needing to know—"But what was I doing inside a carpetbag left in the woods?"

Father sat beside me once again and patted my hand consolingly with his larger one, which had grown quite cold with his story-telling.

"Long ago, when I was still a young boy, a girl was mauled to death in those woods, probably by nothing more Supernatural than a bear or a wolf, but because no one had ever seen bears or wolves lurking there, the discovery of this poor, slaughtered child put the fear of Hell into our townsfolk. Ever since then, the woods have been called haunted and presumed to be a home to evil spirits.

"In their ignorance, the villagers conceived of a means of keeping this Evil at bay. They decided amongst themselves that these evil forces might be appeased and driven away by a sacrificial offering—someone's . . . unwanted child, left out there on the edge of the woods in a carpetbag. I don't know how to explain this to one so young and innocent as yourself, but there are times when young women . . . young mothers . . . find themselves expecting a child that is . . . not welcome. Perhaps they already find it difficult to feed all the hungry mouths in their brood . . . or perhaps the young mother has no husband, no home to offer this babe growing in her womb, who has no business coming into this world other than it is the nature of love, be it random or abiding, to bear fruit. There was one such child, unwanted, who was given up to be put out there . . . and, so it was said, was found drained of blood the next morning. The offering was apparently respected: there were no more attacks. Despite their shared burden of guilt, the townsfolk began to feel safe again . . . and then, one day, someone went walking along the dirt road by the woods and happened to see an empty carpetbag sitting there at the foot of that strange, ungodly tree . . . unfastened, its mouth open wide. The bag didn't belong to anyone known in the village, so its meaning was as obvious as it was ominous: the woods were demanding another child. In this unspeakable chain of history, I am ashamed to say that you—dear, beloved boy—was one of those children.

"Women were forced to bear children, to keep this unholy tradition on-going, in the name of the greater safety and well-being of all. And when such crimes were no longer tenable here, the local men took to their wagons and rode out, looking into neighbouring villages and counties for an unwanted child—and carrying with them persuasive sums of money. As a young man, I was appalled . . . could no one see that these infants were being eaten alive by ordinary animals? When I grew up and became the vicar of this accursed village, my feelings about this arrangement became well known and, consequently, I began to hear less about it. Until I laid eyes on you, wailing with terror inside that carpetbag, I had succeeded in fooling myself into believing that this bargain with the Devil had become a thing of the past and was no longer in session.

"So, yes, when I found you, I felt a terrible fear spread like ice through all my vitals. I plucked you from the mouth of that carpetbag and ran with you all the way back here to the vicarage. You were already about a year old and trussed up like a prize hen with thin, strong hemp . . . I was so upset by the whole experience that I became a bit unhinged myself and barred our doors, should those monsters come for you. Not the monsters that supposedly lived in those woods . . . but the real monsters. The ones who put you inside that bag."

"*She* gave me away," I sneered—meaning Moira, my mother, pronouncing the word *she* as though it was the filthiest obscenity.

"Moira?" Father replied, speaking aloud her detested name. "No, dear boy, your mother *did not* give you away. You were *taken* from her. She told me the story, that day when she saw you in your spectacles and recognised . . . I suppose, the man who once, a long time ago, had forced himself upon her. She told me that, when you were first born, you meant the world to her, that you were like the good thing that came out of the bad. You must appreciate—as I am sure will become easier for you, as you grow older—that Moira was a simpleton. She knew that she was not very bright; she was born to drinking parents, and, when she was still just a girl, she took some nasty blows to the head from a drunken father. She was taken out of her home and placed in an orphanage, where those who tended her were no less abusive. I told you about the night she spent in the cellar with the rats . . ."

Father reached under the lip of my breast-pocket and stroked Jolly with a long and curling finger.

"When she grew up and was able to leave that place," he went on, "it was not long before she caught the eye of a young—and apparently bespectacled—man who seized possession of her body . . . she not knowing any better, and being raised to defer to the demands of men . . . and that is how you came to be. It's a terrible thing, but life can arise from violence as well as from love. I am so . . . dreadfully sorry to have to share these horrible things with you, lad," he interrupted himself, squeezing my hands together inside his own, "but I think you are old enough to know. And I have not yet told you . . . everything. Now please remember, as I tell you the rest, that your soul is in no way diminished, or lesser in value than any other, because your flesh and blood are not sanctioned by Man's law."

"Yes, Father," I promised, listening with rapt attention.

"Those men who took to their wagons and roamed the countryside in search of a suitable appeasement—it was they who found Moira—and that is when they found you. Moira's monster of a father sold you to them for whisky money, literally tore you from her arms as she stood there, incredulous . . . The poor wretch had neither the strength nor the presence of mind to fight back, resist, or do anything but weep.

"She was so appalled by what had been done to her that she left the place where she was born and became a wanderer, taking work and accommodation wherever she could find it, but always packing up and leaving whenever she formed new attachments, lest someone steal from her or take advantage of her or otherwise break her heart again—all the time believing that you, her only child, were dead—left as bait for the dark."

And then Father finished by saying: "She did nothing to deserve your hatred, my boy—can you not see that?"

Dr. Seward's Diary.

2 JUNE, EVENING.—A critical session with Renfield today, which revealed the circumstances of his birth and adoption (as he understands, or prefers to understand, them) and occupied very nearly the entire afternoon.

After relating a conversation between himself and the vicar, in which the patient was shown that the hatred he had turned against his true mother—which had formed the very foundation of his personality in so many ways, from his "outsider" status to his identification with the animal world—had no factual basis, he fell into a deep and contemplative silence.

I allowed the two of us to dwell in that silence for as long as it suited the patient, not knowing where it would take him or with what thoughts our silence would eventually be broken. Five minutes is increasingly used by people as synonymous of no time at all, but to spend five minutes in silence with another human being can be a profound experience. I watched as Renfield searched his inner landscapes for an adequate response to that which he had unearthed from memory.

He eventually broke the silence with a simple declarative sentence: "Of course, I knew better than to believe that old fool."

CHAPTER XX

Dr. Seward's Diary.

3 *JUNE.*—Watkins reports a violent incident with Renfield this morning. When the patient was served a bowl of hot porridge for breakfast, he railed at the guard and threw the cereal against his wall. He has been accepting some food, mostly hot cereals, for a while now, but he refuses to eat anything unless it is served with a generous side-portion of honey or sugar. In this case, it was sweetened in our kitchen and Watkins himself tested it before serving the patient—but Renfield threw a fit anyway, insisting on his right to sweeten his own food to his own taste.

Growling and grumbling, he spent the next several hours absorbed in the reading of his Bible. Renfield does not approve of being observed at his devotions; whenever any of us happen to peer inside his room, he slams his Bible's cover shut—as Watkins says, "Like there was naughty postcards inside."

2:30 *P.M.*—I was afraid of this: Renfield has refused to continue his oral history to-day. Yesterday's talk, undertaken in a manic and boastful temper, ultimately yielded too much information for his liking. To-day he is back to his secretive, covert self. I don't believe it would be advisable to have him dragged here and insist on his co-operation. The only thing for me to do is to hold my ground for the present and allow him the space in which to ruminate on my role and stance within his process.

11:20 P.M.—What an extraordinary, devastating day this has been! Just when I imagined I was finally beginning to comprehend this madman—just when I thought I was finally on the point of laying bare his psychological motives—my eyes have been forced open to an entirely new strata in the complexion of his behaviour.

Where to begin? During the vacant hour I had scheduled for the continuation of Renfield's oral history, I decided to take advantage of a suddenly open afternoon by taking a walk around the grounds. It was necessary for me to avoid the side of the building where Renfield might spy me from his window, as I was determined to continue with him *exactly* where we had left off, with no incidental, intermediate encounters to interfere with the climax we had reached. It was a perfect June day and the white wicker chairs on our lawn were filled with patients and one or two visitors. To calm my vexation, I decided to have a cigarette and found a place well shrouded in hanging vines where I felt confident of not being observed by others.

The tobacco was indeed calming, and as the cigarette grew shorter between my fingers, I found myself smiling at the gossip being exchanged nearby by Huntley and Black—

two Cockney attendants in my employ, whose voices and conversations I have been known to imitate for the amusement of Arthur and Quincey and anyone else who cares to listen. These are not educated men, but they are not without experience, as they were saying in turn, each man doing his best to top the other in this department. They talked about their lives (unhappy stories which made them laugh—the healthiest response to bad luck, perhaps) and the women they had known (of whom they spoke with similarly ribald humour). As I was on the point of stamping out my cigarette, one of them exchanged the topic of the moment for one even less seemly: detailed descriptions of our patients' slops.

This is certainly not my idea of uplifting conversation, and I was on the point of taking my ears elsewhere when Huntley sought to trump his friend's description of Mrs. Welkins's expenditure by relating the even more nauseating contents of Renfield's bucket.

"You want to see somethin' like to make you doubt yer own 'ead," promised Mr. Huntley, "cock yer eye in that Bible man's slop bucket someday, eh wot?"

"Bible man? What Bible man?" enquired Mr. Black.

"The looney on the main floor, 'es the one," Mr. Huntley explained, with the air of a man who had all the information.

Mr. Black identified Renfield by name, adding a question mark.

Mr. Huntley continued: " 'At's the one! Now *there's* a queer bird, ay? Eiver screamin' his 'ead off, or buryin' it in his Bible, like. Talks about 'the Master' and 'ow 'e's coomin' back. Now don't get me wrong, 'arry—I bend me knee at church o' Sundays like any God-fearin' soul, but there's summat un'ealthy about finkin' at it all day 'n all week long, don't 'cha fink? A fella could go bonkers 'r preachy—an' this little bleeder's *boaf*."

"And this has *what* t' do with his bleedin' slop bucket?" enquired Mr. Black.

"Just that this un reads 'is Bible so 'ard 'e's got it comin' out both ends! 'Is slops was big an' lumpy-like as burnt-skin potatoes, but I's lookin' at 'em close . . . you knaow, jus' lookin' . . . an' I sees this white . . . all these white specks like in there, in 'em. An' I looks a bit closer, an' there—plain as blinkin' day—is the words *thou art*. Now you knaow me, 'arry. I may not read much in the way o' books but I can sure as 'ell read *thou art* when I sees it! Ba-loody 'ell! An' I looks at anuvver wit' these specks in there and there's the word . . . *smote*! Now *thou art* you might find in your books of whatcha call art 'istory, but friend 'arry, you could read all the blinkin' books in the world from 'ere to tomorra an' never fine a book uvver than the Bible that 'as a word like *smote*. Nobody smotes nothin' but God 'Isself."

"Now wait a minute," Mr. Black insisted. "Are you tellin' me that Mr. Renfield like . . . voids the Bible out 'is bowels, natural? 'Cause I'd 'ave to say *thou art smote* don't sound like no Bible Scriptures I ever 'eard."

"I didn't say the man shits complete sentences," Mr. Huntley argued. "He musta chewed 'em all up like, the pages, and they coom out confetti!"

By the time Huntley said those last words, I had turned the corner and my two hands were tight around his suspender straps. The poor, indecorous fellow recognised me at once and blanched. He thought I was angered by his colourful conversation and about to violently reprimand—or perhaps dismiss—him, but I had only one urgent thought in mind: to discover if he had any evidence whatsoever to support his claims. But then I understood that I had no need for whatever proof might be in the pudding, so to speak, of Mr. Renfield's slop bucket. The only proof that would truly validate my suspicion was in his room.

I raced into the house and directly to Renfield's quarters. I paused outside his door and caught my breath, so as not to alarm him or put him on guard, then knocked on the trap. When he told whoever it was to go away, I did not do as he suggested.

"Now, Mr. Renfield," I said upon entering, "is that any way for a civilised man to speak?"

Renfield was sitting on his bed, holding his Bible so tightly that the pink skin of his knuckles seemed to whiten before my very eyes.

"You forget, Doctor Seward," he alerted me, "I am anything but a civilised man. I look down my nose at your . . . 'civilisation' from the true regency of the higher animals. You will please leave my den."

I smiled indulgently, hoping that he would not anticipate what I was there to discover. I said, "You know, that Bible, which you seem to prize so highly, was not written by animals. On the contrary, I would say that it is perhaps the ultimate distillation of the human spirit, one of the greatest achievements of human civilisation."

"Oh, would you?" he chided me.

"Yes, I would," I confirmed. "And yet, in our discussions, you have found so much fault with the Bible, haven't you? Its views on the uncleanness and soullessness of animals, its endorsement of animal sacrifice. And yet you spend so much time with it."

"It is the work of more than one author," Renfield argued. "I am not in agreement with them all. But, when I read their work, be it right or wrong, I feel myself in the company of the man I called Father."

"Jesus Christ, or the man you called 'the old fool'?" I asked him.

"I thought I told that idiot Watkins that I am in no humour to discuss such things to-day! Whatever will you do, good doctor, without the details of my life story to distract you?"

"Oh, the things I usually do to relax. Walk . . . read . . . I may even sketch."

"I didn't realise that you fancied yourself a draughtsman!" Renfield exclaimed.

"I don't, not really," I insisted. "I merely find that drawing is a good exercise in the development of one's attention to detail."

"I see," he sneered. "The Good Book frowns on art, you know."

"It does?"

"Well, representative art, anyway—though I would have expected such an expert as yourself to know this. The Lord forbids us to embellish upon His own creations, which are His own. What men call art, the Bible calls idolatry. Deuteronomy, 4:15. Man should not aspire to do better or even to do worse in the rendering of the Lord's miracles. And so my advice to you, my good doctor, should you feel inspired to put your pencil to paper this afternoon, is to draw only what you cannot see in this world. For some reason, the Lord stakes no proprietary claim on our expression of whatever we may find in the dark wells of our own souls."

"That's very interesting, Renfield," I said. "I've read the Bible myself, but I have no recollection of such passage. Would you mind if I looked it up for myself?"

As I held out my hand to receive his Bible, Renfield's chiding expression darkened to that of a cornered rat. Moving slowly, he gripped his Bible more closely to his body, leaning over it, curving his shoulders forward and hollowing his chest, as if wishing to absorb it into the protective labyrinth of his own physiognomy while holding me at bay.

"Please, Renfield," I reprised, maintaining a bright and courteous tone of voice. "I promise to return it directly. I want only . . . to look inside."

It was at this moment that Renfield, who had wound himself into a coil in the upper corner of his bed, sprang at me like a cobra. I was on my back on the floor before I knew what had happened; he was kneeling over me, straddling my chest, striking me repeatedly on my head and face with his Bible, which he continued to grip tightly with both hands.

"It is *mine*!" he shouted. "They were *promised* me!"

Just as I was on the point of losing consciousness, Watkins and Hardy were suddenly in the room in their white coats, interfering with the blows and disengaging Renfield from my body.

"Pry that Bible away from him!" I managed to say.

Renfield made an astonishing show of strength against the two strong men, but it was short-lived—not only because

Watkins and Hardy managed to extract the book from his vise-like hands, but because neither side could hold for long against the other. The Bible went flying, and landed open beside me on the floor.

I suppose I had foreseen what I then saw, though without fully comprehending its purpose. Evidently, judging from the proof which lay before me, Renfield had worked assiduously to gouge out the interior of his Bible by picking at the pages with his fingertips and literally devouring, bit by bit, over a period of days, a few hundred sheets of Holy Scripture. These bits are what had been noticed in his stool. What I had not foreseen was the purpose behind this covert procedure, though as I record these words, I am beginning to appreciate that the truth was there to be seen all along.

Spilling out of the book's meticulously made hollow was a large pile of dead flies, as many as sixty in all. I looked at them, spilling out of the book in profusion, and they told me nothing. I looked at Renfield, rapidly weakening in the tight hands of the two guards, and he returned my look with the infinitely sorrowful expression of a man whose every last secret—personal, religious, carnal—has been forced out into the light; the face of a man all but destroyed.

"Good God, man—what are these?" I demanded, gesturing towards the pile of unmoving legs and wings.

Renfield stood there, cowed and slumping between Watkins and Hardy, his lowered eyes rolling up until they met and locked with mine. I am loath to say this, but I noted what may have been a glimmer of victory there, which, if true, was encouraged no doubt by my damned inability to decipher the evidence placed in such quantity before me. Renfield was not fool enough to swagger, to parade his triumph, but neither was he completely effective at concealing his merriment at my ignorance. What he had apparently feared most had come to pass, but I could not see what he assumed was plain to see.

With an air of embarrassment—which I believe to have been insincere, Renfield finally confessed: "Those . . . are my . . . pets."

"*Your pets?*" I said, collecting myself. "However . . . however did you manage to collect so many?"

At which point Hardy offered: "I think moybe this explains our friend's sweet tooth."

Of course! Capital! That is why Renfield became so perturbed when his porridge was not served with extra honey or sugar. He was using it to bait these insects, which he proceeded to smother in his Bible!

As I turned back to Renfield, I saw that his eyes were still on me—but now there was murder in them. Slowly, with an air of menace, he raised his limp arms, in the grip of the two guards, and then flung them both aside like dolls as he sprang towards me once again. I put my arms behind my back and tried to scramble away from his attack, spider-like, but in a split second, he was upon me and clamping two sweaty hands about my throat. Then, with equal spontaneity, his aggression subsided, and he disengaged from me, cupping his hands together as though holding something captive inside.

"So sorry to have frightened you, Doctor," he apologised, rising to his feet before the two astonished attendants, still sprawled across the floor, "but you had such a nice big fat one crawling on you. I had no time to explain—these are very quick ones, despite their girth. I simply must have it."

"Bind him," I instructed the attendants, who scrambled into action and found no resistance from the patient as they shoved him into his strait-waistcoat.

I could see it all now. Renfield was using the sugar and honey brought to him from the kitchen to collect flies, which were being bred by the thousands from the decaying refuse and other organic detritus abounding on the abandoned neighbouring property! I thought also of the cleaning cloth which had been passed to him by the cleaning girl Beryl— but to what end, this madness? To what end?

Until I can learn more about the role these flies play in Renfield's mania, the only thing I can do is indulge him for the time being and double my vigilance.

CHAPTER XXI

Commentary.

"Indulge him for the time being and double my vigilance"! *What a young fool I was!* At this point in my story, I can no longer blame my errors of judgement on personal or narcotic distraction. Lucy and her mother were now far away from town at their summer-house in Whitby; Arthur was also away, attending to the needs of his father, Lord Godalming; and the heed demanded by Renfield's case had impressed upon me the critical necessity of remaining focussed at all times. Thus, the recording of his oral history and my studies of its transcripts succeeded in weaning me away from more dangerous indulgences, by satisfying all my needs for rigourous distraction.

I thought I was comporting myself as the very soul of vigilance, yet as I compile and re-visit these transcripts from half a century ago, I can see—even at my advanced age—that I should have reached out much sooner to Professor Van Helsing, at the very first suggestion of a Super-natural element in the case. But how was I, a young man of twenty-five, to recognise a madman's recollections of an idealised woman who could fulfill all his needs as an emissary of the Un-Dead, bent on seducing him into perpetual servitude? And how could I be expected to take seriously a patient's baleful warnings that these personal stories, dating from the 1830s or thereabouts, could represent any sort of active national threat some fifty years hence? I may have been a doctor, and an experienced one for my age, but in such otherworldly matters, I was a layman like anyone else. Van Helsing could have saved us. Had I known to summon him earlier, he would have had the opportunity. The blame can only be laid at my door-step.

As this tragic narrative continues—Renfield's and mine—it now reaches the point where my diary entries begin to play a more prominent role in the plot of the book *Dracula*. Therefore, a certain amount of the material to follow shall be familiar to those readers acquainted with Mr. Stoker's "novel." What will not always be familiar is the context in which this information originally appeared in my un-edited records, as well as certain passages—sometimes lengthy—which I withheld from that project.

The reader will note the absence of any diary entry for 4 June. My records show this was a Thursday. As I have no recollection of that day, I am left to assume it was consumed watchfully rather than actively—that is, wastefully. In the wake of my discovery of Renfield's secret use for his Bible, he found other secrets to keep; a new wall was erected between us. Although I allowed him to keep his flies for the moment, in the hope that they might reveal something important about the particular demons plaguing his mind, it was no matter; he lost all interest in continuing the recording of his oral history. This sudden and prolonged interruption left his story poised on the very threshold of unshared information which I knew must have been galvanising to his madness— that is, he had led me to the point of his discovery about his true origins, but not beyond, to the disclosure of how he re-acted to this shattering information . . . how he dealt with the details suddenly volunteered by the vicar . . . how he coped with the devastating revelation that Moira, his mother, was not truly to blame for his circumstances, though he had tortured her throughout her last minutes of life on this very selfish presumption.

My next diary entry finds me treading water, floundering and resorting to overview without Renfield's active input. The space which is seen to accumulate between subsequent entries is even more indicative of my failure, as is my gradual return to pining for Lucy. More wasted time, but a terrible and ironic God would grant my wish to see her again.

Dr. Seward's Diary.

5 JUNE.—The case of Renfield grows more interesting the more I get to understand the man—not that I presume to have come anywhere near to fully achieving that goal. He is such a mercurial subject for study . . . one moment entreat-ing, even grovelling . . . the next moment proud and boastful. And yet he does possess certain characteristics that could be said to be constant. **He has certain qualities which are very largely developed: selfishness, secrecy, and purpose.**

I wish I could get at what is the object of the latter. The chances of this, in the wake of the incident in his room, would seem to be less than zero, given his refusal to speak with me. **He seems to have some settled scheme of his own, but what it is I do not know.** It would seem to have something to do with the story of his life and his fascination with the ruins of the Carfax estate. Renfield is a loathsome, unknowable creature in many respects, yet also strangely pathetic. **His redeeming quality is a love of animals, though, indeed, he has such curious turns in it that I sometimes imagine he is only abnormally cruel. His pets are of odd sorts.**

Just now, as I recorded earlier, **his hobby is catching flies.** I had another look inside his Bible today and he has managed to collect quite a few more since yesterday. **He has at present such a quantity that** he can barely close the cover of his Bible and **I have had myself to expostulate.** I was curious to see how his compulsion would resolve itself, in its own time, but when faced with the sheer quantity of them, amassed in no more than twelve hours—the dull houseflies, the iridescently gleaming blue bottles, and so forth—I became equally inquisitive about how important this dead pile might be to his state of mind. The only way to determine their value was to suggest to Renfield that he part with them, and then step back to gauge his reaction.

"Mr. Renfield," I told him, "I believe in indulging our patients as much as possible to ensure their contentment, but having slept on it, I have come to the conclusion that this hobby of yours is neither particularly healthy nor to be encouraged. Therefore, I must insist that you dispose of your collection."

To my astonishment, he did not break out into a fury, as I expected, but took the matter in simple seriousness.

He thought for a moment, and then said, "May I have three days? I shall clear them away." This request, on the surface of it at least, indicated a measure of attachment to his menagerie, as he could not simply clear the dead things away but needed time in which to disengage himself from it, bit by bit. **Of course, I said that would do. I must watch him.**

9 JUNE.—Once again, in order to gain insights into the patient's covert thinking, I had his tea drugged and borrowed his notebook. What I found were not specific answers to my questions, but there were some curious new entries.

From Renfield's Notebook.

I have committed the sin of pride. I made a boastful reference to His name and gifts in conversation with the doctor. The Master is displeased. The wine of our communion once flowed in plenty but now is limited to one sustaining drop per day. If I try to take more than my allotted share, cannot keep it down. It is enough to live, but not enough to live forever! Do not forsake me, Master!

I live only to serve the Master! But without strength and alertness, how am I to worship? How am I to pave the way for His righteous victory?

Please, O Lord and Master, send me thy answer!

I was sitting on the floor of my room, repenting my wicked tongue. I looked at the palms of my hands, feeling abandoned. I studied all the lines and creases etched there in the skin of my palms, by my life—the life which my Master has governed since its earliest days. In the centre of both hands I saw an X. And this X was but the crux of a larger design in the shape of an hour-glass. The markings were the same in both of my hands. A profound discovery.

I closed my eyes and thought long and hard about the hour-glass, which put me in the mind of Milady's elegant figure. I began to visualise how the sand of an hour-glass pours from the top through a narrow waist at the middle, then spills through, grain by tiny grain, to amass the same fullness below.

My thoughts along these lines were disrupted by the inane chatter of the attendants in the corridor. The two idiots were talking about how certain foods were defensive against illness, as citrus foods and juices have been discovered are deterrents to scurvy.

I like Hardy better than Watkins, though neither of them is fit to lace my shoe—he said there was wisdom in foods that Man hasn't had time to think about. Watkins agreed, talking about how chicken soup helps a cold and that someday, someone will figure out how to put that goodness in a pill that people can take every day to stay well. Then Hardy said yes, but it wouldn't taste near as good as the chicken soup.

These idiotic natterings helped me to see how I might meet the challenge placed before me by the Master. If this denial was intended as a punishment, I would prove myself resourceful and take what was rightfully mine by the means that were available to me. Surely the Master could not deny me that! And then it occurred to me—what if my meagre allotment was not the Master's divine punishment—but His test? A test of my mettle! Perhaps the Master means to teach me to think strategically, as He and other great military generals do?

If this is so, then I am bound to please the Master, for has there ever been a stratagem more elegant in its simplicity than this?

```
x x x x x x x x x x x x x
  x x x x x x
   x    x    x
     x    x
        x
     x    x
   x    x    x
  x x x x x x
x x x x x x x x x x x x x
```

In this way, one might contain the worth of a score and more!

Master! Is this the answer? Have I pleased Thee?

If so, please send me a sign . . .

The Master has sent me a confirmation in His own unmistakable hand-writing! As I came back into my room tonight, I found a little spider with the most wondrous hourglass etched on its back!

Dr. Seward's Diary.

ADDENDUM.—The man is simply mad, a never-ending font of macabre fantasy. A spider such as Renfield describes does exist, but it is highly venomous and found nowhere in England. It would not surprise me, though, if he had found some sort of spider in his room . . . and loving all little creatures as he claims, was using the dead flies from his Bible to feed and make a pet of the damned thing.

18 JUNE.—He has turned his mind now to spiders, and has got several very big fellows in a box. He keeps feeding them his flies, and the number of the latter is becoming sensibly diminished, although he has used half his food in attracting more flies from outside to his room.

1 JULY.—His spiders are now becoming as great a nuisance as his flies, and today I told him that he must get rid of them.

He looked very sad at this, so I said that he must some of them, at all events. He cheerfully acquiesced in this, and I gave him the same time as before for reduction.

He disgusted me much while with him, for when a horrid blow-fly, bloated with some carrion food, buzzed into the room, he caught it, held it exultantly for a few moments between his finger and thumb, and before I knew what he was going to do, put it in his mouth and ate it.

I scolded him for it, but he argued quietly that it was very good and very wholesome, that it was life, strong life, and gave life to him. This gave me an idea, or the rudiment of one. I must watch how he gets rid of his spiders.

He has evidently some deep problem in his mind, for he keeps jotting down things in his little notebook. Whole pages of it are filled with masses of figures, generally single numbers added up in batches, and then the totals added in batches again, as though he were focussing some account, as the auditors put it.

8 JULY.—There is a method in his madness, and the rudimentary idea in my mind is growing. It will be a whole idea soon, and then—oh, unconscious cerebration, you will have to give the wall to your conscious brother.

I kept away from my friend for a few days, so that I might notice if there were any change. Things remain as they were except that he has parted with some of his pets and got a new one.

He has managed to get a sparrow, and has already partially tamed it. His means of taming is simple, for already the spiders have diminished. Those that do remain, however, are well fed, for he still brings in the flies by tempting them with his food.

19 JULY.—We are progressing. My friend has now a whole colony of sparrows, and his flies and spiders are almost obliterated. When I came in he ran to me and said he wanted to ask me a great favour—a very, very great favour. And as he spoke, he fawned on me like a dog.

I asked him what it was, and he said, with a sort of rapture in his voice and bearing, "A kitten, a nice, little, sleek playful kitten, that I can play with, and teach, and feed and feed and feed!"

I was not unprepared for this request, for I had noticed how his pets went on increasing in size and vivacity, but I did not care that his pretty family of tame sparrows should be wiped out in the same manner as the flies and spiders. So I said I would see about it, and asked him if he would not rather have a cat than a kitten.

His eagerness betrayed him as he answered, "Oh, yes, I

would like a cat! I only asked for a kitten lest you should refuse me a cat. No one would refuse me a kitten, would they?"

I shook my head, and said that at present I feared it would not be possible, but that I would see about it. His face fell, and I could see a warning of danger in it, for there was a sudden fierce, sidelong look which meant killing. The man is an undeveloped homicidal maniac. I shall test him with his present craving and see how it will work out, then I shall know more.

10:00 P.M.—I have visited him again and found him sitting in a corner brooding. When I came in he threw himself on his knees before me and implored me to let him have a cat, that his salvation depended upon it.

I was firm, however, and told him that he could not have it, whereupon he went without a word, and sat down, gnawing his fingers, in the corner where I had found him. I shall see him in the morning early.

20 JULY.—Visited Renfield very early, before the attendant went his rounds. Found him up and humming a tune. He was spreading out his sugar, which he had saved, in the window, and was manifestly beginning his fly catching again, and beginning it cheerfully and with a good grace.

I looked around for his birds, and not seeing them, asked him where they were. He replied, without turning round, that they had all flown away. There were a few feathers about the room and on his pillow a drop of blood.

I said nothing, but went and told the keeper to report to me if there were anything odd about him during the day.

11:00 A.M.—The attendant Hardy has just been to see me to say that Renfield has been very sick and has disgorged a whole lot of feathers. "My belief is, Doctor," he said, "that he has eaten his birds, and that he just took and ate them raw!"

11:00 P.M.—Since he continues to refuse to speak to me, I gave Renfield a strong opiate tonight, enough to make even him sleep, and took away his notebook to have another look at it. I found no new stories nor recounted dreams, indicating that the continuation of his story is something that he is struggling to keep well removed from his own consciousness. What I did find in his book were more baffling mathematical figurings, as well as this peculiar rumination, which struck me as authentically sermon-like.

From Renfield's Notebook.

Catch as cat can, the fly feeds the spider, which is grub for the bird, which is meal for the cat, which is prey for that which can pounce on the cat, and I live in the House that Jack Built.

'Tis same for the worm, fodder of fish, whose flesh is for men's feasting, until man's flesh, frail and waning, becomes fodder for worms, ashes to ashes, mud to mud.

The world is a garden, Mother Nature yielding bountiful foods from her soily bosom. Eat vegetables till you vegetate and die, to be put under the soil to dazzle the mulch, thank you very mulch. What nobody tells you is that there has always been this other way—the true way of Nature, as is easily observed—the age-old process of the large growing larger . . . how? By feeding on the small. Survival of the biggest. It is surely part of the Divine Plan, for why else would such meager little diddems reproduce so fast and so fecund unless some were intended to live on and breed, while the rest have no greater destiny than to be caught and consumed? It is a process reaching back, round all yesterdays, to the very beginnings of time. Encroaching creatures breathing down the necks of lesser life-forms, connecting mouth to tail in an endless drama of life and death, self and sacrifice. Fun!

If eating dead vegetables brings about vegetation and death, should not the eating of live things—the swallowing, without chewing, of whole lives—perpetuate life? Is this what the Master means to tell me?

Only this planet knows the full account of our secrets—but it's the biggest and hungriest animal of them all, and it isn't telling. As it spins on, its whirling erodes and devours the beast that fed on the cat who ate the bird who pecked the spider who swallowed the fly—and it has become what it has eaten. Its oceans are a great, curving mass of wrinkled elephant skin; the straw heaped upon its heaths is like the woolly hump on a camel's back; its trees in winter are like snakes, green salient scales forming on their barky limbs in summer; the rivers veining its crust akin to the burrows of moles or ants.

This great, lumpen, growling planet is nothing more than an organ within the larger body of space, perhaps a stomach, in which we are all Jonahs nurturing the fantasy that we are free men when we are, in point of fact, swallowed food—the crumbs of hope and dream, ripe for evacuation to make ready room for more.

Dr. Seward's Diary (cont).

I shall have to invent a new classification for Renfield, and call him a zoöphagous (life-eating) maniac. What he desires—I now reckon—is to absorb as many lives as he can, and I can now see he has laid himself out to achieve it in a cumulative way. As he noted in an earlier entry of his notebook, Renfield has it in his head that he can achieve immortality by denying himself the blood from his heart and taking blood only by other means. I have witnessed him eating a fly and, from this, as well as the bird feathers he wasn't quite able to digest, it can reasonably be surmised that these "other means" are his smaller forms of life.

However, for some reason—because he did something to displease his so-called "Master," perhaps by referencing Him directly in his conversations with me—he was ordered to fast and forbidden to partake of more than one life per day, which was not enough to sustain him at peak capacity. Therefore, he seized upon a plan—illustrated in his notebook with the hour-glass schematic—to absorb the blood of many while digesting only one, as suggested by the hour-glass diagram in his notebook. If he was permitted to eat only one fly, he discovered that he might access a maximum of value by feeding ten flies to eight spiders, then feeding those eight spiders to four birds, and then the four birds to one cat. Here we have the explanation of the upper half of the hour-glass, with the lower half reflecting the values he might absorb from such an experiment.

But what would have been his later steps? It would almost be worth while to complete the experiment. It might be done if there were only a sufficient cause. Men sneered at vivisection, and yet look at its results to-day! Why not advance science in its most difficult and vital aspect, the knowledge of the brain?

Had I even the secret of one such mind, did I hold the key to the fancy of even one lunatic, I might advance my own branch of science to a pitch compared with which Burdon-Sanderson's physiology or Ferrier's brain knowledge would be as nothing. If only there were a sufficient cause! Shall I let him have a cat and see how he proceeds? I must not think too much of this, or I may be tempted.

How well the man reasoned! Lunatics always do within their own scope. I wonder at how many lives he values a man, or if at only one. He has closed the account most accurately, and to-day begun a new record. How many of us begin a new record with each day of our lives?

To me it seems only yesterday that my whole life ended with new hope, and that truly I began a new record. So it shall be until the Great Recorder sums me up and closes my ledger account with a balance to profit or loss.

Oh, Lucy! Lucy, I cannot be angry with you, nor can I be angry with my friend whose happiness is yours, but I must only wait on hopeless and work. Work! Work!

CHAPTER XXII

Dr. Seward's Diary.

19 AUGUST.—Strange and sudden change in Renfield last night. About eight o'clock he began to get excited and sniff about as a dog does when setting. The attendant was struck by his manner, and knowing my interest in him, encouraged him to talk. He is usually respectful to the attendant and at times servile, but tonight, the man tells me, he was quite haughty. Would not condescend to talk with him at all.

All he would say was, "I don't want to talk to you. You don't count now. The Master is at hand."

The attendant thinks it is some sudden form of religious mania which has seized him, but I explained that such talk was nothing new in Renfield's case. Nevertheless, we must look out for squalls, for a strong man with homicidal and religious mania at once might be dangerous. The combination is a dreadful one.

At nine o'clock I visited him myself. His attitude to me was the same as that to the attendant. In his sublime self-feeling, the difference between myself and the attendant seemed to him as nothing. It looks like religious mania, and he will soon think that he himself is God. He already considers himself immortal.

These infinitesimal distinctions between man and man are too paltry for an Omnipotent Being. How these madmen give themselves away! The real God taketh heed lest a sparrow fall. But the God created from human vanity sees no difference between an eagle and a sparrow. Oh, if men only knew!

For half an hour or more, Renfield kept getting excited in greater and greater degree. I did not pretend to be watching him, but I kept strict observation all the same. All at once that shifty look came into his eyes, which we always see when a madman has seized an idea, and with it the shifty movement of the head and back which asylum attendants come to know so well. He became quite quiet, and went and sat on the edge of his bed resignedly, and looked into space with lack-lustre eyes.

I thought I would find out if his apathy were real or only assumed, and tried to lead him to talk of his pets, a theme which had never failed to excite his attention.

At first he made no reply, but at length said testily, "Bother them all! I don't care a pin about them."

"What!" I said. "You don't mean to tell me you don't care about spiders?"

To this he answered enigmatically, "*The Bride maidens rejoice the eyes that wait the coming of the bride. But when the bride draweth nigh, then the maidens shine not to the eyes that are filled.*"

He would not explain himself, but remained obstinately seated on his bed all the time I remained with him.

I am weary tonight and low in spirits. I cannot but think of Lucy, and how different things might have been. If I don't sleep at once—chloral, the modern Morpheus! I must be careful not to let it grow once again into a habit. No, I shall take none to-night! I have thought of Lucy, and I shall not dishonour her by mixing the two. If need be, tonight shall be sleepless.

LATER.—Glad I made the resolution, gladder that I kept to it. I had lain tossing about, and had heard the clock strike only twice, when the night watchman came to me, sent up from the ward, to say that Renfield had escaped. I threw on my clothes and ran down at once. My patient is too dangerous a person to be roaming about. Those ideas of his might work out dangerously with strangers.

The attendant was waiting for me. He said he had seen him not ten minutes before, seemingly asleep in his bed, when he had looked through the observation trap in the door. His attention was called by the sound of the window being wrenched out. He ran back and saw his feet disappear through the window, and had at once sent up for me. He was only in his night gear, and cannot be far off.

The attendant thought it would be more useful to watch where he should go than to follow him, as he might lose sight of him whilst getting out of the building by the door. He is a bulky man, and couldn't get through the window. I am thin, so, with his aid, I got out, but feet foremost, and as we were only a few feet above ground landed un-hurt.

The attendant told me the patient had gone to the left, and had taken a straight line, so I ran as quickly as I could. As I got through the belt of trees I saw a white figure scale the high wall which separates our grounds from those of the deserted house.

I ran back at once, told the watchman to get three or four men immediately and follow me into the grounds of Carfax, in case our friend might be dangerous. I got a lad-der myself and, crossing the wall, dropped down on the other side. I could see Renfield's figure just disappearing behind the angle of the house, so I ran after him. On the far side of the house I found him pressed close against the old iron-bound oak door of the church.

He was talking, apparently to someone, but I was afraid to go near enough to hear what he was saying, lest I might frighten him, and he should run off.

Chasing an errant swarm of bees is nothing to follow-ing a naked lunatic, when the fit of escaping is upon him! After a few minutes, however, I could see that he did not take note of anything around him, and so ventured to draw nearer to him, the more so as my men had now crossed the wall and were closing him in. I heard him say . . .

"I am here to do your bidding, Master! I am your slave, and you will reward me, for I shall be faithful! I have wor-shipped you long and afar off! Now that you are near, I await your commands, and you will not pass me by, will you, dear Master, in your distribution of good things?"

He is a selfish old beggar anyhow. He thinks of the

loaves and fishes even when he believes he is in a real Presence. His manias make a startling combination. When we closed in on him, he fought like a tiger. He is immensely strong, for he was more like a wild beast than a man.

I never saw a lunatic in such a paroxysm of rage before, and I hope I shall not again. It is a mercy that we have found out his strength and his danger in good time. With strength and determination like his, he might have done wild work before he was caged.

He is safe now, at any rate. His cries are at times awful, but the silences that follow are more deadly still, for he means murder in every turn and movement.

Just now he spoke coherent words for the first time. "I shall be patient, Master. It is coming . . . coming . . . *coming!*"

So I took the hint and came too. I was too excited to sleep, but this diary has quieted me, and I feel I shall get some sleep tonight.

20 AUGUST.—The case of Renfield grows even more interesting. He has now so far quieted that there are spells of cessation from his passion. For the first week after his attack, he was perpetually violent. Then one night, just as the Moon rose, he grew quiet, and kept murmuring to himself. "Now I can wait. Now I can wait."

The attendant came to tell me, so I ran down at once to have a look at him. He was still in the strait-waistcoat and in the padded room, but the suffused look had gone from his face, and his eyes had something of their old pleading. I might almost say, cringing, softness. I was satisfied with his present condition, and directed him to be relieved. The attendants hesitated, but finally carried out my wishes without protest.

It was a strange thing that the patient had humour enough to see their distrust, for, coming close to me, he said in a whisper, all the while looking furtively at them, "They think I could hurt you! Fancy me hurting you! The fools!"

Am I to take it that I have anything in common with him, so that we are, as it were, to stand together? Or has he to gain from me some good so stupendous that my well-being is needful to Him? I must find out later on. To-night he will not speak. I wanted so to get him to unburden himself to me that I went ahead and offered to get him the kitten he had petitioned for. But even the offer of a kitten or even a full-grown cat will not tempt him.

He will only say, "I don't take any stock in cats. I have more to think of now, and I can wait. I can wait."

After a while I left him. The attendant tells me that he was quiet until just before dawn, and that then he began to get uneasy, and at length violent, until at last he fell into a paroxysm which exhausted him so that he swooned into a sort of coma.

22 AUGUST.—Three nights has the same thing happened, violent all day then quiet from moonrise to sunrise. I wish I could get some clue to the cause. It would almost seem as if there was some influence which came and went. Happy thought! We shall to-night play sane wits against mad ones. He escaped before without our help. Tonight he shall escape *with* it. We shall give him a chance, and have the men ready to follow in case they are required.

23 AUGUST.—"The expected always happens." How well Disraeli knew life! Our bird, when he found the cage open, would not fly, so all our subtle arrangements were for naught. At any rate, we have proved one thing, that the spells of quietness last a reasonable time. We shall in future be able to ease his bonds again for a few hours each day. I have given orders to the night attendant merely to shut him in the padded room, when once he is quiet, until the hour before sunrise. The poor soul's body will enjoy the relief even if his mind cannot appreciate it.

Hark! The unexpected again! I am called. The patient has once more escaped!

LATER.—Another night adventure . . . Renfield artfully waited until the attendant was entering the room to inspect. Then he dashed out past him and flew down the passage. I sent word for the attendants to follow. Again, he went into the grounds of the deserted house, and we found him in the same place, pressed against the old church door. When he saw me, he became furious, and, had not the attendants seized him in time, he would have tried to kill me.

As we were holding him, a strange thing happened. He suddenly redoubled his efforts, and then, just as suddenly, grew calm. I looked round instinctively, but could see nothing. Then I caught the patient's eye and followed it, but could trace nothing as it looked into the moonlit sky . . . except a big bat, which was flapping its silent and ghostly way to the west. Bats usually wheel about, but this one seemed to go straight on, as if it knew where it was bound for or had some intention of its own.

The patient grew calmer every instant and presently said, "You needn't tie me, Doctor Seward. I shall go quietly!"

Without trouble, we came back to the house.

Commentary.

Such a memorable night! Which is fortunate, because it kept me much too busy to keep a record of it, and not long after this, of course, matters began to accelerate.

Having apprehended him, the attendants and I escorted Renfield back to his room at the asylum. As the door was unlocked and swung open, the poor fellow turned to me with considerable anxiety and pleading, dog-like eyes and said, "Please, Doctor—not here! Might we not spend the hours till light together in the chapel? I haven't the energy to defend myself, and I would feel ever so much safer there!"

"Safer?" I repeated. "From what?"

"From my own shadows," he answered after a short deliberation.

I thought this a most extraordinary reply and nodded to the attendants to escort him to the chapel. Though Renfield had been rampantly mischievous earlier that evening, I intuited from his demeanour—which had greatly relaxed since his apprehension—that the worst was over for this night, save perhaps in the vein of spoken revelations. I sensed that he might be of a mood to finally press on with his story, to divest himself of some very deeply held secrets—and I understood that, to get at them, it would be necessary for me to trust him. So there were no shackles, but I ordered the attendants to remain on call outside the door for the duration of our visit—and I scribbled a hasty note for a messenger to carry to Ralph Morrison, who lived not far away, asking him to return to the asylum and meet us in the chapel at once.

I broke the initial silence by saying, "Do you know, Renfield, there are some people whom you know from the very first instant you meet them, and then there are others whom you come to know gradually. It is very nearly four months now since we first met and, in that time, you have shared a great deal of yourself with me—and yet, after episodes such as I have had with you recently, episodes like to-night's, I am left to feel as though I do not know you at all. You taunt me, you thwart me, you flee from this shelter to a neighbouring property that is structurally unsound and dangerous to inhabit . . . you go knocking on an old church door that hasn't been opened to any needy soul in a century or more, neglecting this very chapel which stands just down the hall from your room . . . and then, when you are finally apprehended, you turn to me and beg for my company and the protection of my chapel."

"Consider yourself fortunate," he said. "You have only two of me to bother about. Imagine how it is to serve a Master with four faces! I am not unsympathetic to your plight, Doctor."

"So there is hope for us yet?" I asked, jokingly, to lighten the mood.

"Don't be ridiculous," he shot back. "Even when one has the expectation of living forever, the concept of hope does not necessarily enter into it. You are still a young man, Doctor—shall I tell you something you might not otherwise discover until you reach my age?"

"Certainly."

"I would imagine that you, like me, lead a life that is divided, shall we say, between outward action and inward contemplation. Introspection, they call it. I always favoured introspection over action, and I have spent a good deal of my life looking within. Within, my friend, is nothing but an empty abyss. Our purpose is to fill it, not to explore it. It is not for us to see or understand God's work. The answers to our probings exist outside and above us, altogether out of our hands."

"Yes, I know," I said.

"You know?" he echoed with visible shock. Then, more calmly: "Well, I did not—and thus I wasted a good deal of my life, looking inside myself and finding nothing, until I ceased to believe in everything."

"Did you ever have a chance to discuss this with the vicar?"

"No," he answered. "I might have done someday, but . . ."—and then he added in a very tiny voice—". . . I killed him, you see."

This is what I needed to hear, at long last. "Renfield," I said, leaning forward, "would you be willing now to repeat that statement, with Morrison as a witness—and perhaps continue with your story to-night?"

"Must you torture me?" he asked, weeping into his hands.

"That is not my purpose."

Suddenly Renfield's face jerked up, out of his hands,

streaked with tears. His dishevelled face, a veritable mask of tragedy, contorted with a queer smile which I imagined to be the smile of Judas at the moment he accepted his pieces of silver.

"Do you realise where He is now?" he asked, almost giddily. "Do you realise what He is doing? What He is *in the act of doing*?"

I thought he had turned delirious and was still talking about the vicar . . . but now, all these years later, I can appreciate that Renfield was experiencing a rare moment of lucidity, and that the pronouns of his pronouncement were capital in nature. As I can now determine by comparing the date of this conversation to those of the other chronicles found in Mr. Stoker's book, Renfield was risking his own life to caution me that his Master, Count Dracula, was at that very moment in England . . . in Whitby . . . taking advantage of Mina Murray's absence from the scene to boldly enter into Lucy's room and feed upon her maiden blood.

"Please, Renfield," I repeated, ignoring his words. "May I?"

"Of course," he said irritably. "What have either of us to lose now?"

CHAPTER XXIII

Patient's Oral History.

I feel closer to Father sitting here. There were times, as a boy, when I would sit in the church, when Father was nowhere about, and look at the stained-glass windows and the icons and the altar and feel his presence all around me, like the folds of his cloak. It is true that I killed him, but I don't feel it was murder; I had no intention of killing Father—I loved him, and he was the only person in the whole world who loved me. In the act of killing him, I was cutting my last connection with the world, don't you see? One cannot be a friend of God and be a friend of the world, the Bible tells us that.

I could not tell you what I was feeling as Father sat there on the edge of my bed, leaning over me in his dark cloak, explaining to me that I had not been abandoned by my mother . . . that I had been taken from her forcefully to be handed over to monsters of the dark . . . that none of my circumstance had been her fault. But I ask you, what does a mother's love mean without a mother to give it? My mother was no mother to me as she lived and breathed, and

I had condemned her for it. The last words she heard in this life were addressed to her by me, her own child, as I condemned her to the worst circles of Hell! I had driven rusty nails into her wrists and feet with my tongue, and now Father was telling me that she was blameless? How could I retract those words, those nails, now? I never had a real family—only a series of God-fearing folk who refused me, abused me, who cast me out, who told me lies. *Lies, lies, lies!* There was but one constant in my childhood, Doctor, and that was my hate and resentment for the bitch who had abandoned me, left me without a place in the world I could call my own! I was miserable before she came, I was miserable after she came—and now that I had finally known the satisfaction of emptying my bladder on her grave, was I now to spend the remaining years of my life in abject misery . . . because I had misjudged her? *No! I reject it! I reject her! I hate you, Moira! Never will I call you Mother! I hate you and I reject you!* And I *cannot accept* what you tell me, Father! *I refuse to accept* that I was ever loved . . . *I refuse to accept* that I was not abandoned . . . *These are the things by which I know myself . . . these things are what I am . . .* and if you deny these things, if you take them from me, *I am nothing!* You leave me with *nothing!*

Did I actually say these words to him, before I swung my bed-side lantern at his head? Or after? I can't remember . . . My only recollection is of walking out of the burning vicarage in my night-shirt, with nervous Jolly in my pocket, and cursing Father in my thoughts because he would not be making good on his promise. Never would he buy a notebook for me now, the little book which he had promised to me, in which I might reject my demons and ensure my peace of mind. Instead, he left me to be torn apart by the teeth of the secret things inside me. Hell is paved with good intentions, to borrow from the good Samuel Johnson. All Father really ever gave me was a name . . . Yes, he gave me a home, but he took it away from me twice, which left me feeling tentative there even when I came back to live at the vicarage for the last time . . . only a name . . . and yet he was a foundling too, as he often told me himself. Was the name we shared even his to give? Another thing about myself I will never know . . .

Wait . . . I remember now. Before I swung the lamp, I asked Father, "Has Milady left for the evening?" He said yes, that she had only just gone . . . That is when I swung the lamp at his head. The blood didn't come out right away, not till I was standing over him. What I said then surprised me. I said, "Slap me, will you?" I left the vicarage without looking back; I could tell from the oranging of the air that it had caught fire. I didn't care, as I had no reason ever to return there. My life was in tatters and my actions, and my reaction to them, had shown me the true meaning of horror . . . a horror so terrible in its truth I dared not admit it to myself . . . until this very moment, all these years later!

By these signs did I know that I had arrived at the destined moment when I must find Milady and follow her, when I must present these facts to her, so that she could keep her promise by freeing me of my human prison and the contract which all beings of flesh and blood must sign with death.

Jolly and I walked to the roadside and looked in all directions for some trace of Milady, the path I had chosen. My heart leaped as I caught sight of her shadow growing smaller against the star-shot horizon, moving in a lurching gait made more macabre by her widow's weeds, towards the open field and the dark and gnarling woods beyond, where we had our first encounters.

I knew that Milady did not like to be accompanied or followed, so I kept a respectful distance. As I think back on this episode, it becomes embarrassingly obvious to me that Milady was quite aware that she was trailed by two shadows—one her own, and the other young and plump and watchful, thinking itself ever so crafty as it scurried behind tree and rock and shrub. Once we reached the field of the cat's tails, waving to and fro in the strange light, it became impossible for me to conceal myself because there were no longer any obstructions to shield me from her view. Likewise, there was nothing to come between her and my view of her, yet I managed to lose sight of her nonetheless. Instead of walking directly across the field to the woods, as I expected, she inclined to the right, approaching her destination obliquely—by initiating a coil-like path of concentric circles. The grain in the field was only waist-high, but as I watched her turn into that first circle, she appeared to vanish into thin air.

Desperate to follow, I ran—Jolly bouncing in my pocket—out into the open and entered into the trail she had trampled into the cat's tails, so that I might follow her exact course. She had to be there, I told myself, because she had flattened the very path I was walking—and also because, once I had stepped inside that path, I became more acutely aware of the colours I had denied myself, in all their variety; the night was pooled from the deepest and most luxurious blues and the bending grain blazed all about me as the most glorious gold.

As I turned the first curve in the spiralling coil Milady had left behind her, the back of her once again came into view—but only long enough for me to see her in the distance, turning yet another bend, winding herself tighter and tighter towards her ultimate destination. I had no choice but to continue moving forward; indeed, I felt myself being pulled forward . . . and I became afraid that I had inadvertently bungled into the same sink-hole of existence I held over Moira's head in her last moments of life. Was I so tied by blood and skin to that woman that she could drag me down through the same hell-pit I had described for her? And that cawing sound! Was it nightbirds I was hearing, gossiping to one another in the high branches about the boy lost out there in the cat's tails? Or was it the triumphal sound of my dead mother's laughter, rising up from the hollow I would find all too soon beneath my bare feet?

As I rounded the last of the bends described in the reeds by Milady's wide skirts, the sound became quite easy to identify—it was the muffled yelp of a baby, coughing and crying—and there was Milady too, no longer going anywhere but turned in my direction and looking frankly at me. She was seated on a surface of flattened cat's tails before the wooded background which had been the scene of my recurring dream—framed, as it were, by the open maw of the forest. There, at the foot of the large tree to her right, I could see a carpetbag—*her* carpetbag—its fabric thumped by something within, so that it appeared to beat like an excited heart. The baby was inside, kicking and crying.

"Why have you followed me here, my pet?" Milady asked me with surprising placidity, ignoring the cries issuing from behind her.

"I mean no offence, Milady," I said, pressing my hand to my breast-pocket to calm Jolly. "You once told me, after I had suffered enough, when my life was in tatters, I might discover the secret of breaking free of my human cage and achieving immortality. I *have* suffered enough, Milady. I have taken my own life this night—not by killing myself, but by destroying everything that held any meaning for me."

"I see."

"This is the moment you told me must pass before it would be possible. You are all that I have now, Milady . . . and so I followed you."

"Look around you, my pet," she commanded. "Do you recognise this place?"

"Yes, Milady. From a dream."

"And before that?"

"Before that?"

"*Long* before that. Before everything."

"Before everything, Milady, I can remember only the dark—and being very, very afraid."

"So you *do* remember," Milady smiled.

She rose and walked towards the woods, where she knelt at the foot of the tree—her dress spreading out beneath her like a dark pool—and opened the mouth of the bag by pulling apart its twin wooden handles. She reached inside. What she removed was indeed someone's baby, not a newborn but perhaps a year old—the source of all the crying I heard when I arrived. There was no thick covering now to muffle its cries, which rent the night's starry sheet with a knife-edge of terror.

Milady rose to her full height, cradling the baby in her arms. "The dark you remember," she explained, "was the darkness inside this carpetbag . . . and the terror you felt was the terror of my approach."

"Father told me about the carpetbag," I confessed, "but I didn't believe him."

"He told you the truth," Milady assured me, "and you can believe the vicar with your own eyes, because this child is you, my pet," she said, lowering it back inside the carpetbag.

Milady made a harkening gesture and seemed to dissolve into the shadows of the moment. Almost at once, a tall young man of the cloth came walking along the road in the moonlight. His hair was darker and there was slightly more meat on his bones, but I knew in my stomach that I was looking upon Father, as he was once upon a time. I stood there watching, unable to intervene in what had already happened, as he discovered the carpetbag, looked inside it—and then turned in the direction of the village and cursed its people under his breath. He removed his cloak and lay it on the ground, removing me from the bag and laying me thereon, folding it over and around me as swaddling. As I stopped crying, I began to cry. I wept as I watched Father raise me into his arms and, with marvellous pity and resolve, follow the dirt road in the direction of what was now surely a skeletal ember.

As Father departed, Milady emerged once again from the shadows. "You were meant for me, boy—for the woods and all that is wild, but as you can see, the vicar *intervened*."

"Father . . ."

"You were meant for me," Milady continued, "but that man took you from me and raised you as his own. And you see the misery his selfish actions have brought upon you? The life you have lived is a mystery, but you understand, in your heart, that your destiny has been thwarted. You have yearned all these years for the magic I alone could have given you, *would* have given you. Yes, my pet, *I* could have been your mother."

"So I was right to follow you?" I asked, with rising hopes.

"Perhaps," she said mysteriously. "What will decide whether your actions were wrong or right is what you choose to do now."

"What choice do I have, Milady?"

"You can wake from this dream . . . or you can live it, by accepting the destiny that the Master has chosen for you."

"And how do I do that?"

"Remember what I told you. Once your life is in tatters . . . when you have discovered the true meaning of horror, so terrible in its truth that you cannot even admit it to yourself . . . you must subject yourself to one more burden of *unimaginable horror*. Are you ready to do that for me? For the Master?"

"How am I to do that, Milady? I have nothing."

"You have *something*," she reminded me.

Her meaning was brought to my attention by the wriggling of Jolly in my pocket. He was right over my heart, like my own heart-beat. I reached into my pocket and brought him out into my hand. He was my heart, my soul, my conscience, my little fat man, and I loved him so. "I couldn't hurt Jolly," I objected.

"You cannot *imagine* hurting Jolly," she corrected me. "And yet, if you want to be with me, and with our Lord and Master, you must."

I ran towards Milady with my hand extended, but my flesh and blood and bone passed right through her—she was but an illusion, yet a persistent one.

"What you hold in your hand, my pet, is of this world," she told me. "That animal is not something that loves you, but the last bar of your human cage. It is the last thing separating you from me—from the destiny that was always yours. Twist that last bar out, my child, and join me. Don't you know how I long to hold you to my breast?"

I looked at Jolly and turned my eyes to Milady as my hand began to squeeze. Even through my tears, a down-pour which seemed to melt the entire world, I could see the image of Milady gaining substance as I felt my hand enclosing a mortal struggle. I dared not look away from Milady and I did not look, and the longer I squeezed, the easier it was to do. I wanted to prolong neither its pain or my wait, so I gave all my strength to the tightening of my hand and—still, without looking—felt the miracle of life and personality depart into another world, where such things could be, while I was left holding a limp rag of fur and flesh and bone. I never cried so hard as I did at that moment.

Her arms, already around me, were quite solid—the space between us was now traversed. She smiled down on me as no other woman's face had ever smiled down on me—as a star smiles down on you when you make a wish.

"Cry for joy, my pet," she said. "You are free."

"I'll never die?"

"You will never die," she confirmed, extending a fingertip to stroke the line of my brow, the bridge of my nose, the curve of my cheek.

I hugged her very tightly, and my hug was returned. "You and I shall erase the past," she announced with such finality that everything, save the two of us, seemed to recede from my senses as she spoke those words. "We will turn back the clock, you and I, and pretend that you are once again the babe in my carpetbag . . . and I have just found you, just as I was always meant to find you . . . and I have lifted you out and placed you in my lap . . . and I am smiling down on you, the mother you have always wanted, the mother you needed, the mother you should have had."

She held me close—close enough for me to see the tiny hairs on her face, close enough to hear the beating of her heart, but I heard nothing—and, though I felt no warmth conveyed from her physicality, there was immense warmth emanating from her spirit, for lack of a better word, as she held me close. Then the look of a wished-upon star vanished from her features, as she assumed a more serious aspect of responsibility and purpose. Leaving the cradling of me to a single strong arm, she reached up to her lace collar, which she proceeded to unbutton along a series of six, seven, eight black buttons that extended down to her waist. There was a flash of pallid skin within the moony-blue shadows she wore and she reached inside them to to extract a single pale breast, plump and heavy, which she laid at my lips. Its pale purple nipple looked as fully engorged as one I had seen in the past. I gazed upon it in helpless disbelief, half afraid to accept it for fear that, somehow, I might be mistaking the nature of Milady's invitation even now.

Then her beautiful skin, as pale as moonlight, began to darken. I moved closer as her shadow flexed and took me under its great wing, where the nipple, darkening still, stood out like a clearing in a forest of whorling black and brown hairs that blew away like thistle down as it emoted . . . as it expressed a white bead of temptation left to tremble at its tip . . . and I closed my eyes in surrender and drank . . . yes, I drank deep of its thickness, of its sweetness . . . "Yes, my pet" . . . my ears warming, growing hotter and sprouting hair, my muscles relaxing, my mind swooning . . . yes, yes . . . I took and took as much as I wished, took of its sweetness until its sweetness turned bitter, a metal taste . . . and then I pulled away, the flow splashing me as it turned from white to pink, then from pink to red . . . but I had waited so long for this, I did not want to stop . . . nothing would take this from me now, not even death itself . . . so I latched on again and I took and took and took . . . "Sweet pet" . . . she said, holding me close . . . *Oh! smile on me, my little lamb!* I drank it yes the white . . . *For I thy own dear mother am*, He said . . . yes the pink . . . *My love for thee has been well tried* . . . the red yes oh yes . . . *I've sought thy father far and wide* . . . *I know the poisons of the shade; I know the earth-nuts fit for food* . . . *Then, pretty dear, be not afraid. We'll find thy Father in the wood.*

Dr. Seward's Diary.

24 AUGUST, EARLY.—As Renfield spoke the last hundred or so words of this morning's confession (the last of them recollected from Wordsworth), his tone ascended from one of curious remembrance to something more incantatory—a surging towards religious rapture, or perhaps masturbatory fervour. This was not a seductive or persuasive incantation, but rather a deeply masochistic one; he grunted the words, through his nose and mouth, as though every few words were a chunk of meat he had to tear from his own wincing torso, and he pressed on until he reached a peak of transcendent ecstasy—as if in blessed relief that the pain of that bodily abuse had finally stopped—and then he became remarkably calm, calm and still.

There was something ominous about his calm, and as I looked upon his sudden suspension of activity with concern, I stared with amazement as his lips parted and a long thread of viscous pink fluid spilled from the edge of his mouth.

At my summoning, the attendants returned the patient to his room. I collected a sample of his sputum from the floor which, upon later analysis, proved to be what rational science would never permit it to be: a spontaneous generation of blood and human milk. The substance was rich in fats and nutrients. Was Renfield able to generate this fluid at will, or only when reminiscing (fantasising?) about this wish fulfilled? If so, it would certainly explain how he had managed to sustain his bulk in his time here, while disdaining our meals.

Could this be the food we did not know about?

CHAPTER XXIV

Commentary.

Morrison's transcription does not lie: as the end of Renfield's recitation loomed near, he followed the recitation of Milady with the clarification "*He* said." My younger self again disappoints me in that I did not take immediate note of this transmutation of pronoun, which I then assumed to be nothing more than a sign of delirium from a man on the point of a mental and physical break-down. Knowing what I know today, I am now of the opinion that poor Renfield, in the course of his nursing—his fantasy!—witnessed what "Madame Vulpes" had promised him: the revelation of his Master's third and penultimate face—a male face, which he was destined to see at the moment he accepted the terms of his ultimate destiny.

The face of Count Dracula.

Also knowing what I know today, I cannot help but draw a parallel to that horrific scene I would later stumble upon—in the heroic company of Professor Van Helsing, Jonathan, and Quincey—as we intruded on the ghastly scene of Mina taking unholy sustenance from a gash in Dracula's breast. To drink of his cold blood, which could magically spill freely from a nail's incision yet not flow through his veins, made her as one with Dracula's keen senses, and it was her shared seeing and hearing with this monster that ultimately led us to him and enabled his destruction.

Had I known then what I now know! Renfield had previously described himself to me as a "vanguard" whose role was to serve as his Master's "eyes and ears" . . . but I presumed these, at the time, to be little more than the narcissistic rantings of a religious maniac. But now, as I peruse these old materials and compare the dates they bear to those appearing on the diary entries published in Mr. Stoker's book, I can see—to my horror—that Renfield informed me that the Carfax estate was no longer "orphaned" on the very day that the contracts pertaining to the property's sale were signed in distant Transylvania!

In essence, just as Renfield was secretly aware of Dracula's every move—thus engendering a division of consciousness that, in modern parlance, would be considered schizophrenic—it could well be that, during my interviews with Renfield, Dracula himself might have been sitting across from me, his eyes boring into me from the other side of my patient's soul, auditing meetings which I assumed to be privileged. Of course, at this stage, Dracula had nothing whatsoever to fear from Renfield's indiscretions. For all anyone knew, they were nothing more than the ravings of a madman. But the time would come when Renfield would rebel against his puppet master . . . when in retribution all of his marionette strings were severed like the main arteries channeling blood in and out of one's beating heart . . . and, in the midst of that dreaded confrontation, would he be shown the dreaded fourth face of his chosen Lord and Master.

I made certain that mine would be the first face Renfield saw upon recovering consciousness. He slept only fitfully and awoke approximately four hours later. He appeared quite distressed to find himself back inside his room and pleaded with me to take him out of there, to take him back to the chapel or to my office. Watkins and Hardy were back on duty by this time, and I instructed them to escort Renfield to my office and remain there on guard. By this time, Morrison had gone home to bed with my blessing, and rather than summon him back, I decided to record our conversation with the help of Mr. Edison's invention. It was deucedly awkward, having to pause every four minutes to change cylinders, but I did well at keeping the length of our interruptions to a minimum.

Patient's Oral History.

R. M. R.—*You must imagine that everything I have told you is a pack of lies.*

J. L. S.—*Whether they are lies or not, I know them to be true to you . . . and they can convey the truth, sometimes. Besides, I know perfectly well that there are more things in Heaven and Earth than are dreamed of in my philosophy.*

R. M. R.—*Don't bother yourself with the Heaven ones.*

J. L. S.—*Renfield, listen to me. I cannot leave you in that field of cat's tails. The story you have told seems quite complete in itself, and it makes rather a happy ending—for you, at least. But I know that there is no such thing as a truly happy ending; you had to come down from your bliss at some point. You may or may not be an immortal, as you claim, but as sure as you sit before me, I know that your life continued amongst the living.*

R. M. R.—That is true. When I awoke from my swoon in that field of cat's tails, I could see all the colours of the world again. I was healed and whole, but I was alone. I worried that Milady had abandoned me, as mothers are known to do, but I heard her voice inside me reassuring me that I was not alone, that I need never be alone again. I will not leave you comfortless; I will come to you.

As you will remember, I had left the vicarage wearing only a night-shirt with no shoes or stockings. I had nothing but the night-shirt on my back . . . with Jolly in my breast-pocket. He was still there, but unmoving—no longer a person, more like a thing in my pocket like a wallet or a handkerchief—and we left the field of cat's tails and started walking back in the direction of the vicarage.

To judge from the quality of the light, it must have been early morning—but which morning? Had it been the morning of the fire, I imagine that parts of the vicarage would still be burning or smoking or still hot to the touch at the very least . . . but the ruin we eventually reached was cold and ashen and skeletal. There were no gawkers from the village, looking on with pious and triumphal faces. There was only one person at the site of the conflagration—a little boy, raggedly dressed and quite a bit younger than myself, playing and making jagged laughing noises as he danced to and fro, as if playing the part of a flickering flame. We exchanged no words. Above the devastation, whorls of bats were wheeling about in mad patterns—lost now that our bell-tower had fallen and the house with its rafters and its garden arbours had burned to the ground.

I crossed the threshold of the vicarage and stepped onto carpets of ash, which were cool and comforting to my feet. Every room was a shell of what it had been, burned down to its structural bones—heavy oaken planks made thin as spent match-sticks. I ambled through the ghost-house in a daze, amidst animals foraging around in the quest for stray edibles, recognising the remains of the kitchen, the library, the shelf wall where Milady had moved the patch of sunlight. Everything on which I set eyes was a punch in the gut, forcing a regurgitation of memories I was damned to recognise as . . . happy.

I found the stairs that went down to my bedroom, buried under a roasted door and some rubble. As I lifted these out of my path, flies floated up and out like nasty cinders. The cellar's stone walls had ensured that its general floor-plan remained intact. Here I descended into the scene of my crime, its ceiling now made largely of sky. Avoiding the centre-piece of horror, I looked upon the heat-blasted metal framework of my bed, my blackened gutted mattress, the ashes that were once my clothes, a couple of melted treasures, the few surviving pieces of the shattered lamp . . .

Then—when I knew I could avoid it no longer—I turned my eyes on Father, who lay on the ground in a lattice-work of early-morning light, his remains covered in flies. Flies of all sorts were making use of him, creeping inside his nasal cavity and out of a hole surrounded by his char-blackened teeth. I felt a convulsion of love for him. Alone of everyone I had ever known, he had sought to protect me from the worst elements in this miserable and misshapen world—its loathesomeness, its ignorance, and its lovelessness—the very elements that inspired him to want to lead people towards the God he had accepted as his personal saviour. I had called an end to his life and all his good works because he thought the time had come for me to know better, and I knew in what was left of my soul that I owed him something.

I lowered myself to kiss him. The tears from my eyes reached his blistered cheek before my lips, and I saw my tears merge with his remains to create swirls like chocolate and tar. My lips were pursed but my grieving needed air, and as my lips parted, some flies rushed into my mouth! I recoiled, gagging on the flies but also swallowing some of them inadvertently.

After that, Jolly and I could not leave my old room fast enough. As we climbed the stairs back to ground level, wondering whatever was going to become of us now, something quite unexpected—if not miraculous—took place. In the approximate area which had once been Father's office, I saw— hovering at roughly a knee's height above the ground—something as blue as the bluest water you have ever seen, but it was rising up in one spot . . . and crackling! It was a will-o'-the-wisp—*one of the blue flames of legend which Milady had told me about!*

As you may remember, Doctor, these are a phenomenon produced when the treasures buried deep in the earth give evidence of themselves, but it only occurs once per year—on the night of Saint George, which was in April or May . . . but this was later in the year! April and May had already passed! I decided to investigate. The flame did not disappear as I came closer, and it burned with perfect coolth, allowing me to touch it, penetrate it, step inside it. I began to dig at the rubble on the ground with my own two hands. There, under a heap of damage and detritus, I found a blackened metal strong-box, which I forced open. It contained all of Father's savings, perfectly intact.

As I stood there, counting it—there was close to one hundred pounds—I chanced to look outside the standing framework of the office window, which looked out at the churchyard. *There I saw other burning wills-o'-the-wisp!* These were of many different shades of blue, mostly lighter but some deeper and more insistent—all the shades from azure and cyan to beryl and sapphire, I told myself—and as I thought of those very words, it was like Father himself had forgiven me and was talking to me, encouraging me to go out there and find the resources to survive without him, as it would not be easy. And feeling his forgiveness in the direction of my senses, I sank into a heap on the ashen floor and wept once again for all I had lost.

When I recovered myself, I hid the strong-box for the time being and climbed the stone wall into the churchyard, where I went directly to the bluest of all the blue flames. It hovered above the grave of a boy called Rhys Malvern, who had died less than a year before of pneumonia. I had known him, gone to school with him, once upon a time; he was one of the few children who never wronged me, because he was a chubby like me. I did not want to dig open his grave and see what time had done to him, but after all that I had been through, to do this was not so awful. I had done worse; I would do worse. I found something to dig with and stepped inside the flame and began to dig, eventually unearthing Rhys's coffin.

Under its lid, I found a skeleton wearing a suit that was approximately my own size, complete with shoes. A bit on the mouldy side, they were, but something to wear was the most important thing I could have found, after money. Half an hour before, I had nothing—but now I had a suit and shoes and enough money to take care of me for a while.

I shed my night-shirt and watched it waft away like a ghost on a soft breeze, as I redressed in Rhys's stinky things. There were other wills-o'-the-wisp in the churchyard, but I decided to leave them be. Before abandoning the vicarage for good, I looked around a bit more and found—in the rear of a burned bureau drawer which had fallen to ground level when the second floor collapsed—a perfectly preserved handkerchief embroidered with Father's initials, *my* initials, which I wrapped around Jolly to keep him safe and warm. He was feeling cold, and I knew the weather would be turning soon. With that, it was time for us to leave that godless place and move on to other godless places.

J. L. S.—And you survived.

R. M. R.—I survived.

CHAPTER XXV

Commentary.

With that simple statement—"I survived"—I presumed that Renfield's story had now been fully told, but as I was about to find out, the telling of that story—*the real time telling*—was only just beginning.

On 31 August, exactly one week after I made those phonograph recordings, I received a plaintive letter from Arthur informing me that Lucy—who was now back from Whitby—had fallen ill. He was quite concerned about her and made doubly worried by a confidence shared with him by Mrs. Westenra that she was suffering from a disease of the heart and was not long for this world. He dare not share his worry with Mrs. Westenra for fear of upsetting her and prompting an attack, so he wrote to me instead, pleading with me to look in on them—as a friend above all, but, if necessary, also as a professional. Because Arthur impressed upon me that he was aware that he was asking a great deal, I knew the situation might be even more serious than he was allowing and made the trip into town.

Lucy's wan appearance worried me, but her manner was perfectly gay and up-beat . . . until we were left alone; then it was like watching all the air and colour drain out of a festive party balloon. I felt honoured that she would make no pretences about her true feelings when the size of the whole wide world was reduced to just her and me, and I listened with rising alarm as she told me about reverting to her childhood habit of sleepwalking when she was away at Whitby. There was something decidedly unhealthy about her aura, but I felt she was not physically ill. Therefore, I judged that whatever was proving so debilitating to her must be either mental or spiritual in origin.

These were the realms of my old mentor, Professor Abraham Van Helsing, and so I wrote to him at once with a full description of her symptoms and a plea for his opinion. I was taken aback when he replied to my letter in kind and also in person, his sudden presence in London expressing a far greater sense of emergency than was conveyed by his cool and calming communication. I took him to Hillingham, where he performed an examination of Lucy. As long as we were in her company, and that of her mother, my professor's mood was charming and light, but the moment we could speak to one another in confidence, he stunned me with this assessment: **"This is no jest, but life and death, perhaps more."** He had recognised the cause of Lucy's depletion, though the name of our opponent was still unknown to us at the time.

In the meantime, Renfield's story continued. His demons were on the march.

Dr. Seward's Diary.

4 SEPTEMBER.—Renfield still keeps up our interest in him. He had only one outburst and that was yesterday at an unusual time.

Just before the stroke of noon, he began to grow restless. The attendant knew the symptoms, and at once summoned aid. Fortunately the men came at a run, and were just in time, for at the stroke of noon he became so violent that it took all their strength to hold him. In about five minutes, however, he began to get more quiet, and finally sank into a sort of melancholy, in which state he has remained up to now. The attendant tells me that his screams whilst in the paroxysm were really appalling. I found my hands full when I got in, attending to some of the other patients who were frightened by him. Indeed, I can quite understand the effect, for the sounds disturbed even me, though I was some distance away. I made the decision to have Renfield moved below-stairs to our padded room for as long as his railing persisted.

I took the opportunity of his re-location to skim the latest additions to his notebook, which were almost entirely mathematical in nature.

It is now after the dinner hour of the asylum, and as yet my patient sits in a corner of his new quarters brooding, with a dull, sullen, woe-begone look in his face, which seems rather to indicate than to show something directly. I cannot quite understand it.

LATER.—Another change in my patient. At five o'clock I looked in on him and found him seemingly as happy and contented as he used to be. He was catching flies and eating them, and keeping note of his captures by making nail-marks on the edge of the door between the ridges of padding.

When he saw me, he came over and apologised for his bad conduct and asked me in a very humble, cringing way to be led back to his own room, and to have his notebook again. I thought it well to humour him, so he is back in his room with the window open. He has the sugar of his tea spread out on the window sill, and is reaping quite a harvest of flies. He is not now eating them, but putting them into his Bible, as of old, and is already examining the corners of his room to find a spider.

I tried to get him to talk about the past few days, for any clue to his thoughts would be of immense help to me, but he would not rise. For a moment or two, he looked very sad and said, in a sort of far-away voice, as though saying it rather to himself than to me:

"All over! All over! I told you too much and now He has deserted me. No hope for me now . . . unless I do it myself!" Then suddenly turning to me in a resolute way, he said, "Doctor, won't you be very good to me and let me have a little more sugar? I think it would be very good for me."

"And the flies?" I said.

"Yes! The flies like it, too, and I like the flies, therefore I like it."

I procured him a double supply, and left him as happy a man as, I suppose, any in the world. I wish I could fathom his mind.

MIDNIGHT.—Another change in him. I had been to see Lucy, whom I found much better, and had just returned, and was standing at our own gate looking at the sunset, when once more I heard him yelling.

I reached him just as the sun was going down and, from his window, saw the red disc sink. As it sank, he became less and less frenzied and, just as it dipped, he slid from the hands that held him, an inert mass, on the floor. It is wonderful, however, what intellectual recuperative power lunatics have for, within a few minutes, he stood up quite calmly and looked around him.

I signalled to the attendants not to hold him, for I was anxious to see what he would do. He went straight over to the window and brushed out the crumbs of sugar. Then he took his Bible, and emptied it of flies outside, and threw the hollowed Book out the window in their wake. Then he shut the window and, crossing over, sat down on his bed.

All this surprised me, so I asked him, "Aren't you going to keep flies any more?"

"No," said he. "I am sick of all that rubbish! Halo of flies, Bible of lies!"

10 *SEPTEMBER.*—True to his word, Renfield has shown no signs of interest in resuming his insect collection. What could be behind this reversal of events? It is not every day that a dipsomaniacal patient throws away his bottle, or a nymphomaniacal one voluntarily locks herself into a chastity belt! Hardy tells me that he saw flies buzzing freely about the patient's room to-day without him showing them any mind whatsoever—with no feigning about it.

Since the completion of his oral history, two weeks ago, my own relationship with the zoöphagous patient has become less intimate and more officious. Perhaps he feels that he might as well be done with his flies, as I have done with him? He will not speak of it and will not be questioned. His manner is depressed and dejected, and he no longer seems interested in baiting me in his old, accustomed way. On the contrary, he complimented me the other day when he happened to observe that John was the name of the Lord's personal favourite. He then proceeded to boast—if a man with such minimal energies can be said to boast—that he could recite very nearly the entire Book of John from memory, if he cared to do so. *"Then Jesus said unto them,"* he quoted, proving himself, *"Truly, truly, I say to you, unless you eat the flesh of the Son of Man, and drink his blood, you have no life in you."*

Something in his internal landscape has changed . . . what, I do not know and he is not likely to tell me.

17 SEPTEMBER.—I was engaged after dinner in my study posting up my books, which, through press of other work and the many visits to Lucy, had fallen sadly into arrear. Suddenly the door was burst open, and in rushed my patient, with his face distorted with passion. I was thunderstruck, for such a thing as a patient getting of his own accord into the study of the chief superintendent's private quarters is almost unknown.

Without an instant's notice, he made straight at me. He had a dinner-knife in his hand, and, as I saw he was dangerous, I tried to keep the table between us. He was too quick and too strong for me, however; for before I could

get my balance, he had struck at me and cut my left wrist rather severely.

Before he could strike again, however, I got in my right hand and he was sprawling on his back on the floor. My wrist bled freely, and quite a little pool trickled onto the carpet. I saw that my friend was not intent on further effort, and occupied myself binding up my wrist, keeping a wary eye on the prostrate figure all the time.

When the attendants rushed in, and we turned our attention to Renfield, the spectacle of him positively sickened me. He was lying on his belly on the floor licking up the blood which had fallen from my wounded wrist, like a dog. He was easily secured, and to my surprise, went with the attendants quite placidly, simply repeating over and over again, "The blood is the life! The blood is the life!"

I cannot afford to lose blood just at present. I have lost too much of late for my physical good, in providing transfusions for Lucy in Arthur's absence, and then the prolonged strain of her illness and its horrible phases is also telling on me. I am over-excited and weary, and I need rest, rest, rest. Happily, Van Helsing has not summoned me, so I need not forgo my sleep. To-night I could not well do without it.

Commentary.

It was on the date of 18 September, not long after the death of Lord Godalming, that I also received word of the untimely death of Mrs. Lillian Westenra. It was at this time that I left Carfax Asylum for an indefinite period to watch over her daughter at Hillingham in the company of Arthur and Professor Van Helsing.

The atmosphere of that time was rife with unpleasant co-incidence; just as Arthur had learned of Mrs. Westenra's heart condition and the illness of his father on the same day, this day of black news was further darkened as I later learned of the unexpected death, on the same date, of Mr. Peter Hawkins, solicitor—by opening a letter written to Lucy by Mrs. Wilhelmina Harker. The very day before his death (or so Lucy told me), Mr. Hawkins—without wife or family of his own—invited Jonathan and Mina, newly married, to share his house in Exeter with him, where they would live for the rest of their lives. I did not know him well, but it is not necessary to know someone long before recognising them as good.

Another good man is my associate Pat Hennessey, in whose dependable hands I left my duties at Carfax Asylum during my indefinite leave of absence. It was during this period that I received the following relevant correspondence from him. I remember, under the oppressive circumstances, feeling grateful for its comic value. Had the account he describes happened under my watch at the asylum, I would likely have been perturbed, but seeing the mis-hap related from afar nearly made me smile.

Report from Patrick Hennessey, M.D., M.R.C.S.L.K., Q.C.P.I., etc. to John Seward, M.D.

20 September.

My dear Sir:
In accordance with your wishes, I enclose report of the conditions of everything left in my charge. With regard to

the patient Renfield, there is more to say. He has had an-other outbreak, which might have had a dreadful ending, but which fortunately was unattended with any unhappy results.

This afternoon, a carrier's cart with two men made a call at the empty house whose grounds abut on ours, to which, you will remember, the patient twice ran away. The men stopped at our gate to ask the porter their way, as they were strangers.

I was myself looking out of the study window, having a smoke after dinner, and saw one of them come up to the house. As he passed the window of Renfield's room, the patient began to rate him from within and called him foul names. The man, who seemed a decent fellow enough, contented himself by telling him to "shut up for a foul-mouthed beggar." I opened the window and signed to the man not to notice, so he contented himself after looking the place over and making up his mind as to what kind of place he had got to by saying, "Lor' bless yer, sir, I wouldn't mind what was said to me in a bloomin' mad-house. I pity ye and the guv'nor for havin' to live in the house with a wild beast like that."

Then he asked his way civilly enough, and I told him where the gate of the empty house was. He went away, fol-lowed by threats and curses and revilings from our man. I went down to see if I could make out any cause for his anger since, except his violent fits, nothing of the kind had ever occurred. I found him, to my astonishment, quite com-posed and most genial in his manner. I tried to get him to talk of the incident, but he led me to believe that he was

Tim Lucas

*completely oblivious of the affair. It was, I am sorry to
say, only another instance of his cunning, for within half
an hour, he had broken out through the window of his
room, and was running down the avenue.*

*I called to the attendants to follow me, and ran after
him, for I feared he was intent on some mischief. My fear
was justified when I saw the same cart which had passed
before coming down the road, having on it some great
wooden boxes. The men were wiping their foreheads, and
were flushed in the face, as if with violent exercise. Before
I could get up to him, the patient rushed at them, and
pulling one of them off the cart, began to knock his head
against the ground. If I had not seized him, I believe he
would have killed the man. The other fellow jumped down
and struck him over the head with the butt end of his
heavy whip. It was a horrible blow, but he did not seem to
mind it and seized him also, struggling with the three of
us, pulling us to and fro as if we were kittens. You know I
am no lightweight, and the others were also burly men. At
first he was silent in his fighting, but as we began to master him, and the attendants were putting a strait-waistcoat
on him, he began to shout, "I'll frustrate them! They
shan't rob me! They shan't murder me by inches! I'll fight
for my Lord and Master!" and all sorts of incoherent ravings. It was with very considerable difficulty that they got
him back to the house and put him in the padded room.
One of the attendants, Hardy, had a finger broken. However, I set it all right, and he is going on well.*

*The two carriers were at first loud in their threats of ac-
tions for damages, and promised to rain all the penalties*

of the law on us. Their threats were, however, mingled with some sort of indirect apology for the defeat of the two of them by a feeble madman. They said that, if it had not been for the way their strength had been spent in carrying and raising the heavy boxes to the cart, they would have made short work of him. They gave as another reason for their defeat the extraordinary state of drouth to which they had been reduced by the dusty nature of their occupation and the reprehensible distance from the scene of their labours of any place of public entertainment. I understood their drift, and after a stiff glass of strong grog, and with each a sovereign in hand, they made light of the attack, and swore that they would encounter a worse madman any day for the pleasure of meeting so "bloomin' good a bloke" as your correspondent. I took their names and addresses, in case they might be needed.

I shall report to you any matter of interest occurring here, and shall wire you at once if there is anything of importance.

> *Believe me, dear Sir,*
> *Yours faithfully,*
> *Patrick Hennessey.*

This letter was written, and was received by me, on the twentieth—branded into my memory as the day when Van Helsing told me, unequivocally, that Lucy was dying. I think too much of my darling to want to condense or paraphrase material that I have already taken great pains to record—it could only lose its immediacy—so here follows the essential details from my diary of that date.

Dr. Seward's Diary.

20 SEPTEMBER.—Only resolution and habit can let me make an entry to-night. I am too miserable, too low spirited, too sick of the world and all in it, including life itself, that I would not care if I heard this moment the flapping of the wings of the Angel of Death. And he has been flapping those grim wings to some purpose of late, Lucy's mother and Arthur's father, and now . . . Let me get on with my work.

I duly relieved Van Helsing in his watch over Lucy. We wanted Arthur to go to rest also, but he refused at first. It was only when I told him that we should want him to help us during the day, and that we must not all break down for want of rest, lest Lucy should suffer, that he agreed to go.

Lucy lay quite still, and I looked around the room to see that all was as it should be. I could see that the professor had carried out in this room, as in the other, his purpose of using the garlic. The whole of the window sashes reeked with it, and round Lucy's neck, over the silk handkerchief which Van Helsing made her keep on, was a rough chaplet of the same odourous flowers.

Lucy was breathing somewhat stertorously, and her face was at its worst, for the open mouth showed the pale gums. Her teeth, in the dim, uncertain light, seemed longer and sharper than they had been in the morning. In particular, by some trick of the light, the canine teeth looked longer and sharper than the rest.

I sat down beside her, and presently she moved uneasily. At the same moment there came a sort of dull flapping or buffeting at the window. I went over to it softly, and peeped out by the corner of the blind. There was a full moonlight, and I could see that the noise was made by a great bat, which wheeled around, doubtless attracted by the light, although so dim, and every now and again struck the window with its wings. When I came back to my seat, I found that Lucy had moved slightly, and had torn away the garlic flowers from her throat. I replaced them as well as I could, and sat watching her.

Presently she woke, and I gave her food, as Van Helsing had prescribed. She took but a little, and that languidly. There did not seem to be with her now the unconscious struggle for life and strength that had hitherto so marked her illness. It struck me as curious that, the moment she became conscious, she pressed the garlic flowers close to her. It was certainly odd that whenever she got into that lethargic state, with the stertorous breathing, she put the flowers from her, but that when she waked she clutched them close. There was no possibility of making any mistake about this, for in the long hours that followed, she had many spells of sleeping and waking and repeated both actions many times.

At six o'clock Van Helsing came to relieve me. When he saw Lucy's face, I could hear the hissing indraw of breath, and he said to me in a sharp whisper.

"Draw up the blind. I want light!"

Then he bent down, and, with his face almost touching Lucy's, examined her carefully. He removed the flowers and lifted the silk handkerchief from her throat. As he did so he started back and I could hear his *Mein Gott!* as it was smothered in his throat. I bent over and looked, too, and as I noticed some queer chill came over me. The wounds on the throat had absolutely disappeared.

For fully five minutes Van Helsing stood looking at her, with his face at its sternest. Then he turned to me and said calmly, "She is dying. It will not be long now. It will be much difference, mark me, whether she dies conscious or in her sleep. Wake that poor boy, and let him come and see the last. He trusts us, and we have promised him."

I went to the dining room and waked Arthur. I told him as gently as I could that both Van Helsing and I feared that the end was near. He covered his face with his hands, and slid down on his knees by the sofa, where he remained, perhaps a minute, with his head buried, praying, whilst his shoulders shook with grief. I took him by the hand and raised him up.

"Come," I said, "my dear old fellow, summon all your fortitude. It will be best and easiest for her."

When we came into Lucy's room I could see that Van Helsing had, with his usual forethought, been putting matters straight and making everything look as pleasing as possible. He had even brushed Lucy's hair, so that it lay on the pillow in its usual sunny ripples. When we came into the room, she opened her eyes and, seeing him, whispered softly, "Arthur! Oh, my love, I am so glad you have come!"

He was stooping to kiss her when Van Helsing motioned him back.

"No!" he whispered. "Not yet! Hold her hand, it will comfort her more."

So Arthur took her hand and knelt beside her, and gradually her eyes closed, and she sank to sleep. For a little bit, her breast heaved softly, and her breath came and went like a tired child's. And then, insensibly, there came the strange change which I had noticed in the night. Her breathing grew stertorous, the mouth opened, and the pale gums—drawn back—made the teeth look longer and sharper than ever. In a sort of sleepwalking, vague, unconscious way she opened her eyes, which were now dull and hard at once, and said in a soft, voluptuous voice, such as I had never heard from her lips, *"Arthur! Oh, my love, I am so glad you have come! Kiss me!"*

Arthur bent eagerly to kiss her but, at that instant, Van Helsing—who, like me, had been startled by her voice—swooped upon him, and catching him by the neck with both hands, dragged him back with a fury of strength which I never thought he could have possessed, and actually hurled him almost across the room.

"Not on your life!" he said, "not for your living soul and hers!" He stood between them like a lion at bay.

Arthur was so taken aback that he did not for a moment know what to do or say, and before any impulse of violence could seize him, he realised the place and the occasion, and stood silent, waiting.

I kept my eyes fixed on Lucy, as did Van Helsing, and we saw a spasm as of rage flit like a shadow over her face. The sharp teeth clamped together. Then her eyes closed, and she breathed heavily.

Very shortly after she opened her eyes in all their softness, and putting out her poor, pale, thin hand, took Van Helsing's great brown one, drawing it close to her, she kissed it.

"My true friend," she said, in a faint voice, but with untellable pathos, "My true friend—and his! Oh, guard him, and give me peace!"

"I swear it!" he said solemnly, kneeling beside her and holding up his hand, as one who registers an oath. Then he turned to Arthur, and said to him, "Come, my child, take her hand in yours, and kiss her on the forehead—and only once."

My impulse was to spare myself this ultimate pain by looking away, but I did not. Their eyes met instead of their lips, and so they parted. Lucy's eyes closed, and Van Helsing, who had been watching closely, took Arthur's arm, and drew him away. Lucy's breathing became stertorous again, and all at once it ceased.

"It is all over," said Van Helsing. "She is dead!"

I took Arthur by the arm, and led him away to the drawing room, where he sat down, and covered his face with his hands, sobbing in a way that nearly broke me down to see. In a few days time, he had lost the man who had been his Father—his past—and the woman who was to be his wife—his future. What remained of his present, as only I knew, looked upon him quite helplessly, jealously and ruefully, and oh so very hateful of itself.

Commentary.

Lucy's funeral was hastily but lovingly arranged to coincide with that of her mother, and in another remarkable and bittersweet coincidence, the return to London of Jonathan and Wilhelmina Harker.

Mrs. Harker (then Miss Murray) had travelled from

Whitby to Hull, from Hull by boat to Hungary, and then by train to Budapest—all in the duty of fetching her fiancé, who, months after travelling to Transylvania to complete the sale of the Carfax estate, had been found wandering through the countryside in a state of shattered mind. Mina found him "a wreck of himself" at a hospital there, which had summoned her. On 24 August, Jonathan pressed his diary into Mina's hands and—calling her by her full Christian name, as he had only done before when asking for her hand in marriage—beseeched her to read it in full before binding her future to his. She read the entries pertaining to his Transylvanian sojourn and arranged to be married to Jonathan that very day.

As the Harkers returned to London and were riding through Hyde Park, Jonathan was reportedly stricken by a glimpse of a man coming out of a shop: **"I believe it is the Count, but he has grown so young! My God, if this be so! Oh my God, oh my God!"** (*Mina Harker's Journal.*) And thus we came to know the name, nature, and most likely address of our common enemy, though there was still no sign of life at Carfax Abbey.

On 29 September, the day after they were to become man and wife, Arthur—along with Professor Van Helsing, Quincey, and me—visited Lucy in the crypt where she had been laid to rest. In an exercise of unthinkable horror and rigourous self-discipline, we performed the obscene yet Godly acts that needed to be done to make her rest eternal.

We were now warriors of Christ, baptised in blood as we restored peace to our beloved. The loss of Lucy, not to mention the necessity of seeing her beauty mutilated to effect the salvation of her soul, would have been enough to lay waste to my strength and fortitude were it not for the coincidental beginning of my friendship with Mina Harker. She, even more so than Jonathan, seemed to me a kindred spirit, industrious and enterprising—a truly progressive woman. An experienced typist, she was fascinated by my use of the Edison phonograph as a diaristic tool, and I gave her a demonstration; during those days of Jonathan's convalescence and so much loss of life, we were both grateful to each other for the opportunity of ordinary, everyday intercourse. On 30 September, Mina volunteered to transcribe the diary entries I was rapidly accumulating on phonograph cylinder. Of professional necessity, I shared with her only my personal documents—withholding those which pertained to Renfield's oral history.

Dr. Seward's Diary.

30 SEPTEMBER.—After lunch Harker and his wife went back to their own room, and, as I passed a while ago, I heard the click of the typewriter. They are hard at it. Mrs. Harker says that they are knitting together in chronological order every scrap of evidence they have collected. Harker has got the letters between the consignee of the boxes at Whitby and the carriers in London who took charge of them. He is now reading his wife's transcript of my diary. I wonder what they make out of it. Here it is . . .

Strange that it never struck me that the ruin next door might be the Count's hiding place! Goodness knows that we had enough clues from Renfield! The bundle of letters relating to the purchase of the house were with the transcript. Oh, if we had only had them earlier we might have saved poor Lucy . . . *Stop! That way madness lies!* Harker has gone back, and is again collecting material. He says that, by dinner time, they will be able to show a whole connected narrative. He thinks that in the meantime I should see Renfield, as hitherto he has been a sort of index to the coming and going of the Count. I hardly see this yet, but when I get at the dates I suppose I shall. What a good thing that Mrs. Harker put my cylinders into type! We never could have found the dates otherwise.

I found Renfield sitting placidly in his room with his hands folded, smiling benignly. At the moment he seemed as sane as anyone I ever saw. I sat down and talked with him on a lot of subjects, all of which he treated naturally. The recording of his oral histories have evidently served a cathartic purpose for the patient; he comported himself as thoroughly purged of anger and frustration. He then, of his own accord, spoke of going home, a subject he has never mentioned to my knowledge during his sojourn here. In fact, he spoke quite confidently of getting his discharge at once. I believe that, had I not had the chat with Harker and read the letters and the dates of his outbursts, I should have been prepared to sign for him after a brief time of observation. As it is, I am darkly suspicious. *All those outbreaks were in some way linked with the proximity of the Count.* What then does this absolute content mean? However, after a while, I came away. I mistrust these quiet moods of his, so I have given the attendant a hint to look closely after him, and to have a strait-waistcoat ready in case of need.

CHAPTER XXVI

Dr. Seward's Diary.

SAME DAY, LATER.—I got home at five o'clock, and found that Godalming [Arthur, having attained the title after the death of his father] and Morris had not only arrived, but had already studied the transcript of the various diaries and letters which Harker had not yet returned from his visit to the carriers' men, of whom Doctor Hennessey had written to me. Mrs. Harker gave us a cup of tea, and I can honestly say that, for the first time since I have lived in it, this old house seemed like home.

When we had finished, Mrs. Harker said, "Doctor Seward, may I ask a favour? I want to see your patient, Mr. Renfield. Do let me see him. What you have said of him in your diary interests me so much!"

She looked so appealing and so pretty that I could not refuse her—and there was no possible reason why I should, so I took her with me.

When I went into the room, I told Renfield that a lady would like to see him, to which he simply answered, "Why?"

"She is going through the house, and wants to see everyone in it," I answered.

"Oh, very well," he said. "Let her come in, by all means, but just wait a minute till I tidy up the place."

His method of tidying was peculiar. He simply swallowed all the flies and spiders in the boxes before I could stop him! It was quite evident that he feared, or was jealous of, some interference. When he had got through his disgusting task, he said cheerfully, "Let the lady come in," and sat down on the edge of his bed with his head down—but with his eyelids raised so that he could see her as she entered. For a moment I thought that he might have some homicidal intent. I remembered how quiet he had been just before he attacked me in my own study, and I took care to stand where I could seize him at once if he attempted to make a spring at her.

Mrs. Harker came into the room with an easy gracefulness which would at once command the respect of any lunatic, for easiness is one of the qualities mad people most respect. She walked over to him, smiling pleasantly, and held out her hand.

"Good evening, Mr. Renfield," said she. "You see, I know you, for Doctor Seward has told me of you."

Renfield made no immediate reply, but eyed her all over intently with a set frown on his face. This look gave way to one of wonder, which merged in doubt, then to my intense astonishment, he said, "You're not the girl the doctor wanted to marry, are you? You can't be, you know, for she's dead."

Mrs. Harker managed her own personal feelings for Lucy

admirably. Without so much as a flinch, she **smiled sweetly** as she replied, "Oh no! I have a husband of my own, to whom I was married before I ever saw Doctor Seward, or he me. I am Mrs. Harker."

"Then what are you doing here?"

"My husband and I are staying on a visit with Doctor Seward."

At this, Renfield blurted out, "Don't stay!"

"But why not?"

I thought that this style of conversation might not be pleasant to Mrs. Harker, any more than it was to me, so I joined in, "Renfield, how did you know I wanted to marry anyone?"

His reply was simply contemptuous, given in a pause in which he turned his eyes from Mrs. Harker to me, instantly turning them back again: "What an asinine question!"

"I don't see that at all, Mr. Renfield," said Mrs. Harker, at once championing me.

He replied to her with as much courtesy and respect as he had shown contempt to me. "You will, of course, understand, Mrs. Harker, that when a man is so loved and honoured as our host is, everything regarding him is of interest in our little community. Doctor Seward is loved not only by his household and his friends, but even by his patients, who, being some of them hardly in mental equilibrium, are apt to distort causes and effects. Since I, myself, have been an inmate of a lunatic asylum, I cannot but notice that the sophistic tendencies of some of its inmates lean towards the errors of *non causa* and *ignoratio elenche*."

I positively opened my eyes at this new development.

Here was my own pet lunatic, the most pronounced of his type that I had ever met with, talking elemental philosophy! I wonder if it was Mrs. Harker's presence which had touched some chord in his memory. If this new phase was spontaneous, or in any way due to her unconscious influence, she must have some rare gift or power.

We continued to talk for some time, and seeing that he was seemingly quite reasonable, Mrs. Harker ventured—looking at me questioningly as she began—to lead Renfield to his favourite topic. I was again astonished, for he addressed himself to the question with the impartiality of the completest sanity. He even took himself as an example when he mentioned certain things.

"Why, I myself am an instance of a man who had a strange belief. Indeed, it was no wonder that friends like Doctor Seward were alarmed, and insisted on my being put under control. I used to fancy that by consuming a multitude of live things, no matter how low in the scale of creation, one might indefinitely prolong life. I held the belief so strongly that I actually tried to take human life. The doctor here will bear me out that, on one occasion, I tried to kill him for the purpose of strengthening my vital powers by the assimilation with my own body of his life through the medium of his blood—isn't that true, Doctor?"

I nodded assent, for I was so amazed that I hardly knew what to either think or say, it was hard to imagine that I had seen him eat up his spiders and flies not five minutes before. Looking at my watch, I saw that I should go to the station to meet Van Helsing, so I told Mrs. Harker that it was time to leave.

She came at once, after saying pleasantly to Mr. Ren-field, "Good-bye, and I hope I may see you often, under auspices pleasanter to yourself."

To which, to my astonishment, he replied, "Good-bye, my dear. I pray God I may never see your sweet face again. May He bless and keep you!"

1 OCTOBER, 4:00 A.M.—Just as we gentlemen were about to leave the house with the intention of breaking into Car-fax Abbey, an urgent message was brought to me from Ren-field to know if I would see him at once, as he had something of the utmost importance to say to me. I told the messenger to say that I would attend to his wishes in the morning; I was busy just at the moment.

The attendant added, "He seems very importunate, sir. I have never seen him so eager. I don't know but what, if you don't see him soon, he will have one of his violent fits." I knew the man would not have said this without some cause, so I said, "All right, I'll go now," and I asked the others to wait a few minutes for me, as I had to go and see my patient.

"Take me with you, friend John," said the professor. "His case in your diary interests me much, and it had bear-ing, too, now and again on our case. I should much like to see him, and especial when his mind is disturbed."

"May I come also?" asked Lord Godalming.

"Me too?" said Quincey Morris.

"May I come?" said Harker.

Bemused but feeling better for their companionship, I nodded, and we all went down the passage together.

We found Renfield in a state of considerable excitement, but far more rational in his speech and manner than I had ever seen him. There was an unusual understanding of himself, which was unlike anything I had ever met with in a lunatic, and he took it for granted that his reasons would prevail with others entirely sane. We all five went into the room, but none of the others at first said anything.

His request was that I would at once release him from the asylum and send him home. This he backed up with arguments regarding his complete recovery, and adduced his own existing sanity.

"I appeal to your friends," he said. "They will, perhaps, not mind sitting in judgement on my case. By the way, you have not introduced me."

I was so much astonished, that the oddness of introducing a madman in an asylum did not strike me at the moment, and besides, there was a certain dignity in the man's manner, so much of the habit of equality, that I at once made the introduction: "Lord Godalming . . . Professor Van Helsing . . . Mr. Quincey Morris, of Texas . . . Mr. Jonathan Harker . . . Gentlemen, this is Mr. Renfield."

He shook hands with each of them, saying in turn, "Lord Godalming, I had the honour of seconding your father at the Windham. I grieve to know, by your holding the title, that he is no more. He was a man loved and honoured by all who knew him, and in his youth was, I have heard, the inventor of a burned rum punch, much patronised on Derby night. Mr. Morris, you should be proud of your great state. Its reception into the Union was a precedent which may have far-reaching effects hereafter, when the Pole and the

Tropics may hold alliance to the Stars and Stripes. The power of Treaty may yet prove a vast engine of enlargement, when the Monroe Doctrine takes its true place as a political fable. And finally . . . what shall any man say of his pleasure at meeting Van Helsing? Sir, I make no apology for dropping all forms of conventional prefix. When an individual has revolutionised therapeutics by his discovery of the continuous evolution of brain matter, conventional forms are unfitting, since they would seem to limit him to one of a class. You, gentlemen, who—by nationality, by heredity, or by the possession of natural gifts—are fitted to hold your respective places in the moving world, I take to witness that I am as sane as at least the majority of men who are in full possession of their liberties. And I am sure that you, Doctor Seward, humanitarian and medico-jurist as well as scientist, will deem it a moral duty to deal with me as one to be considered as under exceptional circumstances."

I think we were all staggered. I contented myself with making a general statement that he appeared to be improving very rapidly, that I would have a longer chat with him in the morning, and would then see what I could do in the direction of meeting his wishes.

This did not at all satisfy him, for he said quickly, "But I fear, Doctor Seward, that you hardly apprehend my wish. I desire to go at once—here, now, this very hour, this very moment, if I may! Time presses and, in our implied agreement with the old scytheman, it is of the essence of the contract. I am sure it is only necessary to put before so admirable a practitioner as Doctor Seward so simple, yet so momentous a wish, to ensure its fulfillment."

He looked at me keenly, cupping a balled fist with a relaxed hand, and seeing the negative in my face, turned to the others, and scrutinised them closely. Not meeting any sufficient response, he went on, "Is it possible that I have erred in my supposition?"

"You have," I said frankly.

"But I wish to go home!" he insisted.

"Where is 'home'?" I asked directly—but, at the same time, as I felt, brutally. Naturally, Renfield had no answer for this.

Van Helsing was gazing at the patient with a look of utmost intensity, his bushy eyebrows almost meeting with the fixed concentration of his look. He said to Renfield in a tone which did not surprise me at the time, but only when I thought of it afterwards, for it was as of one addressing an equal, "Can you not tell frankly your real reason for wishing to be free tonight?"

Renfield shook his head sadly, and with a look of poignant regret on his face.

The professor went on, "Come, sir, bethink yourself. You claim the privilege of reason in the highest degree, since you seek to impress us with your complete reasonableness. You do this, whose sanity we have reason to doubt, since you are not yet released from medical treatment for this very defect. If you will not help us in our effort to choose the wisest course, how can we perform the duty which you yourself put upon us? Be wise, and help us, and if we can, we shall aid you to achieve your wish."

He still shook his head as he said, "Professor Van Helsing, I have nothing to say. Your argument is complete, and if I were free to speak I should not hesitate a moment, but I am not my own master in the matter. I can only ask you to trust me. If I am refused, the responsibility does not rest with me."

I thought it was now time to end the scene, which was becoming too comically grave, so I went towards the door, simply saying, "Come, my friends, we have work to do. Good-night."

As, however, I got near the door, a new change came over the patient. He moved towards me so quickly that, for the moment, I feared that he was about to make another homicidal attack. My fears, however, were groundless, for he held up his two hands imploringly, and renewed his petition in a moving manner. As he saw that the very excess of his emotion was militating against him, by restoring us more to our old relations, he became still more demonstrative.

When he found that his appeal would not be successful, he got into quite a frantic condition. He threw himself on his knees, and held up his hands, wringing them in plaintive supplication, and poured forth a torrent of entreaty, with the tears rolling down his cheeks, and his whole face and form expressive of the deepest emotion.

"Let me entreat you, Doctor Seward, oh, let me implore you, to let me out of this house at once! Send me away how you will and where you will! Send keepers with me with whips and chains! Let them take me in a strait-waistcoat, manacled and leg-ironed—even to gaol!—but let me out of this room! You don't know what you do by keeping me here. I am speaking from the depths of my heart, of my very soul! You don't know whom you wrong, or how, and I may not tell. *Woe is me! I may not tell!* By all you hold sacred, by all you hold dear, by your love that is lost, by your hope that lives, for the sake of the Almighty, take me out of this and save my soul from guilt!" Here he came to a stop—and then, once again, a renewed outburst: *"Can't you hear me, man? Can't you understand? Will you never learn? Don't you know that I am sane and earnest now, that I am no lunatic in a mad fit, but a sane man fighting for his soul? Oh, hear me! Hear me! Let me go, let me go, let me go!"*

I thought that, the longer this went on, the wilder he would get, so I took him by the hand and raised him up. "Come," I said sternly, "no more of this, we have had quite enough already. Your soul, your soul, your soul. What about the other souls at risk? Now to your bed and try to behave more discreetly."

He suddenly stopped and looked at me intently for several moments. Then, without a word, he rose and, moving over, sat down on the side of the bed. The collapse had come, as on former occasions, just as I had expected.

When I was leaving the room, the last of our party, he said to me in a quiet, well-bred voice, "You will, I trust, Doctor Seward, do me the justice to bear in mind, later on, that I did what I could to convince you tonight?"

CHAPTER XXVII

Dr. Seward's Diary.

SAME DAY, LATER.—Harker is out, following up clues, and so are Lord Godalming and Quincey. Van Helsing sits in my study poring over the record prepared by the Harkers. He seems to think that by accurate knowledge of all details he will light upon some clue. He does not wish to be disturbed in the work, without cause. I would have taken him with me to see Renfield, only I thought that, after his last repulse, he might not care to go again. There was also another reason. Renfield might not speak so freely before a third person as when he and I were alone.

I found him sitting in the middle of the floor on his stool, a pose which is generally indicative of some mental energy on his part. When I came in, he said at once, as though the question had been waiting on his lips. "What about souls?"

"What about them, yourself?" I asked.

He did not reply for a moment but looked all around

him, and up and down, as though he expected to find some inspiration for an answer.

"I don't want any souls!" he said in a feeble, apologetic way.

The matter seemed preying on his mind, and so I determined to use it, to "be cruel only to be kind." So I said, "You like life, and you want life?"

"Oh yes! But that is all right. You needn't worry about that!"

"But," I asked, "how are you to get the life without getting the soul also?"

This seemed to puzzle him, so I followed it up, "A nice time you'll have sometime when you're flying out here, with the souls of thousands of flies and spiders and birds and cats buzzing and twittering and moaning all around you. You've got their lives, you know, and you must put up with their souls!"

Something seemed to affect his imagination, for Renfield put his fingers to his ears and shut his eyes, screwing them up tightly just as a small boy does when his face is being soaped. There was something pathetic in it that touched me. It also gave me a lesson, for it seemed that before me was a child, only a child, though the features were worn, and the stubble on the jaws was white. It was evident that he was undergoing some process of mental disturbance, and knowing how his past moods had interpreted things seemingly foreign to himself, I thought I would enter into his mind as well as I could and go with him.

The first step was to restore confidence, so I asked him, speaking pretty loud so that he would hear me through his closed ears, "Would you like some sugar to get your flies around again?"

He seemed to wake up all at once, and shook his head. With a laugh he replied, "Not much! Flies are poor things, after all!" After a pause he added, "But I don't want their souls buzzing round me, all the same."

"Or spiders?" I went on.

"Blow spiders! What's the use of spiders? There isn't anything in them to eat or . . ."

He stopped suddenly at the word *drink*.

Renfield seemed himself aware of having made a lapse, for he hurried on, as though to distract my attention from it, "I don't take any stock at all in such matters. '*Rats and mice and such small deer,*' as Shakespeare has it, 'chicken feed of the larder' they might be called. I'm past all that sort of nonsense. You might as well ask a man to eat molecules with a pair of chopsticks, as to try to interest me about the lesser *carnivora*, when I know of what is before me."

"I see," I said. "You want big things that you can make your teeth meet in? Like my poor wrist, I suppose! Perhaps we could do better than that . . . How would you like to breakfast on an elephant?"

"What ridiculous nonsense you are talking?"

He was getting too wide awake, so I thought I would press him hard. "I wonder," I said reflectively, "what an *elephant's* soul is like!"

The effect I desired was obtained, for he at once fell from his high-horse and became a child again.

"I don't want an elephant's soul, or any soul at all!" he

said. For a few moments he sat despondently. Suddenly he jumped to his feet, with his eyes blazing and all the signs of intense cerebral excitement. "To Hell with you and your souls!" he shouted. "Why do you plague me about souls? Haven't I got enough worry and pain to distract me already, without thinking of souls?"

He looked so hostile that I thought he was in for another homicidal fit, so I blew my whistle.

The instant, however, that I did so he became calm, and said apologetically, "Forgive me, Doctor, I forgot myself. You do not need any help. I am so worried in my mind that I am apt to be irritable. If you only knew the problem I have to face, and that I am working out, you would pity and tolerate and pardon me. Pray do not put me in a strait-waistcoat. I want to think and I cannot think freely when my body is confined. I am sure you will understand!"

He had evidently self-control, so when the attendants came I told them not to mind, and they withdrew. Renfield watched them go. When the door was closed, he said with considerable dignity and sweetness, "Doctor Seward, you have been very considerate towards me. Believe me that I am very, very grateful to you!"

I thought it well to leave him in this mood, and so I came away.

Commentary.

Though I had no way of knowing this at the time, Renfield's surprisingly tender expression of gratitude would mark the last of our private conversations.

Dr. Seward's Diary.

2 OCTOBER.—I placed a man in the corridor last night, and told him to make an accurate note of any sound he might hear from Renfield's room, and gave him instructions that, if there should be anything strange, he was to call me.

Before going to bed I went round to the patient's room and looked in through the observation trap. He was sleeping soundly, his heart rose and fell with regular respiration.

This morning, the man on duty reported to me that, a little after midnight, Renfield was restless and kept saying his prayers somewhat loudly. I asked him if that was all. He replied that it was all he heard. There was something about his manner, so suspicious that I asked him point blank if he had been asleep. He denied sleep, but admitted to having "dozed" for a while.

It is too bad that men cannot be trusted unless they are watched.

Today, Harker is out following up his clue, and Art and Quincey are looking after horses. Godalming thinks that it will be well to have horses always in readiness for, when we get the information which we seek, there will be no time to lose. Van Helsing is off to the British Museum looking up some authorities on ancient medicine. The old physicians took account of things which their followers do not accept, and the professor is searching for witch and demon cures which may be useful to us later.

I sometimes think we must be all mad and that we shall wake to sanity in strait-waistcoats.

LATER.—We have all met again. We seem at last to be on

the track, and our work of to-morrow may be the beginning of the end. Renfield's moods have so followed the doings of the Count, that the coming destruction of the monster may be carried to him some subtle way. He is now seeming quiet for a spell. Is he?

"GOD! GOD! GOD!"

Wait! That wild yell seemed to come from his room . . .

The attendant has just come bursting into my room to tell me that Renfield has somehow met with some accident. He found him lying on his face on the floor, all covered with blood. I must go at once . . .

CHAPTER XXVIII

Commentary.

The death—no, the murder—of my patient R. M. Renfield left me grief-stricken and deeply so, though I would not realise this until some time after his Master had been destroyed and my thoughts slowly returned to being my own.

Without Renfield and the conundrum he presented, there was nothing more to distract me from my thoughts of Lucy—which were now the thoughts of her victimisation, her death, her Un-Dead preying on small children as the dreaded "Bloofer Lady" of the newspapers, and, ultimately, the terrible means by which her soul was freed from Dracula's captivity. I nearly died from over-indulgence of morphine and surely would have done, if the good Patrick Hennessey had not recognised my symptoms and intervened, saving me from the dire sink-hole within myself.

As for Renfield, he was swept up like broken glass to be dumped into a pauper's grave. I intervened to make arrangements for a proper service and burial and headstone; it is true that he tried to destroy us, and made an attempt on my own life in the process, but in the end, he was as valiant a crusader as any of us in the war against Count Dracula. As I provided what few details I could to his death certificate, I hesitated over the blank space requesting the decedent's Christian name and felt very strongly that he needed the protection of one before we parted for ever. He was ultimately laid to rest under the full name of Rhys Malvern Renfield. May no fire find him, be it blue or red.

As he had intimated to me, that last time, as he regained consciousness with all of us assembled around him, I found his notebook inside his right trouser pocket—partially soiled with the blood he had lost but still readable.

I close this tragic document with the final entries inscribed in his own struggling hand . . .

From Renfield's Notebook.

If I could but take all the pain out of myself and leave it here upon this page, where it might be absorbed into the abstraction of language! If I cannot succeed in doing this, have I the right to call this effort successful? I was promised I could discharge my demons and devils into a book such as this, so why is it not accomplished?

The Master was devious to place me here, where no one will listen to me. No one will heed my warnings, being the warnings of a madman, though my only wish now is not for myself, but to see that the sweet lady who spoke to me is protected! Only I know how He looks upon her, how He covets her because I saw it with my own eyes; only I know how her voice delights His ears like a music of bells, because I heard them too! Only I know the stirrings He felt—and only I could feel them as one still living!

She spoke to me, took my hand. She made me wish that

I could be anything but what I am. O give me my freedom that I may set us all free—but this kind lady most of all!

I must effect some change for the better . . . I gave my death for the Master, but if I am now to give my life as well, as I feel bound to do, may I live on at least in the memory of a single deed that was not repugnant.

I address these pages to Doctor Jack Seward, my friend and benefactor . . . I may be a pawn but I am not a fool, least not a perpetually sleepy one, so I have reason to believe that you have been putting something in my tea and juice to gain access to this notebook.

I trust it has been, and will continue to be, helpful to you as the nature of your cause—this battle in which you find yourself embroiled—becomes more apparent. Know that in no way do I regard your peeks into this book as a betrayal of my trust; on the contrary, I only wish I could have been of greater assistance to you.

By the time you read these words, I imagine that I shall be far from here, whether in Heaven or Hell I do not know. There is much I have not yet told you, and I may now never have the opportunity unless I seize upon this moment of clarity to tell you all I can, here and now.

I never had the opportunity to tell you how I managed to survive through the many years—indeed, decades—which followed that morning when I left my village, wearing a dead boy's suit and carrying poor Jolly in my pocket—so I seize that opportunity now, because I am dreadful of what the coming hours may hold for me.

Part of the answer lies in the phenomenon of the blue

flames I described to you. These are the means by which those who follow the Master and share His goals finance their devotions. Surviving into adulthood required a certain amount of stealth and dishonesty, I must own . . . but, by the time I was twenty-five, I had amassed a great deal of wealth, all of it wrested from the ground and much of it plucked from the hands of the buried dead—enough to sustain my existence comfortably, indeed to insinuate myself into certain corners of London society. By day I lived on an equal footing with men of wealth and influence, and by night, I would use my manicured hands to dig at the damp ground like a mole for items of importance dropped and forgotten: coins, jewels, gold-encrusted keepsakes, even papers of entitlement. Each night, I would leave my comfortable house and walk until I could see, alone out of everyone walking the streets of London and environs, those wondrous flickering flames of blue—and grieve as, inevitably, they began to dim.

This dimming was my signal that the time had come to "renew my vows," if you will pardon the blasphemy. The fading of the flames meant that it was time for me to find another small animal to prey upon, one innocent and trusting of me as dear Jolly had been. Only the taste of blood would bring Milady back to me, *the taste of Milady* back to me. Sometimes it was easier than others to find animals, but it was never easy to do away with them; you know how I feel about the little creatures.

Sometimes as I was out walking, a lost puppy would attach itself to me and follow me home, and I would have no choice but to take it in. There is one I remember particularly: a black spaniel whose name-tag read "Samson." He could not have been more than four months old, and it had plainly been some days since he had his last meal. Abandoned, most likely. I was holding out, do you see, and a couple of months in arrears with my rent, at the time; I was being threatened with eviction when he latched onto me so eagerly. I took him home with me and resisted my impulse—*no, my duty!*—for one night, and then two, just for the sake of his sweet companionship. He broke my heart with his affections, which were initially quite desperate, almost as desperate as his need for nourishment. As I gave him some suitable food, he was so witless with joy at the prospect of dinner and a little love that he jumped convulsively between his bowl and me, licking both gratefully. I could not help but imagine that this was how I must have looked to Milady, that night in the field. Once Samson began to trust my hospitality, he settled down and we rested together on my sofa, both of us breathing in deeply of a shared moment of profound contentment . . . which is always the most blessed time with animals . . . and then I took him up and embraced him, weeping, until I snapped his neck and tore his flesh and drank my fill of him. The next night I dined in the best restaurant in London and raised a glass of the finest French champagne to that little dog's memory.

When I was first brought into your care, Doctor, I looked destitute because I had resisted my calling for nearly two years, so appalled was I at what I had become. I lost everything during those two years, everything I had accumulated over the past forty. I walked until the soles of my shoes had nearly worn away, until my coat stank of the unwashed man it protected from the elements, until my trousers were torn and shiny. I would sleep in public parks, under bridges, in abandoned houses, even gardens with the other homeless children of the night—dogs, cats, foxes, mice, some of them huddling close to me for warmth on cold nights, unaware of how sorely they tempted me. But I resisted. I took their love, but not their lives—that is, until that night on the grounds of the Carfax estate. Can you imagine my plight, Doctor—not being able to die, *yet not being able to live*? For I knew that, if I did succumb once again, I would be renewing a contract which bound me to do so again and again.

And regardless of how long I succeeded in resisting the will of the Master, He continued to decide my every movement, do you see? I might never have found Carfax Abbey if I had not seen in my vagabond travels someone in the distance who looked ever so much like Milady. It may not have been the Milady of my past, the one who lives on in my mouth, because there are so many Miladies—all in His service. But this one led me onto the grounds of the Carfax property like an irresistible fragrance or flavour, an old taste from the past—and when I first saw you, good doctor, standing in the midst of this madhouse in your evening finery, I could tell by simply looking at your face that you had seen her, too. It was all a puppet show, of course—a means to bring me here that I might keep watch on His property and gain Him entrance to your asylum and your private rooms and poor Miss Mina, whose photograph He had seen among Mr. Harker's belongings in Transylvania and did ferociously covet.

And though there was nothing I had not sacrificed to find His favour, I did not remain young because the gift of eternal youth was withheld from me until I had made good on my moment of usefulness! I grew old waiting for my moment of deliverance to come. The Master sent me gifts to keep me going . . . gifts that flew, gifts that crawled, gifts that filled my mouth again with mother's milk . . . but after I had spoken of

383

Him to you, I could make use of no more than one per day. The madness became greater, the arc of the sun intolerable to my disposition. Perhaps He was testing me, or perhaps He was merely being cruel and showing me who was Boss . . . but then, in my craftiness, I struck upon the idea of feeding ten to eight and eight to six and six to three and three to one, so that for each fly I was allowed to eat, it was equal to ten. When I had proved my strategic talents to the Master, he forgave me and allowed me spiders . . . and then birds . . .

He was always a mist to me, a mood or an atmosphere, sometimes no more than a glint in Milady's eye . . . I did not see the Master in his human form until he came here—here to my room, last evening—the moment for which I have lived more years than I care to admit. How I adored Him! But He brushed past me, wanting only my invitation to enter—as though I were naught but a red carpet! I may be worthless and a weakling, but I tell you, Doctor, I have given too much of myself, of my soul, to be treated like that.

They say that madmen have the strength of ten. Tonight, for the sake of Miss Mina, I shall allow myself to dwell on my thwartings and my frustrations and all that I have lost and sacrificed so that I may be at my maddest—and then I shall dare to match my strength against His. I do this for Miss Mina and for the memory of my late mother. In the moments when I am most myself, such as now, I cannot forgive myself, knowing that I wronged her so terribly and unforgivably.

Whether to-night I should win or lose, I beg of you, my friend—who has struggled to understand me, as I have struggled under a will much greater than my own to understand myself—*pray for me*.

CODA

In that day mankind will cast away their idols of silver and their idols of gold, which they made for themselves to worship, to the moles and to the bats, to enter the caverns of the rocks and the clefts of the cliffs, from before the terror of the Lord, and from the splendor of His majesty, when He rises to terrify the earth.

—Isaiah 2:20–21

Afterword by Martin Seward.

The Book of Renfield was completed by my great-grandfather in 1939 but never published—not in his lifetime, nor in the years when his son or his son's son were alive and in possession of its raw materials.

According to various papers in my possession, Jack Seward found the road to publication blocked by the success of the Bram Stoker novel *Dracula*. When my ancestor decided in the mid-1930s that sufficient time had passed since Renfield's death to make the larger account of his story known, London publishers took him to be a laughingstock for insisting that the late Mr. Stoker (who died in 1912) had merely lent his name to a variety of authentic diary and epistolary scraps written by others. He received no support from Mrs. Florence Stoker, as it was in her best interests to perpetuate that version of events for the remaining years of her widowhood. An interested publisher was eventually found, but Mrs. Stoker threatened legal action against the company, were the book to include any of the diary entries actually written (that is, recorded) by Doctor Seward, which had previously appeared in the pages of *Dracula*—which were then, of course, under the iron-clad protection of her copyright. Florence

Stoker died in 1937; three years later, Jack Seward found his own way to life's secret egress, a victim of the London blitz of September 7, 1940.

It was a triumph for fiction and a triumph for Dracula.

When I inherited my ancestor's manuscript and its related materials upon the death of my father in April 1995, I had the only reaction to their existence possible for someone who had grown up with the inescapable media image of Count Dracula: I convinced myself that it was all someone's idea of a joke.

My father, you see, had kept this chapter of our family history very much to himself; it was never so much as whispered about between my parents, so far as I could overhear, and I heard more pass between them in my time than a son should. As I opened aged morocco bindings and rifled through sheaves of transcription, and, above all, as I learned how to play wax cylinders on my ancestor's still-operable Edison phonograph, my mind struggled to assimilate everything by concocting more easily digestible lies by way of explanation. Had this Doctor Seward, my great-grandfather, cultivated a sophisticated sense of the absurd while running his asylum for the insane in Purfleet? In order to vent professional steam, did he, in his spare time, concoct this material as a sort of before-its-time, multimedia farce?

As I continued to plow through it all, seeking to understand it, such explanations failed to satisfy and I became increasingly absorbed in the material, its depth and variety—which included Ralph Morrison's careful transcriptions, etched in fading trails of fountain pen, and the typescripts made by Mrs. Harker. But my final understanding of the documents was clinched by my ancestor's surviving diary cylinders, which could not be forged and corresponded—exactly at times—to the journal entries ascribed to a character of his exact name in Bram Stoker's "novel" of 1897.

As the truth of the materials dawned on me, I had the sensation of having touched pitch and been defiled—which Anthony Burgess once described as the responsibility of all good novelists. Being a novelist myself, I know all too well how lies can be made to look legitimate, and I wanted very much to believe that this is what my ancestor had done. Taking the step of believing in the veracity of my bequest meant accepting that everything I thought I knew and understood of my rational world—a world wherein monsters such as Dracula exist only in literature or on film—was false. The only reason I could conceive for such prevailing falsehoods to be in place was that, somehow, the monsters (that is, those secular or political forces for whom literature and film conceived such monsters as metaphor) had won. As Professor Van Helsing had cautioned, that people do not commonly believe in the Supernatural is perhaps its greatest defense.

My ancestor admitted to surrendering to an old morphine addiction while preparing *The Book of Renfield*; my own defilement, as I became better acquainted with my bequest, took the no-less-destructive form of an extreme and bitter cynicism. I felt myself in possession of a great truth unknown as truth to others, and ultimately unsharable with anyone. It was the same despair that might also be felt on a daily basis, for all I knew (or know), by living, tight-lipped people who know the true identity of JFK's assassin or assassins, or whether or not extraterrestrial vehicles did in fact once crash in the Arizona desert.

Even now, I find that whenever I am faced with anything fictional, especially fiction of a more shocking variety, I begin to wonder if the whole construct might not be a proverbial sugar pill, a palliative to ease lite-similes of difficult truths still to come down the gullets of a sheeplike public. It wouldn't surprise me if more documentary evidence were forthcoming someday from my father's attorney—papers, for example, that might prove beyond doubt that Renfield did not die at Carfax Asylum but had instead moved to America, where he assumed a new identity—Walt Disney perhaps— another man, after all, who kept company with a mouse, a mouse who helped him to amass a fortune, a fortune that he used to erect a castle on the Western coast of the new conti- nent, thus completing the arc of Vlad Drakul's plans for worldwide conquest! Who was to say that such a conquest wasn't successfully carried out under our very noses? Tokyo Disneyland opened its gates in 1983—at approximately the same time Disney began to relinquish its formerly wholesome image by releasing films with PG-13 and R ratings. A case *could* be made . . .

Such flights of whimsy were my only means of coping with the otherwise unfaceable concept that this myth, this bogeyman Dracula—who so permeates our culture in Hal- loween costumes, on cereal boxes, in movies good, bad, and ridiculous—was rooted in the fact of a royal hellion who had crossed the ocean from his depleted country to England, who fed upon bloodlines very close to my own to sustain himself, and spoke with his dying breath the family name of Seward.

Accepting that *Dracula* was not a novel by Bram Stoker—but rather a true account by various authors of a thwarted attack on British soil by legions of the dead, spearheaded by a bloodthirsty Middle Eastern conqueror—meant that I would also have to accept Dracula's pride of place in popular culture—in the movies I loved, the Aurora model kit I built as a child, Count Chocula, and the rest of it—as implicitly dangerous, since it enticed people of all cultures to befriend the image of what my ancestor had called "the Un-Dead"—in effect, to let down their guards and welcome it into their homes.

It was once said that Bram Stoker's *Dracula* was second only to the Holy Bible as a source of material for motion pictures, and today, the Holy Bible almost certainly lags in second place. I asked myself: Had Dracula, despite his demise, somehow succeeded in besting Van Helsing, my grandfather's father and his valiant friends? Had he not once again survived his own death and become immortal?

With these thoughts dogging my consciousness, I began to feel that my bequest had been presented to me as a sacred duty. I put aside the novel I was writing and dedicated myself to the task of salvaging my ancestor's shattered dream. I set to work on preparing a sample chapter/outline presentation, built around Jack Seward's Foreword, which my agent sent around with the hook that *The Book of Renfield* could be readied for publication to coincide with the coming *Dracula* centenary in 1997.

To our great disappointment—though Stoker's book had not once been out of print in the near-century since its initial publication by Archibald Constable and Company—no one in New York's Publishing Row was interested in acknowledging, much less celebrating, *Dracula*'s centenary. Waiting for takers for *The Book of Renfield* was like waiting for Godot. When the *Dracula* centenary finally rolled around, the city condescended to play host to a Dracula Centenary Festival, where the attendees voted Frank Langella the greatest screen Dracula of all time.

I subsequently put the artifacts of my inheritance out of sight and out of mind and resumed work on my abandoned novel, which I was never able to finish, so furious was I that the world preferred to persist in its contented thinking that Dracula, like Marlowe's Hell, was just a fable—or, worse still, a romantic leading man.

Years passed and then an unimaginable disaster befell New York City. In the wake of that catastrophe, while searching for news on the Internet, I happened to discover an article by a fellow New Yorker that brought my feelings back into focus and gave me the courage to try again. It follows with the author's kind permission:

"A perfect agony of grief": DRACULA 9-11-01
Posted on the Mobius Home Video Forum
(www.mhvf.net)
by: Richard Harland Smith, 10/03/2001, 12:15:49

Well before the events of September 11, 2001, I had made a pact with my girlfriend Barbara that we would read Bram Stoker's Dracula together, she for the first time, me for the (I don't even know) 5th, 6th, 7th time. As many of you know, we are New Yorkers and were stuck in London on the day of the attacks on the World Trade Center and the Pentagon. Four nervous days followed, full of anxious waiting, frenzied telephoning, and lots of walking around London not knowing what to do.

Since I've been back in Manhattan, I have found myself at a loss to focus my attention—but cracking Dracula again, I was instantly swept away by the adventure, by the wealth of details and the brilliantly executed mood of menace. As I read on, however, I found the experience of revisiting this book to be much more than the diversion I had anticipated.

In a nutshell, Dracula concerns a group of (mostly) young people who have entered adulthood purely by dint of chronology; they have not been tested, nor have they passed (it would seem) any essential rites of passage. Within a short space of time, however, these innocents find themselves face up against a series of events that are unbelievable even to their own eyes, and thrust into a situation that is seemingly unendurable, against an enemy who seems unconquerable.

Sound familiar? In the telegrams and diary entries of Jonathan and Mina Harker, Jack Seward, and Abraham Van Helsing, I was quick to recognize the letters, e-mails, and phone calls my friends and I have been trading for the past three weeks. And in the unabashed emotions that these characters express for one another—sentiments I once thought, in a gentler time, to be a bit treacly for my postmodern tastes—I instantly recognized feelings I have been of late expressing openly.

"I comforted him as well as I could. In such cases men do not need much expression. A grip of the hand, the tightening of an arm over the shoulder, a sob in unison, are expressions of sympathy dear to a man's heart." (Jack Seward, Chapter 13)

Walking around the city of New York these days, I have seen some very strong emotional reactions from people here; I've seen a lot of giddy denial, but more often a tearing down of emotional barriers supposedly hardwired to gender . . . and scenes not unlike Mina Harker's exchange with a grieved Arthur Holmwood:

"In an instant the poor dear fellow was overwhelmed with grief. It seemed to me that all that he had of late been suffering in silence found a vent at once. He grew quite hysterical, and raising his open hands, beat his palms together in a perfect agony of grief. He stood up and then sat down again, and the tears rained down his cheeks. I felt an infinite pity for him, and opened my arms unthinkingly. With a sob he laid his head on my shoulder and cried like a wearied child, whilst he shook with emotion." (Chapter 17)

Reading late last night, I even discerned in Van Helsing's briefing to his comrades thoughts familiar to anyone who has watched the news feverishly for some plan of action from Washington:

"How then are we to begin our strike to destroy him? How shall we find his where, and having found it, how can we destroy? My friends, this is much, it is a terrible task that we undertake, and there may be consequence to make the brave shudder. For if we fail in this our fight he must surely win, and then where end we?"

It would be intolerably glib to compare the architect of our misery to the fictional Count Dracula, but I'm finding this 104-year-old novel to be remarkably timely, and as such remarkably comforting. The phrase "loss of innocence" has been tossed around a lot (too much) in the media since 9/11, and while I don't know if what we lost that day was truly innocence or perhaps just ignorance, I want America to endure and her citizens to be safe. I feel certain of very little these days, but I will throw in (as Quincey Morris might put it) with Bram Stoker, when he avers (through the sweet voice of Mina Harker):

"The world seems full of good men, even if there are monsters in it."

Though I assume that Mr. Smith's words were widely read and appreciated, I had the feeling that they had been written for my eyes alone. Finally, after being online for a decade, the Internet had given me some sustenance for my soul, rather than merely spending—or siphoning away from—my life and time.

Like Mr. Smith, I had lost a friend in the September 11

attacks, but I was also able to read his posting from the unique standpoint of being related to someone it mentioned by name—the flesh-and-blood descendant of a man who is remembered today, if at all, as a character of fiction.

I am one of those Geminis who can only do one thing while I am doing another. As I first discovered Mr. Smith's posting on the Mobius Home Video Forum, I happened to be simultaneously watching CNN's continuing coverage of the search for Osama bin Laden out of the corner of my eye (with the closed captioning activated on my TV screen, in case I needed to "hear" anything) and listening through headphones to a CD-R I had burned on my Philips deck, for the sake of convenience, from one of Jack Seward's phonograph cylinders.

As my eyes toggled between a fellow New Yorker's disarming portrait of life lived in the shadow of an incomprehensible disaster and televised replays of people being pursued through the streets of Manhattan, through puddles of blood, by camcorders and colossal, inescapable clouds of vaporized steel and glass and human remains, the following words flowed into my ears on a crackling wave traveling across more than a century:

"You would help these men to hunt me and frustrate me in my design! You know now, and they know in part already, and will know in full before long, what it is to cross my path. They should have kept their energies for use closer to home. Whilst they played wits against me, against me who commanded nations, and intrigued for them, and fought for them, hundreds of years before they were born, I was counter-mining them. And you, their best beloved one, are now to me, flesh of my flesh, blood of my blood, kin of my kin, my bountiful wine-press for a while, and shall be later on my companion and my helper. You shall be avenged in turn, for not one of them but shall minister to your needs. But as yet you are to be punished for what you have done. You have aided in thwarting me. Now you shall come to my call. When my brain says 'Come!' to you, you shall cross land or sea to do my bidding."

Here, my ancestor was recording into his phonographic diary the words of Count Dracula, as they had been hurled at him and his companions by Mina Harker in the wake of his foiled assault upon her, the attack which had so memorably left her "Unclean! Unclean!" When I first read this passage in *Dracula* (which was required reading during my sophomore year of high school), I had wrinkled my nose at the staid, antiquarian phrasing—but, as I heard the same words spoken on this cylinder, in a voice only two steps removed from the Un-Dead source, Jack Seward's quaking elocution as he stammered through those words of imperial command was impossible to accept as anything but authentic, and terribly moving in its struggle to remain unbroken and dignified.

I had the unhappy experience of hearing that tremor a few times at first hand in the course of my forty-odd years: once, coming from my own mouth as I was asked by local news reporters to describe what I had seen and felt when a man standing beside me in a Queens subway station had thrown himself onto the tracks before an oncoming train—and again, more recently, coming from the mouths of people I had randomly met on the streets or on the stairwell of my own building, who engaged me in incredulous, clinging conversation, as people make when they need to forge new bonds in the wake of a loss so inconceivably vast. No one could fake the special tremor peculiar to a voice that had witnessed violent death up close—and mind you, these cylinders dated from a time when the world was infinitely smaller, when one had to physically cross oceans before earning the epithet, "worldly." Such emotion wasn't something that people in Jack Seward's day could have merely picked up from a Meryl Streep picture on television; it had to be earned the hard way.

The combination of these three things, that day in early October—the Mobius posting, the news broadcast, and the cylinder recording—helped me to recognize that I was now inhabiting a world in which *The Book of Renfield* must exist, not only for me but for everyone. It needed to be made ready for publication, whether the end result saw print in my lifetime or not.

Today, more than a century after its first printing, Bram Stoker's *Dracula* remains arguably the most relevant and progressive publication of its period. I believe the world may now be more receptive to the story told by *The Book of Renfield*, having witnessed not an act of God but an act of fanatics who presumed to force the Hand of God. I believe that people have been slapped by this event and learned, perhaps for the first time in their lives, to respect death—or may learn it yet, before the next devil arises from a parched homeland to feast on blood needlessly spilled by the young.

It is crucial that we remember Dracula not as a pale romantic played by Frank Langella or Gary Oldman, as someone who dressed like a head waiter and made women swoon by speaking to them of his eternal love. Dracula was not an Elvis rebel in a black leather duster to be longed for like a decadent dessert, but a plague upon humanity ultimately put to permanent death by my ancestor and those closest to him. Dead, yes, but the appetites that gave shape to Dracula live on: the thirst for blood and power, the need for world conquest, death and destruction, horror and apocalypse. Renfield also endures, in the legion of religious and political zealots who believe they can survive the apocalypse by helping to invite it, by standing nearest its epicenter—only to discover that they, themselves, are the first to succumb to its shock waves.

There is one last piece of documentation to be presented before I can call this good deed done: a typed transcript of what is described, by handwriting in the margin (not Morrison's), as the final meeting of Jack Seward and Lucy Westenra. Offered as an Appendix, these pages are undated, making it impossible to insert them in the manuscript according to proper chronology—nor, in all honesty, have I been able to determine whether this episode was a waking dream, as Jack himself suspected it might be, or if my illustrious ancestor spent his later years exorcising his demons vis-à-vis the art of fiction.

I have done as I believe he would wish me to do, by leaving the final verdict undecided—and open to your interpretation.

Martin Seward
New York City, NY
21 June 2004

Appendix.

TYPESCRIPT CARBON, UNDATED.—As I woke from my nap in my office chair, I found that night had fallen. Fog, having drifted through an open window, rolled mid-way between the floor and ceiling, as at a men's smoker. To my surprise, Miss Lucy Westenra was seated opposite me, in the chair usually occupied during our meetings by my patients, placid and smiling.

I could scarcely believe my eyes or my wakefulness. Was Lucy really there? I was hesitant to speak, for fear of scattering this pretty picture of her like a reflection in splashed water . . . but she spoke for me:

"Dear Jack! You looked so contented, napping there, I told myself it would be a pity to disturb you."

"I wasn't nearly so contented as . . . I wasn't contented at all, I assure you. You surprise me, Lucy! To what do I owe this unexpected pleasure?"

"If a man pledges his eternal friendship to a girl and she suddenly never sees him again, she begins to wonder," she said, without fully closing her mouth after the last word. "I was worried about you, to be quite honest, and I needed to see that you were all-right."

"All-right?"

"All-right . . . with what had been decided," she explained.

I fell silent and glum. I thought to myself, If I could only hold this silent and glum posture indefinitely, I might hold her here for ever and achieve my happiness, after all.

"I suppose it depends on your definition of 'all-right,'" I said pensively, eventually. "I've been keeping busy, trying to concentrate on my work here at the asylum, trying to get lost in other people's worlds."

"Lost in other people's worlds," she echoed playfully, like the spoiled child she always was. "And what happens to yours in the meantime?"

"Nothing terribly much," I admitted, "but right now, my own world is more about looking backwards than looking ahead to the future. And since I am of that inclination, I might as well be looking backwards at someone else's past, where it might actually do someone some good."

"Jack, honestly! How can you do good by getting lost in someone else's past?"

"Oh," I said, "by helping them to face things they would rather not face—perhaps things they have ceased to think about, things they have ceased to remember they are at war with." Then I chuckled, apologising: "Forgive my grammar. I'm still a bit . . ."

Lucy leaned forward in her seat, pushing her beautiful face out towards mine, much as she had done that night at Lord and Lady Remington's soirée.

"Do you know why I turned you down, Jack?" she asked.

The directness of her question was hurtful, but I tried not to let it show.

"Because you don't love me?" I hazarded.

"To tell you the truth," she answered at length, "I haven't known you long enough to ask myself whether I do or not. I do feel . . . *tenderly* towards you—*quite* tenderly—but mostly because I am touched by how nervous you are when you're in my presence. A doctor, the head of this important establishment, a respected man in his community—but, when you're with me, you're like a bashful little boy."

"That is very interesting," I said, knowing this to be perfectly true.

"Not so interesting, but very *flattering*," she clarified. "There is also this constant fidgeting. The reason I turned you down is because of your nervousness, your fidgeting. You would not place a bird that had fallen from its nest into trembling hands. I believe you do think you love me, Jack, and it is more than obvious that you are attracted to me, but I think—and this is the ultimate truth of the matter—that you fear me too much to really love me. And I could never accept the proposal of a man who didn't love me, who couldn't see past my pretty face to the person I really am behind my looks, behind my sex."

"Well, well," I chuckled nervously at her daring speech. "We *are* speaking directly to-night, aren't we?"

"Well, is there any reason now to continue playing courtship games?" She smiled frankly. "There are no more walls between us. Look at yourself: I am sitting right here, looking my prettiest, alone with you, and you are not fidgeting about in the least. You have finally become comfortable with me, as comfortable as I always needed you to be. You have finally become, truly, my friend."

401

I nodded in confirmation once, twice, thrice. *That is true, that is true, that is true.*

As Lucy eased back into her chair, looking as calm as a cat, we regarded one another in frank appreciation for a period lasting perhaps minutes. When I next felt the need for words, I confessed to her, with a pained smile, "I think of you terribly often, you know."

"Is it possible that I misjudged you?" she asked, her expression falling in such a way that my heart reached out to her.

In an effort to retain my composure, I picked up a pencil from my desk and used it to drum on my crossed legs.

"What do you mean?" I questioned her. "What makes you think you could have misjudged me?"

"Because," she explained, "I can tell, by the way you speak, that when your thoughts turn back to me, it weakens you. I weaken you simply by sitting here, don't I?"

I put the pencil down, seeing that my drumming was less the cavalier gesture I intended to project than an advertisement for my anxieties, and one I did not wish risking Lucy's notice. I leaned forward, resting my crossed arms on my desk. I needed to show Lucy my strength and so I gave her my candour.

"You refused my proposal, Lucy," I scolded her, albeit gently and civilly. "What right have you now to rifle through my secrets?"

"And what right have you to hold me here," she countered, "when even poor Arthur has let me go?"

It was a most excellent question, but one for which I had no ready answer. In time, I thought of this one: "Because things that were, are possibly easier to part with than the things that never were."

She seemed to understand this remark, even if it brought her no particular satisfaction. "I have regrets too, you know," she confessed in time. "I was going to marry a lord. I was going to be Lady Godalming."

We sat together in silence, pondering this notion, as black winds rustled the boughs of white trees outside the open window, in a dream world where wolves ran and bats flew in ever-convoluted circles and vortices. It was getting very late.

"Shall I stay awhile longer?" she asked.

Did I dare to answer her? Would the bubble burst?

"Oh yes, Milady."

About the Author

TIM LUCAS is the author of the novel *Throat Sprockets* (1994), which topped several year's best lists and was praised by *Kirkus Reviews* as "a virtuoso performance." In the decade since this remarkable debut, he has worked as editor and co-publisher of the award-winning monthly magazine *Video Watchdog* (www.videowatchdog.com) and written for such international publications as *Sight and Sound*, *Film Comment*, and *Cahiers du Cinéma*. His nonfiction works include *The Video Watchdog Book* and *Mario Bava—All the Colors of the Dark*, an epic biography of the Italian film director thirty years in preparation. A popular authority on horror and cult movies, Mr. Lucas has penned the liner notes for more than thirty different DVD releases, recorded several audio commentaries, and appeared as an on-screen commentator in various documentary programs including the A&E series *Biography*. He is currently pursuing yet another career—as a screenwriter—and his first script has been optioned by a major American director. He lives with his wife, Donna, and three perpetually hungry cats in Cincinnati, Ohio.

The Book of Renfield

1. Have you read Bram Stoker's *Dracula*? If so, do you think reading *The Book of Renfield* has enriched your appreciation and understanding of that novel? If not, were you able to follow the story and appreciate Lucas's novel on its own?

2. Throughout the story, Jack begins to notice parallels between himself and Renfield. What do they have in common? How do Renfield and Jack begin to reflect and influence each other? What significance does this growing connection have for the novel?

3. Jack's life is punctuated by the abuse of morphine. What makes him turn to "the arms of Morpheus" and how do you think his periodic addiction affects his perception? Do you think Jack is a reliable narrator?

4. Renfield tells of events that are at once sad, horrifying, and fantastical. Are you able to draw a line between those things he truly believes and those lies he tells Jack?

5. Jack is at turns disgusted with and sympathetic to Renfield. How do you feel about Renfield? How responsible is he for the direction his life takes? What events or people

shaped him into the kind of person that Dracula would turn to for help in executing his diabolical plans?

6. Though we at first believe that Renfield exists only to do the bidding of his "Master," we come to realize that Renfield has, in fact, struggled with his allegiance to Dracula all his life. Why does Renfield continually betray Dracula and, ultimately, reject him? Do you think Renfield is able to redeem himself before his death?

7. Though the main characters of this novel are men, the female characters seem far more powerful. Who are some of these powerful women, and what kinds of power do they wield? Why do you think the author chooses to portray such a dynamic between the sexes?

8. *The Book of Renfield* is a snapshot of a time period and culture as much as it is about universal human experiences. What did you learn about Victorian England that you didn't previously know?

9. Jack's great-grandson, Martin Seward, tells the reader that he wants to publish *The Book of Renfield* because "the appetites that gave shape to Dracula live on." How do you feel about his relating the events of this novel and of *Dracula* to the September 11 attacks? What reasons does he have for doing so?

10. *The Book of Renfield* is presented as a collection of transcriptions and diary entries so as to give the effect of its

being a "historical document." Why do you think the author chose this form for his novel?

11. Martin Seward's Afterword explains that *The Book of Renfield* is a warning to modern readers who, in their comfort and complacency, have forgotten that Evil once walked the earth and can return at any time—in fact, that it may never really have gone away. Do you think this warning transcends the fictional context of the novel? Does the message resonate for you? What might have prompted the author to use his novel in this way?

12. The final entry of the novel is a conversation between Jack and Lucy, seemingly after her death. How does this entry fit into the story? What significance do Jack's final words, "Oh yes, Milady," have?

Discover more reading group guides and download them for free at www.simonsays.com.